I heard a door close and whei

"I believe I'm being followed. Actually, I'm quite positive I am."

"Same stalker that gave you the card?"

I shook my head, then stopped realizing he couldn't see me. "No, it's not him. There's two of them, and they've been there each time I've turned around. Now they are standing outside the shop I'm in."

"Where are you? Are you safe at the moment?"

"Yes. I'm in a changing room." I glanced down to see I still held the two dresses the clerk brought and hung them up.

"Really? That's interesting, I've never had a call from a changing room before."

I sat down. "I'm so happy to tick that off your new experience list. What do you suggest I do?"

"Well... I'd have to see what you're trying on to help you decide..." He chuckled. "Just use your transporter."

Closing my eyes, I sighed. "I would, if I hadn't left it at home."

Another door closed. "You know we gave that to you to carry *with* you in case you needed it, and it seems you do."

"Yes, yes I know. I forgot it." Something I would regret from this day on. "When I did my check before I left... wallet, yes, phone, yes... it seems I'm not used to remembering little transporter thing to another realm."

He sighed, "don't distract me with sass, I'm thinking."

I stood up again, feeling very anxious. "Can't you just pop here and get me?"

Chase snorted, "I'd have to have been there before to do that, and I'm not in the habit of visiting women's changing rooms, however entertaining the idea is."

"Oh," Another fact I should have probably asked. "I didn't realize."

"Don't despair, duchess, I'll get there. Tell me where you are in terms of large landmarks."

He was just going to walk down the street to find me? "What... what if they know you? I mean, if they know who you are? Your size draws attention, not to mention your golden locks and flirty little beard... you will be recognized."

"Worried for me? That's very touching." He paused. "For the record, my beard is not flirty... it takes adorning my face quite seriously."

Also by J. Risk

THE ALTEREALM SERIES
1 *The Huntress*
2 *The Seer*
3 *The Empath*
4 *The Witch*
5 *The Chronos*
6 *The Warrior*
7 *The Telepath*
8 *The Healer* (coming soon)
9 *The Kinetic* (coming soon)

Writing As: Jacqueline Paige

Dreams
Three steamy stories that started with a dream

Curses
Two tales of curses.

After the Silence
Volume 1 Bree

ANIMAL SENSES
1 *Heart*
2 *Scent*
3 *Passion*

MAGIC SEASONS ROMANCE
1 *Beltane Magic*
2 *Solstice Heat*
3 *Harvest Dreams*
4 *Autumn Dance*
5 *Winter Mist*

SINGLE TITLES
Solitary Witchling
Salvation
Café Serenity

The Empath

Alterealm Series

Book 3

By J. Risk

Family tree at the end of *The Seer*

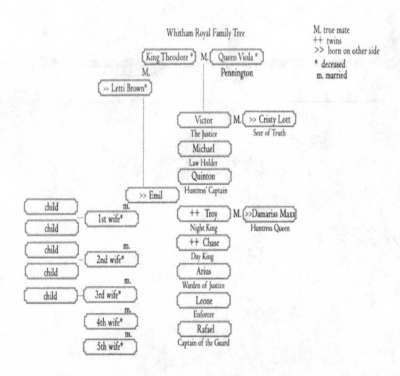

Whitham Royal Family Tree

M. true mate
++ twins
>> born on other side
* deceased
m. married

King Theodore * | M. | Queen Viola *
M.
Pennington

>> Letti Brown *

Victor | M. | >> Cristy Lott
The Justice | | Seer of Truth

Michael
Law Holder

Quinton
Huntress' Captain

>> Emil

child

1st wife *

child

++ Troy | M. | >>Damariss Maxx
Night King | | Huntress Queen

child

++ Chase
Day King

2nd wife *

child

Arius
Warden of Justice

child

3rd wife *

Leone
Enforcer

4th wife *

Rafael
Captain of the Guard

5th wife *

Published by FRP
Copyright © 2018 Roxane Kerr
Edited by Gaele L. Hince
Cover art by: Off the Wall Creations

Updated 2020

ISBN- (paperback) 978-1-7773723-7-8
ISBN- (digital) 978-1-7773723-6-1

Prologue

Clutching her daughter to her chest, she opened the door wide enough to peek out into the hall. Eva was shaking with fear. How could she have forgotten to keep her arm covered? The exhaustion must be wearing on her to overlook such a thing. Checking three times to be certain none of the other boarders were awake and the hallway was empty, she slipped out the door and bolted to her room.

Closing the door quickly, she turned and set the infant in the middle of the bed. They had an hour to get to the train platform, she wasn't taking a chance on being late. It had been nerve-wracking few days, waiting to get papers signed that would clear them for travel.

She had been terrified through the entire process that they would ask her to remove her jacket. When the doctor had finally decided she and her child hadn't been exposed, and were displaying no symptoms of the virus, she had almost fainted with relief.

Her heart skipped a few beats, thinking what would have happened if they'd been denied. There were camps filled with those afflicted. And each time the medical trucks passed, they carried others to the quarantined areas. It was horrifying, what the country was going through. To survive the years of war and then have millions fall ill with some deadly influenza. She only glimpsed the headlines of the newspapers as she passed them in her travels, but it was everywhere, it seemed.

Moving to the mirror, she studied her reflection. Her cheeks were hollowed and dark circles were under her eyes. The months of stress and worry were catching up to her. She sighed, her white cotton shirtwaist wasn't stained, but the wrinkles were adding up. How many days had she been wearing it now? If there had been more time, she would have given it a rinse, but she couldn't risk missing one of the few trains still running out of the city. "Lord knows my brassiere and bloomers are in desperate need of a rinse as well," she whispered to the scared woman looking back at her. Smoothing a hand down her skirt, she smiled, thankful it was a little longer then current fashion dictated, as her stockings were beyond any condition that a mere washing could remedy.

Her heart ached as she looked at the tattoo covering the length of her left arm. She touched it gingerly and closed her eyes, willing the tears not to fall. He had to be all right. She didn't know what was taking so long, but she knew that he would come back to her. When he did manage to cross back over, the caretaker of their building would give him the message, then he would come and get Alona and her. *Please, Levi, come soon.*

The baby's soft whimper made her open her eyes. She turned and smiled. "Not to worry, love, your daddy will find us at your aunt's." Going over, she sat on the edge of the bed and looked down at her child, her whole world. "We have to go, I don't have a choice. The sickness is spreading, and if we stay here any longer," She let out a ragged breath, "we won't be able to get out." Alona was a beautiful baby, she looked so much like her father. Picking up her bonnet, she placed it on the child's head, over her thick black hair. "You're my strength, little one, never forget that." The baby watched her with pale eyes. She was certain they were going to be the same pale green his were, well when his weren't red that was.

2

Leaning down, she kissed the soft cheek. "I would be lost in a sea of despair if I didn't have you my precious Alona." It was the truth. The only thing that had prevented her from dissolving in the constant pain of being without him, was their child. While she'd been growing inside her, Eva knew she had to overcome the feelings of grief and continue on until he returned for them.

Tucking the blanket around the baby, she reached over and picked up her worn satchel. Getting her coin purse out, she dumped the contents in her hand and counted. The train fare was going to cost nearly seven dollars, which was the most expensive thing she'd done in as long as she could remember. After that they'd have to get by on what was left, which would be a week's grocery money, maybe two, if nothing unexpected came up. Putting the money back in the purse, she snapped it shut and tucked it safely into her bag.

"You'll like it in the country, doll, once you learn to walk, there's so much to explore." She gathered up the few items not in the suitcase and folded them. Glancing around to be sure nothing was missed, she picked up her jacket and gloves. It was quite warm today, but she had no choice, her arm and hand had to be covered. Telling those curious enough to ask that her husband had died in the war was one thing, and that usually brought a halt to any further questions. Explaining why she had a tattoo that covered the length of her arm, well, that was unexplainable. The scandal it would cause would not end well, something like that was unheard of and completely unacceptable. Levi had said in his world the tattoos were a wondrous and cherished thing. She couldn't wait to see his world.

She missed him with all she had. For months she'd worried that something had happened. Was the outbreak where he was too? Had something happened to him? He told her he would know if she was harmed through the connection of their tattoo, so she had to hold onto the belief that the connection went both ways. She knew he lived, but couldn't understand what was taking him so long. He had to go back to arrange for her to come with him, then they could be together always.

Until he did return, she had to make certain their child was safe and happy. They hadn't discussed children, but he was such a loving man, Eva was sure the surprise of being a father would be something he would welcome.

Tucking her hair up under the embroidered velvet toque, she studied the woman looking back at her. "Just a few more days and you'll be safe, and won't have to worry about someone finding out." She nodded to herself and then turned to pick up her daughter. Cradling her in one arm, she smiled down at the beautiful face as she made sure her mouth was lightly covered by the blanket. They'd managed to avoid infection this far, she wasn't taking chances. Hooking the satchel on the same arm, she opened the door and picked up her case. Taking a deep break, she exhaled and stepped out into the hall.

She had to hold onto the hope that her sister was well. If the sickness had reached the country, there were no other options to take... they'd be lost.

Chapter One

I had spent close to one hundred years staying away from anything that would draw the attention of others. Which, due to the fact I didn't age, was not an easy task. Six months ago I'd moved, an unfortunate necessity, done so people didn't notice that I didn't age. Since then, staying in the shadows didn't seem to be working.

It started when a crazy woman with fantastically bright red hair, and a chaotic array of emotions grabbed me in the club and dragged me out. Since that moment, everyone seemed to be noticing me.

I thought she was completely bonkers, who wouldn't be with so many emotions oozing from her every pore, until I discovered what she said was true. Someone did appear to be after me.

I spent three weeks going to an abandoned fish factory, after painting an x on the wall. Insane, I know, but I did just as she'd told me to do, if I needed help. I went there because the chaotic one had told me her friends could help me, and that they were like me.

That, as far as I knew, was impossible. Yet she knew my eyes changed to red, and when they did my mouth filled with fangs. If I hadn't felt the truth seeping from her, I would have walked in the other direction. After many years of believing I

5

was the spawn of Satan, I was too curious to not find out. I needed to know if it was true. Were there others like me?

When she finally showed up at the factory today, minus the red hair, I thought I'd go meet her friends and see for myself. Of course, I thought the meeting would take place in some out of the way café or concealed location. I did not foresee being zapped, or whatever had just happened, to some room in the blink of an eye.

Now I stood in an empty, drably beige room, unable to figure out what was going on and feeling nauseous in the worst way. I looked at Crissy, she was closing the lid to the watch thing on her arm that she'd pushed to bring us here. I debated on grabbing it from her and pushing the button, so I could get back home to pack up and move, again.

A tall man with gorgeous, long black hair that rivaled my own, came running into the room. He slid to a stop and crouched down with his arms out giving me a cautious look, like I might bolt for the door. And go where? I thought.

"How do you feel? He looked me up and down, his grey eyes filled with worry. "Any pains?

He had one of those watches like Crissy's in his hand. Did I want to try to grab it? He was a large man, so maybe not in my current state. I stared at him for a few seconds and then reached for the blade on my back. Closing my hand around the handle, I scowled at him. "I feel... confused..." My stomach lurched again, so I put my other hand over it hoping I didn't throw up on this stranger. "And I want to throw up." I backed away from him and watched him carefully. "Where am I? Who are you?" I looked to person responsible for this. "Crissy, what the hell is going on?"

Crissy blew out a breath and nodded. "I know. Transporting sucks. My stomach still hates it."

"Transporting?" I glanced at the man again, then shook my head. "Like *beam me up*, transporting?" She gave me a blank look, so I looked to the man to see him smirking.

"No." He sobered. "Not like that at all."

"It's okay, this is the best place to meet since no one can follow you here." Crissy tried to reassure me.

I was debating on giving her friend a few more moments to convince me. That I couldn't pick up any emotions from his was... unusual, to say the least. I could see emotions going through his eyes as he studied me but couldn't *feel* any of them.

"Cristy." A large, redheaded man came running into the room. With the way he was dressed, he looked like he was going to battle. And I don't mean military dress, I mean Samurai meets Blade, black leather, head to toe, large sharp weapons sort of dress. He immediately went to Crissy and hugged her into his large body and kissed the top of her head. *That* I hadn't anticipated. The gentle expression in his eyes bought him a minute's free pass before I lost it on him, or everyone else.

"I will get to the *why* and *how* you got to the other side... later. My heart stopped when you hung up." He touched her cheek in a loving way.

Crissy bit her lip and looked up at him. "Sorry. I just knew I had to go back today, but I didn't know why. Until I did." She smiled at him while pointing at me.

He straightened away from her and gone was the softer look. Replaced with an ice cold assessment, but once again, I could only see his emotions and not feel them.

He looked me up and down for a moment. "Clearly, she is meant to be here, or she'd need a device." He raised an eyebrow at me. "How are you feeling?"

I glared at him, "Like I've entered the twilight zone."

The one with the black hair snorted but didn't comment.

"Victor, she was waiting for me. She keeps seeing that guy that chased her—" Crissy sighed, "from when I got my scar."

He hugged her against his side but was still rigid standing there. "Has he approached you?

I shook my head, "I don't hang around to give him the opportunity to strike up a conversation."

He inclined his head, saying nothing else.

"Crissy, are you all right?" The woman that had come to get Crissy when she passed out in the alley came running in.

She stopped when she saw her and placed a hand over her heart. "When Victor went screaming by to get here, I thought you'd been..." she paused when she saw me. "Oh. Awesome! You were finally there."

"So, it seems." How many people had Crissy told about me?

The blonde cleared her throat and looked at the others, "So, maybe we could... oh I dunno, go to the dining room, or somewhere other than the landing room?" She rolled her eyes at me and mouthed 'men'.

I couldn't pick up a single emotion from her either, which intrigued me even further. I'd never been near this many people and not sensed emotion. "I would like to know more about this man following me." I looked at Crissy. "Why is he following me?"

She pouted, "I don't know. It hasn't shown me that, but I do know he's not good."

I looked at her, unable to figure out what she meant. "If you don't know, who does?"

"I know who can find out." The black-haired one said. He grinned at the one still holding Crissy close. "We can get Troy to ask his buddies we picked up after Criss was hurt."

My head snapped back to Crissy. "They hurt you?"

She blew out a breath. "Some magic," she waved a hand around, "whatever it's called, was stuck in my back." Frowning, she glanced up at her man before looking back to me. "It hurt so much. It's gone now, the rune has locked it out forever." She nodded.

If I hadn't felt the truth oozing out of her and all over me, I would have demanded they please take me home. I didn't know what she was talking about, but I was living proof that other types were possible in this life. I held up my hand. "I will just... take your word for all that."

The blonde exhaled loudly and then stepped over and put out her hand. "I'm Daxx. I never did thank you properly for keeping an eye on Crissy when she blacked out in the alley."

I looked at her hand and then shook it briefly. I still picked up nothing from her, a very rare occurrence. "Things tend to be eventful when Crissy is around."

She snorted, "You have no idea." Turning, she motioned to the man that had come running in first. "This is Arius," then to Crissy's man, "and his brother Victor."

Both men inclined their heads briefly but made no move to come closer.

"Let's go to the dining room, grab a coffee or something and figure out why those guys are after you." She suggested.

Before I could decide, another tall man came in. He had short black hair and pale blue eyes. My only thought was that I was usually the tallest person in the room. Seemingly, the males here were all of the large variety.

He stopped in the door and looked me up and down. "Is this who we've been watching for all these weeks, Crissy?"

Crissy nodded enthusiastically. "I brought her back, she said they're following her."

Raising an eyebrow, he glanced at the device Arius held then back to me. "Obviously, she's meant to be here."

At some point, I would have to clarify why they kept saying that. I turned back to Daxx. "You said something about coffee?" I still didn't know where I was, but I wasn't leaving until I knew what the hell was going on, and if they could tell me *what* I was while I was here, that would answer a question that had plagued me for seventy-eight years.

Chapter Two

We moved to a large dining room. Large may have been understating it, I'd seen restaurants smaller than this room. There was a long, polished wooden table with chairs surrounding it. On the walls were portraits of ancestors, judging by the fact that the males in the room resembled the people in the portraits in one way or another.

I sat there looking around at the seven men, still a little shocked they were brothers. What woman in her right mind would keep going after giving birth to the first few? Incredible, was my first thought. Well done, mom, was the second. Each one was a varying degree of good looking, from cute-baby-faced to ruggedly-hot. It seems the genes were good on this side of whatever they called it.

"Sorry I'm late. Am I late? I think I'm awake at night instead of day, this past week has been hell on my system. I've been to more locations in this realm this week than I have in a hundred years." A man said wandering in a different door than we had used. He was identical to the man Daxx was with, except he had a goatee. He looked like he'd just crawled out of bed. Not that I'd tell him, but half-asleep looked good on him.

Walking toward the table, he stopped and looked at me and then around to the others. "What have I missed? We seem to have an extra body today." He looked around again. "A female body."

"Nothing wrong with your observational skills." I said quietly.

He grinned, a real player's smile at me. "And she's *sassy*." Holding a finger up, he winked at me. "Let me get coffee and wake up, then I can keep up with a bit of sass." Turning, he went and sat down.

I glanced to Troy. "How many brothers are there?"

"There's eight of us. This is Chase..." He shook his head. "Actually, there's nine, but one we haven't even met... the one from your side." He motioned to Crissy. "She's trying to find him."

Crissy nodded enthusiastically. "The man in the club I was looking for."

I nodded, remembering our last bizarre meeting in the club. My side and their side. Side of what, I debated on asking.

Crissy pointed to the quiet Arius. "He looks almost identical to Arius, only with shorter hair."

I studied him for a moment. "I think I may have seen him at the club, but not recently." A male as striking as that, you couldn't help but notice.

"I hope he hasn't vanished again." Crissy said with a sigh. "It wasn't easy going through three hundred years of records to track him down."

"He's three hundred?"

She nodded.

"I guess I'm not that old..." I stopped talking. It wasn't like me to give away anything about myself. I didn't know what was with this group, but as far as I could tell they were emotionless. I picked up a few spikes of emotions, but they were nothing compared to what I was used to. Instinct told me to run, but my mind was way beyond curious.

"How old are you?" Daxx asked me.

I studied her for a moment, not sure if I should answer.

"Alona, it's okay." Crissy nodded. "

I stared at her. "How do you know that name? I haven't used it in—" I blew out a breath, trying to remember how long. "I don't know how many years."

"Oh." She bit her lip. "I don't know how I knew, I just did."

"What name are you using now?" Victor asked as he wrapped his arm around Crissy's shoulder.

I still couldn't see how those two ended up together, but he clearly cared for her. "I have been using Isabell for the last six months, before that it was…" I waved my hand around, it wasn't important. "Another name."

Crissy looked at me for a moment, an odd look on her face. "You don't look like an Isabell."

I smirked. "Most people don't stop to see if you look like your name." Not that I became well enough acquainted with most people to share my name of the moment.

"Alona is your birth name?" Michael asked me, leaning back against the wall and crossing his arms. He reminded me of a cop. Did they have cops here?

"Yes."

He nodded for a moment. "Do you know who your parents were?"

I shrugged. "I am assuming a man *and* a woman." I crossed my arms and studied him. I didn't know these people, I was not revealing anything until I knew what they were all about.

He sighed and then seemed to drop the hard appearance. "I only ask because we are trying to figure out how residents from this side got over to the other side, and apparently frequently enough to have relationships."

"Getting a woman pregnant isn't exactly a relationship."

"You knew your mother than?" Leone asked, his tone much more compassionate than his cop-like brother.

"Yes, until she died from a broken heart when I was ten. Then I was shuffled off to the orphanage." I shook my head. "I didn't care for it, so I didn't stay very long."

Chase snorted but didn't say anything.

"There's a pattern." Crissy said softly.

Victor looked down at her, appearing to wait patiently for more.

She pointed to Daxx and then me. "We were all in the system." Taking off her backpack she opened it while talking quietly to herself. "I need to look in my book, maybe I can piece more together."

I realized then that the others weren't really paying attention to her.

The big hearted one, Quinton, I think his name was, got up and came down to sit across from me. "I can't imagine what you've gone through, over there and not knowing who you really were."

"You have no idea." I glanced around at the others trying to decide how much to share in order to find out more. "Crissy said her friends," I waved my hand toward the others, "were like me... how like me?"

He smirked. "Your eyes turn to what color?"

I leaned back in the chair and studied him for a few more seconds. "Red."

Grinning, he waved his hand around, "then you're the same as all of us, except Chase and the girls."

I turned to look at Chase, his eyes were bright yellow. He shrugged.

"I see." I clasped my hands in my lap for a moment and thought about that. A whole group, possibly even culture, that were like me. Maybe my mothers' stories weren't delusions after all. "My mother spoke of my father, saying he had to get permission and arrange for her to go back with him." I glanced at him. "I guess she wasn't imagining it."

The cute one, Rafael, sat down. "There's no way he'd be denied bringing someone over if there was a child."

I cleared my throat softly. "He didn't know about me. My mother found out after he left to make arrangements. He never returned."

"When was this?" Michael asked, not looking so hard and cop-like now.

I took a deep breath and exhaled it slowly. "I was born after the war," I looked around for a reaction, "the first one, during the influenza pandemic." Mentioning my age didn't even phase them. Which was a strangely comforting thing, I realized, to not be the oldest being in the room for once.

The twins both swore at the same time.

"During the transport ban." Michael said looking to Victor, who nodded.

"Transport ban?" Daxx asked.

Her man leaned closer to her and wrapped his arm around her. "During the outbreak, we had to ban inhabitants from crossing over, we're just as susceptible to disease and have many humans living here." He glanced at his twin. "We were trying to protect our own."

My heart started beating twice as fast in my chest then it should. I held my hand over it, hoping to slow it down. "Are you saying my father *couldn't* come back to my mother?"

"It's quite probable." Victor told me as he stood up. He started undoing buckles and then took the large swords off his back and hung them on the chair and then shrugged out of his jacket.

My heart jumped into my throat and I scrambled off the chair in a very ungraceful way and pointed to his arm. Covering my mouth, I shook my head. It couldn't be. "Where—*why* do you have that tattoo?" His eyes were green...

He held out his arm and looked at it and then to me, confusion on his face.

"Oh," Crissy jumped up and pulled her arm out of her jacket and held it out, "we both have it. See." She held out her arm.

Shaking my head, I backed up. It couldn't be.

Victor paused and looked at me. "I can assure you, my mark is very recent and I have never had any dalliances on the other side."

"Alona? Did your mother have one? A tattoo down her arm?"

It took a second for it to register that Chase was speaking to me. I looked at him, still not sure if I could speak and nodded my head yes.

"Shit." He looked at his twin. "They were mated."

"Wouldn't he have told someone, so he could go get her?" Michael asked looking angry.

Victor shook his head looking upset as well. "I would think he would. Even with the ban, that would have been allowed."

"They couldn't have done the blood rite…" Troy mused quietly, "without it, living apart that long would…"

"Cause one to slowly go insane? With long bouts of depression?" I asked, trying to stay calm. I didn't understand much of what they were talking about, but I did grasp one thing. My mother hadn't been lying.

"Yes." Troy said softly, compassion bleeding from his every pore.

Daxx looked like she was going to cry. "I can't imagine it."

"Even if he'd been over there illegally… any of us would have allowed him to go back to find his mate." Quinton looked to Victor, "Right?"

Victor nodded, a very thoughtful expression on his face. "Did your mother ever tell you his name?"

I shook my head. "Not that I remember. All I know, is that I have his eyes."

"Michael, go talk to the doctor and see if there's any record of a male displaying symptoms of a mate loss during that time, hopefully he keeps accurate records. Also, get him to pull the history of all males we lost during that epidemic." Victor turned back to Troy. "Do you still have records for any that applied to bring someone over during that period?" He glanced to Chase, "either of you?"

Troy rubbed the back of his neck. "We do, but I can't see him having applied and being denied whilst bearing the mate's mark."

"Is there a chance he did go over and got sick there?" Daxx asked.

"We'll have a record if he didn't return." Victor said, then dropped a quick kiss on Crissy's head and walked out of the room.

I just stood there, trying to process all of this. My father hadn't just bailed on my mother and me, at least that was my take on it. Everything I thought I knew for close to a century was now altered. I felt like the walls were closing in. "I think..." I looked around trying to decide. "I'd like some time..." I glanced at the door. "How do I get home?" I looked at Crissy, who turned and looked at Daxx.

"Are you sure you should go back if they're following you?" She asked me cautiously.

I'd forgotten about that. "I will be fine. I'll just stay at my apartment." I took a deep breath and then exhaled. "I need some time away to process."

"We're going to see if we can find him." Troy offered softly.

I nodded. Find my father. "I appreciate that, I truly do. I'll give you my number..." I remembered the *sides*. "Will my number work? Can you call..." I didn't know how to even ask.

"It will." Daxx nodded. "I'll give you mine also, if you need me or have questions you can call me."

Taking my phone out of my pocket, I handed it to her. "Please just put it in my contacts." It felt as if my insides were quivering in shock.

"We'll let you know if we find out anything." Chase came over and stood a few feet from me, his hazel eyes assessing my current state.

I wished him luck with that, as I wasn't even sure what I was feeling right now. "Yes. That would be lovely." I nodded again, just wanting to get out of here.

"Add my number, kitten, if that guy shows up she can call me. I'd like to have a *chat* with him." He turned to look at Troy, who nodded like he'd spoken to him, then glanced to Arius. "Give her the transporter, so she can get back here if she needs to in a hurry." Arius stood up and handed it to him. Opening it, he showed me. "Just push that button, while wearing it..." he smirked, "anyone you are touching will come back with you, *but* if they're not meant to be on this side, they will most likely die in a few minutes if they're not wearing it..."

That I understood. I looked to Crissy and opened my mouth. "I could have died?"

"Oh my gosh..." She whispered. "Is that what happens? I kept forgetting to ask."

"It's okay, cutie, Alona is meant to be here—you saw her, so we were sure she was safe too." Chase assured her.

I took the device he held out and looked at it. There was only one button, so no chance of making a mistake. "It brings me to that room?"

"It does." He tucked his hands in his pockets.

"How do I leave?" Daxx held out my phone, so I took it and put it back in my jacket pocket.

His hazel eyes kept moving over my face, and I couldn't pick up on the emotions going through them as they did. "I'll take you back, just tell me where."

I glanced to Crissy. "Can't Crissy take me back?"

Chase shook his head, "No, only members of the royal family can without a device, she may be able to without... but..." he turned and looked at Crissy for a second, "I don't see Victor rushing to find out until she can focus on one thing at a time."

"I see." I wasn't at all comfortable with the idea of anyone knowing where I lived.

"It's okay, really. If it wasn't, I would have killed them all by now." Daxx put her hand on my back and then her eyes widened. I felt her feeling the blade between my shoulders. She smirked. "A girl's best friend."

I nodded once. "Absolutely."

"Anyone else feel like we've missed something?" Quinton asked.

Sighing, I turned around and pushed my jacket off my shoulders, so they could see the dagger hidden on my back.

When I heard enough noise to let me know they had seen it, I put my jacket back on a turned around. "A girl can't be too careful." I shrugged.

Chase grinned wide. "Do all women over there carry concealed knives? I mean, seriously, the men don't stand a chance."

I gave him a puzzled look. "Only the smart ones, I suppose."

"I think he's talking about this." Daxx pulled a small curved blade from behind her back. "I don't go anywhere without my little raptor."

I understood what he meant now, but still needed to get out of here. "Do you need an address, or what... to take me back?"

He shook his head. "Daxx probably could by address, I don't know that city well, it has to be somewhere I've been to get there."

"Just get me back to the old factory and I will get home from there." I told him, hoping that was good enough.

"Wait." Crissy came rushing over and hugged me briefly. "I'm sorry about your mom and dad." She gave me a heartfelt look.

I inhaled sharply, her emotions smothering me. "Thank you. I've had decades to get over it. Mostly." I stepped back, as I tried to build a barrier to block out some of her emotions. I nodded to the others in the room. "Thank you, all. I'm sure we'll be in touch soon." I glanced at Chase, more than ready to get out of here, even if it was with a strange man.

"I'll be back shortly," he said and glanced at his twin. Giving me a half smile, he put his hand on my arm. "Close your eyes, or you'll get dizzy."

I paused for a second and then closed them.

Chapter Three

The rolling of my stomach told me he'd done whatever it was to bring us back. I opened my eyes as he stepped away and put my hand over my stomach. "Is it like that every time?"

Chase tucked his hands in his pockets. "I think your body gets used to it." He shrugged. "I've been doing it for a few hundred years, so I can't remember." Looking around, he motioned to a platform that had once been a loading dock. "Here, come sit for a minute. Once you've got your bearings I'll go back."

I nodded and went over and sat down. "This isn't quite the day I had planned when I woke up."

He snorted and sat down a few feet away from me. "That's my moto lately." He blew out a breath, "especially since cutie... Crissy, came along."

I exhaled slowly, breathing to relieve my churning stomach. "I believe that. I can't quite get a sense of her yet."

"I wouldn't count on ever getting one, not really, she's one of a kind." He grinned. "Which is why I'm thankful and eternally grateful that she put my uptight oldest brother in his place." With a half shrug, he watched me. "All I know is if she says duck, we duck, if she says run... we don't ask why because we're running."

I took a deep breath, encouraging the queasiness to settle. "It is an odd match." What he said registered. "She can see what's going to happen?"

Chase shrugged. "Fate seems to know who we need as a mate, so you can't argue with that. As for Crissy, I don't know how it works, just that she sees a lot and it's always right, even if we don't always understand what she says."

So much made sense to me now, with Crissy always spouting confusing things about seeing, but not until she saw. I studied him for a moment, he wasn't the player he appeared to be when not in front of his siblings. "Fate selects the mates, it's not your choice?"

"No." He smirked, "which is probably a good thing or there would be matches that didn't belong together for eternity all over the place." Pushing his still messy hair back from his face, he gave me a serious look. "There is no divorcing a true mate."

I still couldn't grasp that there were others as old, or older, than I was. I'd given up hoping for that a long time ago. "Well, fate is a cruel bitch to have done what it did to my mother."

With a sobering look, he inclined his head. "We'll find out what happened. I know it doesn't change the outcome, but at least you'll know."

"I have a lot to think about. I hated my father for what he did to her..." I sighed, "And, even though I loved my mother, I always believed she was—that she had misconstrued the truth to avoid facing true facts."

A look of contemplation was on his face. "I can't even imagine what you've been through." He waved a hand around. "To come into the change over here, without knowing," he blew out a breath, "it shouldn't have been that way."

I could feel the slightest touch of empathy coming from him, which somehow made me feel better that I'd sensed any emotion from him. "I came into... *the change* during the war, the second one, while helping in the medical camps. I was twenty." His eyes widened. "Of course, the horror of wanting to bite the injured didn't sit well with me, so I fled and I've never looked back since." He sat there, his hands clasped in his lap, hazel eyes searching my face, listening. I couldn't even remember a time when I had someone who listened to me. "Although, now finally knowing I'm not the spawn of Satan may be worth knowing the rest."

He chuckled, "Nope, you're perfectly normal." He rolled his eyes, "okay not over *here*, but in Alterealm you are just like the rest of us." Chase paused to asses me with those pale eyes of his again and then stood up. "Here we're the nightmares of this side, witches, mages, seers, mind readers... it's just normal life for us over there."

I knew my eyes were wide as I digested that. "Extra... abilities go with it?"

"For many, not all." He winked. "I was given the gift of my charm instead of a psychic power."

I cleared my throat, "so you're still working on perfecting that gift then?"

"Oh, the burn of that sassy tongue." He held his hand over his chest.

"Your eyes go yellow, so you don't have to bite people?"

He smirked, "only if I want to. No, I'm not an essence feeder, no fangs required."

Essence feeder. Is that what I was? I found that somehow comforting. I detested the taste of blood and yet was still drawn to bite into flesh, never knowing why. Only knowing that my health suffered if I didn't. It dawned on me I still hadn't found out the reason I'd gone over there in the first place. "I'm sorry, but I was distracted meeting brother after brother," I shrugged, "no one explained why that man is following me, or who *they* are."

"Most likely they want to recruit you, if that's the case then they know you're not as you appear to be. If the eyes are yellow, don't get close enough to let them stare into your eyes. If their eyes are purple, be somewhere else, fast. Those are the two to watch out for." He rubbed his hand over his jaw. "They are team bad, we're in the midst of a good versus evil war between this realm and ours."

Just my luck, to end up in something like that. "You and your brothers are the good?"

He rolled his eyes at me, "of course we are. I'm offended you'd have to ask." Chase looked around us, then motioned to the device I still had. "Use that if you have need, call if you have questions." I nodded and he bowed in a regal way and was gone, before I could say a word.

I stared at the spot he had been, then looked down at the device I held. "What have you landed in this time?" I pondered out loud. Checking to make sure no one was around, I got up and headed to find a cab.

I spent the entire day, well into the evening, sitting in my apartment digesting everything I'd found out. I wasn't alone in my strange ways, in fact, there was an entire *realm* of others just like me. I can't say I was disappointed to not be as unique as I'd thought I was a day earlier. I still wasn't ready to think in terms of different realms existing simultaneously though.

If what Chase had said was any indication, having extra abilities was normal as well. Of course, having help about ninety years ago to learn to cope with it all would have saved me a lot of heartache. When I'd first started absorbing the emotions of others around me, I'd thought it was due to my mother's never-ending pain and depression. After she passed, it didn't take long for me to discover it was every single person around me. Until today, when those brothers had been all but impossible to read emotions from. I had to wonder if all others like myself were like that or was it just them.

Perhaps once I got to know more about them, I could inquire about others with my issue, and see if there was a better way to cope with it. Mind you, I hardly ever became too overwhelmed now, and hoped the days of throwing up and passing out were over. I was owed some sort of good luck.

For an hour I'd tried picturing the moment of meeting my father, if he was in fact still alive. I honestly didn't know how I felt about. It may not have been his doing, and I knew this now, but still, seeing a man that had tormented my mother by—marking her, I suppose was the correct term, and then leaving her. Did I want to set that aside and see him? I didn't know.

I paused in thought and stared out the window. What if they did figure out who he was and he had relatives still living? I'd never had any sort of family that I remembered. My aunt and uncle had died shortly after my mother had gone to them, when I was a baby. Aside from them, there was no living family. I didn't know how to be part of a family. I didn't even know how to be around people on a social level.

There have been very few people I had allowed myself to get close to over the years, always ending with me watching them die while I remained the same. I couldn't do that again. Soaking up other emotions was one thing, drowning in my own… too reminiscent of my mother's life to me.

I did know one thing: I was never allowing myself to be marked or mated, or whatever the technical term for it was. Ever. I would not submit myself to that kind of torture and pain willingly.

The longer I sat here brooding, the more I remembered things they had said. The royal family could only transport without a device, being one of the things I recalled. Royal family? Naturally that lead me to think of monarchy and all that, but with all the new things I was learning, it could mean something different. If this kept up, I would have to start a list to remember my own questions.

My phone made a strange noise, so I went to go get it and see why. I'd only ever used it to call a cab, order Chinese food and keep an eye on the stock markets. A few good investments over the years had kept me from having to earn my keep among people that smelled like dinner as they drowned me in their feelings.

I had a message from Daxx. Sitting down, I studied my options, not quite sure how to open it or reply. I tapped on it and it opened.

Just checking that you are okay, before the testosterone crew start asking.

I smiled. I could like her, I thought. Hitting 'reply' I typed carefully so I wouldn't hit a wrong button.

I am. I haven't left my apartment. I clicked send and stared at the phone, feeling oddly excited to text someone.

That sounds like fun. At least Crissy and I have her tower to hide in.

Pausing I wondered what kind of tower that would be. One more question to add to the list.

I only have a penthouse in a high security building. No tower.

Okay you win. The men are stomping around demanding answers, so hopefully we'll have some for you soon.

Answers. The question that remained was, did I want to know them?

I believe I have more questions then I will ever have answers for.

LOL! I can relate to that! Learning about Alterealm was like a bad acid trip for me… still is some days.

LOL? I debated on asking, but it was a small matter of pride at my age to not feel like an idiot. I would look on the internet later as to its meaning. The internet knew everything.

Yes, it is quite a bit to digest.

Troy is looking for me. I have to go. Call if you need me or have the answer now kind of questions.

A second one arrived before I could think of a reply.

And Crissy says if you see Emil (lost brother that looks like Arius) to grab him and push your button.

I honestly wasn't sure if she meant that or how to respond, so I typed back, *I will and thank you I shall call if I need to.*

A little yellow smiley face was the only reply I got back.

Setting the phone down, I looked at it. That was something I suppose, to have had my first conversation by text message at ninety-eight years old. I chuckled to myself. I needed to get out of my head for a while so I could think more clearly about, well, everything.

Getting up, I went and looked out the window down over the city. I lived in a clean, upscale neighborhood, full of well-heeled citizens that kept to themselves. For that reason alone, when I needed to feed I went to a less savory area of the city. The area, I just realized, that if I hadn't gone to, I never would have met Crissy. If one could call a strange woman dragging you from a club a meeting.

Sighing, I turned back and grabbed my phone. I needed to go sate my need for essence, I now had a name for it, I realized. Before I became needy and anyone seemed appealing. I'd discovered long ago, going to a bar or club where most were intoxicated was the best way to find those easy to feed from, it helped that their emotions were simpler to deal with.

Staring at the little device they'd given me, I picked it up and tucked it in my pocket—just in case. I'd never had a fast way out before, so it would be ridiculous not to take it. My dagger was the last thing I made sure was on my person, then I put on my jacket and left to get a cab.

Chapter Four

I stood at the dark end of the bar, turning the drink in my hand, watching all the action around me. As odd as it seemed, this place was familiar and that brought comfort. The bartender, Jorge, knew me, and I always sensed confusion from him. I suppose I didn't blend in well with the crowd that preferred this location, but I liked it. There were five different exits, and that was better than any other spot I had found.

It wasn't late enough to have the usual crowd falling over each other, but there were a few good prospects I was keeping an eye on. It had taken a few decades to hone the skill of selecting the right person. Of course, the sixties had been the easiest by far to find someone to share a few non-sexual close moments with, but that time was long gone.

I'd like to say I'd always kept it platonic, but that would also be a lie. The years could be lonely and the occasional night of lying to yourself was allowed and forgiven. Mostly. The least complicated person to select was a female. Men always expected more. If my *other realm-ness* involved being able to place a trance on my victims, that would have made life so much simpler, but sadly it did not. I knew this after trying when I first thought I was a vampire. The moments in my youth had been strictly trial and error.

The bartender came down and leaned across the bar. "I'll never figure it out." He grinned at me. "What you are doing here."

I offered him a genuine smile. "You wouldn't believe it if I told you." He reminded me of a biker, but was in fact a big teddy bear, well, toward me he was. I had seen him step in to settle patrons down, and anyone that crossed him was lacking in intelligence, to say the least.

He stood there looking at me for a moment, then raised his hands and backed away. "All right Ms. Mysterious, we'll leave it at that." Tapping the gouged-up bar beside the glass in my hand, he smiled. "If you ever drink that, let me know." With a wink, he turned to look after another customer.

In all the visits here, I'd never yet drank what I ordered and he knew it. I leaned back into the dark space and looked around to see if anyone new had arrived. Would it be too much to ask for someone half passed out in a dark corner? I wasn't in the mood for having to spend an hour finding a way to get what I needed and get home.

A man I had briefly spoken to the week before came in and looked around. He was a low-life scavenger as far as I was concerned. Pure bottom feeder. As least he knew not to approach me again with his sad ideas. I watched him go to the other side of the room. Once assured he was avoiding me, I looked around again.

The light reflecting off a bald head I was starting to know a little too well caught my eye. It was the man with the yellow eyes. Again. I knew he didn't know where I lived, as I hadn't seen him near there, but anytime I crossed that bridge to this side of the city, there he was. I watched him sit at the other end of the bar and look around. As long as I stayed where I was, I would be hidden in this shadowed corner. Of course, that didn't help me accomplish what I had come here for.

Chase had said not to let him get close, there was no worry of that happening. I still needed to know why he was following me to begin with. 'Good versus evil war between realms' didn't exactly tell me anything. In fact, most of what

Chase and his brothers had said made little sense. I had to find out, or I would need to find a new location to look for essence donors, which could take weeks. Chase had to said to call if I saw him again, that, I didn't see happening.

Pulling out my phone, I opened up the messages from Daxx earlier. She was the only one that didn't seem to speak in riddles, or in Crissy's case, mass confusion. Hovering my fingers over the screen, I debated if I should. Sighing, I typed out, *if I were to see that man following me again, what would you advise me to do?* Then tapped send.

If it were me? I'd get in his face and ask him what was up with the stalking. And then the guys would get pissy at what I did. Winking yellow smiley face. *Guess you left your penthouse?*

I couldn't help smiling to her message. I sent back. *I had some things to attend to.*

You need backup? Say where and I'm there.

Did I? That was a whole new possibility for me, having someone to help me if I required. I looked over at the bald *stalker*, he sat there still looking around. Essentially, I was going to be stuck in this corner until he left, and if the past encounters meant a thing, he wouldn't leave until he tried to follow me.

I answered Daxx. *I'm not sure if I do. However, I would like him to stop following me.* It was a few minutes before she replied.

Crap. Raf read over my shoulder and I've been grounded. Frowning yellow face. *Raf says he'll be happy to come to get rid of your stalker.*

Raf? How did anyone keep them all straight? I messaged back. *Which one is Raf?* If it was the cop-like one, I didn't want him showing up, or the one that was Crissy's man.

LOL the big sweetie. Blond, blue eyes.

The LOL again. I glanced around while holding the phone, trying to decide. *Can he be inconspicuous?* I asked her.

"Tell her yes." Raf said, as he sat down on the stool beside me.

I just stared at him. How did he get here so fast?

He shrugged. "Wasn't hard to figure out where you'd be to *attend* to things." He smiled at me.

The bartender came over and set a drink in front of him and gave him a nod, then looked at me and smiled. "It's becoming clearer now." He laughed and went back in the other direction.

Realizing I still held my phone, I closed the screen and put it in my pocket. I looked Rafael over and was thankful he was in jeans and didn't have any large weapons hanging from him.

He raised an eyebrow at me, "I know how to blend." He grinned wide. "So where is our stalker?" Raf asked without looking at me.

Did he read minds? I should ask Daxx about these brothers and their *gifts*. I leaned back into the darkness and nodded toward the end of the bar. "He'll sit there until I get up and then will attempt to follow me."

Taking a drink, he took a few minutes to study him. "So how do you want to play this?"

I held my glass and turned it a few times, watching the liquid move as I did. "Do you always come to the aid of strange women?" I looked back to him. He gave me a smile that would make any female's knees weaken.

"It's what I do best." He winked at me.

"I see. Is that your gift, as charm is Chases?"

He laughed. "Don't let his teasing fool you, being king of half of our side is a job he takes seriously."

A king? He was a king? "Only half?" I had to ask.

Rafael rolled his eyes. "It's a very long story and history. We have two, Troy and Chase. Later we'll talk about it if you like." He nodded to the bald man. "What are we doing about him?"

I had so much to learn. "I'd like to know why he is following me."

"If I were any of my brothers, I'd tell you hell no and persuade you to leave." He shrugged, "but I'm not. Why don't you go ask him and I'll lurk nearby?"

"Really?" I looked back to the man we were discussing. "Chase said not to let those with yellow eyes close."

Nodding, he leaned in until our faces were a mere six inches apart. "That would be *this* close."

I looked into his blue eyes for a second and then he leaned away again. "If he gets that close, I'd have to poke out his eyes."

He grinned and motioned down the bar. "I'll be close enough if you need me." His eyes moved over my face for a moment. "Just flick your hair back off your shoulder if you want me to step in."

I ran my hand over my hair that fell close to my waist, making sure it hung in front if I needed to *flick* it. Taking a deep breath, I nodded and got up. With long strides, I walked toward the man and he watched me take each step. There was no smile on his face, or even a friendly look, when I sat on the stool closest to him. "You seem to be everywhere I go." I said loud enough for him to hear.

Dark eyes moved over my body, making my skin crawl. "I have friends that would like meet you." He finally looked back to my eyes. "They think you'll be interested in hearing what they have to say."

I couldn't sense any emotions from him and was sure that was a good thing as far as he was concerned. "So, stalking me is your way to persuade me to agree?"

His facial expression didn't change. "You make it very hard to approach, when you're running the other way."

"A girl can't be too careful when strange men approach." Without feeling what he was, I couldn't tell if he was like every other pervert out there or not.

Giving me a slight nod, he reached in his pocket and pulled out a card. "If you're interested, call here."

I took the card and looked at it, there was only a number. "That's all I get? How do I know if I'm interested without details?" When I looked back up, his eyes were yellow. I leaned further away, making sure he wasn't close enough to do whatever that meant.

"To work with many others like yourself? I think that would be intriguing." He said, and then his eyes went back to dull brown.

"I see." I held up the card. "And what do I say if I call this number?"

"Just tell them you need to speak to Lou." He grinned a half smile. "That's me." With that he got up and headed for the exit.

I sat there holding the card and watching him leave. If I'd known it was going to be that simple I would have spoken to him several weeks ago. Rafael came over and sat on the stool he'd just left. I flipped the card around and showed him.

His brows drew together. "They're handing out cards?"

I shrugged. "I thought it odd."

He snorted. "And epically stupid." Glancing around, he turned back and gave me a soft look. "We need to go tell Victor."

"You mean back over there?" I wasn't sure I wanted to do that again.

Rafael nodded. "Unless you'd like him to come here and soak up some of the night life with you."

I still hadn't fed, but supposed I could hold off for an hour or so, if needed. That man I had just talked to had something to do with Crissy getting hurt, and I would feel guilty if I didn't help her... mate, seek some sort of retribution. Giving Raf a hesitant look, I nodded. "I guess I could go back, I mean, who doesn't love wanting to throw up."

With a laugh, he stood up and tossed some money on the bar, then held out his hand. "I'll try to do it slowly for you."

"There's a slowly?" He gently tugged my hand as he went to the back exit.

Once outside he looked around and then patted his chest. "Rest your head against me and close your eyes, breathe slow, deep breaths."

I gave him a skeptical look.

He smirked. "It's not a line, I swear."

Looking him up and down, I debated on it for a moment. "I suppose you wouldn't need to use a line very often."

He chuckled. "I don't think I can answer that without it sounding wrong."

I stepped closer and took a deep breath. "Just breathe slowly?"

He touched the back of my head, so I would lean against his chest. "It's worse for some people, getting used to it." His hand didn't stroke me or anything, he just held it there.

Chapter Five

My stomach rolled and I knew he'd done whatever it was they did to bring us to the other side.

"Just keep your eyes closed for a second." He said softly.

"I'm not sure... oh, Raf, you're back." I heard Daxx.

Opening my eyes, I stepped back, regretting that as the movement brought a wave of nausea with it. I realized we were in the big dining room, and quickly sat in a chair and put my head on the table.

"Alona? Are you all right?" She was now right beside me.

"Yes." I took slow breaths trying to breathe through it.

"Her system is very sensitive to transporting." Rafael informed her.

Lifting my head, I looked at him. "I'm sure most bodies have difficulty adapting."

"I got so dizzy sometimes when I was getting the hang of it." Daxx said and then sat down.

I noticed her large mate standing behind her. "I spoke to my stalker and he gave me this." I set the card on the table, then noticed I'd crushed it in my hand when Rafael had brought us back. Flattening it, I glanced to Troy. "If I'm interested in working with others like myself, I'm to call, *Lou*, at this number."

He reached around Daxx and picked up the card. "They give out cards?"

"That's what I said." Raf chuckled.

Troy flipped it over to look on the back. It was blank.

"It should say team bad with a logo on the other side." Rafael told him with a grin.

Troy set the card back on the table and straightened. "I'm—I have no words. I can't believe they're handing out cards."

"Sorry for my absence, dears, Ira was a bit under the weather the last few days."

A shorter woman with strawberry blonde hair twisted up in a chignon came into the room. Waves of loving emotions swamped me, even from this distance.

"I didn't even know you could get sick." Daxx said sounding amazed.

"It happens, love, we're still susceptible beings over here." She stopped and looked at me. "Hello, dear, I'm Mitz."

"Mitz, this is Alona." Rafael informed her.

"Oh, the one Crissy kept seeing." She paused and looked at me carefully. "Stomach doesn't like transporting? I have some tea that will take care of that." She gave me a nod.

I offered a weak smile. "Anything to settle my stomach would be lovely."

"Is Ira back on his feet? The guard house doesn't run nearly as well without him." Troy asked her.

She nodded. "He's fine. He was just being a man, love, nothing to worry over." Turning, she went back through the door she'd come out of.

"What does that mean?" Troy asked.

Daxx snorted and then smiled at me. "Males tend to exaggerate the slightest sniffle."

Troy frowned. "I'm sure you're mistaken."

Laughing, she got up and patted his big chest. "Of course, a king such as you, would never exaggerate anything."

"Does anyone ever *use* their office anymore?" The cop-like brother came in waving papers in the air. "I went to Victor's, Leone's and yours," he pointed to Troy, "they're all empty."

Rafael waved his phone in the air. "That's why they invented these little things so you can call people instead of chasing them down."

"Why were you looking for us, Michael?" Troy asked while hugging Daxx.

He stopped and looked at me, and then down to the papers in his hand. "I didn't know you'd be back so soon."

"She called for backup and managed to get us a lead all in one night." Rafael informed him, grabbing the card off the table, he held it out to him. "Team bad is handing out cards."

Frowning, Michael took the card from his hand and looked at it. "They're giving out cards? Well, at least we know their intelligence is not a priority we need to worry about."

Crissy came racing in the door. "Your back! I was so worried. When I'd seen it, I wasn't sure, but now that I see you, I am." She nodded very excitedly while looking at me.

"Deep breath, Crissy and tell us that *with* the missing pieces, please." Daxx told her.

I felt somewhat better knowing I wasn't the only one that didn't understand her.

"I saw Alona's eyes, only now that I see her I know they weren't *her* green eyes, they were the same, but different." She smiled. "And a little piece of a paper." She frowned, then her eyes widened. "Oh, and a cave glowing orange... only I think that's just lighting and it's not really glowing and may be more of an old alley then cave..."

I looked away from her to see the others were taking every word she said very seriously. I didn't even know what she was telling us.

"Hey." She almost hopped over to Michael and pulled the card from his hand. "This is the piece of paper that was in my head. The numbers are the same." She smiled at him. "How did you know?"

Michael looked from her to Daxx, "Call everyone. Now."

Daxx nodded, she already had her phone in her hand when she paused. "Chase too?"

The men in the room exchanged looks.

"He needs to be kept up to speed." Troy said finally.

"Okay," she mumbled, "but he's going to be cranky, us waking him up early, again."

I glanced at Rafael. "I feel like I've missed something quite important."

Grinning, he sat down in the chair beside me. "You get used to it." Patting the chair on the other side, he looked at Crissy. "Sit and write down anything important we need to know."

She nodded and pulled her backpack off. "I was in my tower after Daxx left and it came to me all at once."

I watched for a few moments as Crissy began scribbling in a notebook. "At some point, someone will explain whatever she said, yes?"

Rafael nodded. "Yeah. Once we translate it."

Whoever could translate that, I wished them luck. At least, while she was scribbling in her notebook the emotions weren't pouring off her.

"Here you go, love." Mitz came in carrying a cup. "This will settle the body nicely after shifting it over here." She gave me a sweet smile.

The only time in my life I'd felt the emotions she was giving off was when my mother used to hold me and hum softly at night. I took the cup and smiled. "Thank you." I meant it too, not just for the tea. In a world too full of people, I spent most of my time trying to build barriers to block out emotions I didn't want. Feeling one that made me remember love and caring was an emotional wave I was in no hurry to rid my system of.

Michael and Troy were on the other side of the room now talking quietly, looking at the papers he'd been waving around.

Arius and Leone came in, both dressed as Victor had been, dark leather and large weapons. I had to wonder if we hadn't gone back in time to a more medieval period. Either that, or this war they were fighting was grossly and personally violent, unlike the push-of-a-button battles today's society thought normal.

"Victor will be here shortly." Leone said as he shrugged out of the series of straps holding the weapons on his back. "We had a few trying to lay claim to the farms on the other side of the wasteland," he shook his head. "No idea why they'd want those."

"The ones on a three-year rest?" Troy asked

Arius nodded. "Yes, those."

"Private or commercial use?" Troy asked crossing his arms over his chest.

Leone sat down and rubbed a hand over his short hair. "Pretty sure for commercial use."

Troy didn't look pleased with that. "They're on a rest period for a reason. If we don't let the nutrients in the soil replenish, we'll have the wastelands all over again."

"That's what happened to the wastelands?" Daxx asked setting her phone on the table.

"More or less." Arius answered, and then he saw me and bowed his head. "Welcome back."

"Do we need to increase patrols? Maybe set up a new squad, with everything else we're chasing... do we need to have someone else deal with the lands?" Troy asked looking every bit a ruler now.

"Are you insinuating we can't do our jobs, brother?" Victor asked walking in with long strides. He was all in black leather again, minus the swords on his back.

"I would never assume such a thing." Troy told him.

Victor nodded and walked to Crissy and glanced at what she was writing in the book. Leaning down, he kissed the top of her head and then straightened. "For what purpose was this meeting called?"

Rafael leaned back in the chair and looked up at him. "It's kind of a mix n' match of what Michael discovered, little sister saw, and Alona was given."

Victor studied him for a moment and then looked to Troy. "Perhaps someone with a grasp of the English language could tell me."

Mitz came in carrying a tray with a small mountain of sandwiches on it. "I'll be back with coffee." She set it down and left again.

"Perfect timing." Quinton said as he walked in and went right to the food. Grabbing a few he sat down. "Struck out on that tip for the location of more followers." He said not looking at anyone.

"It was deserted or entirely wrong?" Victor asked and sat down beside Crissy.

"Deserted." He answered between bites.

"It's like they're moving from our side to the other side now on a regular rotation to keep us guessing." Arius said as he helped himself to the food.

I had no idea what they were talking about, so I chose just to sit there and remain invisible. I leaned closer to Rafael. "At some point, something someone says will make sense to me, yes?"

He chuckled. "We can hope." Shrugging he grinned at Daxx. "Sometimes I don't even understand."

I doubted that, but it was sweet of him to try to put me at ease. I took another sip of the tea. I'm not sure what blend it was, but it was helping my stomach a great deal. Later, I would enquire as to the leaves used. With nausea being something that plagued me often, it would be nice to have this on hand.

Chase appeared in the doorway that Mitz kept going in and out of. His hair was mussed like he'd been sleeping. In his hand was a large steaming mug, most likely full of coffee. "You know," he looked around slowly at the men, "if you were decent brothers, you would let a king sleep occasionally." He huffed out a breath and walked in, taking the first chair he came to. "My captains seem to be running my half of the realm more than I am since Marcus went rogue and ruined my sleep schedule."

Troy rubbed the back of his neck. "It's been trying for everyone, Chase, but it's not that early. You'd be up in a few hours."

Chase took a sip from his mug and then gave him a half nod. "I had trouble sleeping..." he waved his other hand around, "brain decided analyzing life was more important." Raising his cup, he paused when he looked at me. Setting it down he sighed. "Now I know I'm exhausted when I don't even see a lovely woman in the room." He smiled at me. "Welcome back, duchess."

Daxx snorted. "Uh oh, you're stuck with us now, you've been nicknamed by the royal flirt." She pointed to Crissy, "meet cutie and I'm kitten."

I glanced at her with wide eyes. "I'm not sure about either of those, but I am most definitely not the duchess type."

She laughed again. "Says the woman who was texting me from her *pent*-house."

"As entertaining as all of this is, could we please get to the reason we were called here? I have a few leads I'd like to look into before this day is done." Victor said sounding annoyed.

"Oh my gosh." Crissy's head popped up and she looked at me. "I think you were the baby I saw." She looked to Victor and then Daxx. "I told you, after my text about it." She exhaled a loud breath. "It makes sense now."

I know my mouth was open, but I honestly didn't know what to make of that. I glanced to Daxx and then Rafael.

He shook his head. "It gets easier."

Mitz came in with an urn and set it on the table and then brought a cup to Crissy. "Just give a shout if you need anything. I have to get the kitchen straightened up after being away."

"Thank you, Mitz." Troy said and then sat down and motioned to the others to sit. "First, Alona spoke to the man that's been following her and brought back something interesting."

Rafael picked up the card and held it out. "He gave her a card and told her to call the number if she wanted to work with others like her."

"You're serious?" Chase said over his cup. He glanced at me. "You what, just went up to him and he gave you a card?"

I nodded. "I wanted to know why he was following me, so I asked." I motioned to Rafael. "Rafael was there in case I required aid."

Chase gave his brother an odd look for a few moments. "You thought that was a good plan? Put her in reach of someone like that?"

"I warned her how far to stay from him, and I was literally five steps away, watching the entire time." He defended his choice.

Chase's jaw clenched, but he inclined his head and then took a sip of his coffee without speaking.

"I can't believe they're handing out cards." Quinton said, pausing a sandwich halfway to his mouth. "Is there just a number?"

Michael snorted. "No, brother it says *to find us follow the trail of bread crumbs*. Of course, it's just a number."

"Can we trace the number?" I asked. I didn't know much about such things, but it was in the movies often enough.

"It will most likely be a cheap burner, but we can try." Michael said, then glanced to Troy.

"I'm guessing if it's not Alona calling, the call will be dropped and the number will vanish."

"Are you saying we need to use her as bait?" Chase all but hissed at his brother.

Michael gave him an odd look. "No, I'm saying if they've been following *Alona*, gave *Alona* the card, if it's not *Alona* on the other end of the phone it becomes a new dead end." He huffed out a breath. "I know we woke you, but stop being like a bitchy fifth grader."

Chase glared at him. "I am nothing like a child."

Rafael chuckled quietly beside me. "You know being an only child sounds appealing sometimes."

Shaking my head, I glanced to him briefly. "I can't say these many siblings would have been welcomed, but being only one is quite empty at times."

"Let's just come back to the card and what we're doing about it. If she calls him back too quickly, they will be suspicious, at least I would be after having to chase her down." Daxx suggested softly. "I want to know what Criss saw. She's put us in the right place at the right time before, I have faith that wherever she saw is where we need to be.

Victor nodded. "Your thoughts about the card seem most likely." He placed his arm around Crissy's shoulder. "Tell us what you saw, heart."

She smiled up at him. "The card, well, it was a piece of paper with numbers to me, but they are the same numbers." She tapped her notebook, "I wrote them down before I left the tower so I wouldn't forget."

Victor kissed her forehead. "You never forget anything."

Crissy sighed, "that's true. I thought I'd seen Alona's eyes, only it wasn't hers, which is good, because they looked angry and hollow, can eyes look hollow?" She frowned for a moment, "but they were the same other than that."

Everyone turned to look at me. I didn't know what that could mean. "My eyes always look like they are now, as far as I know. Perhaps a little less confused, but the same."

"I don't think she was seeing your eyes, but a relative with eyes the same." Michael offered and then tapped the papers he'd been carrying. "I was searching empty offices because I found out about your father." He glanced to Troy, who nodded. "In the time during the transport ban, we only had one male go over and not return," he held up his hand before anyone could speak. "Yet, the serial number on his transporter has been used since then."

"What does that mean?" I put my hand on my chest, not sure if I wanted to know more. My heart was already speeding up.

"He went over looking for your mother and didn't come back for months, but the transporter was not returned, and

41

then it was used a few years later." Michael rubbed and hand over the scar on his face. "In the chaos of the ban and preventing the sickness from spreading over here, somehow it was completely overlooked."

"Didn't we lose several of the guards that monitor the landing rooms to the sickness?" Arius asked with a solemn tone.

Victor nodded. "We did. They were exposed when others came back and exposed them. It was a few weeks before we knew it had happened."

"That would explain not keeping track of all the devices." Chase said quietly, but his eyes didn't leave me during the whole conversation.

"What...what your saying is my father did apply to go back, and went to find my mother." I could barely form a sentence. Everything I thought I'd known was wrong. "My mother left the city, she left word with the building caretaker, for when he returned..." I covered my mouth with both hands and stared at the table before me. He had returned. The room was silent, no one spoke or moved. I tried to process the fact that my mother had died waiting for a man that couldn't find her.

I looked back to Michael. "You're certain it was him?"

Michael nodded. "It is the only application for a male to bring his true mate to Alterealm."

"And his name?" Was this really happening? Was I going to finally know after this long what my father's name was? I had asked my mother many times and each time I did it caused one of her depression periods, so I had given up asking. Even as young as I was, I somehow was able to grasp that it hurt her to speak his name.

"Levi." Michael said close to a whisper.

I covered my mouth with a shaking hand. "I need a moment. Excuse me." I pushed back from the table and went out the closest door. I found myself standing in the long hallway they had brought me through when Crissy had spontaneously hijacked me to this world. I just stopped and stood there looking down the long hallway. My father's name was Levi and he had wanted my mother, maybe he would have wanted me also.

I felt someone come up behind me. "Alona?" It was Daxx. "I'd ask if you were all right, but I understand the shock all this must be."

A tear rolled down my cheek. "I thought my mother was insane and made up this story to make it acceptable that she'd conceived me out of wedlock." I wiped the tear away. "I'm normally not the weeping type."

She stepped around so she could see me. "I'd be bawling my eyes out if I were you." Her emotions were genuine. "I didn't know either of my parents." She tucked her hands in her pockets and I was thankful she wasn't the hugging sort, or I would have crumbled completely. "I would give anything to know why they gave me up."

I nodded. "I, at least, had my mother for ten years." It wasn't much, but it was more than she had. "I can't go back in just yet." I cleared my throat and tried to compose myself. "Is there a chance he's alive still, is that what they were getting to?"

"I'm not sure, but if Crissy saw his eyes, then I would say there's a chance."

Closing my eyes, I exhaled slowly. "This is so overwhelming."

"I understand that. I grew a tattoo on my back out of nowhere one day, and then five years later I find myself here as the prophesized huntress and queen of Alterealm."

My eyes popped open and I looked at her, even more surprising was she was telling the truth. "I suppose you understand quite well then."

She nodded and then smiled. "Someday I'll tell you the whole story."

"There's more than that?"

With her eyes huge she nodded again. "Yep and some days I still don't believe it happened." She pulled up her sleeve to show me her mate tattoo. "But it's not like I could forget."

43

I found the crushing pressure on my chest easing. "I'll be sure to have plenty of wine on hand."

She snorted. "A few shots of JD would help too."

Taking a deep breath, I exhaled slowly. "Thank you. You would think with my age, I could take news like that in stride, but it swamped me for a moment."

"I'll throw you a life preserver anytime." She grinned. "How old?"

I exhaled sharply. "Ninety-eight, and I hate saying it out loud."

She laughed. "Yeah 'cuz you look soo old." She rolled her eyes. "At first glance, you look twenty-nine, tops."

I frowned. "Really? That's depressing."

Motioning to the dining room, she smiled. "I'm really anxious to find out where Crissy saw. It usually means I get to go kick some ass."

I turned to go back in. "You fight with the men?"

"Damn right I do." She went back in the room.

"Interesting."

Chapter Six

The meeting went on for an hour more. A location that Crissy had seen needed to be found before anything further could happen. Michael was going to see if he could locate my father through the device he'd never returned, and everyone agreed doing nothing with the number given to me for a day or two was advisable.

I sat there as long as I could, but I was starting to smell everyone in the room, and taking a bite out of someone was an ever-growing possibility the longer I sat there. I made sure not to interrupt anyone before sitting forward in my chair. "I really must go, I have things to attend to." I stood up.

Crissy smiled. "Oh, you need to feed. It makes sense now... I couldn't understand why you would be in *that* club..."

I felt my face flush.

"I don't think she wishes to discuss it, heart." Victor said quietly.

Rafael rubbed the back of his neck. "If that's why you're going into danger, we can help with that," he pulled out his phone.

I know my jaw dropped. "Wait..." I didn't know how to say it. "You have what... dial up...

over here? Like a pizza delivery?"

"Uh…" Quinton smirked, "kind of it's uh…"

"Remember that time… oh, wait, mixed company." Rafael nodded and stopped talking.

Leone shook his head.

Michael grinned. "Vic is so old he's outlived some of the…" He cleared his throat and then sat back as if he'd realized what he was going to say and decided it wasn't wise.

Crissy leaned against Victor's shoulder. "I should send them all a thank you note, for looking after him for all those years until I came."

Victor raised his eyebrows and looked at his brothers with a smug look on his face.

I wasn't sure how I felt about that. "I don't think I'm ready," I waved my hand around. "I'm not comfortable…"

"Stop you guys. Alona has known about this place for a day. It's a lot to digest, give her some space." Daxx told them, in a tone that meant business.

"I can take you back, Alona." Arius offered getting up. "Just let me change. It's my turn to check the club for Emil."

"Thank you." I grimaced when I remembered. "I'm not looking forward to the nausea, but I do need to return."

"I'll be back in five minutes." He nodded and then walked out into what I now realized must be the kitchen.

"Be right back." Chase said and followed him.

I stood off to the side observing the interactions around me. They really were a functional family unit. I hadn't had much experience with this up close in my life, but had always watched it from afar when it wouldn't be noticed.

Mitz came in and set more food on the table. I had to wonder if she worked around the clock just keeping them fed. I hadn't met any parents yet, but I felt she was close to a mother to them all. With a caring smile on her face, she came over and held out a little pouch to me. "It's the blend I use to settle the stomach."

I took it. "Oh, you are a lovely woman."

She patted my hand. "You will get used to traveling back and forth, love, I'm sure of it." With a nod, she turned and went back to her kitchen.

I wasn't sure about that, but I hoped she was right. Clearly, if I wanted to learn more about myself I would have to come back here.

"Ready?" Arius came in from the hallway.

I nodded and looked at everyone left in the room. "I will talk to you soon." I glanced to Michael. "Thank you."

"I'll let you know if I find out more."

I realized Arius went out into the hallway and followed him.

He stopped outside the door and smiled at me. "To the club, or did you want land closer to home?"

He'd changed into jeans and a dress shirt, with his hair pulled back. He still wouldn't go unnoticed, but he wouldn't shine like a beacon either. "How do you know I don't live near the club?"

He smirked. "If you live in a penthouse, I *know* you don't live on that side of town."

I exhaled quietly. "No, I don't. The club is just the easiest place to find someone."

"I'll help tonight." He winked. "I don't know much of the other side of the city, so give me a big landmark to aim for."

I thought for a moment. "Do you know the buildings lit in blue at night, on the east side of the bridge?"

He nodded. "I do."

"I live across from there."

"Okay." He patted his chest. "Rest your..."

"Does that really work?" I gave him a suspicious look.

He glanced back to the dining room and smiled. "It does. Leone and I used to take girls over when we were younger."

"I see. I won't tell."

Chuckling he shook his head. "Troy and Chase taught us, so it's not a secret. Well, maybe from Victor. But I suspect he wasn't always so proper."

I took a deep breath and held onto the little pouch Mitz had given me. Stepping closer, I put my head on his chest and closed my eyes. At least they all smelled good. His hand rested on the back of my head and then my stomach lurched.

"Keep your eyes closed and breathe for a moment." He murmured.

I'd learned what sudden movement did the last time, so this time I complied. I still felt woozy, but it wasn't hitting me in waves. "I'm afraid to move." I confessed.

He chuckled. "There's no hurry."

Opening my eyes, I assessed how I felt, surprised it wasn't too bad. "I might live through this." I said as I slowly lifted my head off his chest. "I'm still a little off, but nothing like before."

Arius nodded. "It still hits hard when I have to pop and run in the same motion." He shrugged. "I just got used to it."

I looked around and realized he'd put us squarely in a darkened location, out of the glow from the streetlights. "Do you ever land in a crowd?"

He shook his head. "Not yet, but it's bound to happen someday." With a sweep of his hand, he motioned to the restaurant across the street. "Do you have a preference? Male or female?"

I looked over to see a group of people coming out. A couple said good night and then started walking down the street. "I usually pick female because they don't get touchy feely."

He grinned. "There won't be any of that with my help."

I was intrigued now. We started to follow the couple. "Why is that?"

"I have a gift."

I looked at him briefly. "One like Chase's charm, or an actual one?"

Laughing quietly, he put his hand behind me so I would walk a bit faster. "Oh, no mine is quite real." He pulled out his phone and then walked quickly toward the couple.

"Excuse me, I think we're lost. The map says we're in the right place, but I can't find the address we need."

They couple stopped and the male came toward him. "I swear the maps on phones never make sense."

"Tell me about it." Arius said looking at his phone. When the man came up beside him, he put his hand on his shoulder and looked at him for a moment. The man just stood there. As the woman approached them, Arius turned and put out his hand. "Hi." She took his hand and he looked at her face briefly and then she just stood there.

Turning, he grinned at me and motioned to the shadowed awning of the next building. I gave him a puzzled look but went over to it.

When I got there, he was leading the couple toward me, with just a hand on their arms. "You have about two minutes before they're back with us." He said quietly.

I know my eyes were huge and I had questions, but this was the easiest choice ever.. I took the man's arm and turned him into the shadowed corner. He even let me tilt his chin up so I could get to his neck.

Licking across my bite, I moved away and turned to see Arius grinning at me. With a wink, he walked the woman over and put her arms around the man's neck and backed up. "Let's go."

We quickly crossed the street. I glanced back, but kept going. "What if they're not a couple?"

He paused in step. "I hope they're not brother and sister. That will mean years of counselling." He chuckled.

I motioned to cross when we were back where we'd started. "How did you do that?"

Tucking his hands in his pockets, he walked beside me. "I can suggest things to people." He shrugged. "Most people."

I paused and looked up at him. "I would have loved that gift about seventy years ago. It's been a constant struggle to find ways…"

"It's not always a good thing." He grinned, "Okay it was fun as hell when my brothers and I were younger." He frowned. "And I think I'm the reason there are no pets in the royal chambers now."

I realized we were getting closer to where I lived, and I needed to decide if I would tell him that. "It's much more useful than what I have been handed, trust me." I stopped and looked down the street to the building I lived in.

He stopped and looked in the direction I was. "You can trust me, but I suppose everyone says that."

I did want answers. I studied him for a moment, I couldn't completely feel his emotional state, but I also didn't pick up anything dangerous from him. "How do you feel about wine?"

"Fondly." He smiled.

"I just had a case imported. I'd be willing to share in exchange for a few answers." I started walking toward the entrance.

"I can't say no to that." He had no problem keeping up my speed as I walked, his long legs striding confidently at my side.

"Lovely."

The security guard gave Arius an odd look, but I paid well for privacy and discretion, so not a word was uttered as we got on the lift.

"How did you land a place like this?" He walked around the sitting area that over looked the city.

Taking off my boots, I set them by the door. "I start looking for the next location as soon as I move. This place was put on reserve for me long before there was a need."

He paused and looked out the window. "That's a hard way to live."

I didn't know how to explain my life to a man that had been surrounded by an entire population that knew and accepted what they were. "I suppose to you it would be, but self-preservation required that I become well versed in vanishing."

Arius settled on a chair I often sat in to look out at the city. It was a wonderful view.

"Is white agreeable, or would you prefer red?" I took off my jacket and placed it on the sofa. I left the blade strapped to my back. I only took it off when I was alone.

"Whichever you're in the mood for will work for me." He gave me an easy smile. "Haven't had a lot of time to just relax since Marcus went rogue."

Another question I needed to ask, what Marcus going rogue meant, exactly. "I'll just be a moment."

Pouring two glasses of my preferred mellow white, I took it out to him.

He was looking around casually, probably trying not to seem rude. "I have to wonder if my lost brother is doing as well as you are." Taking a sip, he nodded. "That is nice."

I settled on the chair across from him and realized I'd never had company here. Holding the glass between my hands, I gave him my opinion. "If he's had three hundred years of living here, I'm sure he's gotten good at it."

Leaning back, Arius sat quiet for a moment. "Hopefully he's good at the right things."

I hadn't thought of that. "Yes, I suppose that could be a concern." Taking a sip, I watched him just sit there and watch me. He wasn't very vocal, if the long silences were any indication.

"I'm just trying to figure out how you live like this." He smirked.

"Ah, well, I realized right after the seventies society seemed to recycle. Trends, lifestyle, clothing, each cycle was the same, only a little more modern each time." I motioned around us, "So I tried my hand at predicting what would be the next *big thing* in the markets." I smiled. "After a few mishaps, I got it right." I shrugged, it was more or less the truth.

"You got all this playing the stock markets?" He tilted his head, a look of doubt on his face.

"Oh, I don't play. It's not a game to me. It's the difference between living with a measure of security that I require, or turning into a quivering basket case."

"How so?"

I thought how best to explain it. "I don't handle being around others well. Where your *gift* is something you can choose to use or not, mine allows no choices." I took another sip and let the flavor of the wine sit on my taste buds while he considered what I'd said.

Taking a drink, he motioned to me with his glass. "I don't have Troy's ability to look inside a mind, so you're going to have to give me more to go on if you want me to understand."

I leaned forward. "He can do that?"

Arius nodded. "With most, yes."

Sitting back again, I shrugged. "That's intriguing, and so much cooler than the burden I bear."

"Like Crissy, I imagine. She can't shut hers off either."

Sighing, I set down my drink and clasped my hands in my lap. "I'm feeling guilty now, I thought she was just a bit off-center."

Arius chuckled. "She's that too. Her life wasn't easy, but she made the most of it, in her way."

"I don't know about that, or her visions, only that she feels about ten different emotions a second, it's quite overwhelming."

Placing his glass on the table, he leaned his elbows on his knees. "You're an empath?"

"Yes." I shrugged, "at least that's what my research says. My label is an *intuitive empath*, but I'm sure they've never had a case like mine for their research. I'm more of an emotional sponge."

His brows furrowed. "And you can't shut it off?"

I shook my head. "Not completely. I've learned how to build a resistance to it, erect a psychological wall best describes it, but sometimes even that doesn't work."

Leaning back, he studied me. "I can't even imagine having to feed and ward off an emotional onslaught at the same time."

"The first few years of perfecting the selection was, well, let's just say I was ill often. At that point, I soaked up every emotion anywhere near me."

Blowing out a breath, he shook his head. "Wow, I don't even know how you've managed." He smiled. "If *Lou* had of tried to feed off you, I guess he would have got more than he'd bargained for."

"How do you mean?"

"The yellow eyes mean they're emotion feeders, for lack of a better name."

I sat there looking at him. There was such a thing? Others that actually wanted what I was cursed with? "Really? So, your brother, Chase?"

He nodded. "Yeah and he's turned it into a skill, he can use it against someone as much as he does for sustenance."

I couldn't even picture that. "That's intimidating."

Arius snorted. "Don't tell him that. He already thinks he's perfection." Sobering, he shook his head. "I'm sorry, you had questions and I've been doing more asking then answering."

I smiled. "No, that's perfectly fine. I'm still learning about all of this—everything, that I didn't know existed." I blew out a slow breath. "I still can't quite grasp the idea that my father may still be alive."

He rubbed his temples and then held up a finger. "Pause for one moment. I need to call older brother before he gives me a migraine."

I must have looked as puzzled as I felt because he grinned.

"My brothers and I can demand each other's attention through our family blood bond, and right now he is calling, probably to check that you made it home safely."

"Oh." I motioned so he would call. The very idea they could do that was astounding, but with all I'd been finding out the past day, I wasn't even sure if it was on the high scale of amazing or a lesser one.

Arius stood up and pulled out his phone.

I sat staring out the window, not wanting to eavesdrop, but he didn't move out of the room either.

"She's fine. Yes, we're just sitting talking." He chuckled. "No, not at the club."

I picked up my glass and took a sip, still trying to seem like I wasn't listening in.

"I helped her feed, and before you ask no, not some low-life from the club." He made a sound of exasperation. "Is there a problem I'm not aware of?"

Getting up, I decided I would top off our glasses. I moved past him to the kitchen and got the bottle.

"We're sipping wine and talking, Chase, stop sounding like I'm fifteen."

I smirked, unable to resist as I stepped by him to refill his glass.

Walking back toward the window, he rolled his eyes at me. "I'll be heading back shortly, I'm exhausted and you need to go do something like, oh, take care of daywalker business or something." He hung up and tucked the phone in his pocket. "I think one of our kings needs a vacation. He's very moody today." Sitting down, he picked up the glass and gave me an appreciative nod.

I set the bottle on the table and sat down again. "I'm sure his responsibilities are many. I don't quite understand this two kings and half a realm thing."

Nodding he sat there for a moment. "I'm trying to think of the easiest way to explain it." He took a sip and the exhaled loudly. "Alterealm, in the time of my grandfather's and father's rule was not a peaceful place. So, all criminals were put on one side," he shrugged, "more or less. The real dangerous ones were imprisoned, obviously. That was during my father's rule." Arius rubbed his jaw and then smirked. "I'm trying to remember my history lessons."

I smiled, never having had suffered through much schooling myself. Everything I knew had been learned through my own hard lessons, from reading to the math that helped me amass the money I lived on.

"It's very complicated to explain all at once, it was prophesized that twins would be born into the royal family every five hundred years and from there they would rule equally…"

"Your brothers are the first pair of twins?"

He nodded. "So, the sides were split, day and night. Meaning if you're from the daywalker side, your day time is actual day time. On the night side your day time hours are technically in the middle of the night."

"Oh, I see. Chase griping about sleep loss makes more sense now."

Arius laughed, "Chase always gripes about that, even when nothing disturbs his sleep."

"So, the sides have nothing to do with whether a person is an essence feeder or emotions?"

He shook his head. "No, nothing to do with it at all. Everyone on his side aren't bad, it's just easier to monitor trouble during the daylight hours… so, day king and night king were born."

I took a drink and thought about it. "It's quite ingenious if you think about it." A few more things came to mind. "Each of you brothers have leading rolls in the maintaining of these kingdoms?"

Nodding, he took another drink of the wine. "Yes. Victor is our justice. Basically, any decision, verdict, or punishment handed out goes through him."

"That explains his cold and rigid demeanor."

Arius grinned. "He's always been stiff, that I remember, but he was two hundred and fifty when I was born, so he may have just been set in his ways by then."

The mere fact that he mentioned age like it was nothing special, reminded me that I wasn't alone in the ageless plight.

"Quinton is now one of the huntress's captains, so he's chasing down people on both sides of the realm, and on this side as well."

"Daxx is the huntress, yes?" I took a sip, finding this all very intriguing.

He nodded. "Yeah. She was a bounty hunter on this side, so she still comes back to track down people when needed." He smirked. "She just likes kicking ass, so she'll use any excuse to do it."

"Yes, I caught that in something she said already."

He took a drink and savored it for a moment. "Michael is like our lead detective, he's the law that works closest with Victor."

I chuckled. "I thought he looked like a cop." I grimaced. "I've spent more time than I'd like to admit eluding them…" I motioned with my glass, "before I figured out how to feed unnoticed, that is, not because I'm a criminal."

"He does look like a cop, you're right." Grinning, he took a deep breath. "Leone is our enforcer, so he tracks down anyone breaking actual laws. Rafael is like the leader of the guards, but works with Leone and Michael a lot."

"And you? What is your official purpose?"

He smirked. "I am usually in charge of the cells, our prison, but I help whichever brother is in need." He shrugged. "Our prisoners can't escape, so it's a boring gig." Picking up the glass, he winked. "And I like fighting as much as my brothers, so I tend to go where the action is."

"I gathered fighting was a favorite activity by the sheer number of weapons you all carry."

Arius laughed, "Says the woman with a blade strapped to her back."

I shook my head. "Oh, I am not fond of fighting, but self-defence is required from time to time, so I got good at it." I glanced around the room. "I haven't always had a secure building to live in, so anytime I was able to study with masters of the combat arts, I have."

Tilting his head, he studied me for a moment. "That sounds intriguing." Then his brows furrowed. "How are you able to fight, wouldn't there be a backlash of pain, from your opponent's feelings?"

Blowing out a breath, I nodded. "Yes. It didn't take many skirmishes in my life to realize I couldn't stick around afterward."

"No doubt." He shrugged. "But it's good you can take care of yourself. We had to work with Crissy about defensive moves." He shook his head. "Just so we all aren't half out of our minds with worry when she is out of sight."

"I suppose you have all lived long enough to perfect your combat skills."

He grinned like an eager child. "Next time you're on my side, I'll show you the royal family's practice room. Maybe you can show me what you've learned."

I inclined my head and grinned. "Perhaps."

His phone chirped, so he pulled it out and checked it. "I'm afraid I need to go. I'm needed at the cells." He sighed loudly. "I don't know if I helped with your questions or not." He stood up.

I nodded. "I'm understanding more and more." I got to my feet. "It's going to take me some time to absorb all of it."

He offered me a sincere smile. "No doubt. Finding out that things you thought were absolute aren't, actually can be a bit of a shock."

I flipped my hair back from my face. "Considering that a few days ago I thought I was a spawn of Satan and my father deserted me... yes, there's some adjustments to make with all of this."

He chuckled. "You are definitely not satanic, there's too much good in you." He winked. "Call me tomorrow, after it's dark here is then my day, if you have any questions." He shrugged. "I'll help where I can."

"Thank you. I do appreciate you taking the time."

"Anytime." He gave me a regal bow and then was gone.

I had been about to say I didn't have his number then he

vanished. I stood there looking at where he had been standing. I wasn't sure if I was in a nightmare or a dream, or even if I wanted to wake up and find out at this point. Seeing the rest of the wine in the bottle, I decided my best action would be to finish it and go to bed.

Chapter Seven

Ducking into the next shop, I paused long enough to grab something off the rack and quickly went into the changing room. After I closed the door, I leaned against it, trying to calm down. Without even looking at what I'd taken, I hung it up and closed my eyes. Maybe it was just paranoia, I thought, even though I didn't believe it. Why did I think speaking to the Lou person meant no one would be following me now? Naïve wasn't like me.

I pulled off my sunglasses and opened the door a crack and peered out. They were standing outside the store, waiting. I was definitely being followed. Now what?

I'd gone out early this morning, because it was the quietest time. To keep my resistance to emotions working well, I had to expose myself. Having learned that if I stayed in seclusion, emotions would smother me when I did go out again.

I sat on the bench, trying to think through my options. I hadn't brought the little transporter thing, so that left an easy exit out of the question.

Someone knocked on the door. "Do you need help?"

I glanced at what I'd grabbed. "I'm trying to decide if a lighter color would suit me better." It was the first excuse I could come up.

"I can bring you a few more options." The saleswomen told me.

"That would be lovely, in a medium please, maybe large for the extra length?" I stared at the dress again, I could probably wear it.

"I'll bring both, ma'am."

"Lovely." I had more pressing matters than a new dress. How was I getting out of here?

Pulling out my phone, I opened the contacts and was about to call Daxx, then remembered it was daytime. Logic predicted, if she was mate to the night king, she most likely slept when he did. That left the other king and the only other number in my contacts. I doubted the Chinese restaurant and my stockbroker would be of any help. Biting my lip, I tapped Chase's name and hit dial. I suppose even having a king to call was something, even if I was uncomfortable.

"Duchess, this a surprise."

"For us both." I glanced at the door. "I seem to have a situation."

The women knocked on the door. Opening it a crack, I smiled and took the two dresses she offered. I lifted a finger, hoping she was intelligent enough to see I was on the phone whilst supposedly trying on dresses. With her best sales clerk smile, she nodded and walked away.

"What sort of situation do you have?"

I heard a door close and wherever he had been, it was now quieter. "I believe I'm being followed. Actually, I'm quite positive I am."

"Same stalker that gave you the card?"

I shook my head, then stopped realizing he couldn't see me. "No, it's not him. There's two of them, and they've been there each time I've turned around. Now they are standing outside the shop I'm in."

"Where are you? Are you safe at the moment?"

"Yes. I'm in a change room." I glanced down to see I still held the two dresses the clerk brought and hung them up.

"Really? That's interesting, I've never had a call from a change room before."

I sat down. "I'm so happy to tick that off your new experience list. What do you suggest I do?"

"Well… I'd have to see what you're trying on to help you decide…" He chuckled. "Just use your transporter."

Closing my eyes, I sighed. "I would, if I hadn't left it at home."

Another door closed. "You know we gave that to you to carry *with* you in case you needed it, and it seems you do."

"Yes, yes I know. I forgot it." Something I would regret from this day on. "When I did my check before I left… wallet, yes, phone, yes… it seems I'm not used to remembering little transporter thing to another realm."

He sighed, "don't distract me with sass, I'm thinking."

I stood up again, feeling very anxious. "Can't you just pop here and get me?"

Chase snorted, "I'd have to have been there before to do that, and I'm not in the habit of visiting women's change rooms, however entertaining the idea is."

"Oh," Another fact I should have probably asked. "I didn't realize."

"Don't despair, duchess, I'll get there. Tell me where you are in terms of large landmarks."

He was just going to walk down the street to find me? "What… what if they know you? I mean, if they know who you are? Your size draws attention, not to mention your golden locks and flirty little beard… you will be recognized."

"Worried for me? That's very touching." He paused. "For the record, my beard is not flirty… it takes adorning my face quite seriously. I'll be just fine. Give me your location. Exit the changing room, but don't leave the store until I call you back." I heard another door close. "The phone won't work during the transport.

"But your beard…" The idea of my being responsible for one of their kings landing in trouble didn't sit well with me.

"Duchess if you're suggesting I shave it off, we're going to have our first spat."

I huffed out a breath. "Very well." Biting my lip, I tried to stay calm. "I'm east of the bridge, a few streets south of the river... there's a large park at the end of this street..."

"Ok, I know that park. Give me a moment."

He hung up. I stared at the phone and then shook my head, still not sure if calling Chase had been a good idea. Glancing at the dresses, I grabbed one and left the room. The clerk met me before I reached the cashier. "I'll take this one." I gave her my best smile, despite my heart jumping inside my chest.

She was handing me my change when the phone rang again.

"Still in the shop?"

I accepted the bag. "Yes."

"I'm walking in that direction now, but as I don't know your shopping habits, I need you to walk out and head toward the park. Don't look at them, or so much as pause. I'll be on the phone the whole time."

Putting on my sunglasses, I went to the door. "I'm leaving now."

"Just walk out and come toward me. I'm the one with the flirty beard."

I smiled, even though I was having trouble breathing. The two men didn't even look away, just waited until I walked by. I glanced to the window of the shop and saw their reflections, they turned to follow me.

"They still on you?"

I could hear the cars through the phone, echoing what was around me and knew he was close. I looked back to where I was going. "Yes."

"Hmm, I think I know why they're following you."

My heart stuttered in my chest. "You do?"

"Yes. You look stunning today. Miles of raven locks shining in the sunlight... and I have to say I'm a big fan of tall boots on a woman, and you wear them so well duchess.

I'd be following you too if I didn't have to try to get a good look at these idiots."

Without turning my head, I glanced at everyone walking toward me and didn't see him. Then I saw something across the street that caught my eye. He stood, leaning against a lamp post on the corner opposite me, like he didn't have a care in the world. If he'd thought dark glasses would make him less conspicuous, he was mistaken.

"Don't you take anything seriously?" I kept walking, slowing down a slight bit, so I could see what he intended to do.

"Serious and brooding was last century, I'm trying something new and different for this one. Keep going to the park, sit by the lovely flower garden near the entrance."

I glanced at him briefly, if it weren't for his light hair and size, he would have blended in dressed in casual dark pants and a white button-up shirt. "At least you not in black leather looking like you're going to war."

He chuckled. "Leather chafes in the warm sunlight. I'll meet you at the park shortly." He hung up.

I paused and looked at the phone, debating on turning and see where he went, or at the two following me, but decided perhaps some things were best unknown to me. Walking faster, I hurried to the park.

When I reached it, Chase was standing by the flower beds waiting for me. He held out a hand toward me.

"Let's lose these guys, then I can take you somewhere safe."

I took his hand, and he walked quickly to the trees in the center. I had to almost run to keep up with his long strides, which was a first for me.

He glanced at me over his shoulder, "As soon as we reach that tree, I'm going to transport us elsewhere."

I nodded, I would take the nausea over the threat of being followed.

The moment we were close enough, he tugged on my arm, bringing us to the hidden side of the tree. Wrapping his arms around me, he hugged me against his body and then my stomach plummeted inside me.

I took a moment and just stood there with my eyes closed, trying to breathe through the tidal wave of nausea that hit me.

"Sorry about that being so abrupt. They were getting closer, and I didn't think you wanted to chat with them."

Exhaling slowly, I opened my eyes. "That's fine. Thank you." Backing up, I swallowed the nausea down and looked around us. He had brought us to the fish factory.

"I didn't know where else to go." He motioned across the river. "I know you live over there, but I have no idea where."

I put my hand over my churning stomach. "I can take a cab from here."

"Was that shop near where you live?"

I nodded. "It's in that neighborhood, yes."

"Then I'll accompany you back."

I studied him for a moment, not entirely sure if I wanted to take him to my home. "Is that really necessary?"

Taking off his glasses, he looked at me for a moment. "They know the area you live in, duchess."

I felt ridiculous not having realized that fact. I didn't know what was going on lately, but I seemed to have gotten lax in my safety precautions. I would have to think about that later to figure out why. "I see your point." Turning, I pointed to the street. "We'll get a cab from over there."

With a regal nod, he motioned for me to go first. "So, you just felt the need to run out and buy new clothes today?"

I sighed, "No, an outfit wasn't on my mind when I went out." I lifted the bag containing my new dress. "I only purchased this as a ploy to stay in the shop, I have no idea if it will even fit me." We crossed the street and I kept walking to where I knew the cabs would be.

"Just out for a mid-morning stroll then?" He kept pace with me easily.

I shook my head, still preferring not to talk because my stomach wasn't at all settled yet. "No."

When I stopped by the corner, he stood in front of me, his hazel eyes moving over me slowly. "I'm just trying to figure out why you'd put yourself at risk."

"I just needed to go out. I try to get out once a day, otherwise staying in seclusion becomes too easy." I was glad I still had my glasses on, so he couldn't see me looking back at him much the way he was at me. Chase was a very striking man. Reminding me of statues of Greek gods, with his strong jaw line and flawless composure. Then again, he'd had more than a century to hone looking that good. I still wasn't sure of his age, but if last century had been his brooding one, as he'd put it, then he was at least in his second or third. That, was still something I never thought to do, consider someone older then myself.

"You look at me much longer and I'm going to be getting ideas... ones that may get me stabbed." He said with a smirk.

I spotted a cab and waved it down. "I somehow don't think my dagger would deter your thoughts and ideas." The cab pulled up to the curb.

"You would be correct, duchess." He opened the door and motioned for me to get in, then put on his glasses and got in behind me.

The ride to my building was a silent one and although I couldn't see his eyes, I could feel them on me.

I was thankful the security guard was different than the night before, or I would look like a tramp, bringing a second man up to my home in less than a day.

Chase stopped and stood just inside the door. "Most definitely several steps up from the place Daxx called home."

I set the bag down and shrugged out of the light jacket I wore. "Oh?"

"Mmm," he wandered in further and looked around, "hers was more the size of a closet, and I'm fairly certain it was infested by at least one type of pest, if not more."

I smiled and motioned for him to look around. "I've lived in my share of places like that. During and right after the war were the hardest times."

He went over and looked out the large windows. "I can imagine it was difficult to find somewhere safe at that point." Turning, he went over to a painting on the wall.

It was the only one I owned, but when I'd seen it, I had to have it. The artist had taken a single child and painted a scene all around her. She was completely surrounded by a crowd of people, yet utterly alone. I supposed I related to it a little too much.

"This is quite a piece." Chase glanced at me over his shoulder. "A picture that says a thousand words, and not one of them in earnest…" he said softly.

I went over and stood beside him and looked at it. "It was a bit of an impulse buy, I just knew I had to have it the moment I saw it."

"Possibly you were relating to the scene it depicts?" He asked with a careful tone.

I tilted my head and glanced at him. "Perhaps. I have always had a weakness for helping children though. Men fight their battles for land or gain, but it's always, absolutely always the children that suffer for it." I released a shaky breath. "I find myself drawn to the poorer neighborhoods no matter where I call home. I like to do what I can to ease their struggle, even if it's only in a small way."

"A noble cause." He agreed, watching me.

"That's how I found this painting. I was in one of those areas, on the other side of the bridge, and happened on this quaint little gallery. At first I thought it would be filled with desperate attempts at art, and was pleasantly surprised to see the works in it were… far above average…" I paused, thinking of where that gallery had been. I looked to him and then back to the painting. "Oh, I think I may know something useful…"

"Regarding?" He crossed his arms and looked down at me.

"An orange alley, surrounded by stone buildings and walkways." I pointed to the painting, "When I found this, I was encouraged to explore further because it was breathtaking, the way the light reflected off the stone and archways down this alley... which was most likely once a popular location for a market... more than a hundred years ago."

"That's not surprising, that you'd discover the location cutie saw... fate is weaving us all together like a cloth lately." Pulling out his phone, he frowned at it. "I'm afraid it's about four hours too early to even think of waking the others." Chase smiled, "I'm much more considerate of causing them sleep deprivation than they are me."

I smiled back. "I'm sure you are. It can't be easy living an opposite schedule to your family."

He shrugged. "I've had years to grow used to it."

I wasn't sure if he meant to wait those hours here with me, but my stomach was finally settling and reminding me that I hadn't eaten. I motioned to the kitchen. "I was going to make a light lunch. Would you care to join me?"

He looked surprised. "I would love to. I'm quite fond of eating."

I rolled my eyes, "I'm sure you all are, judging by the size of all of you." I turned and went to the kitchen. "I can honestly say it was odd, not being the tallest person in the room when I met all of you." I turned, and he was right behind me, his eyes looking at my boots.

"I think you cheat and add a few inches with those boots." He smirked.

I looked down at the boots that went almost to my knee. "I confess, they are a favorite of mine." I glanced back to him and then went to the fridge. "Being born in a time when women had to cover nearly every inch of skin, it was quite exhilarating when these were acceptable. The shoes available in the thirties through the fifties were most uncomfortable."

He smirked. "I recall the fashion flipping once the sixties arrived, much to society's dismay."

I laughed and made a face. "I don't know who decided bell-bottoms were a good idea, they were tacky looking things."

He snorted. "I was rather entertained by the go-go dancers though."

Setting ingredients for a salad on the counter, I closed the door and gave him a knowing look. "I'm sure you were." I started cutting vegetables for the salad, hoping he wasn't opposed to one. "I don't mean to pry, but I am curious…"

Chase leaned back against the counter and crossed his arms, watching me.

"How is it you and your brothers," I smiled at him, "I'm fairly certain I am the youngest on the list."

He smirked. "You are."

"How is it you've lived a hundred, or hundreds, of years and never settled down? Only two of you eight have partners." I got a bowl out of the cupboard. "I understand that here, with longevity being much shorter than where you live… at least, I'm assuming there are women that live to your ages.

Chase chuckled. "There are women." He sighed and stared at the cupboard. "That is a very complex answer, let's just say fate is controlling the entire scenario presently." Reaching over, he took a piece of the pepper I had just cut and put it in his mouth. After he chewed it, he gave me a brief glance. "I recently had my heart crushed because fate is a taunting bitch, so if it's agreeable, perhaps we could discuss something else for the time being."

I paused in what I was doing and gave him a heartfelt look. "I'm sorry if I brought it up. I had no idea."

He made a noise conceding to my apology. "I am mostly over it. Just tender, due to the trickery of it. *But* my brother has his queen, so in that, all of us must be thankful."

I wasn't sure what he meant by that. I did feel, very fleetingly, his grief before it was gone in a flash. "Daxx is quite the woman. I like how blunt she is."

He chuckled. "Yes that she is." Pushing away from the counter, he went around and sat on the stool on the other side of the island. "I feel partially responsible for the loss of your parents. I was one half of the whole that issued the transport ban."

I stopped and looked at him. "Thank you for the sentiment, but I don't see as there's anyone to the blame. It was circumstances beyond anyone's control. I'm not sure how it was where you and your family were, but I read all the information in the archives when I was older, and it was pure madness on this side."

"That's very gracious of you." He gave me an odd look. "You are not as jaded by a hard life as most others would be."

Taking a moment to consider that, I turned to get some cheese out of the fridge. "If I were to allow hard feelings to control my actions, I wouldn't have the energy to focus on living... And when I realized I may very well have more than my share of years compared to others, I decided to do some good while I had that extra time." Slicing it I arranged it on the plate, then turned to get some crackers. "Your serious tone with me is unexpected," I told him over my shoulder, "what would your siblings say?"

Chase laughed softly. "Rest assured, they know a beast lies in wait behind the comical quips."

Getting some bowls and cutlery, I set them on the counter beside the salad. "I am a bit envious, I suppose is the word... that you've had so many brothers to weather the years with." I pulled a stool from the end of the island to sit across from him, feeling more secure with the island between us. There was something about him that put me on edge, where being alone with Arius hadn't bothered me as much.

Sitting down I motioned for him to help himself. "The years for me have been very hollow at times, especially once I understood that I would always outlive any partner in a serious relationship."

He was quiet for a moment, busying himself with a portion of the food. "Have you paused to think about the fact that you don't need to flee to a new location now?" Chase stopped and looked at me, his hazel eyes moving gently over my face. "You can use your own name forever now, as well."

I folded my hands in my lap and looked at him. "If I were to go to the other side and stay there you mean?"

He shrugged. "More or less. We do have others that live on this side for a large part of the year." Waving his hand around at my home, his eyes didn't leave mine. "Those that do, swap homes, changing ownership on this side so no one notices their failure to age, but yes, I was referring to the fact that you could come over and live among others just like you, where you didn't have to worry about feeding, living in the shadows and moving constantly."

I took a bite and thought about how I felt as I chewed. "While living here can be trying at times, I do good where I can, and help those less fortunate." I pointed my fork at him and smiled. "It took many missteps to get where I am now."

Getting up, I selected a bottle of red wine from the rack and gave him and inquiring look while holding up the bottle.

He nodded. "Please."

I turned to get the opener and when I stepped back around, he was right there. I hadn't even heard him make a sound.

He took the bottle and the opener out of my hand and made fast work pulling the cork out. Setting it on the island, he went back around and sat down. "Can I persuade you to take a vacation on *my* side perhaps?" He leaned over his plate giving me a serious look. "At least until we find out why they are so determined to have you."

Setting the glasses down, I poured the wine. "I hadn't considered that. There is nothing special about me, so I have no idea why they're being so persistent."

He smirked. "I'm sure there is something special. You aren't going to like the other option if you insist on staying here."

I sat down. "What do you mean?"

"I will have to assign you a guard. I would have brought one of mine with me today, but most of mine wouldn't blend in well in your neighborhood."

"A little too rough to hide among the yuppies?" I smirked.

"I do love the words that come out of your lips." He nodded. "Yes. Cutie says they all look like pirates, so I'll have to find one that cleans up nicely." He continued eating.

"Do you really think I need a body guard?"

His hazel eyes moved over me. "I do."

The idea of having a guard meant I would have to constantly erect mental barriers to block their emotions. "May I consider this?"

Chase incline his head in that regal way, seeming every bit the king when he did so. "You may."

I busied myself eating for a moment. "So, what happens when everyone is awake and you tell them I've been to the," I paused to remember what Crissy called it, "orange caves Crissy saw?"

He nodded and then took a sip of the wine. "If Daxx knows where it is, we go check it out. If she doesn't, you take us there to go check it out."

"Check it out, like walk in the alley and look around, or full battle wardrobe, check it out?"

He smirked. "Most likely the second. If cutie's seen it, then it's probably another faction of Marcus' followers. They're not very receptive or welcoming when they see any of us."

I played with the stem of the glass and thought about that. "What if she saw it because it had something to do with the man that gave me the card? She saw that as well." The idea that she could see and predict things was amazing to me.

Cocking his head to the side, he raised an eyebrow at me. "What if it has something to do with your father, he was in her head then, too."

I took a sip of the wine, giving myself a moment to consider that. "So, your saying it's better to go prepared for anything, then be caught unaware."

He nodded slowly. "Something like that."

We sat there eating quietly for a few moments. I was thinking of what it would mean to my life if my father was found. I wasn't sure what Chase was thinking about, but he had a most curious expression in his eyes as he watched me.

Setting his fork down, he picked up the glass and studied me briefly over the rim. "Would the availability of human essence be one of the reasons you'd want to stay on this side?"

I honestly hadn't seen that question coming. "I'm not certain why you would think that, I actually abhor having to feed, I think with the availability of the meals on dial-up over there, it is much less troublesome."

He looked surprised. "So, there's no pleasure in the way you sustain yourself?"

I must have conveyed my shock in his question, because he shook his head.

"I'm sorry. I'm just… I'm trying to find the draw of this side. One of my brothers has struggled for over thirty years with an addiction to human essence. I just wondered if it were the actual substance, or the means he's developed for taking it."

I opened my mouth and then closed it again, trying to find a helpful answer. "I've never felt the need to take more than the absolute minimum I require—but *my* circumstance is quite complicated out there and just," I waved my hand around, "biting someone, for me, except when they are passed out isn't for me."

His brows furrowed together. "Okay, I'm going to put a bookmark there and come back to it in a moment. I suppose what I'm wondering is, what's the difference? I mean, I have a fondness for human emotions because most are stronger, but, I definitely don't have a preference of specie." He smirked, "gender, yes, specie no." He pointed a finger at me. "I've asked my essence feeding brothers as well, and they aren't inclined one way or the other either… so don't feel I'm putting you on the spot…"

"No. I understand, you just want to help your brother."

He nodded quickly. "Yes. He's been disappearing a lot lately and I'm wondering if he's back-sliding or faltering." He rubbed a hand over his face, looking suddenly weary. "I've already suffered through helplessness watching three other brothers through difficult, traumatic events... I'd really like to aid Leone again in any way I can."

I was quite taken aback by this. First appearances led me to believe he was never serious and took everything lightly. Now, I realized I had completely misread him. "I would love to help you, truly I would, but as I have no knowledge of the difference between human and... non-human essence, I can't be of very much assistance."

"Really? So, you've only fed from humans then, or would you know if it were one from my side?"

I opened my mouth, and then shook my head. "I have no idea. So much I thought I knew has been changing these last few days."

He shrugged. "True enough." Sipping the wine, he smirked at me over the glass. "If anything useful comes to mind, please call. I'm out of ideas how to help him. For years, we forbade him from coming over here, but we have many humans on our side too, so it wasn't a huge deterrent."

I offered him a gentle smile. "I will think about it and let you know if anything comes to mind."

Chase suddenly smiled at me. "Now, about this biting people who are passed out. That's not very sporting."

I rolled my eyes at him. "It's not a sport to me, it's an unfortunate necessity."

"Hmm, when I thought you were already mysterious, you step it up a notch, duchess." He winked at me. "I like a challenge."

I felt my face flush. "I'm not trying to challenge you." I told him quietly.

"Oh, but you are. A new unknown puzzle to solve." He leaned over the island, so he was much closer to me. "And now you're sitting there blushing and intriguing me further, yet your eyes are telling me off limits—you are *definitely* challenging me, duchess, and you aren't even trying." He sat back. "I like it."

Picking up our dishes, I got up and took them to the sink, needing a moment to decide how to respond to the flirty man reappearing so quickly after the heartfelt discussion. When I turned around, he was right behind me. Whatever else this man was, he was also a predator.

Chase made a sound of annoyance in the back of his throat and pulled out his phone and looked at it. He sighed. "We'll have to pick this up again later. I have to get back." He backed away from me, his eyes not leaving mine. "Would you like to come back now? I can bring you back in a less abrupt way then the device can."

I shook my head. "I'll be fine here, I have some stock reports to ponder and strategize some new investments."

He inclined his head as if to acknowledge, then spoke. . "Please refrain from shopping trips until I can find a suitable guard. It may take me some time."

I exhaled a breath, realizing I had been holding it. "I think I've had enough shopping experiences for today."

He grinned. "Good. Please put the device *on*, so you have it available all the time."

I glanced to where it sat on the counter. "I will."

"I will let you know when the others are awake. Thank you for lunch."

Then he was gone. Again. I just stood there, would I ever get used to someone just vanishing in front of my eyes? I somehow didn't think so.

Chapter Eight

I paused outside the building I had arranged to meet Lou at. It was a restaurant, and not in a bad part of town, as I thought it might be. I'd actually worried it would be in the orange alley Crissy had seen. Biting my lip, I checked my pocket again for the device, making sure, for the fifth time, I had it. I was going to put it on my wrist but thought they may know what it looked like and recognize it.

I wasn't entirely sure I should have called him, but the brothers hadn't taken the card, and I wanted answers. The idea of having to live with a bodyguard or be afraid to leave my apartment didn't sit well with me. I had been alive these many years without someone dictating what I could or couldn't do.

My plan was simple; speak to the man, find out why people were following me and make a graceful exit. If I found out more to help bring those to justice for harming Crissy, it was a double win. In this case justice meant Victor, literally, so no one could get upset if I helped.

Simple.

Yet I was still seriously apprehensive about this meeting. Taking a deep breath, I willed my feet to carry me into the restaurant.

As soon as I stepped inside, I saw where Lou was sitting. I motioned to him as I went past the hostess. I was a bit surprised that team bad not only handed out business cards but dined in fine restaurants as well.

Lou nodded to me as I sat down. He was dressed very differently from when I had seen him in the club, now wearing casual clothes to suit this establishment. He still looked intimidating, regardless of what he was wearing.

"I was surprised you called me."

"Wasn't that the purpose of giving me the card?" He only nodded. "I was intrigued by what you said." I shook my head when a waiter came over and offered to pour some wine.

Lou waved him away.

I gave him a polite, but cold smile. "I'm also curious as to why you have people following me."

The expression on his face told me two things. He was surprised I brought it up, and that I had realized I was being followed. I felt better knowing that he under-estimated me.

"For your safety, I assure you."

I studied him for a moment, trying to figure out what his place was in this war, he wasn't a leader that much I knew, his face gave away too much. "Oh? From whom?" I raised an eyebrow, trying to appear more nonchalant than I was feeling. "Until you started following me, no one ever paid me any notice."

He played with his wine glass as he studied me, between glancing around the room. "You left with a red-headed woman…"

They had been watching me longer than I'd realized. "You mean the crazy little one? She was completely freaked out over something, I left with her because I was concerned for her well-being. I lost her in the alley. She accosted me a second time at the club to tell me you were following me… and she was right. I haven't seen that red head since." Which was the complete truth, Crissy had dyed her hair, and it was no longer red.

"As far as we know she's dead." He told me sounding sure of his information.

I wasn't about to tell him otherwise, but I would be passing that information along. "Oh, that's disheartening." I sat there and looked at him for a moment more. "So, you have people following me because a street waif accosted me in the club? I hardly perceive that as a threat."

He cleared his throat. "No. Much more than that, but it's too complicated and not something I can get into presently." He glanced around at the patrons in the restaurant.

"I see. Well, I am quite capable of looking after myself, but thank you for your concern. Your men are not required." I started to stand up.

"Wait." He leaned forward. "Please." He added hastily.

I sat back down and waited. I couldn't get a read on his emotions, but he was very nervous, which confirmed my earlier thought that he was someone's lackey in this.

"I'm sorry," he said quietly, "it's been very tense lately. Hard to tell who to trust since Marcus was taken."

I gave him a blank look. "And Marcus is?" I honestly didn't know that answer as no one had explained that to me, only mentioned it in passing.

"Very important in all of this." He said looking stressed.

Clasping my hands in my lap, I tried to look relaxed. "And where was he taken?"

The stress on his face grew. "As far as we can tell, to the cells, along with many others."

Shaking my head, I looked at him hoping I was portraying boredom in my expression. "All of this tells me precisely nothing."

He took a deep breath and let it out in a loud whoosh. "Would you like to meet others like you?" He smirked, "okay, they're not exactly like you—as you have something extra special, but I can tell you when working with us, you will never have to hide who, or what, you are again."

I squinted at him. "I'll admit, I'm curious."

Lou's round face lit up in a smile. He raised a finger at me. "Are you claustrophobic?"

I couldn't suppress the look of shock on my face.

He shook his head. "Like tunnels. Do you have a fear of being underground?"

I gave him a skeptical look. "Not that I've ever found, but I can honestly say I've never really been in an underground tunnel before."

He sat back and I could see he was thinking something through. "It's easier to travel and stay off the radar using the tunnels."

"Oh, I see." I just sat there, not sure what to do next. It wasn't as if I could ask him to tell me the location.

Nodding, he waved to the waiter. "I'm going to take you there."

The entire time he was paying for whatever he'd had, I was wondering if I should go with this man. Briefly, *very* fleetingly I considered texting Chase about what I was doing, but something told me he wouldn't approve.

When he motioned for me to follow him, I was surprised when we left out the back of the restaurant into the narrow delivery street behind it. I followed him, having more doubts with each step. If it weren't for the nervous emotion pouring from him, I would have turned around and gone home.

"We need to take a cab back across the bridge," he said over his shoulder, "there are no tunnels under the river."

For that I was thankful. The idea of being under the river was concerning. Getting into a vehicle with this man was however, not going to happen. "I'm not comfortable riding in a cab with you." I told him, leaving no room for argument in my tone. "I don't get close to people I don't know." It was the truth, I hadn't been close to anyone, nor gotten to know a single soul in the last twenty years.

He stopped and looked at me for a moment and then nodded. "I understand." Turning, he looked toward the river. "I will wait at the café where the road splits before the bridge." He gave me a look. "Five minutes, then I'm gone."

Giving him a slight nod, I watching as he hailed a cab. Once it pulled away I motioned for the next one. The fact that he had agreed surprised me, and made me nervous. He seemed willing to agree to anything to get me to go with him.

As the car drove over the bridge, I opened the screen on my phone to text Chase, deciding that someone knowing where I was may be useful... should I have need of assistance in a hurry.

I sent him. *I called Lou. He's taking me to the tunnels to meet others.*

Exiting the screen, I checked that the volume of the phone was off and put it back in my pocket. Receiving messages from one of the Alterealm Kings would probably not win me any brownie points where I was going.

Paying the driver, I got out and had no problems seeing Lou's large form waiting for me beside the café.

He smiled when I walked toward him. "I really thought that was a line you had used to dump me."

Offering a polite smile, I tried to look shocked. "A girl can't be too careful around strangers."

Making no further comments, he turned and walked into the narrow alley. Stopping, he motioned to what looked like a cellar door. "I asked if you were claustrophobic because we've had a few people freak out before we could get them to the location." Lifting the door, he stood there waiting.

I looked down worn cement steps that led into darkness.

"There are lights after the first thirty feet. I'll use my phone so we can see until then."

There was no way I was walking down there into the blackness with a strange man behind me. "I'll follow you." I told him. I was seriously debating on listening to the voice inside my head, the one that was telling me this was a bad idea. Unfortunately, unless I wanted them to keep following me, I didn't see any other option.

I stood at the bottom in the dark while he closed the door. "How far are we going in these tunnels?"

The light from the phone didn't illuminate a large area. "All the way." He said as he walked by me.

I had no choice but to follow closely if I wanted to see where I was going.

"These tunnels are endless under the old part of the city. It's allowed us to move around freely with many exits to get us where we need to go."

I avoided getting too close to the walls. "There's a lot of you then?" He didn't shine the light anywhere but where we needed to step, and I was all right with that, knowing there would be spider webs and rodents in this dismal space. I'd had my share of living in places with those.

"Around three hundred, give or take."

I stepped on something that wasn't stone and cringed. "Really? There are that many like us?"

He led me around a corner and I was pleased to see better lighting, so I wouldn't have to stay too close to him.

"They're not all like us, we have many humans that work for our cause as well."

I watched a rodent scurry into a crack in the wall and was wishing for less light again. "I'm sorry, but wouldn't they be putting themselves at risk… to be fed on?"

He paused so fast, I almost walked into him. "We have very strict rules, no feeding off the humans *with* us—unless they offer." His brows furrowed. "Which isn't very often, unfortunately." He started walking again. "We had a feeding co-op" he chuckled, "for lack of a better way to describe it. Somehow the royals found it though, so we're trying to set up a new one now."

I remembered I was supposed to be clueless. "The royals?" The tunnel we were now in had that old, musky odor and I tried to inhale through my nose as little as possible.

"The royal brothers from the other side. We have no idea how they keep finding our locations." He grinned at me over his shoulder. "Which is why we spread out, so they can't find all of us."

I tried to look impressed. "That seems wise." I stumbled over stones protruding from the floor, catching my balance, I thought of something to keep him talking. "Did you say the other side? As in opponents against your objective?"

He stopped suddenly again. "You really don't know do you?" Making a noise in the back of his throat, he started walking again. "I can't believe how many we've found that didn't know." He snorted. "So much for their strict transport polices."

I could hear water trickling and wondered if we were near an underground river. I hoped it was a river and not sewer drainage. "How much further? This odor is not pleasant."

"Almost there." He said, but kept moving. "It's not so dank once we get there. The witches have cleansed it."

I stopped. "Witches?"

He chuckled again. "You have a lot to learn."

Checking behind me, I started walking again. "So it would seem."

When he stopped, I looked around his large frame to see an old wooden door. "Don't wander away, there are many areas only specific people are allowed to go."

I nodded. "I wouldn't care to get lost down here."

He opened the door, on the other side was another long set of stairs leading down. "It opens up into chambers once we reach the bottom." When he realized I wasn't going to go first, he turned and started down the stairs.

"I had no idea all of this was under the streets." I said as I watched where I placed my feet.

"Not many do, which makes it perfect for us." He looked around at me. "We won't have to hide for much longer."

"I can say that may be a good thing, being down here is somewhat confined." I mumbled.

"We're almost there, then it's more open."

I didn't reply, focusing on the steps and avoiding the many cracks and divots in them.

Once to the bottom, we went through another old door and I was shocked to see we were in a large chamber with several doors around it, some open, some not. "This is surprising."

He grinned. "Isn't it? I don't know what this was used for way back when, but there are rooms off this that are perfect for what we need now. Motioning for me to follow him, he walked by a few other beings sitting along one wall.

I wasn't able to pick up many emotions from them, so they couldn't have been human. We went by one door and I glanced in to see a few people working on something at a roughly made wooden bench.

"Lou."

I turned to see a man coming out of another doorway. He was tall, like the brothers, and I was taken back when he looked at me with eyes reflecting purple in the low lighting. Something Crissy said to me about avoiding purple eyes came back to me. and I had to force myself to stand there and act like I didn't have a care in the world, otherwise I'd be running up the stairs we'd just come down.

"Excuse me." Lou said, looking apprehensive.

I nodded. "Not to worry I'm not going to go anywhere on my own." I stood there looking around, trying to see what was behind the other doors, while listening in on their not so quiet conversation. They may have been close to whispering it, but in the soundless space it may have well be shouting.

"What are you doing?" The man hissed at him.

"Marcus told me we had to have her with us," Lou looked over to me, I smiled. "I had to be straight with her, she's smart."

The man took his arm and turned him so his back was to me. "Did Marcus say why?"

"No, Davis, and I didn't ask." Lou sounded nervous now.

They moved a few more feet away from me, probably thinking they couldn't be overheard. I studied the old stonework, trying to appear as if it fascinated me.

"Where are we with production?" Lou asked.

I knew then, he wasn't as clueless as he led me to believe.

"We're out of parts, we can't get them on this side. Our contact inside has vanished, so I'm guessing he's cooling his heels in a cell." Davis told him in a very hushed tone. "But we have a plan in place to get Marcus and Erin back."

"We have someone on the inside there?"

Davis made a noise that more or less implied Lou was an idiot. "No. None of ours could work in there. We're going to offer them a trade they can't refuse."

Lou leaned down closer to him. "Who do we have they'd want that badly?"

I was distracted when three children came running out one door and into the door beside it. There were children down here? With them? I focused to hear more.

"No one yet, but we will soon." Davis said, sounding very happy.

Lou straightened up. "What do I do with her until we know why Marcus wanted her with us?"

I glanced away when Davis looked at me.

"Show her around I guess, don't pressure her. Just don't let her see too much for now." Davis turned back to the room he'd come out of.

"Got it." Lou told him and then turned back to me and motioned me over.

I went over. "Is everything all right?" I asked hoping I wasn't as nervous as I felt.

Lou nodded. "Yeah, just business."

I smiled and then glanced to the door the children had gone in. "There are children down here."

"Yes." He smiled. "Human and otherwise." He motioned to the door they had gone in. "They won't grow up not knowing what's going on."

My heart was jumping around in my chest, just thinking how that would have been. "They're very lucky then." I followed him to see the door led to another hallway. "Are their parents here as well?"

"Some are. Some we traced their parentage, so they could turn out to be human or like us… we'll have to wait and see." Stopping he opened another door and motioned me in.

I followed quickly, feeling anxious and not sure why. We stepped into a large chamber that was set up like a huge dining hall. A rough wooden table went down the center of it with fifty chairs, I guessed, around it. At the one end sat seven individuals. Quite large men and a quick look told me they were in fact not ordinary humans. They had no problems with showing the color of their eyes. Three had red eyes, two were yellow and to my surprise one had white eyes and one had eyes that were green. I had no idea what the last two could do, but wouldn't be getting close enough to find out.

"Hey, Lou. Who have you brought us?" The one at the end of the table asked him, while leering at me.

Lou straightened to his full height, sending them a cold look. "This is Isabell. I'm just showing her around today."

I had to look to the floor when I realized he didn't know my real name. Small blessings where I could take them, I decided.

"Don't be shy, darlin', come join us. We're waiting for the others to arrive, so we have time." The one with green eyes said with an inviting smile.

I discovered one thing, not all that were like me could shield their emotions. I was picking up several different emotions now, and not of one of them were one I welcomed. "Perhaps another time. I'm sure Lou has more to discuss with me."

There was a few chuckled.

"I'm sure he does, darlin'." The man replied.

With a move of his large hand, Lou motioned to the door. I didn't pause as I quickly moved back out through it.

"Sorry about that. I didn't know they would be there." He mumbled.

I was still trying to rid myself of the emotions I'd picked up. "That's fine."

He turned and headed through another doorway into a long tunnel. "There are areas down here that will be much quieter. I can see if one of the women are around, to help fill in some blanks for you."

Before I could reply, a large group of men began to fill the tunnel. I couldn't count how many there were, only that they were all large as they passed by us. Malevolent emotions hit me so hard, I almost stumbled. I tried to keep walking, get out of this closed-in space. Darkness clouded my head, filling every recess of my mind. Feelings so pitted with violence and malicious desires flooded into me. They just kept coming, one after the other. I kept my head down, trying to focus on the stones and try to build the barrier up inside my mind to stop any more of them intruding. My stomach was feeling queasy.

"Isabell?"

I realized I had stopped walking and looked up at Lou. "I'm sorry, the walls just closed in on me suddenly." It wasn't a lie, they had done that and more. I could still hear the men but didn't turn to see if they were exiting.

"It happens sometimes." Lou told me.

The barriers weren't working. It was stupid of me to come into an unknown situation and think I would be fine. "I need some air, I believe." I took deep breaths, trying to breathe though the darkness filling me. Why did good emotions disappear in seconds, but anything bad clung on for what seemed like hours?

I felt Lou take my elbow and start leading me somewhere, and I didn't have the strength to stop him.

"There's stairs up to an alley just ahead."

I had to get away from him and out of this place, was all I knew. I stumbled before I realized we were going up stairs, and focused as hard as I could on lifting my feet so he wouldn't have to drag me up them.

"Just a few more." I heard Lou say. Suddenly there was brightness, and the musty odor was gone.

"Just breathe deeply." I heard him say, much closer to me than I would have preferred.

Straightening, even though I couldn't actually see him, I tried for a smile. "I will be fine in a moment."

He chuckled. "I get it. Took me months to go down and stay down there. You'll get used to it, gradually."

"Yes." I said, and silently prayed he'd go away. "I'm sorry about that, I really wanted to know more." I heard a phone ring.

"There will be time for that." He grabbed my elbow again. "Let's just get you in a cab, and we'll pick this up later on."

"Lovely." Was the only thing I managed to say. I took another deep breath and tried to look around, the nausea grew worse before I managed to see a sign that was very familiar. It was the gallery I'd gotten my painting from. I needed to get away from this man, now.

He stopped walking.

I stood there, trying not to sway on unsteady legs.

"Here's a cab." I felt him lead me down the curb. "Take her where she tells you." He told the driver. "I paid him." He told me. "Call me when you feel up to more."

"Absolutely." I told him and smiled what I hoped was toward him. I sat down and was pleased it was on the seat, pulling my feet in, I heard the door close.

The car moved and I knew it was safe to speak. "Just take me around the corner and drop me off please." I said quietly. "No change required."

The motion of the cab wasn't helping me ride through the waves of nausea now hitting me. How could I have been so stupid?

"Is here good?" The driver asked me.

"Is it out of his sight?" I asked, swallowing down the bile threatening to expel its self from my body.

"Yeah."

"Okay." The car stopped, I fumbled for the handle. "Thank you." Tripping up the curb, I looked up and tried to see if I could find a place out of sight. There was an alley with dumpsters. I headed in that direction. "Idiot." I hissed.

I practically fell the last few steps until I was behind the dumpster. Holding my hand on my forehead, I forced my head to stay up and looked around. Nothing but walls here. Good. Reaching in my pocket I pulled out the device. I had to get out of here and that was the only option I had. Never had I been filled with so much evil emotion in my life. My sight was starting to blur, "No, not yet." I huffed out short breaths and fumbled with the strap to get the device on. When it was on my wrist, I yanked my phone out of my pocket and hit the screen.

I was on my knees know, leaning over them, my face almost on the pavement when I finally managed to get the phone unlocked and contacts opened. I hit one of them, not knowing if it was Daxx or Chase, only prayed it wasn't the Chinese restaurant.

"Duchess, what the hell…"

Chase.

"I waited too long…" I gasped.

"Use the fuckin device, *now*."

"Yes." I clutched the phone and fiddled with the cover on the device to open it. As soon as it was, I pushed the button.

My stomach, already churning perilously felt like it rolled over completely, and I knew I was no longer in the alley. I was already sweating and then the shakes started. Resting my forehead against the cool floor, I dropped the phone and tried to pull my arm out of my jacket

"What the… Alona?" I heard footsteps rush to me. "What is it?" Chase asked.

He tried to move me and I whimpered. "Don't move me." I panted. Any motion with this much dark inside me would make me throw up. I was going to throw up at some point, experience told me that, but if I could ride it out until the shaking stopped it wouldn't be as violent or painful.

"Are you hurt?" His voice was right beside my head now. "I can't see if you won't let me." I heard him swear. "Get to the landing room, now." He barked.

"Jacket..." I gulped air into my lungs, "off." I managed to say before another wave of shakes hit me.

I could feel him gently pulling my arm from between my body and legs and tugging on the sleeve. I was sweating profusely now, and just wanted the jacket off. Of course, I knew in a few minutes I'd have the chills and would want it back. One step at a time.

"Chase? Alona?" It was Quinton, at least I think it was him. "What happened?"

"I don't know." Chase said from the other side of me now. "She messaged she'd called Lou and I've been losing my freaking mind trying to reach her, then she calls and ports back here like this." I felt him pull my arm out of the other sleeve.

"Is she injured?" The other voice asked, close to my head.

"I don't know." Chase sounded very upset, but I was drowning in the other emotions so there was no way I could feel his.

"Quinton why did you... holy shit... Alona?" It was Daxx, at least I recognized her voice. "Is she hurt?"

"Don't know." Quinton said. "I don't see any blood."

"Move her and see..."

"She cried out when I tried, and she told me not to." Chase said sounding even more distressed.

I heard a moan and realized it was mine. My stomach was the least of my problems, the pains in my head had started. I clutched my head between my hands and moaned again, maybe it was more like a squeal, but I didn't care.

"Troy, look and see if you can do something." Daxx ordered.

Her voice was close to my head now as well. Another wave hit and I knew someone was trying to mess inside my head. I swung my arm out trying to swat them away. "Don't." I cried.

"Shit." I heard Arius say. "She's an empath." He sounded closer now.

"She's an empath?" Chase asked.

"Alona?" Arius was right beside me now. "Tell us how to help? Were you exposed to too many at once?"

I would have hugged him if I could have moved. "Yes," I hissed and then clutched my head again and tried to pant through it. "Dark." Was all I could manage to say.

"Chase, help her. She's been exposed to too many emotions, bad ones. Help her. You can pull them out." Arius said over my head.

"Get her up, I need to see her eyes." Chase said.

I felt someone grasp me under my arms and pull me up, the whole room started to spin and the pain in my head intensified. I squealed.

"Sorry, duchess." Chase's voice was in front of me now, his tone was softer. I felt a hand under my chin. "Open your eyes, let me help."

"Can't see…" I tried to tell them.

"You don't need to." I could feel his breath against my face.

Clutching my head, I struggled to open my eyes, knowing the light was going to make it hurt more. Panting, I managed to get them open and then the pain started to lessen. The black sludge inside my head was clearing. I could see, and it wasn't the room I saw, it was bright yellow eyes.

"Fuck me." Chase whispered and then moved back from me quickly and sat a few feet away.

The room was still spinning, and I was still shaking, but the pain was gone.

"What the hell were you doing, duchess?" Chase asked sliding further away from me. He shook his head. "Don't touch me for a minute until I get a handle on these." He gave his head a quick shake. "Get her to a room to rest, I don't want to go near her until I'm sure she's not going to feel them from me."

I tried to get to my feet, but my legs gave out.

"Help her for fuck's sake." Chase growled and then raised a hand. "Sorry. Just I need a minute here." He huffed out a breath.

Arius stepped away from him and gently lifted me up into his arms. "I think we'll just give big brother a moment or two." He said, then quickly carried me out of the room.

The chills had started, and I was shaking so hard I didn't know how Arius managed to hang onto me. "T-thank you... f-for... explaining." I said trying to contain the vibrations.

He snorted. "Wasn't really the way I would have preferred it." He walked into a large room and carried me over to the bed and set me down. "I'll be right back." He ran out of the room, most likely to check on his brother.

Daxx and Crissy came running in the door. I put my hand up so they wouldn't come too close and bombard me with concern right now. I still wasn't through with this. Whatever Chase had done helped, but the shock of darkness was still coursing through me.

"S-sorry." I tried to say. "Need space."

They stopped and nodded.

"Do you need anything?" Daxx asked. "Want me to run a hot bath?" She motioned to a door to my left.

I considered that for a moment, never having been in the state to try it before on my own. My stomach rolled and I shook my head. "Not yet." In the time it took for me to take two breaths, I started sweating again. Two of the men came running in the door, but I didn't have time to figure out which ones they were. My stomach heaved, I jumped up and bolted for the room Daxx had motioned to, hoping it was a bathroom.

It was.

As I was leaning over the toilet, my body purging the remaining negative from my system, I felt someone hold my hair back for me. That was appreciated more than they could know, and one less thing for me to worry about. A cold wet cloth was put against the back of my neck and it felt heavenly.

When the straps that held my dagger on my back moved off my shoulders, it allowed me to slump completely and rest my forehead on the cool porcelain. Huffing out a few breaths, I assessed if my body was finished. With weak hands, I tried to stand, and then two strong hands pulled me to my feet. I stood on shaking legs and realized I was looking at a large male chest. It hadn't been one of the women helping me.

"Later, I'm going to be really pissed with you."

I looked up and was shocked to see Chase looking down at me.

He smirked. "Let's get you cleaned up a bit, and then you can lay down."

I nodded and let him lead me to the sink. Lifting me like I weighed no more than a child, he set me on the counter and I was again thankful, because I didn't know if I could stand on my own. With a gentle touch, he wiped my face and neck with a warm cloth.

"I don't know what you were into, but I think it gave me indigestion." He winked at me. "I'm still having to work on settling down."

"Sorry. It was completely unexpected."

He raised an eyebrow. "Don't talk about it just yet, or I will lose this war inside me."

I nodded. I wasn't sure how that worked, but if he said he was struggling with the emotions he took from me, then I wasn't about to make a wrong move that would have me absorbing them again.

Scooping me up against his chest, he walked out and put me on the bed, then sat down and pulled off my boots.

I was a weak as a baby, which was normal after I went through that. "Thank you." I whispered and leaned back against a soft pillow. It was then I noticed we weren't alone. All of the brothers were standing near the door looking at me. "It's okay," I said as loud as I could, "after that purge, I can't pick up any emotions for a few hours."

A few of them moved closer.

"Do you want something to drink? Water, tea, juice?" Quinton asked me.

I shook my head. "I can't put anything in right now."

"What about some blood?" Daxx asked, she motioned to the men. "Their blood helps them heal faster than, well, anything."

I put my hand over my mouth and shook my head again. "No. Please. I abhor the taste of blood. Just the thought of it makes me nauseous all over again."

Arius stepped up to the bed and looked down at me. "Does feeding help?"

I titled my head to look at him from a more comfortable position. "I don't know. I usually pass out for a day or so afterward." Sighing, I gave him a wide-eyed look. "Feeding for me usually means combatting emotions, so trying feed too soon after I've always assumed would put me right back there." I pointed to the bathroom.

"I can't even imagine what you've gone through to survive." Troy said hugging Daxx against his side.

"I diet, often." I said trying to make light of it, even though it has been my life-long curse.

"What if the essence came with no emotion?" Rafael asked me, moving closer to the bed.

I opened my mouth and then closed it and gave him a blank look. "I don't know." I lifted my hand and then dropped it again. "That is not something I've experienced before."

"She's only had humans." Arius said quietly and then shrugged. "Hell, most of us would have a hard time keeping emotions on lock down while someone bit us."

"The only time I can say in my life, since I changed, that there were no emotions… while the person was conscious… was when Arius did his little mind control thing the other night." I informed them.

"Let me get this straight," Chase said in a low tone. "You pick up *all* emotions around you, but you've had to feed off humans… who feel far too much all the time?"

I nodded.

"How the fuck, have you lived this long?" He growled and then raised his hand. "Sorry. Still struggling here." He got up and looked around at his brothers. "I have sucked some pretty bad shit out of people before, usually to scare the holy hell out of them…" He paused as a few of them nodded. "But what I just pulled out of her," he motioned to me, "was the darkest, most vile emotion I have *ever* tasted."

I could tell by their expressions that was quite serious. "I was completely unprepared for it…" I stopped talking when Chase's head snapped around and he glared at me.

"Don't discuss it yet." He said softly.

I nodded and pulled myself more upright on the bed. "I am too weak to discuss any of it at the moment." I assured him.

"Which brings us back, what can we get you?" Arius asked.

Turning, I shrugged. "I can't eat with my stomach like this…"

"You have to do something," Chase said sitting down so I didn't have to look up, "you're shaking still."

"I usually just sleep." I watched his eyes move over my face, not sure what the look meant.

"And you're usually on your own without any other options." He continued to look at me.

"I need coffee, if I'm going to come up with any valid suggestions." Michael said. "We'd just sat down for breakfast when Quinton went racing out of the room."

I looked around, Crissy shrugged.

"I still don't understand it." She said. "We eat breakfast when it gets dark, but Chase has dinner with our breakfast." She nodded. "I've never eaten so often before."

Victor wrapped his arm around her shoulder. "You will never be hungry again." He said as he dropped a kiss on top of her head.

She gave him a look, her eyes huge. "No, I'll be fat instead."

Rafael laughed. "You never stop moving, you burn the calories off three days before you eat them."

She gave him a look, then grinned at him.

"Why don't all of you go to breakfast?" Chase said turning to look at them. "We'll be along shortly, once Alona's stomach has settled."

"Are you sure?" Quinton asked.

Chase nodded. "I need a few more minutes to get a handle on things. I'll sit with duchess until she's steady."

Chapter Nine

After everyone left, Chase turned and studied me quietly for a few moments. "I thought you weren't going out again." He finally said.

"No. I said I'd had enough shopping for the day. I didn't go shopping."

I could see annoyance in his hazel eyes. "You look so drawn, it's very upsetting." His voice was soft again.

"I am very tired and probably couldn't walk to the other side of the room right now." His brows creased. "It's normal." I wasn't used to someone to worry over me.

"And unnecessary."

I shook my head.

"It may have been what you'd have to suffer through when you were alone, but you're not alone now."

The way he was looking at me made my heart beat a little bit faster. I needed to change the subject. "What did Daxx mean when she said your blood heals?"

He leaned back on one hand and looked at me. "True bloods heal quickly to begin with, but royal blood given to others heals them almost immediately."

I pursed my lips together and looked at him. "I do not heal quickly, and I'm starting to feel quite inferior since meeting all of you... which is new for me."

He smirked. "You are anything but inferior." Cocking his head to the side he gave me an inquisitive look. "Would you like to try it?

"Your blood?"

Chase nodded.

I thought about that for a moment. "No, my stomach doesn't like the idea of blood. I've always hated the taste of it."

"Maybe you haven't tried the right blood." His eyes were almost daring me.

Smiling, I gave my head a quick shake. "Perhaps I'll try some time when my stomach is more settled."

"Fair enough." He sat forward again. "So, that leaves two options, and you need to pick one, because it's very upsetting to see you this pale. Eating or feeding."

I didn't know him very well, but I did understand that he was a man that got his way. "I couldn't eat right now, the very thought of it makes my stomach turn."

"That's okay, duchess. I've had moments where my stomach wanted nothing to do with food as well. Although, I had to consume large amounts of alcohol to get that way..." He waved his hand around, "those are stories for another time. You'll feed then."

I knew it wasn't a question. I opened my mouth to decline, politely, and he interrupted me.

"Don't offend my fragile ego by saying no. I have never, in two hundred and sixty years, *ever* let someone feed off me."

I looked at him for a moment. "I find that hard to believe..."

He raised he hand. "I said feed, I didn't say bite... that's an entirely different ending." He winked at me. "If you'd like, I can call someone else..." He pulled out his phone. "It will cause me shame and embarrassment though, if you preferred one of my brothers over me..." He held the phone up, waiting almost patiently.

"I've never fed from someone who expected me to bite them before."

He shrugged. "Then we're even, I've never offered up my neck before."

I bit my lip and looked at him. I didn't know if I could, but I was fairly certain he wasn't budging until I did...

"You're overthinking it." He said quietly. "I can almost hear your mind moving faster than the speed of light."

"You just... consumed a large amount of negativity. Won't that be giving it right back to me?"

He shook his head. "Essence and emotion don't blend. Have faith that I can control the emotions. Trust me."

Taking a deep breath, I thought about how I felt about biting him. He was a striking man, and I'm sure being close wouldn't be a hardship if he controlled the emotions...

"My patience is waning, duchess. Just do it. Then take a shower and see if it helped you. It may do nothing to help you recover... then my ego would be crushed of course, but..."

I put my hand over his mouth so he'd stop. "I'll try it."

He grinned. "Oh, I feel like a teenager right now." He teased.

I exhaled a nervous breath. "Just... stop talking..."

"Do you prefer right or left?" He moved closer to me.

I hadn't even thought of which side. "I... I guess left." I realized I always did bite a certain side.

Getting up, he climbed on the bed and sat on my right. He gave me an abrupt nod and then moved so close I could feel the heat of his body. "Take what you need, not just enough to *get* by." He whispered next to my ear.

I could feel my heartbeat in my throat. I was nervous for the first time in many years.

"You're killing me here," He whispered.

His breath brushed against my throat sending a shiver up my spine, and not in a bad way. I inhaled slowly and could smell his essence, and it was very appealing. I felt my fangs in my mouth. With a quiet sound, he touched the back of my head and pushed me towards him. I bit into him and he hissed softly, but held my head firmly in place, so it couldn't have bothered him too much.

He pulled me against his chest, so our bodies were touching from the waist up. It was a new feeling for me, to be close while feeding, one that I discovered I liked. When I realized I was feeling more pleasure than I should be, I pulled away and licked over the punctures on his neck. His big hand continued to hold me in place for several moments after I finished.

When he finally released his hold on me and leaned back, I found myself looking into yellow eyes. They moved over my face and stopped at my mouth. "I enjoyed that more than I ever thought I would." He confessed, his voice rough, yet soft.

I'm not sure how long we sat there, just looking at each other, but my heart was beating a wild rhythm in my chest by the time he leaned back and the feline-yellow tint of his eyes gave way to a softer shade. .

"How do you feel?"

I nodded. "Better. Thank you."

He grinned. "Don't thank me, duchess, it was my pleasure." He reached out and grasped my chin lightly. "Go shower or soak in the tub, grab anything you like from the closet… it belongs to no one in particular, then send a message and someone will show you to the dining room." His pale eyes caressed my face. "*Then* you can tell us what happened with *Lou*." Letting go of my chin, he stood up and looked down at me, waiting for an answer.

I nodded. "I think I will take a quick shower, thank you."

He backed up a few steps and with an abrupt nod, turned and walked out of the room closing the door behind him.

I put my hand over my rapidly beating heart. "Just when you think you're too old to feel something new." I said quietly and then got off the bed. "*That* was definitely new."

After a quick shower, I found a lovely skirt that fit like it was made for me in the closet, along with some hair clips I wished I'd seen before the shower to keep my hair dry. I was just securing it off my neck when someone knocked on the door. Going over, I opened it to see Arius. He looked me up and down and smiled.

"Shower made you feel better I see." He motioned down the hall. "I was sent to fetch you and show you to the dining room."

I wondered if Chase had told them I had fed from him. If what Arius said meant anything, he hadn't. "I do feel better." I followed him down the hall.

"That was quite the start to our day." He glanced at me out of the corner of his eye.

"Sorry about that. I was glad I had the device or else I would have still been laying behind a dumpster in some alley."

He paused for a moment and looked at me and then shook his head. "Don't tell me until I'm sitting down."

When I stepped into the room, all eyes turned to me.

Crissy smiled and then looked at Daxx. "I told you half the closet would fit her."

Daxx nodded. "She is taller than we are." To my puzzled look, she rolled her eyes. "Long story for later. But you look great."

"Thank you." I looked down at the ankle length black skirt I wore and smiled. "I love this skirt. Most skirts this length I can't wear, they don't have a slit to allow me to walk in my normal stride." I looked up at her and grinned, and then realized fashion talk probably didn't thrill the men in the room.

Mitz came out of the kitchen with a cup and plate of toast. She set them on the table by the chair I stood behind. "Tea and toast for a troubled stomach." She smiled at me before she turned and walked out.

I sat down and glanced down to Chase. He inclined his head so slightly, I doubt anyone else noticed. I smiled.

"You look better than you did. I guess a shower and bit of quiet did the trick." Troy said, smiling at me.

"I feel much better, thank you."

He glanced briefly at his twin and then into the mug he held.

"Feel up to sharing what brought you here in that state?" Victor asked.

I took a sip of the tea, thankful it was the blend Mitz had given me before. "Yes. I actually think I found out quite a bit, although I'm sure most of it will mean more to you than it did to me." I nodded and looked around, noting the unhappy look on Chase's face. Glancing back to Victor, I offered a polite smile. "I called Lou, mostly because I don't want a bodyguard."

Victor nodded. "Chase told us you have others following you."

"Yes, I only planned to speak with him on the phone, when he suggested we meet at a restaurant." I shrugged. "Surprisingly, it was a nice one, near where I live." I waved my hand around. "I thought there was no harm in a place like that."

"I'm guessing you didn't stay at the restaurant." Michael said as he studied me.

I shook my head. "No, and despite how I arrived here, I don't regret it. I don't think you shall either, when I tell you the rest."

Michael waited with a patient expression on his face. .

"Lou is very talkative, in an almost naïve way…" I shook my head, "or I'm a better actress then I thought." I took another sip. "I picked up very nervous emotions from him, so I knew, almost instantly, he was someone's lackey."

"Did you ask him why you were being followed?" Leone asked me.

I nodded. "Yes. He said it was for my own safety." I pointed to Crissy. "He knew you had accosted me in the club twice…" I glanced to Victor, "and they think she's dead."

"Oh." Crissy looked animated. "That rune must work very well."

"Indeed." Victor replied and then looked back to me.

I didn't want to get distracted asking about the rune, but made a mental note to inquire at a later date. "I asked why me, and he said he knew I had something extra special." I glanced around at the others. "Can they know I'm an empath?"

Arius rubbed his hand over his jaw. "You hide it very well, and as far I know there isn't anyone with the ability to pick up on that." He looked to his brothers, none offered anything.

"That is something I'd like to find out." I said more to myself then them. "Lou suddenly decided he wanted to take me to meet the others." I raised my hand before they interrupted. "He was quite uncertain, but it came across as a desperate attempt to impress me, I'm not sure why." I took another sip of tea, trying to keep events straight in my head. "He told me we had to cross back to the other side of the bridge because that's where the tunnels were. The tunnels allow them to move around freely, and stay off the radar. I took a separate cab there, telling him I wouldn't ride in a car with a strange man."

Quinton nodded. "Yes, we've found them in the tunnels."

I remembered how many of them there were. "He says there are around three hundred... members, or whatever they call them..."

That brought all of the brothers into motion.

"Three hundred?" Leone blew out a breath.

"How many have we got?" Arius looked to Michael.

"Last count, a little over a hundred, I think. We caught all those with devices before they crossed..." Michael said shaking his head.

"I didn't anticipate that many." Troy said glancing to his twin.

Chase shook his head. "Nor I. Where did they get that many? We'd notice..."

"Some of them are human." I added, hoping it helped.

Daxx frowned and leaned forward to look down at me. "Humans from our side?"

I nodded. "I took it to mean that. He said they have many humans that are *for their cause* as well." I exhaled slowly, still feeling tense about the next part I was going to tell them. "I've also seen young children there. Lou said some were human, some not. That they'd traced their parentage and found them, and would wait and see if they were special or just human."

"They have children?" Crissy sounded distressed.

"Sounds like they're building a whole community." Rafael said and then sat back in his chair. "Three hundred, with humans and children…"

"Are they using them for feeding? The humans?" Quinton asked sounded angry.

I shook my head. "I don't think so. Lou said they had a feeding co-op, but *the royals* found it, so they're working on setting up a new one." I grimaced, the thought of that turning my stomach. "Did you find one?"

Crissy nodded. "The people were so scared."

I put my hand over my mouth. "They were feeding against their will?" I huffed out a breath, "I mean, knowingly, the people knew what they were being used for?" I looked around. "Are they all right?"

Arius nodded his head slowly. "Yes, I made sure they wouldn't remember."

I huffed out a breath and sat back, resting my hand over my throat. "That… good." I took another drink of the tea trying to settle my thoughts again. "I just need a moment. There's more."

"Are you all right?" Chase asked.

I glanced to him and nodded. "Yes. The reality is just upsetting me." I rolled my eyes. "I know I'm hypocrite. I feed on humans too, but they aren't held against their will, and have no idea." I shook my head. "I can't imagine the horror they felt. It's a paralyzing emotion to pick up, it's like I'm living it with them."

Chase's look softened. "Just take a few deep breaths and try to tell us the rest."

I continued to look at him, while breathing deeply and exhaling slowly. "I'm all right, thank you." Closing my eyes, I tried to remember what else had been said. Opening them, I looked back to Chase. "They don't know how you keep finding their locations, but they've spread them out so you can't find all of them."

Leone snorted. "We've already discovered that."

I waved my hand around. "He made some comment about how he couldn't believe how many others they'd found, and so much for your strict transport polices."

Troy grunted. "We really need to review those."

"The others are like you and born on that side?" Arius asked.

I shrugged. "I suppose that's what he meant."

"Aside from really old ones, Crissy, do you think you can come up with a way to find them?" Michael asked her.

She bit her lip and bounced around in her chair. "I can try to find patterns online, but I don't know."

Everyone turned and looked back to me. "They have witches… they cleansed the chambers so they aren't as rank with that foul odor."

"Witches? Plural?" Quinton looked to Rafael. "Guess the one we caught isn't the only then."

"Wonderful." Rafael said sounding very unimpressed.

"He said they won't have to hide for much longer." I took a bite of the toast to see how my stomach was.

"He said a lot, how long were you with him?" Daxx asked.

I shrugged. "I'm not sure." I looked at Chase. "I messaged Chase when we left the restaurant and don't know how long it was before I very abruptly came here."

"Too long, is how long. I almost lost my mind trying to reach you." He growled, annoyed. then glanced around at his siblings. "It wasn't even an hour."

"Lou is very talky." Daxx noted.

"Yes, he was. Oh, a man with purple eyes…" I looked around to see if they understood that.

"Shit, they have another mage." Arius sighed. "I was hoping Marcus was the last one."

"We knew he'd have more." Michael stated.

"His name was Davis." I told them.

"I know that name." Troy mused. "I'll call Romulus and see if he can give me more information."

"I don't think they thought I could hear them, they were whispering and moved further away… but it was so quiet in that chamber."

"Chamber? They weren't tunnels?"

"Yes, we went through tunnels and then down a long stairwell and it opened into a large area with several other areas, or at least doors, I didn't see in them all."

"Do we have those maps yet?" Victor asked Michael.

He nodded. "Yeah, but there's miles and miles of them to go through."

"I know where we went in and roughly where I came out." I looked down to Crissy. "We came out near your orange alley." I looked to Chase and nodded. "I managed to stay coherent enough to look around, it's near the gallery where I bought the painting."

"Alona visited a gallery near an old market alley that glows orange with the lighting on it." Chase said.

"Oh, are there doors… but it ends at the far end, with an archway of stone?" Crissy asked.

I nodded. "Yes, it's very similar."

She nodded her head and then didn't speak for a moment. "Then I think that it is, I seen it and then Alona ended up there and it was with that man that had the card, I seen as well." She nodded again.

"Ok so we know where the orange cave is." Daxx said and then looked to me. "Is there more."

I nodded. "Yes. This Davis didn't seem happy that Lou brought me down, but Lou said Marcus said they had to have me with them." I looked around at them hoping for some insight as to why. No one looked pleased with the idea, but Chase looked very angry.

"Why?" He asked.

"I don't know. Davis asked Lou the same thing and he didn't know." I exhaled and looked at my cup and then remembered the rest Davis had said. "Oh, they're making something and are out of parts... they can only get on this side, and their contact has vanished, so they can't make any more."

"Bet it was one of the guards or staff Crissy found." Quinton said with a grin.

"So, we've slowed them down from bringing more over from this side, but they're still three hundred strong and rounding up more, from the sounds of it." Victor reminded them.

"Yeah, but the good thing with the ones from that side is they haven't been fighting like we have for hundreds of years." Leone nodded. "That's a good thing."

"No, they just fight with things like *bullets* instead." Daxx stated with heavy sarcasm.

"Is that everything?" Troy asked me, sounding very much like a king.

I was sure they didn't want to hear the rest, but I hadn't gone down there for fun. I shook my head. "When they thought I was distracted watching the children, they said something about having a plan in play to get Marcus and Erin back." I frowned. "They're going to offer a trade you can't refuse, and from what I could tell it's a person they plan on taking soon."

"Fuck! It just keeps getting better." Chase said with a snarl.

"Did they say who?" Victor leaned forward and gave me a hard look.

"No that was all they said about it."

"Who could they take that would make us release Marcus and that witch that tried to kill us all?" Rafael looked around the table.

"I don't know, but Cristy, you are not to go anywhere without Bronx if one of us here aren't with you." Victor said leaving little room for argument.

"Okay. I won't." She nodded.

Troy turned to look at Daxx.

Daxx held her hand up. "Yeah I got it." She didn't look happy about it either.

"I think that's it… oh, they don't know who I really am. Lou called me Isabell, so I don't think they know as much about me as they would like." I picked up the cup and then paused. "And they have men there with white and green eyes, as well as red and yellow… and the purple eyed man." At no point in my existence did I ever think I'd be describing people this way.

It was silent for several moments, each face at the table in deep thought.

"How did you end up coming back that way?" Arius asked me in a quiet tone.

I shook my head. "We were walking down a shorter tunnel," I motioned to the room, "maybe as long as this room and it just filled with very tall men." I nodded to Chase. "Like all of you… they were walking through, and the waves of awful emotions just swamped me. I couldn't possibly have erected barriers that fast to protect myself against it." I took a short breath, "Lou said others felt ill being that far underground, and he'd even had to get used to it gradually, so he put me in a cab, and said to call when I was feeling better."

"He didn't even notice how off you were?" Daxx asked me.

I shrugged, "I was able to fight it as best I could until I made it to the alley and hid behind a dumpster." I glanced to Chase. "Then I called Chase and used the device."

"I think they've been trying to get her to join them for a while, if this Lou was parading her around like a prize." Chase said with a sneer.

"I agree." Michael nodded and looked down at me. "And even though you brought back a lot of intel, going without backup was…"

I held up my hand to stop him. "I'm not some naïve adolescent. I know what I can and cannot withstand." I nodded to Chase. "I had been out earlier to expose myself to emotions, having discovered years ago that if I did so regularly my resistance was higher." I waved my hand around trying to find the best way to explain it. "When he said others, I presumed they were like all of you… I can barely feel a trace from you, it's quite remarkable." I paused and looked at Daxx. "You… you're human, but not… I can barely sense yours as well." I smiled at Crissy. "Except you… you feel everything and nothing at the same time. You almost drowned me that first time you dragged me out of the club."

Crissy nodded and then grinned. "I find it fascinating that you're an essence feeder but feel everyone's emotions… don't you find that fascinating, Chase?" She looked at him.

He watched her for a moment and then scowled. "Seer analysis later, cutie." His hazel eyes turned to me. "I don't know how you've survived this long. Or how you have been out there this long and not known what you are?"

I pushed my cup away and considered his questions. Taking a deep breath, I looked back at him. "Oh, I don't know, I supposed your website… Alterealm dot com, was down the day I searched for never-aging-with-an-inclination-to-bite-necks on the internet." There were a few chuckles, but I met his glare without fear. "No…" I held up my hand and gave my head a quick shake, "when I was looking for *those* answers there was no internet in existence!" I tilted my head and returned his hard look. "By the time there was internet, I was more concerned with managing to live… I have to bite people to survive, *but* when I bite them I feel their pain and fear… yet if I don't, I cease to live." I stood up. "So, I've been doing the best I can, *alone,* for my entire life."

Arius got up quickly. "Practice?"

Several stood, pushing back chairs, as I continued to glare at Chase, who sat there, his eyes not moving from mine. I could see his jaw clenching and didn't need to feel his emotions to know he wasn't happy with my answer.

"Alona, come." Daxx breezed by me and grabbed my arm. "You can watch the men flex and beat on each other."

I glanced down at her. "That sounds appealing. I haven't been able to find a suitable sensei since I moved again."

"Sensei?" She grinned. "You fight. That's awesome."

Daxx and Crissy were rushing me down a hallway when we stopped quickly.

Daxx held up her palm. "High five. The way you put Chase in his place."

I tapped her hand with my own, then Crissy's and grinned.

"You made him speechless," Crissy nodded. "I've never seen that."

Smiling, I hissed out a breath. "He just seems to push the right buttons."

Daxx snorted. "You have no idea."

We began walking again.

Chapter Ten

We stepped in a room, I had expected a large dojo, this was not even close to that. It was a huge gymnasium with an entire wall lined with weapons. I was quite taken back, and maybe a little impressed.

"They seem to be prepared for anything." I murmured to the girls.

Daxx grinned. "This is my favorite room on the planet."

Crissy shrugged and walked over to where the men stood.

Arius stepped away from the group and smiled at me, opening his arms wide. "I'd love you to show me what you've learned from the masters." He placed his palms together and bowed in a formal manner.

Walking around the edge of the mat in my boots, I grinned at him. "I could use a little practice. I haven't found a suitable dojo to stay in form." I was about to take off my boots when someone laughed.

"You're going to fight dressed like that?"

I looked to Rafael and decided I'd leave the boots on for the moment.

Chase smacked his brother on the chest. "Shut up, brother."

I smiled and reached down to pull up the hem of my skirt. "Always." I tucked the corner of it into the waistband and began to walk toward Chase, who looked entirely too enthusiastic about my outfit. "A female opponent wouldn't bother to notice," I glanced to Daxx, who shrugged. "Unless of course their preference leaned that way." I kept walking toward Chase, whose eyes were on my legs, now showing more skin than anywhere else. "But a male, so much bigger than I in strength..." I stopped a few feet from Chase and motioned to my legs. "They'd notice."

Chase grinned wide. "*Yess*, they would."

With a fast move, I stepped toward him and turned quickly, one foot hit the floor beside his feet as I grabbed his arm and flipped his large frame over my body in a single, smooth motion. He hit the matt with a loud thump. I stepped and put my boot on his chest and smiled. "And they'd be very distracted."

He looked at the boot and then smiled up at me. "Completely."

A few around us clapped and the girls cheered.

"Damn did anyone take a video of that?" Rafael asked.

I moved my foot and held out my hand. With a big grin, he allowed me to pull him to his feet.

Crissy bounced in place before glancing to Victor. "Maybe I need a skirt to fight in."

Victor snorted. "Over my dead body."

Frowning, Crissy shook her head. "I don't think you'd have to die for me to get a skirt, Vic."

Pulling her with him they walked away.

"Impressive, duchess." Chase said, still smiling at me. "Although it may be considered cheating."

I leaned down and unzipped one boot. "Using your own weaknesses against you isn't cheating." I took off the boot and reached for the other one.

"I'm surprised you can fight, without the backlash of emotions." Michael mused as he stood there leaning on a long bo.

I sighed as I made sure the skirt was still tucked in. "It took a long time to find a way to fight and protect myself without collapsing under a backlash. Martial arts require great discipline and an almost unemotional focus, so I endeavoured to master all I could." I motioned to the wall of weaponry. "It may not be as brutal as you are accustomed to, but it works to aid me when I require it." I glanced down at my skirt. "I'm normally not dressed this way for sparring, so I will mostly be a bystander today."

Arius motioned to the matt. "Show me how you just did that to Chase."

Nodding I walked by him and then realized without the heels on my boots, I was at a height disadvantage now. Decades of learning would have to help me then.

Watching the way they fought, I realized a few things. They were very good, and meticulous in their study and practice in hand-to-hand combat.

They went through more than one weapon and sparring partner. Daxx was impressive, holding her own against much larger opponents. As for Crissy, anyone intending to harm her would have to catch her first. If I were to describe her technique, I would say it was evasive maneuvers.

Chase bowed to Troy, who then turned to answer Arius' taunts. Their closeness showed in their treatment of one another. It was something I hadn't had the opportunity to observe much in my life.

Placing the large wooden sword back on the wall, Chase came to squat beside me, a serious look on his face.

"Did Leone say anything to you before he left?"

I shook my head. "Only that he was glad I was okay."

He brushed his fingers over his goatee. "Maybe he had a lead to check out," he mused quietly. His pale eyes moved over me briefly. "How are you feeling?"

"I am good. Thank you." I motioned to the others. "Do you do this every day?"

Nodding, he glanced to his siblings. "Most days, yes. Until recently we hadn't had any wars or uprisings, so we practice to stay in shape."

"You're all very good."

He smiled. "Helps to be, so we don't lose." His hazel eyes moved over my face. "Are you hungry, you didn't eat your toast?"

"I was trying to remember everything I found out."

"Mmm," he sighed, "some of it, I could have been happier without knowing." He shrugged. "Like the children being around others like that." Pulling out his phone, he looked at it. "Walk with me to the kitchen? I want a drink before I go back to my office, and hopefully I'll get to bed in a few hours."

We walked for a few minutes without speaking. I couldn't sense what he was feeling, but I could see the worry in his eyes.

"You're worried."

He glanced at me and nodded. "Concerned for Leone, you, and who they have in mind to kidnap to trade for Marcus and the witch."

"I wished I'd heard more."

"No, staying longer, actually, going down there in the first place was a huge risk." He stopped walking and looked at me. "Tell me I'm not going to be awakened because you are there again."

I shook my head, trying not to smile at his expression. "No. I'm planning on sleeping shortly as well. Just as soon as someone takes me home."

"You could stay here tonight." He began walking again.

"I don't feel comfortable with that."

He sighed in a dramatic way. "I figured as much. Arius will take you back. Tomorrow my last remaining personal guard, as Daxx and Crissy have adopted my other two, Sith, will be joining you. I'm afraid he is still very piratical in appearance, but you will be safe."

I was silent as I considered that. Having someone I knew I could trust, in case Lou and those men with him decided they wanted me no matter what, was a good idea. "Thank you. I have no plans on going anywhere tonight or in the morning."

"Good." He turned into the dining room.

Mitz came out of the kitchen and set a tray on the table. "Have a good night, love. I'm off for home for a wee bit."

Chase gave her a warm look. "All the way to the far end of the royal chambers. Say hello to Ira for me."

She gave him a soft, motherly look. "Will do." Glancing at me, she smiled. "I'll see you tomorrow." Then she walked out.

Chase motioned to the tray. "Help yourself. Can't offend Mitz by leaving it untouched."

I looked at it to see a full wine glass, a tumbler of dark liquid and crackers. Picking up the wine glass I took a sip and then gave Chase a curious look.

"Probably your favorite, right?" He smirked.

I nodded.

He picked up the tumbler and grinned. "That's not shocking with Mitz."

"Leone," I said quietly, "he seems like he's steady." I shrugged. "I've seen many addicts including those who are struggling, and he doesn't appear that way."

He gave me a soft look. "I appreciate you saying that, and he does seem like he's solid *but*, he's also had thirty years to get it together and appear to be fine."

I nodded, "Yes, longevity… I keep forgetting I'm the youngest one now."

He chuckled. "Not a bad thing to get used to."

Clearing my throat, I studied him for a moment. "I can answer a question that you asked while we were having lunch today…"

He cocked an eyebrow at me. "Oh?"

I smiled. "Yes. You asked if one donor of essence was better than the other…"

"Donor?" He put a hand over his heart. "I'm wounded you think of me as a simple donor."

"I-I meant the others…"

He smirked. "Is one better than the other?"

"I find humans to be lacking… now." I felt my cheeks heat from my confession.

"Is that so?" He set the glass down on the table. "And why is that?" His eyes were locked to mine. "No emotions interfering? That is wasn't distant and impersonal? Or…" He motioned down his body, "was it the particular *donor*?"

His voice was so smooth it gave me goosebumps. "I'm not certain, it could be all of those combined."

Chase stepped closer and I had to steady myself, so I wouldn't back away from him.

"I'd be happy to help you figure it out," his eyes flicked to my mouth, "having your mouth on me wasn't a hardship for me. Although, if we could try it without the evil emotions and dire need next time, I'm sure we'd both come out of it with more."

I didn't reply immediately, I was too busy telling my body, no. I didn't need any physical distractions in my life at the moment. "It was *pleasant* not having to worry about things."

"Anytime you want, duchess, my neck is yours."

There was barely a foot between us now. "I thought you didn't allow people to feed from you." The way he was watching me, that intensely, made me nervous. I licked my lips. His eyes followed the movement.

"I don't, but I feel you may be the exception to that rule." He whispered.

"I am?"

"Mmm," he inched closer still, "you are."

We were close enough now that I could feel the heat from his body and smell his essence. I glanced at his neck briefly.

He touched my chin, so I would look up at him. His eyes were not quite yellow, but not really hazel either. He growled softly in the back of his throat and took the wine glass out of my hand to set it on the table. Taking my arm gently, he walked us to the furthest corner of the room and turned my back into it. Then he looked down at me. His eyes were completely yellow. My heart sped up.

"I'm not going to feed on your emotions, but I *can* sense them, just so you're aware…"

I hadn't realized that emotion feeders could, but it made sense now that he'd said it.

"You can't go hunting at the club for now, so feeding is going to be difficult." His voice was very rough now.

"I hadn't thought of that." I admitted.

"You feeding, is *all* I've been able to think about," he whispered, standing so close I felt his breath on my cheek. "Feed from me again, Alona."

I swallowed, my mouth suddenly dry and looked at his neck once more. I'd never fed this soon before, of course more would be welcome. Especially from him. I wasn't sure why, and seemed to be unable to think clearly to figure it out.

"A trade," he whispered against my ear, "something I want, for something you want."

I lifted my face toward his. "Which is?"

"Just say yes."

I felt lost in his eyes, despite them being yellow. "Yes."

He growled softly and lightly grasped the back of my head. I felt fangs fill my mouth. I expected him to feed from me, the way he was looking at me, but instead his mouth crushed mine in a frantic kiss. The emotion coming from him was the strongest desire I'd ever felt. Combined with my own, I suddenly felt like I was going up in flames.

Wrapping his other arm around me, he pulled me tight against his hard form as he ran his tongue over my sharp teeth.

With a groan, he lifted his mouth away and pushed my head toward his throat. Swimming in lust, I didn't need any further coaxing and bit into his flesh. He growled and tightened his hold on my waist. I wasn't even sure if I'd done anything to dull the pain of my bite, but he wasn't stopping me, so I must have.

Licking over my marks, I rested my forehead against his shoulder and fought to catch my breath. I realized my arms were wrapped around him, and my hand was holding his hair. I didn't even know when I'd done that.

"If we weren't standing in the most popular room in the kingdoms, I'd explore this much further." He whispered against my ear, a deep, rasping tone.

I lifted my head up and looked at him. "I think that could be dangerous."

Chase grinned a daring smile. "Exactly. Our emotions fueling each other, I expect smoke at the very least." His eyes were slowly turning back to their normal color.

"I don't mix feeding and… flames." I told him quietly.

His eyes lit up and he smirked. "Don't distract me talking like that. Tomorrow, after a sleepless night fantasizing about you, I want to discuss a possible blood bond."

I inhaled deeply, feeling completely sated, in one way at least. "Blood bond?"

He nodded and his hold started to loosen. "Yes, I think if we had one, I may be able to sense when you're overwhelmed, and possibly help." He frowned. "I'm not completely sure if would work, but it may be worth a try."

I grimaced. "All but the blood part."

Chase winked. "You may like it from the right vein, taken in the right way."

I gave him a skeptical look. "I'm not sure about that."

"We'll discuss it. I want to ask the elders and get their take on it first. I don't want to flood you with my own emotions either, which can happen."

"Like a moment ago?"

He chuckled. "Oh, duchess," he backed me into the corner and placed a hand against the wall on either side of my head. "That was both of our desires, not just mine. I held mine in check until yours all but had their way with me."

I felt my cheeks grow hot. "It was surprising." I bit my lip, trying not to think about it, or I'd be acting like a needy trollop. "But, I don't think it's wise, on either of our parts…"

"Let's not label or limit it right now." He placed his hand under my chin, so I would look at him. "Just do me a small favor, until we decide…" His eyes locked on mine. "Keep those sexy fangs out of my brothers, I wouldn't want to have to kill any of them."

I raised both brows at him. "I wouldn't. I'm still shocked I fed from you."

"Twice." He nodded and released my chin. "If I have my way, we're going to explore it many, many more times."

Someone cleared their throat. Chase turned enough that I was able to see Arius standing by the table.

He motioned to the hall. "The others are right behind me."

Chase sighed deeply and moved away from me.

Arius cleared his throat again. "I came to see if Alona wanted to go home, or if she's staying and if she…" he looked from Chase to me then back to Chase again, "wanted help feeding, but I see that's been taken care of."

I looked at Chase's neck to see a smudge of blood on it. My face grew hot.

With a grin, he touched where I had bitten him.

"I'm just…" Arius pointed to the door. "Going to change. Then I'll be back." He turned and quickly walked out the door.

Chase chuckled and then winked at me. "I'll exit via the kitchen so the rest of the hoard don't see my neck." He inclined his head. "Call if you have need, duchess, for anything."

I watched him walk out the door and downed the entire contents of the wine glass, before the others came walking in.

Chapter Eleven

Arius stepped away from me so quickly after we reached my place, I had to sit down so I wouldn't tip over with dizziness.

"Sorry. I forgot." He tucked his hands in his pockets and looked at me, as if he was looking for something.

"Have I broken some rule by feeding from your brother?" It was the only reason I could think of for the look I was receiving.

He shook his head. "No. It's... uh... not that." He grinned. "Chase is a big boy and *way* out ranks me, so he can do whatever he likes. I'm just..." He sat down by the window. "Surprised he offered." His brows furrowed. "Twice, if I'm not mistaken."

"He thought it would help after I was so ill."

"Did it?" He was leaning forward on his knees studying me.

"Yes. Any other time I could never have..."

He waved his hand, "Oh, I realize that." He sighed and sat back, a look of thoughtfulness on his handsome face. "I'm just surprised he did."

"He said he never had before."

Arius snorted. "He wasn't lying. Even when we were younger, or one of us were injured, he'd always shove another neck in our face." He shrugged. "I think it has a lot to do with the fact that out of the eight of us, he's the only one without fangs."

I clasped my hands in my lap. "Oh, I suppose that would make him feel excluded and maybe a bit scorned at the same time."

Arius nodded his head slowly. "It had to be that way though. He is one of the twin kings."

"I don't understand." I motioned to the kitchen. "Would you like some wine?"

He grinned. "You love your wine. Just a little."

I got up. "Yes, I do. I suppose some have a comfort food or habit. I have wine." I brought the bottle and glasses back quickly. "Please elaborate, the twin kings."

He accepted the glass and took a sip. "You have excellent taste in wine." He smiled briefly. "It was prophesized... Alterealm, by the way, is really big on prophecies." He glanced out the window. "Anyway, it was prophesised twin kings would be born, one to rule the day, one the night and every five hundred years after the first new royal twins would come." He looked back to me. "So Troy is the night and Chase is the day."

I found it quite interesting. "They are the first twin kings."

Arius nodded. "It was too much for one king and his guardsmen to rule over, so the years of waiting for the twins were many, so I'm told. I was born ten years after them, so they've always been there."

I took a quick sip. "That's a lot of expectation to live up to."

Tilting his head, he gave me a curious glance. "I hadn't thought of it that way." He took a drink.

As I raised my glass to do the same, my phone started vibrating across the table. Picking it up, I looked at the number. I frowned. "I think it's Lou."

"Answer it." Arius was up out of the chair before I could push the button.

"Hello?"

"Isabell, it's Lou. I was calling to see how you are feeling."

I watched Arius pull out his phone. "Oh, your concern is touching. I'm feeling much better now."

Arius was texting on his phone. Probably informing a brother.

"I think I may have just been overwhelmed today, Lou. With the enclosed space and seeing so many…"

"Yes, yes, I imagine it would be a bit of a shock, considering you didn't know others existed."

Arius was watching me carefully, his expression hard.

"Exactly. I'm going to need a day or so to wrap my head around… all of it."

"Of course. Yes. I completely understand that."

Arius was reading his phone, his jaw clenched. He typed something back, scowling the whole time.

"I was wondering if perhaps we could meet somewhere, other than the tunnels this next time." Arius frowned at me, his brows so drawn together his eyes were barely visible. I walked over to him and held the phone away from my ear, so he could listen.

Lou laughed. "A bit at a time." He said in his loud voice. "So you're not overwhelmed. We can probably arrange that. We're not all in the dark tunnels under the city."

"I can't tell you how happy I am to hear that."

He laughed again. "I'm out of town tomorrow, so I'll call you when I get back."

"That would be lovely."

"Have a good night, Isabell."

"You as well."

He hung up.

Straightening, Arius looked at his phone again. "He really does want to get you, doesn't he?"

"It's as I said." I told him.

Putting his hand to his temple, he waved his phone around. "Just give me a second to appease my king so he gets out of my head."

I nodded and sat down again.

Arius tapped his phone and put it too his ear. "I was not ignoring you. I was listening in on the conversation." He nodded. "Yes. This Lou sounds like he'd do cartwheels and backflips to impress Alona to get her to join them"

I smirked at his description.

He sighed. "No, Chase. He's going out of town, so she'll be fine tonight." He huffed out a breath. "When she suggested meeting somewhere not underground he told her they're not all in dark tunnels under the city, so I think we have an opportunity…" He turned and looked at me. "No, she's sitting right here." Sighing Arius walked over and held out the phone to me, he looked very annoyed.

I took the phone. "Hello?"

"You didn't block your number when you called him?" Chase barked.

I gave Arius a wide-eyed look. "I didn't know I had to do such a thing."

Chase sighed. "I'm sorry for yelling. I didn't expect him to call you."

"Neither did I."

I heard a door shut. "Do you want a guard there tonight?"

I looked to Arius to see him standing with his hands on his hips, looking anywhere but at me. "I don't think that's necessary. I doubt Lou or his friends will push the issue with me. Whatever his purpose or intentions for me are, they don't want me upset."

Chase snorted with annoyance. "You could come back here."

"I think I'll be fine here. The security personnel can't even access my floor. I had my own system installed when I moved in."

"Complete with alarms?"

I nodded. "Yes, very loud alarms."

"Smart girl. Wear your device when you go to bed, any sign of trouble get here."

I sighed. "Fine, yes I will."

He growled quietly. "Give the phone back to Arius, please."

"Good night, Chase." I started walking to his brother.

"Have sweet dreams, duchess."

I held the phone out to a very tense Arius.

Shaking his head, he put it back to his ear. "Yes. I'm not." He rolled his eyes. "Fine. Go to sleep, brother." He snorted. "I'd be happy to bite you—I haven't fed." He laughed and hung up.

Tucking his phone in his pocket he sat down and picked up the glass. "I am supposed to ask if you'd like to come back with me and sleep safely within the walls of the royal chambers." He drank down what was left in the glass.

"I don't think that's necessary." I held up the bottle, he shook he head no. "Is your brother always so…" I waved my hand around searching for the right word, "dramatic?"

Arius laughed. "No. Chase is usually the laid back, annoyingly calm one."

I took a sip. "Perhaps it's the stresses of his position today."

Arius tilted his head and gave me a gentle look. "Perhaps." Getting up, he motioned to the darkness outside. "I have to get back and make my rounds at the cells. Will you be all right? I could have Daxx come over if you'd rather not be alone."

I stood up. "I'll be fine. Alone. It's the with others part I don't know how to manage."

He grinned.

"I'm going to have a hot bath and then go to bed." I looked out the window. "I've never been much of a night person."

"Call if you…" he sighed. "I should give you my number."

I picked up the phone and handed it to him.

Putting his number in it, he handed it back to me and grinned. "Call if you need anything."

"I will thank you."

He bowed his head, and then once again was gone in an instant.

Taking my phone, I went and took off my boots and put them by the door. When I checked to see if the security system was activated, I remembered we hadn't come through the door.

Chuckling quietly, I went into the bathroom and turned the water on to fill the tub. I took off the device and set it beside my phone on the counter.

I was just stepping into the hot water when my phone beeped. Grabbing it, I sat down and then checked to see I had a message from Daxx.

Was told to see if you want me to come there tonight.

I smiled and answered her. *Chase?*

Yep. Do you?

I chuckled softly again. *No thank you. I will be fine.*

Figured. Have a good night.

I thought about that for a moment. *I will. Have a good day?*

LOL I will.

I hadn't even put the phone down when it beeped again. It wasn't from Daxx this time. It was Chase.

Are you sleeping yet?

I laughed. *No not yet.*

His reply came back fast. *I can't sleep either.*

I glanced at the time on my phone. *It's been five minutes since I spoke to you.*

Is that all? Feels like an eternity.

I laughed again and sent back, *only five minutes.*

Why can't you sleep?

I paused to think of something to say, without telling him I was having a bath. I sent back. *Aside from constant messages? I would drown if I went to sleep right now.*

It was a moment before he replied.

You're in the bath?

I sent him. *Yes.*

Naked?

I'd never laughed so much while bathing before in my life. *Do you bathe with clothes on?*

No.

Another one came back before I could type anything.

I can't believe your texting me while naked…I'll never get to sleep now.

I smirked at my phone. *Take a hot, relaxing bath.*

Is that an invite?

I paused to wonder if this was the same growling man that had yelled at me a few minutes earlier.

I'm holding my breath here, waiting.

I smiled and answered him.

No. It's not.

I received a little heart broken in two back. *Chase?*

Yes

Are you even in bed?

It was a moment before he replied.

No. I'm sitting behind my desk looking at stupid reports about grass growth and cattle. Frowny face. *I am NOT a farmer.*

Perhaps reading them thoroughly will help you sleep. I replied with a smirk on my face.

There's a good chance they might. Are you still naked?

I bit my lip and typed back. *No. I got dressed so you could sleep.*

LOL liar.

I sent him back a yellow smiley face.

Swear you will call me if you need anything!

I grinned as I typed back. *I damn well will!*

LOL I'm going to pretend to be a king now.

Play the part well. Smiley face.

Always do, duchess. G'night.

Good night.

I stared at the phone for a few minutes, in case anyone else decided to message me. When no more came, I set it on the ledge by the tub and slid down into the hot water. I didn't know what I was going to do about that fair king. He made me smile, but I needed to consider it before I became attached. He wasn't human with a short life span, a first in my life. Yet I didn't think I could ever open my heart again. There was only so much heartbreak you could handle before shutting out the option in self-protection. I'd reached that point a few decades ago, and I didn't see it ever changing.

Chapter Twelve

My phone rang as I stepped up the curb. It was Chase. "Hello."

"Good morning, duchess."

"Your majesty." I grinned. "Am I supposed to call you that?"

"You are *not*." He made a hissing sound. "So, I have your guard and thought I'd pop in to introduce you, in case you planned on going out *later...* but we seem to be standing here in your penthouse, alone."

I looked over my shoulder, as if he was going to appear there. "You brought a strange man to my home unannounced?" I went up the steps. "What if I'd been standing there in the room naked?"

"Mmm, there's an image." He cleared his throat. "Then I suppose he'd have a beautiful sight to remember after I removed his eyes from his head."

The security guard opened the door for me. "That seems a bit brutal."

Chase growled softly. "That may be due to the fact that you are *not* here. Why are you not here?"

I huffed out a breath when I saw how many others were in the building. "I had to go to the bank and sign papers to transfer some money."

"I see." He really didn't sound happy. "Transferring your money was more important than your safety?"

Stopping, I debated on leaving again and coming back when it wasn't as busy. "Chase, go look out the big window in my sitting room."

"I'm looking."

I smiled at the guard as I just stood there. "See the building across the street?"

He sighed. "The bank?"

"Yes. I walked across the street. All. By. Myself." I had to curb the urge to laugh.

"Don't distract me with sass when I'm trying to be cross with you."

Turning, I checked to see the manager had someone sitting in his office already. With Chase's mood, I decided I should wait, as I may not get back here today. "I'm sorry. While your being cross with me, why don't you put some coffee on for us?" I walked over to wait near the small sitting area, then noticed a familiar pair of grey eyes watching me.

I inhaled sharply. "Do you have your brother following me?"

"What? Which brother?"

Huffing out a breath, I started to walk toward him and then slowed my step when I noticed the way those eyes were moving all over me with great interest. Very unlike Arius. It wasn't Arius.

"Chase?"

"What's wrong?"

I bit my lip and glanced at the man again. "If I put my hand on someone and push the button on my device do they come back with me?

He made an odd noise. "Put your hand on who?" He was almost yelling into the phone.

"Yes or no?"

He growled. "Yes. Now what is going on?"

I smiled at the grey eyed man, with short black hair, I'd thought was longer. He smiled back. "Okay." I was going to hang up and then remembered. "Uh, maybe have someone waiting with a device... in that room I come back in."

"What? Shit!"

I hung up and went right up to him. Crissy was correct in his description, he was almost a mirror image of Arius. Perhaps a little older around the eyes, but there was no mistaking the relation.

"Hello." I smiled sweetly at him and looked him up and down similarly to how he had me. I couldn't sense any emotion from him, which for me, confirmed his identity even more.

He smiled wide in return. "Hello."

Now, how was I to push the button and be touching him at the same time? I looked around and realized I couldn't just pop us out of here in front of so many people. The odd thought of alien stories I'd read came to mind. Some things made more sense lately, in a very obscure way.

Opening the cover on the device, I gave him a smile that may be considered inviting. "Could I..." I bit my lip. "Could I borrow you for a moment?"

He gave me a curious glance, like he was going to say no. I pointed to the enclave that led to a side exit. "Just, can we go over there for a moment?"

His grey eyes gave me a heated look as he looked me up and down again, pausing for a few heartbeats on my exposed legs. "Lead the way."

"Oh, lovely." I smiled again, while thinking I was not cut out for this cloak and dagger business. My heart was thumping in the base of my throat so hard, I was sure you'd see it if you looked.

Once we reached it, we were mostly hidden from the customers, I stumbled into him like I'd tripped. He reached out with both hands and grasped my shoulders to steady me. I pushed the button.

My stomach flipped and I knew it had worked. The hands tightened on my shoulders, squeezing and then were gone.

I opened my eyes to see very angry grey ones looking at me.

"What the fuck, lady." He growled at me in a deep voice.

Before I could reply Chase and a large man appeared a few feet from us.

"Swear on my mother's grave, duchess, I'm putting you in a..." Chase stopped talking and looked at the man beside me. His entire demeanor changed as he straightened to his full height and held his hands out from his body like he was expecting a fight.

Holding my hand over my churning stomach, I looked to the man I'd brought back. "Sorry about that, but are you in pain?"

He scowled at me and shook his head. "No just, lightheaded." He looked from me to the men. "What the hell is going on?"

I nodded. "Good." I looked to Chase. "He'll be all right then?"

Chase didn't look away from him. "Yes. Duchess, call Arius to come here. Now."

"Oh, of course." I opened the screen on my phone and tapped Arius' number. He picked it up right away.

"Alona? Are you all right?" His concern was touching.

"Yes, yes... well your brother is a tad cross with me," I waved my hand remembering there were other more important issues. "Could you come to the..." I frowned and looked at Chase.

"Landing room." He said in a flat tone.

"To the landing room, please. Your presence is required."

"On my way." He hung up without asking a single question.

Neither Chase nor his brother moved or said a word, they were too busy staring at each other. I looked at the guard Chase had with him, he was quite large. No taller than Chase, but much bulkier. I smiled at him. "You do look like a pirate, a dashing one, but still a bit of a ruffian."

"Dashing?" Chase gave me a brief look. He glanced to the guard. "Sith, while I consider firing you, could you do your *job?*"

The man didn't reply, just immediately placed his large body between me and the man I'd hijacked. I wondered if Chase brought me a mute guard. Huffing out a breath, I stepped to his side and looked at the grey eyes still zeroed in on Chase. "I'm sorry for the manner of bringing you here..."

His head snapped in my direction. "Where the hell are we?"

"I got here as fast as I could..." Arius came running in and then stopped abruptly when he saw his lost brother. "Holy fuck." He whispered and looked him over. "Crissy wasn't kidding when she said we look alike."

I nodded. "Yes, one of you may have to grow a flirty little beard so others don't confuse you."

Chase gave me a flat look, one brow raised.

I sighed and stepped toward Arius, while looking at the confused man. "Emil, may I introduce you to two of your many brothers," I motioned to Arius, "Arius and Chase." I waved a hand to the unimpressed king.

"Brothers? I don't have any brothers." He said in a low voice.

I laughed quietly. "You actually have more than your share of them, eight to be exact."

His brows furrowed. "If I had eight brothers, don't you think I would know?"

"It's true," Arius told him, "you have three older brothers and five younger ones."

Emil gave him a wide-eyed look. "Did you say older?" He snorted, "Now I know you're all crazy."

Chase crossed his arms over his chest. "Yes older. Victor is five hundred, Quinton is four hundred and fifty and Michael is three hundred and sixty." He glanced to Arius. "Did I get those right?"

Arius nodded. "I think so, I can't keep them all straight most of the time either."

Emil's face blanched and he suddenly looked like he was going to faint. He shook his head. "It can't be…"

"And yet, it is." Chase glanced at Arius. "Better round up the others, wake them if they're sleeping. They're going to want to know about *this*."

Nodding, Arius pulled out his phone and walked out of the room.

Chase's expression changed and he looked back to Emil. "I know you're as confused as shit right now, and I don't blame you, but please, come join us and we'll fill in the blanks." He rubbed a hand over the back of his neck. "It's a touching tale, really, about a king and an affair he had in another realm."

Emil looked from him to me, and then back to Chase again before inclining his head in the way I'd only ever seen these brothers do. "I'll listen." He said in a rough tone.

"Excellent." He turned to Sith. "Please show my brother to the dining room."

Sith nodded abruptly and held his hand toward the door.

After they walked out, Chase turned to me and crossed his arms over his chest. "You know I can't even be mad at you now, because you found my brother while doing what you weren't supposed to do, right?"

I smirked. "It must have been fate, telling me to go to the bank." I wasn't serious, but he rolled his eyes and then relaxed his stance somewhat.

"You have no idea how fate can be a shocking, controlling bitch." Holding out his hand, he sighed. "Come. We have to try to explain to a man that is three hundred years old that nothing is as he thought it was."

Nodding, I took his hand. "I'm very well versed in how that scenario goes."

When we reached the dining room, Arius was leaning against the kitchen door frame, his arms crossed over his chest. Emil stood at the door we came in, his pose almost identical. "No family resemblance at all there." I murmured, as Chase guided me to the far side of the table and pulled out a chair. I sat down and looked over to see my large, mute guard standing beside the door, watching Emil. I hoped some of the others got here soon, the tension was almost visible in the room. Chase stood behind my chair like a statue.

Mitz came through the door with a coffee urn and then stopped and looked from Arius to Emil. She set the urn down on the table and rushed to Emil. "You're home, finally." Reaching him, she grasped his face in her hands and pulled so he was leaning down to her. "You are the spitting image of your great-grandfather, as Arius is." She sniffled. "I can't believe it's really you after three hundred years." Shaking her head, she sighed. "You never should have been out there on your own that long…"

Emil glanced at Chase with a look of panic on his face.

Chase moved around the table and gently pulled Mitz off the man's face. "We have much to explain to our lost brother, Mitz, maybe a snack would be required?"

"Oh," she nodded her head quickly, "yes. I won't be long." She looked at Emil again and wiped a tear from her cheek and rushed out of the room.

I turned to see Arius looking at one of the portraits. "She's right, we do look like him."

Emil cleared his throat and walked to the other side of the room and looked up at the painting. "How is all of this possible?"

Chase snorted, "If I have to explain the birds and the bees to you at your age, then you…"

"Is there a good reason for dragging us out of bed?" Troy came in with Daxx tucked under his arm. He stopped in the doorway and looked at Arius and Emil. "Oh, my god."

Daxx came over and sat beside me. "Did you find him?" She asked in a hushed tone.

I nodded. "Yes. I pulled a Crissy and yanked him here with me."

"The likeness is uncanny." Troy said quietly.

Arius looked from him to Chase, who was beside him, "Yeah 'cuz that never happens in this family." He glanced to Emil. "This is Troy."

Emil looked him up and down, much like he had the others, but offered no greeting.

"I can't find Leone." Rafael came in, pulling swords from his back as he did.

Emil stepped away from Arius and moved both arms quickly. Two butterfly blades appeared in his hands and it smooth motions he had them both open.

"Fuck *that* was impressive." Raf said with a grin. Then he paused and looked from Arius to Emil and slowly set his swords on the table and held out his hands. "I was just taking them off, not using them."

I noticed all the other males were suddenly hunched and ready for a fight. "Oh, stop it, all of you. Put the toys away." I told Emil.

He glanced at me and then relaxed his stance slightly and flicked both wrists and the blades were folded up again. He cleared his throat and looked at Rafael then to the swords. "Where the hell is this place, where you walk around like that?"

Rafael grinned and looked like he wanted to hug Emil, then glanced to the knives he still held.

"This," Arius said sounding bored, "is your youngest brother Rafael." He looked at Emil's hands. "If you weren't holding those he would be hugging you like a Raggedy Ann doll by now."

Emil looked horrified at the prospect and made no move to put his blades away.

"I'm... you're here... you are... you're really here." Rafael stammered, making no sense.

"So it appears." Emil replied hesitantly.

Chase turned to Rafael. "What do you mean you can't find Leone?"

Rafael looked at him quickly and then back to Emil. "He hasn't been back since practice."

Troy leaned back on the edge of the table, keeping Emil in plain sight. "Have Clairee check to see if he's at the temple."

Rafael nodded. "I called her and left a message."

Michael came in from the hallway, with Crissy almost skipping beside him. He waved some papers in the air. "Crissy knows where to find Emil…" He lowered his hand and looked at the man standing near Arius.

Crissy became animated and then laughed. "Now everyone knows where to find him." She looked at me. "It was you, wasn't it? I knew I seen you both at the same time for a reason." She nodded.

I just smiled in answer, knowing actual replies weren't always needed with her.

Crissy went right up to him and looked up at him. "See, I knew the eyes were a little different, but really the same." She smiled at him. "Do you have fangs?"

"Cristy." Victor growled from the kitchen doorway.

Excited all over again, Crissy motioned to Emil like she was presenting him. "He's found."

Victor was dressed as he had been the first time I'd seen him, all black leather and many pointy weapons. He held out his hand to her and she went over. Dropping a kiss on her head, he nodded to where Daxx and I were sitting. "Go sit over there, please." His tone was soft but his eyes that studied his brother were not. He didn't move until she was beside Daxx, on her knees on the chair, not actually *sitting*.

Victor moved toward Emil, his eyes noting the weapons in his hand. "I suggest putting those away." His tone left no room for discussion. "I'll not have you armed while the women are present."

Daxx laughed. "Yeah 'cuz we're all so dainty and not armed ourselves."

Crissy chuckled and then sobered up when Troy glared at Daxx.

"I'm drowning in the testosterone in here." Daxx said. "Emil meet two of your older brothers," She motioned to where Michael still stood. "Michael, and the big scary one in your face is the eldest brother, Victor."

Mitz came out of the kitchen carrying a large tray of pastries. I had to wonder if she had twenty people in there at all times just in case the brothers gathered. She set the tray down and looked around at them. "All of you sit down. Now." She glanced to Emil. "And put those away. I may not have changed your diapers, but I won't have you disrespecting this home." Turning she froze, her eyes on the swords on the tabletop. "Rafael, get those filthy things off my table."

Raf moved quickly and picked them up and took them to the corner and leaned them there. "Sorry, Mitz." He came back and sat down by the tray.

Chase and Troy were backing away from Emil to the table. They sat down, almost in unison.

Michael, who still looked like he was in shock, went around and sat at the other side of the table as well.

Victor didn't move to sit, he did motion to the table and then watched as Emil walked to the furthest chair and sat down.

Mitz nodded. "That's better." She turned her motherly smile to Emil. "Can I get you something, love?"

He shook his head slowly and then looked around at the others again. "No… thank you."

I watched Mitz give a little nod and then she hurried from the room. I didn't know her place in this family, but I did know she wielded awesome power to keep these men in line.

Emil rubbed a hand over his jaw and looked at me, shaking his head he sat back in the chair. "All of this because of a gorgeous pair of legs." He mumbled.

Chase growled and glared at him.

"Where is Quinton?" Troy asked.

Rafael waved his hand around. "He'll be here in a minute." He said around a mouthful of pastry. "Him and Welsley had to go settle some kind of dispute."

"Everything resolved?" Victor asked in a stiff way.

Rafael nodded. "Yeah, nothing important."

Quinton came in wiping something off the front of his shirt. "They threw food at us," he growled and then froze mid-motion when he saw Emil. "Holy shit, you're real." Shaking his head, he quickly wiped his hand down the front of his jeans and walked over to him with his hand out. "I'm Quinton."

Emil stood up and shook his hand briefly.

Quinton grinned. "Just what I need, another younger brother." He chuckled and then spotted the tray sitting on the table and went toward it.

Emil sat back down and waved his hand around. "How is all of this possible?"

"Strange when you find out you're not the oldest in the room, isn't it?" I said nodding my head slowly.

"And then some." He said quietly. "I don't know where..." he looked around, "here is, but I am waiting for a very important call about my son, so..."

Crissy almost stood on the chair. "From which marriage?" She shrugged, "Not that it matters, any of your sons would be two hundred years old now or older." She nodded.

He frowned and looked at her.

"She," Chase motioned to Crissy, "knows things."

"Are all five of your children like you? Like us?" Michael asked him.

Emil sat back, a solemn look on his face. "No. Two sons and a one of my daughters appear to be like I am." He glanced to me for a moment. "A son from my second marriage and daughter from my third passed away after normal human life spans."

"I'm sorry." I offered him a heartfelt look. "I understand losing people."

He inclined his head and then cleared his throat. "My son seems to be caught up with the wrong sort presently, I have an investigator following him."

"Your phone will work here." I told him. Feeling like that was probably the only fact in all of this I could offer the man.

"What type of wrong sorts are we talking about?" Victor sat forward in his chair, I wondered if he maybe couldn't sit back with the weaponry on his back.

Emil studied him for a moment. "Some low-life group wanting to take over the world or something."

The men all exchanged looks with one another.

"Low-life like they have red or yellow eyes as well low-life, or human gang type of low-life? Michael asked him, looking like he wanted to pounce on something.

He frowned. "I believe most are like me... us." He sighed. "They're telling him some nonsense about a royal family being unjust and controlling..." He shook his head.

"So, you know your children, you have a relationship with them?" Troy inquired.

Emil nodded. "Yes. Once I realized they were like me and didn't age, I thought at the very least I could offer them some sort of guidance."

"That's lovely." I smiled at him. "That they have you."

Chase cleared his throat. "Maybe a bit of history is required here." He looked at his twin. "Your father... our father was the king of Alterealm..." he waved his hand around motioning to the males at the table. "Welcome to the royal family, brother."

"So, Emil's son is on team bad?" Daxx asked glancing to Troy.

Troy nodded. "So, it seems."

"Wait." Emil held up his hand. "This war is true?"

Victor nodded briefly. "Indeed, it is. We had a mage go rogue and has been, for much longer than we were aware, building illegal transport devices so any can go to the other side and stay there."

Michael hissed out a breath. "Most of these should never be on the other side with humans, they will leave a trail of death in their wake."

Crissy nodded. "They had humans, so scared, locked in a cage to feed from."

Emil looked like he was in shock now.

I leaned on the edge of the table. "It's all very overwhelming, to learn." I smiled. "I've only known a few days." I motioned to Crissy. "She found me, much like I did you." I offered him a look of compassion. "Team bad is trying to recruit me as well."

"How old is your son that they've recruited?" Quinton asked between bites.

Emil blew out a breath. "Ellis is two hundred and fifty, or there abouts."

Arius chuckled. "I have a nephew the same age as me."

"Where are your other children?" Daxx asked looking very serious. "Are they with them as well?"

Emil shook his head. "No. Rena lives in the mountains, a few states from here. She prefers quiet. Abraham is here…" he frowned, "there, in the city, but thinks his brother is insane, so he has nothing to do with it."

Chase sat forward and looked to Crissy. "Could they know about his son? That Ellis is related to us? Could that be who they were talking about that Alona overheard?"

Crissy bit her lip and shrugged. "It could be, but I don't think it is." She huffed out a breath. "It took a lot to trace them." She pointed to Emil. "It took a lot to track him. They would have to know about him and his mother's name to even start." She nodded. "And all the name changes, I lost him a few times." She grinned at Emil. "Emmett, Ernest…Eric, I like that name." She looked at Victor. "I want to name our son Eric."

Victor coughed and gave her a wide-eyed look. "We're having a baby?"

Crissy laughed. "No. Why would you ask that?" Shaking her head, she turned back to Chase. "I don't think anyone else can trace his children."

"Good." Chase looked back to Emil. "This is going to be a long day, found brother, we need to fill in all the blanks for you, and then figure out how to get your son out of there, so we don't accidentally kill him."

"I have a question, before we climb into all that." Michael said watching Emil. "Did your mother have a tattoo on her arm? Or any of your wives?"

Emil frowned. "My mother did, which was horrifying for her. None of my wives did. What is the significance of it?"

All the brothers looked to Victor.

"Dad had two mates?" Rafael said sounding shocked.

Victor raised his eyebrows. "So, it would seem. That is one mystery solved." He looked to Emil, "Now to figure out how Emil managed children with women other than his mate."

"Mate?" Emil asked. "I shouldn't be able to have children?"

Quinton sat back. "I still say it's because his mother was human, it must have messed with genetics in some way."

"Possible." Victor said with a thoughtful expression. "However, for now, I think we need to explain as much as he can handle today, for as long as one of us can stay awake."

Several heads nodded.

"Can I listen in?" I asked. "I'm still very lost."

Chase chuckled. "Some days, even I'm lost, and I'm a king."

"I just kill it if I don't understand it." Daxx said with a smirk. "Less thinking that way."

"I'll need to make a few calls if I'm here for the day." Chase said getting up. He spotted Sith by the door. "Sith, you may as well go back to our side and help my captain today."

Sith nodded abruptly and left.

I leaned over to Daxx. "Does Sith speak?"

Daxx shrugged. "I've never heard him talk now that I think of it."

"Lovely." Chase had gotten me a guard that would just be a large silent statue. Was that better than one that chatted with me? I wasn't sure.

Chapter Thirteen

The discussion to educate Emil lasted a few hours. More pieces fit together for me with each additional part shared. I was very curious about all of the prophecies being mentioned. At some point, I wondered if I'd be allowed to see them for myself.

Halfway through the discussion, Leone was discovered in his room sleeping, so worry no longer affected the brother's focus. The night brothers finally had to go to sleep. Emil was taken back with a device of his own, so he could check up on his son. Chase took him back, so I was left sitting in the large dining room alone.

Michael had left the stack of papers he'd been waving around, so I browsed through those while waiting for Chase to return.

I felt him enter the room, before I heard him. That was something I found alarming, that I was that turned into him. I motioned to the papers in front of me. "Crissy is very good at tracking people down." I looked up at him.

He leaned against the back of a chair and nodded. "I think it has to do with her processing more information at once than the rest of us. We're almost sure she has a photographic memory."

I winced. "I would not want her mind."

Chase chuckled. "No, it's a little too busy and full for my comfort."

"Is she going to look for the others?"

He sighed and rubbed the back of his neck. "I don't think we have a choice but to look. It's largely due to our mismanagement that there are people out there, like you, who have no idea what they are."

I smirked. "It's hardly your fault residents from this side had sex with those from the other side."

"Don't distract me with sex talk, duchess." He grinned.

I shook my head, not wanting to talk about that. "Maybe I could help Crissy look. I've had some practice at hiding who I am and moving around."

He nodded slowly, "It may speed up the process. I'll discuss it with Michael and Crissy."

I raised an eyebrow at him. "I don't know how you discuss anything with Crissy."

"Mmm, it's a challenge at times." He grinned, "But I like challenges." His pale eyes moved over my face.

"I recall."

Straightening, he sighed. "Care to come back to my office? I'm not sure what your plans are, but you'll be requiring Sith, and he's on my side presently."

I stood up. "I still have to go to the bank."

"Ah, yes, that reminds me of where we began today." He motioned to the doorway.

Walking past him, I gave him a quick glance. "Is it always so eventful here?"

Chuckling, he looked me up and down. "You seem to be the cause of the *events* the past few days."

I frowned. "You're right. How unlike me."

"My brother was right about one thing."

"Which brother would that be?"

Chase gave me a heated look. "Emil. Your legs are gorgeous."

I looked down at my short skirt and boots. "I love boots. I only wear short skirts to show off my boots."

"You, duchess, can wear a short skirt and boots every day if you wish, I will *never* complain about that." His grin widened. "I may have to remove eyeballs, but I won't protest."

I felt my face flush from the way his eyes watched me. Turning I looked around as we walked. "Is the entire kingdom underground?"

"No, the royal chambers are, for safety, built that way about eight hundred years ago, but the rest is above ground like anywhere else." He stopped and punched in a code on a pad by the door.

On the other side were two large guards. They followed along behind us.

Chase noticed me looking back at them. "More security is required on this side." He motioned down the hallway. "Sometime, when there aren't so many events taking place, I'll show you beyond the miles of hallways."

"I would like that."

Holding a door open, I went in to a large office. The furniture was dark, polished wood, books lined one entire wall, and there was a navy loveseat and chair beside a fireplace. I glanced back to his desk. "Did you sleep on your desk last night?"

He smirked. "No. The reports failed to bore me to sleep." He held up a hand, "but, I do know which breed of cattle is thriving."

"Fascinating."

He shook his head. "No, it's not. Troy and I take turns with those tasks, thankfully next week he'll get to read all the boring reports and give me the summary."

"I think it's quite unique, the double monarchy."

Leaning back against his desk, he shrugged. "I don't know about that, I do know that having only one king would be entirely too much work." He frowned. "Although father seemed to have enough free time to find a second mate."

"Does that happen often?"

His expression was hard. "Not that I'm aware of, and I can't even imagine it personally."

"I've seen what happened to my mother without my father, so I don't know how it would work, to have two."

He shook his head. "I don't even want to contemplate the complexity." He looked back to me, his eyes moving over me slowly.

It was all I could do to not squirm as he studied me.

"And how are you doing today?" He stood up and moved toward me in that slow predatory way. "No ill effects after yesterday's overload?"

I smiled. "No, and I have to say not sleeping for a day or feeling ill for several was a very pleasant and welcome thing." He gave me a heated look. I cleared my throat. "And you? No side effects from taking on all those dark emotions?" I stepped back a few steps.

He shook his head briefly, still moving in my direction slowly. "None. I had a few moments right after where I would have liked to kill something, but they passed."

"Good." I offered a pleasant smile, trying to ignore my pounding heart.

"I'm still struggling with the other emotions." He said quietly.

"Oh?" I went to step back again and realized the loveseat was right behind me.

"Yes, the ones that invade my every thought, the emotions created by you feeding and being close to me." He stopped right in front of me, his eyes locked on mine now.

My face grew hot. "Oh." I put my hands behind me to steady myself. I didn't know why this man played havoc with my body, without touching me, and I wasn't sure I wanted to know.

"I can taste what your feeling right now, duchess." He said softly and then frowned, "I don't like the tinge of fear. I would never harm you."

I inhaled deeply. "You don't scare me, I'm just..." I didn't know how to explain it.

"Feeling things, you've never felt before?" His voice was almost a whisper.

"Yes." I licked my lips. "It's a bit unsettling."

"Mmm," he reached out and played with my hair, running it through his fingers, "it is, but I'd rather have the taste of your desire."

There was only a few inches between our bodies now, part of me wanted to close that distance, but simply because I felt that way, I didn't.

"With all the events of today, a new brother and all that... I haven't had a chance to talk to you about the blood bond."

I swallowed, trying to settle the uneasy feeling the thought gave me. "I'm still uncertain how that would work, or help."

He sighed quietly, "I've felt it before, one not linked to my brothers. Daxx was gravely injured, she almost died, so I gave her my blood to heal her."

"Wasn't that Troy's place?" I didn't know much about mates, but I did notice other males didn't go near the two mated females.

"It was before they were mated and time was of the essence to save her life." He cleared his throat. "It was a bond like I'd never felt before... long story for another time, but during a fight I was able to give her a boost of strength." His brows creased. "Victor was able to block Crissy's visions temporarily when they shared a blood bond..."

I couldn't keep the shock off my face. "That must have taken a great deal of strength on his part."

"I have no doubt it did." He reached out and brushed the hair back from my face with a careful touch. "I'd like to help you."

I felt mesmerized by his steady stare. "I'm quite fine right now."

"Mmm, yes you are."

I picked up a hesitation on his part, I wasn't sure if it was the feelings tugging at him as they were me, or if it was something else. "Why do I feel like you're not telling me something?"

He smirked. "Really? You can sense it?" He frowned, "Either I'm rusty at hiding emotions or you're that good." His smile was wide. "I believe it's the latter, to save my bruised ego." He inhaled a deep breath, and then exhaled slowly. "We're going to need your assistance in finding the orange cave and the entrance you used. Most likely it should happen tonight. If we wait any longer, they may have moved locations again."

"Oh." My heart started thrumming with anxiety. "I didn't know it was decided."

"It wasn't, until about half an hour ago. Emil is worried about his son, and has gone to try to keep him out of the fray. But our main mission will be getting those children out of there."

I nodded. "I most definitely agree with that." I bit my lip. "I may even have somewhere you can take them."

He studied me. "As long as it can't be traced back to you..."

I shook my head. "No, my name is on nothing there."

I could see he was considering what I said. "I will talk to Victor about it. He's not happy that Crissy is going as well, but with the both of you and Daxx, we'll at least have someone to get the children out while we take care of other things that pop up."

"Yes. I can't see those children suffering in any of this, so I'll show you where." I paused. "You don't think they'll associate the location being found with me?"

He shook his head. "We've been finding them all along, so no I don't think they will." He gave me a softer look. "So, back to the blood bond, I don't want to see you overwhelmed again. At the very least I could assist you long enough that you can get clear, if it becomes too much."

"I don't... I mean, you'll be too busy to be focused on me." I didn't want anything to happen to him because I was distracting him.

He touched my chin gently and smiled. "I can multi-task, duchess, no worries there."

Biting my lip, I wrapped my arms around my waist, trying to see how I felt. I wanted to help them, and those children… but if I collapsed because of emotional backlash, I wouldn't be good to anyone. I closed my eyes to concentrate, and then opened them to look at him. "I want to help, I truly do… it's just… for years, close to a decade I thought I was next to a vampire and the very idea of blood…" I gave him a wide-eyed look. "I didn't know it wasn't the blood I was after in the necks I was biting… I would throw up each time…"

He cupped the side of my face in his big hand. "That breaks my heart, duchess, to know you were out there alone without anyone to help you." He stroked my cheek softly with his thumb. "I'm sure we can find a way to get you to take some blood, so it doesn't emotionally scar you." He smiled.

"Do you…" I searched his hazel eyes. "Do you have to take it as well?"

He shook his head. "I think just you from me should work. I don't want you to carry all of my feelings on top of what you already deal with." He smirked. "And I seem to have more feelings the last few days."

The motion of his thumb brushing against my cheek was sending shivers up my spine. "I'll try. Do your brothers know we're doing this?"

He shook his head. "I want you to feed too…" His eyes flicked to my mouth. "You have a glow today; did you know that? I think it's because you actually fed, and weren't starving yourself."

My eyes, without realizing it, looked at his throat. "I shouldn't need to…"

"Later may be a little too busy." His hold on my face became firmer. "I don't want you to take a bite of my guard." He cleared his throat. "Or anyone else, if I'm being honest."

I gave him a curious look. "I don't…"

His brows creased. "I can't explain why right now… I'm still working through that. Just trust that it wouldn't end well if I found your mouth was on another." His look softened.

"There is an explanation, I'd just like to be certain... I've already fallen for fate's trickery once, I don't want to again."

"I don't understand."

"I know... *please* trust me."

I could feel his emotions, or enough traces of them to know he was being earnest and meant what he said. I nodded.

His hazel eyes lit up. "It's not a hardship, is it? To feed off me..." Reaching out, he pulled me by the hip so we were closer. "To be close to me?"

"No," I barely whispered, "I'm just not sure we should... play with fire." It was the truth; the sparks were far too hot when we were close. I had never experienced anything like it before.

He smiled, his eyes on mine. "I'm not afraid to get burned." Letting go of my face, he unbuttoned the white shirt he wore. "I dressed pretty in case I was seen in your neighborhood." He smirked.

I was mesmerized watching his hands slowly reveal his chest. When he tossed the shirt aside, I swallowed and slowly looked back up to his face. His eyes were yellow. "Do... do you need to feed?"

"As much as I'd like to, I need to avoid feeding from you... for now. I'd lose control completely and I don't think we need that right now."

I didn't know what he meant, but nodded anyway. My heart was already beating faster, and I had to clench my hands into fists to not run them all over his muscled chest.

"Your desire tastes so sweet, I am tempted like never before..." He lifted my chin, his hand moving to the back of my head.

Cautiously, he leaned down. My breathing sped up, waiting for his mouth to touch mine.

"Take what you want." He whispered against my mouth.

Unable to resist a second more, I reached up, grasped his hair and kissed him. My mouth immediately filled with fangs. I'd never had such a reaction before. There was feeding and sex, the two were not interchangeable... until now. With him.

He growled deep in his throat and took over the kiss. The moment he did, I felt his desire blend with my own, and my knees trembled from the feeling. I didn't want him to end the kiss. I'd been starved of more than just essence in my life. I craved the heat from his body, the closeness.

Chase wrapped his arm around my waist and picked me up into his hard body. I could feel his arousal and moaned against his mouth. Grasping my head, he dragged his mouth from mine and pulled my head back. He ran his teeth roughly down my throat.

"Gods, I wish I had fangs right now." He moaned against my ear. Pushing my face toward his neck. "Feed from me, now."

I didn't hesitate. When I bit into his flesh, he made a low guttural sound and bunched his hand in my hair, holding my head in place.

Reaching with his other hand, he pulled my leg up and held my thigh against his hip, rocking his body into mine. I opened my mouth and moaned, then licked across my bite marks.

His mouth crushed mine in a hard and demanding kiss, his tongue brushing over my sharp teeth. He suddenly released my head and broke the kiss. With yellow eyes holding mine, I struggled to catch my breath. Grasping the back of my head again, he pushed it toward his chest. "Drink before it heals."

I looked to see a score in his flesh, over his heart, blood was running down his skin. I had no idea when he'd done it.

"Alona, put your mouth on me." He growled low.

I almost burst into flames from his tone. Leaning forward I put my lips over the wound and sucked gently. He groaned and rocked his hips into mine again. His blood didn't repulse me at all, although I'd also never been so turned on in my life, so that may have had something to do with it.

When the wound sealed, I still licked it and then over his nipple, because it was so close to my face.

He hissed out a breath and grabbed my head, kissing me once more.

When he pulled his mouth away, he held me against him and fought to catch his breath. My breathing was just as erratic.

"I don't even think... fire, adequately describes that." He said into my hair. Grasping my face gently in both hands, he looked down at me. His eyes were slowly returning to a pale hazel, just as my fangs were receding. "I have never wanted anyone like I do you." He kissed my mouth softly. "Know that."

"I feel the same," I whispered breathlessly.

Releasing me, he stepped back so there was space between our bodies. "When some of this..." he waved a hand around, "chaos is resolved, you and I need to have a discussion, duchess... a very serious, life-altering discussion."

I had no idea what it could be about, but nodded, unable to think clearly. Blowing out a breath, in hopes it would cool my still too warm body, I remembered he still had no shirt on. I took a moment to let my eyes look over him leisurely.

"*That* is going to land us both in trouble." He said in a rough voice.

I blinked and looked back to his face. "Then put your shirt on." I smirked.

Picking his shirt off the back of the loveseat, he stopped and looked at me, then stepped forward to kiss my mouth firmly. "You need to go, so I can plan a raid." He whispered against my mouth. Backing away, he put his arms in his shirt and started to button it up. "While you were distracting my brother with your legs at the bank..." he glanced at me, "we programmed Sith's transporter to your penthouse. He can take you there or here... but that's it."

I ran my hands through my hair, trying to put it back in place. "I won't be going out today. I have some research to do."

He did up the bottom button and looked back to me. "Research?"

I nodded. "Yes. I have an idea, and want to look into what it would take to bring it to life."

"That's intriguing. Care to share?"

He stood there, his hair mussed, and I was momentarily distracted again. I bit my lip. "Not yet. Let me see if it's feasible, before I discuss it with you and the others."

His eyebrows rose. "Oh, mysterious indeed." He smiled. "Just...if you could try to stay out of trouble for the next few hours, I'd appreciate it."

"You make it sound like I go looking for it.", I replied, arms crossing with a little scowl on my face.

He smirked. "I know you don't, but you do attract it." His eyes moved over me slowly. "With those legs you attract a lot."

I rolled my eyes at him. "So, the blood, does it take time to work or... how does this work?"

Chase moved over and perched on the corner of his desk. "With one exchange like that I can sense your emotions... without having to be near you. So I'll know if you're in trouble."

That was interesting. "Oh, so you can already feel them?"

He shook his head and sighed. "All I can feel right now is my own unfulfilled lust and desire." He grinned wide. "After you leave and I settle down, I will be able to."

I pursed my lips together and studied him for a moment. "I'm glad you're suffering. My own state isn't much better."

He scowled at me. "Don't tell me that or I'll feel inclined to end our *suffering*, and then you will be very angry with me."

I opened my mouth to ask why, but he shook his head.

"But," he held up his hand, "not now. I can't explain it all yet, once I'm certain, I will." Straightening away from the desk, he came over and took my hand and started walking to the door. "Now, let's get Sith to take you home, so I can come up with a plan for tonight, so we're not all just running around in tunnels." He smiled at me. "I will call you when the others have awakened, so you can show us where." He kissed my mouth quickly and opened the door. Sith was standing on the other side of it. "Sith, I have to go to the cells, please take, duchess home now." He turned to me, a soft look on his face. "I'll see you soon." He winked.

I nodded. "Yes, for breakfast dinner."

He chuckled. "Now you're getting it."

Chapter Fourteen

I paced out of my office. Which was actually a second bedroom containing a desk, table and two chairs. Going into the kitchen, I glanced at my silent guard still standing by my door. It was a bit eerie that he just stood there.

I looked from the coffee maker to the wine rack, trying to decide if it would be wise to drink with the impending raid later today. "It would probably be frowned upon if I were tipsy for this... raid." I said to myself. I set up the coffee maker and then paced out to the sitting area while it brewed. Hopefully Liza would respond to my email in a timely manner.

Going over to the window, I crossed my arms and stared down at the street. My nerves were on edge, which wasn't a feeling I was comfortable with. Although, the fact I was going to be involved in a *raid* later may have a lot to do with my restlessness. I had never intentionally put myself in that position before. I turned and straightened the pillows on the sofa I never used.

"You should find something to take your mind off it." Sith's deep voice told me.

I shrieked and jumped back. Holding my hand over my heart, I glared at him. "You talk."

His mouth moved and I was almost certain he was smirking. "Yes."

"Well then..." My phone started vibrating across the island. Giving him a firm look, I went over and answered it.

"Duchess, what's wrong?"

I looked around the room, half expecting Chase to appear. "Nothing."

"I got a sudden feeling of distress..."

"Oh... it was nothing. Sith spoke and nearly gave me a heart attack." He could feel that reaction I had?

Chase chuckled. "Mmm, he's a man of few words, unless he's been drinking and I wouldn't advise that, it's counterproductive to why he's there."

"I see that now." I glanced to the man standing there like a statue again. "I didn't even know he could speak." His mouth quirked again, confirming it was indeed a smirk.

"I don't select guards for their great conversational abilities..." I heard other voices in the background. "If you're well, I'll let you go."

"I am." I nodded and walked to the kitchen to check on the coffee.

"Hopefully missing me at least." He said softly.

I grinned. "Possibly."

"You are hard on a man's ego, woman." He said in a light way.

I smiled. "King or not, you can't have everything easy."

He snorted. "Call if you need me."

"I will." I hung up the phone and set it on the counter and then turned to look at the man standing there. I pointed a finger at him. "Why have you not spoken until now?"

He shrugged. "I talk when necessary." He shifted and looked less frozen in place. "My king is quite talkative, usually I just need to nod my head, a lot."

I chuckled. "He is chatty at times."

Sith chuckled and nodded his head.

Turning I looked at the coffee maker. "Would you like a coffee?"

He nodded again.

"Good." I got two mugs down and then turned to eye him again. "How are you at puzzles?"

His dark eyes gave me a surprised look. "Puzzles?"

"Yes." I poured the coffee. "I need distraction, or I'll be a basket case by tonight, so you can help me figure out this confounded puzzle I bought thinking it was a good idea." I motioned to the sugar, he shook his head. "Cream?" Again a no. "I'm about ready to dump this puzzle into the bathtub and set it on fire."

He grinned. "I could help." He looked to my door. "There's not much action here."

Picking up the mug, I took it over and held it out to him. "I prefer solitude and less action in my life."

"You've succeeded then." He took the mug and followed me to my office.

Reaching it, I motioned to the table. "I thought a thousand pieces sounded challenging when I purchased it." I walked over and looked down at it. "Of course, being a sunset, the entire thing is all the same color with only small variances in the hues..." I glanced at him over my shoulder, "I've only managed to properly fit about a hundred pieces... it's very frustrating."

Coming over, he looked down at the puzzle and then glanced to the box with the picture on it. "Well, I'd say if you wanted a challenge, you found it."

"Exactly. Grab the chair." I set my coffee down, checked the screen of my laptop to see if I had mail and then dragged the other chair over. "Are all residents from your side so good at masking their emotions?"

He sat down and studied the pieces I'd sorted with similar patterns on it. "I'm not sure." He picked up one and turned it, holding it over the pieces I had already fit together. "Probably not, just those disciplined in fighting are, more than others I'd imagine... or perhaps the scholars..."

I watched him pick up a different piece and look at it. "I'm so happy you talk." I smiled when he glanced at me and grinned. "I was dreading long hours of you standing by my door."

Pausing, he looked at me. "My job is to keep you safe and well." He shrugged. "I didn't know you wanted conversation."

I bit my lip and thought about that. "I'm finding I want things lately that I never have."

His dark brown eyes assessed me for a moment. "Chase told me of your past, it must have been hard."

I nodded and then blew out a breath. "That's a gentle description."

"You seem to have done well, though."

"Anything can be accomplished if you fail enough times."

He chuckled and then grunted as he fit a piece together. "Eight hundred and ninety-nine to go."

I laughed and turned my attention to the annoying pieces on the table in front of me.

~

I stood back from the table and looked around the large dining room. The brothers and several other large men filled the room.

Sith stood beside me, his arms crossed over his chest. I noticed a large 'pirate' standing behind Crissy in much the same pose, concluding that must be her guard, Bronx.

I could pick up a few emotions in the room, usually simple spikes before they were gone. It was something I wasn't used to, being in a room filled with people and not drowning in emotions.

Shaking my head, I turned my attention back to the conversation.

"Alona's friend, Liza, will be here with a van." Chase tapped the map. He glanced to a man beside him. "Anthony, you're to stick with the van and the children until otherwise notified."

He nodded.

Anthony was the least intimidating guard Chase and his twin could find. I insisted on it. I didn't know all the details, but I didn't want the children or Liza in danger... or scared to death of their guard.

"Cristy, Daxx and Alona will stay near this exit until the children are located." Victor glanced at his mate. "Their guards *will* remain with them."

I wasn't sure what that meant, but if a man as hard as that told me in that tone to do something, I would be inclined to follow his request.

"If anything goes wrong," Troy said looking to Daxx, "you ladies use your transporters and get out of there."

Crissy taped the device on her wrist and nodded enthusiastically.

Leone came rushing into the room, everyone stopped and looked at him.

"Brother, you're late." Arius announced.

Leone rubbed his short-spiked hair. "Sorry, I slept in."

Quinton straightened away from the table. "Are you okay?"

Leone nodded. "Yeah, I think I'm just messed up because I never know when to be awake or asleep anymore."

Chase snorted. "Welcome to *my* hell." He motioned to the map. "Do we need to explain the details?"

Leone glanced at the map and then looked back to his brother. "We go in stealthy, kick ass and come home?"

Chase grinned. "Yes." He motioned to me. "The ladies will be getting the children out to a van waiting here." He tapped the map.

Leaning over the table, Leone looked to where he pointed. "Got it." Straightening, he went toward the kitchen. "Let me inhale some coffee and I'm good to go."

Everyone turned back to the map. I watched Chase look toward the kitchen, concern on his face.

I smirked at my statue. "Don't move, I'll be right back."

He smirked, but that was the only sign made that he heard me.

I walked around the large bodies to the kitchen. Leone stood at the counter a cup in his hand. I could feel confusion pouring off him. "Despite your assurances to your brothers, I can feel what your feeling." I said softly.

He turned to look at me, his brown eyes moving over me slowly. "You mean the clusterfuck that is my head right now?"

I smiled. "More or less."

He sat down on the stool. "I don't know what's wrong with me lately..." he glanced to the dining room, "I see the looks from them, they think I'm tempted again..." He gave me a curious glance. "I have an addiction..."

I nodded. "I'm aware."

Leone blew out a breath. "Figured you'd be in the loop. It's not that though..." he shook his head again. "But, I don't know what it is."

I went over, feeling the need to reassure this man. "What's happening?"

Rubbing his hands over his face, he dropped them and huffed out a breath. "It's like dreams... that I don't just have while I'm sleeping... but when I do sleep they're clearer." He grimaced, "but not, because I still have no idea what they're about." He sighed. "I can't believe I slept through meeting my own brother."

"I'm sure you'll have the opportunity to meet him..."

Serious eyes turned to me, "Do you think I'm going crazy?"

His eyes were filled with so much fear, I had to work to keep it out of my head. "I don't think that's it." I frowned. "I've seen how that works and what you're experiencing is not that."

He studied me for a moment and nodded. "Voices in my head isn't exactly normal either."

"Male or female voices?" Chase spoke from the doorway.

Leone stood up quickly, like it wasn't acceptable for his brother to see him vulnerable. "Uh, female."

"Interesting." Chase mused and then came into the room. "Are you up to joining us tonight? Maybe you should go see the doctor…"

Leone shook his head. "No. I'm good. I need the distraction to get out of my own head." He gave his brother a solemn look. "I'll go see the doc if it continues."

Chase nodded. "Talk to Troy later, maybe he can take a look inside your empty head and see what's going on."

Leone smirked. "Yeah, okay." He looked down at what he was wearing. "I'm going to go change."

Chase inclined his head and watched him leave. "Thank you." He said softly, his hazel eyes connecting with mine. "For coming to check on him."

I crossed my arms over my chest, taking a deep breath. "His emotions are quite strong. Confusion, fear…"

"We'll figure it out. He probably wouldn't have told one of us though, so again, thank you." His eyes moved down over me, taking in the tall heelless boots and skirt I wore. "I had thought you were only teasing me wearing the skirt earlier, but you weren't."

I looked at what I was wearing. "No. Although it took four outfits to find one Sith deemed battle worthy."

Chase frowned. "I didn't give you a guard to *bond* with and have fashion showdowns."

I shrugged. "I'm sure he was just appeasing me, I was… am, very unsettled with this."

Sighing, he stepped closer and touched my cheek lightly. "If we didn't need you to lead us through the start and confirm we're in the right location … and to get the children out… I wouldn't ask this of you. There are so many damn tunnels in that location, we could end up wandering around for days."

"I want to help."

"And you have, finding somewhere for the children to go."

I sighed. "I hope they're still there and all right."

He kissed my mouth softly and then straightened. "I must change. Sith will take you to the armory. We'll all meet there."

He kissed my mouth again quickly, giving me a soft look before turning to walk out.

Chapter Fifteen

The armory contained more weapons then the practice room, only none were the wooden type.

"Do you want a blade?" Sith asked, his brows furrowed.

I shook my head and reached up under the back of my jacket to pull my dagger out.

The surprise was clear on his face. "You wear that all the time?"

I knew he was wondering if I'd had it on while we were at my place.

"Yes, unless I'm sleeping… then it's under my pillow."

He looked down at it, a curious expression on his face.

"Oh," I pushed the release on the handle and my dagger split into two thin daggers.

"That's just cool." He said grinning.

I smiled up at him. "I found it in a small oriental shop years ago."

"You're a constant surprise, duchess."

Turning, I watched Chase walking over. My heart paused, when I took in the sight of him. He wore black leather from shoulder to boots. A tight vest revealed not only his very well sculpted chest, but toned muscular arms. A moon pendant rested just below his collar bone. It took a moment for me to even see the weapons. Two blades were crossed on his back as well as one on his thigh and another on the opposite hip.

He held out his arms and paused, knowing I was ogling him. "I do bad *very* well." He smirked.

"Indeed, you do."

Sith cleared his throat and stepped away.

Chase looked at the blades in my hand and held out his. "May I?"

I handed them to him. He studied them for a moment and then fit them back together and turned it over in his hand. "A lovely, deceptive toy." He motioned for me to turn around. "I'm assuming you know how to use them?"

I nodded. "When required."

He put them back in the case on my back. "If you use them tonight, then Sith isn't doing his job." His tone was very low and lethal.

"I'm sure I won't have to." I assured him as calmly as I could, despite the speed my heart was racing. I wasn't sure if it was what we were about to do, or from his closeness.

He made an odd noise in his throat and turned me to face him. "If it's too much for you, use this." He lifted the arm my transportation device was on.

I huffed out a breath and nodded. "I will."

His hazel eyes moved over my face with a gentle look. "Now, I have something I'd like you to wear." He swallowed like he was nervous. "It's a bit presumptuous on my part, but please accept it … and I promise explanations will follow… at a later date."

I could see a look of vulnerability in his eyes and was surprised. That was something I'd never pictured him giving in to. "All right." I gave him a soft look.

He opened his hand, in it lay a silver necklace with a small pendant. It was a tiny Sun with a small moon beneath it.

"It's lovely." I touched it lay in his palm.

"Will you wear it for me?" He didn't so much as breathe as he waited for me to answer.

I nodded and he heaved a sigh of relief.

Undoing the clasp, he of the pendant around my neck and then leaned over to fasten the clasp. "It has a great meaning among Alterealm residents, and I don't want anyone to disrespect you... even in the slightest. This will ensure they do not."

When he straightened, I placed my hand over where it rested against my skin.

He looked at it for a moment, a look I didn't understand on his face.

"Are we ready, brother?"

I turned to see Troy and Daxx coming over to us.

"Always, brother." Chase told him.

I noted Daxx wore a similar pendant, and Troy a larger one of the moon. It must be a symbol used among 'team good', I thought with a smile.

Troy paused and glanced at the pendant I wore and looked to his brother with an eyebrow raised. With a nod to Chase, making me think they could communicate nonverbally, Troy smiled and smacked Chase on the shoulder in a rough, brotherly way.

"Ready?" Daxx asked me.

I blew out a breath. "Not entirely, but let's get this done."

I stood and glanced around the corner at the van. The whole process of bringing the small army to the two locations appeared as a practiced process by the brothers. I found out from Sith that witches would cloak their presence from the public until they were in the tunnels.

If I wasn't living all of this, I would have had the perfect plot for a fantasy novel, if I was inclined to be creative.

Liza agreed to wait in the van, with Anthony standing guard nearby.

Daxx got my attention from the top of the stairs and nodded to me. Crissy who was a few feet away gave me a serious look. "Guess it's our turn."

I glanced at the long blade strapped closely to her leg and nodded. Before I could change my mind, I went down the orange alley to Daxx.

"Took them a minute to find the right tunnel. Tim's waiting at the bottom."

"I wasn't seeing clearly when I came up."

She shrugged. "There's only one that leads into a cavern like you described. The guys will be reaching the other entrance right now. We need to hurry."

As soon as we entered the tunnel below, I knew it was the one in which the emotions had swamped me. I began to prepare for the onslaught I knew would be waiting at the other end. I'd been close to enough fights in my life to know that the emotions ran from one end of the spectrum to the other. Glancing behind, I saw Bronx and Sith following close behind. Anyone that thought to come up behind us didn't stand a chance.

Daxx paused at the door. "Ready?"

I nodded, not wanting to break my concentration by talking.

Daxx motioned to Tim, who opened the door. Before I stepped into the chamber I could hear the clash of metal on metal. A new feeling I hadn't often had come over me, concern, for the men I knew the strikes would be aimed at.

As I crouched down near to Daxx at the door, I felt energy flood into my mind. "Oh." I touched my head.

"You okay?" Crissy asked.

I nodded. "Yes. I think Chase just added a wall inside my head to help keep emotions out."

Daxx glanced at me, an eyebrow raised. "Little blood-bonding going on?" She shook her heard. "You'll have to share the details later…"

Tim suddenly stepped in front of us, his large sword blocking someone else's from swinging down on us. "Girl talk later, huntress?" He grunted, and then blocked another attempt.

"Shit. Right." Daxx rolled and came up behind the man trying to cut Tim in half. There was a quiet popping noise and then the man vanished. A small device in Daxx's hand snapped back to rest on her belt. She gave me a wide grin. "Cool, huh?"

I looked around, not able to recognize any of the men I knew in the swarm of bodies. They were seriously outnumbered. "What now?" I asked.

"How do we find the kids?" Crissy whispered moving closer me.

Daxx shuffled back closer to the doorway. "Don't ask me. I'm usually out there rushing into the shit while the men do all that tough posturing crap."

Tim snorted and stepped toward a man coming in our direction. As soon as he did, Sith took his place in front of us.

"Daxx." Rafael called out as he kicked some man in the chest to knock him back. "Kids ran into that room..." The man charged at him again and Rafael blocked his attack again, kicking him back. "Where the guy with the axe is standing." He said quickly before swinging his sword at his opponent.

Daxx straightened up and looked around. "Axe... axe..." She moved trying to see through the commotion of bodies moving in every direction. "Dammit. What's with these guys and battle axes? Seriously." She pointed.

Following the direction she indicated, I saw the man she was referring to. He was huge, even by the standards of the brothers. He held a two-sided axe. I'd never seen one in person before, and from this glance, hoped to never again. His eyes were glowing green. I moved along the wall to where Daxx was, Crissy following right behind me. "What do green eyes mean?" I asked her.

"Uh..." She looked to Crissy.

Crissy shrugged. "I keep forgetting to ask."

"Hold on, let me ask my blocker." Daxx said.

Tim knocked a man down just as she stepped away. Daxx ducked down and used the box on the downed man and he vanished.

"Can I get one of those?" I asked Crissy.

She frowned. "No. I wanted one too."

"That's disappointing."

"Tim." Daxx got his attention. "Green eyes? Bad for me?"

Tim stepped into another man's swing. "Very bad for you." He grunted when their blades clashed.

Daxx came back and squatted down. "Green eyes, very bad for us."

"Hey," Sith hissed. I looked up at him to see his eyes glowing green. "*Some* are bad for you."

I couldn't hide my surprise, and pointed to the man with the battle axe.

He turned and mumbled something about 'damn axes'.

Bronx went by him and shrugged. "Could be worse, could be a whip."

I wasn't sure how a whip could be worse than a sharp double-sided axe, but now wasn't the time for questions.

After Daxx popped Tim's opponent to wherever they went, they came back over.

"Tag team? She asked him.

Tim glanced to the man with the axe. "Royal rumble may be more appropriate." He motioned to the other two guards to go.

Again, I had no idea what that meant. Staying close to the wall, I looked around at the others. The brothers were not executing the graceful moves they did during practice sessions. They used a great deal more force and malicious intent. The fierceness of their battle was heart stopping. I glanced around for Chase, needing to know he was all right.

He was fighting with *two* others, a blade in each hand. The expression on his face was cold. as he focused solely on keeping their weapons from touching him. I had no idea how he was doing that while helping me not pick up emotions. There was a great deal more to this man than I had realized.

"Thing of beauty, right?" Daxx asked beside me again.

"I don't know about that, but it is impressive."

"Yep, come on the guards are clearing a path for us." She pulled a second small blade from her back then glanced to Crissy. "Go up."

Crissy nodded. "Okay." She whispered and then ran toward the wall ten feet from us.

I was momentarily stunned to see her fast climb it, then start walking across an old wooden beam toward the room we were trying to reach. Turning, I spotted Victor, and he also glanced up, fully aware of where his mate was.

Snapping out of it, I pulled the knife from my back, just in case I'd need it. "Better be prepared." I mumbled and followed. Tim was behind me, I heard his guttural grunt and knew he was preventing someone from reaching us. Bronx and Sith took on the man with the axe, Daxx stayed back looking for an opening to get to the room or use her box, I wasn't sure which.

She turned to look at someone and a man came running toward her with a large curved blade. Stepping fast, I rushed at him and dropped down to kick out his foot. As soon as he faltered, I jumped back up and grabbed the arm with the blade and flipped him over my body. He landed on the stones on his back. With my dagger held toward him, I stepped and put my boot on his throat.

"Eva?"

I looked at his face to see green eyes so like my own looking up at me.

"Got him." Daxx said and gave me a nudge so I'd remove my foot. She used the device and he vanished.

"Who the hell is Eva?" She asked, turning to check behind us.

I stared at the floor where he had been. "My mother." I told her.

"Oh shit." She looked around. "He's safe, that sent him to the cells."

Someone grabbed my chin, I jolted to see Chase looking at me.

"Is it too much?" His brows were drawn.

"I think we just sent her father to the cells." Daxx told him.

His hazel eyes held compassion. "Alona, get the children to safety."

I jerked out of his hold and then nodded. "Yes."

He winked at me and stepped back.

I turned to see him step back into the fray of bodies. I looked to Daxx. "Let's go." Feeling a new determination, I glanced to see Bronx and Sith still fighting with the axe man. "I think they need help."

Daxx grabbed my arm and ducked as a bo went over her head. "We *are* the help." She told me.

"Oh. Of course." We hurried toward them, stepping around any that got in our way. I glanced up to see Crissy attached to a harness from the beam above the door we needed to get in. "Can Crissy jump down and distract him somehow?"

Daxx nodded. "Yeah."

I huffed out a breath. "Get your little box thing ready. If we can get him down, he needs to vanish."

She grinned. "Good to go."

"Whenever Crissy is ready." I ducked low to the wall and inched in that direction trying to watch Crissy and all around me at the same time. Bronx and Sith were looking quite winded now. Glancing up, I saw Crissy nod to me.

Straightening, I stepped quickly past Daxx. "This is going to hurt." I said more to myself then her.

Crissy dropped down and kicked out, she missed his body but managed to connect with the axe and knock it from his grip. Which was one less thing to worry about— losing a limb or being beheaded.

Taking that opportunity, I ran at him and jumped up executing a two-footed flying kick. Landing it high on his chest, he fell to the floor. As I caught myself from hitting the stones, Daxx slid by me, her arm out with the box in hand. The large man vanished.

Jumping up, Daxx nodded to me looking thrilled. "Nice!"

Rafael came over. "Smooth moves, sister." He grinned at me and opened the door.

Jamming my dagger down into my boot, I went in the room behind him. There were six children huddled in the corner. None were older than ten.

I went over, determined their fear wouldn't overwhelm me. "Hi." I smiled. "We're going to get you out of here." Their fear spiked. I turned to see Tim and Sith in the doorway. "I even brought fierce pirates with me to protect you."

"Cool." One of the small boys whispered.

Nodding, I held out my hand. "Come. My friends will keep you safe. We have a nice house for you to live in."

Crissy was by the door and took a little girls hand. "Run fast." She told them. "Don't stop or look around. Okay?"

A few nodded.

Sith moved forward and picked up the two smallest ones. "Hang on tight." He told them. Tim gave him a nod and moved to cover him.

Rafael moved back out the door. "I'll clear the path."

As we stepped through the doorway, I was surprised to see several of the brothers there, keeping anyone from reaching us.

A little boy took my hand and squeezed it. I could feel his fear and leaned down to whisper. "The ones in black are my friends and came here to get you."

"That's good." He nodded. "I don't like it here."

"Let's run." I suggested. He nodded.

As we reached the door to the tunnel I felt a warm feeling fill me. I glanced over my shoulder to see Chase watching me. A swing from a blade barely missed his head as Quinton pushed closer, fighting someone.

I sent Chase a brief glare, hoping it conveyed he needed to pay attention. With that, we turned and ran into the tunnel to the stairs. I may completely fall apart later, but we had managed to save and change six children's lives.

I could live with that.

Chapter Sixteen

I stood in the landing room with Daxx and Crissy. We'd come back right after the children were safely away with Liza and Anthony. Of course, Tim had to negotiate with Daxx to keep her from charging back down to fight. I'm not sure what he used to get her to come back with us, but she finally conceded.

Currently I was standing here trying not to think about the man calling me by my mother's name. I wasn't succeeding so far.

Crissy was in a corner bouncing a small ball against the wall and mumbling to herself. Daxx and the three guards didn't seem bothered by it, so it wasn't my place to ask if it was normal. I was coming to realize the oddest things, where she was concerned, were perfectly fine.

"I hope they find some useful clues down there." Daxx said out of the blue, breaking the silence. "We're out of places to look." She turned to me. "Have you heard from that Lou guy again?"

I shook my head. "Not yet, but if he's found out what just happened tonight, he may be otherwise occupied."

She smirked. "Yeah. Like running around and screaming, 'oh shit we're gonna…'"

Rafael and Leone appeared.

Both were ragged looking. Rafael was holding his side. He looked all three of us over to check our state of health.

"You hurt?" Daxx asked him.

He shrugged, looking annoyed. "I'll be fine in a few hours. Got caught in the crossfire."

Leone patted him on the back. "I appreciate your ribs taking that blow for me."

With a snarl Raf glanced at him. "Don't mention it, that's what brothers are for."

"Where is everyone else?" Daxx looked very anxious.

"Some were checking other tunnels or chambers." Leone said, stretching his arm and wincing. "Victor, Michael and our kings are going over some papers that were found."

"Anything useful?" I asked, hoping it to be true.

Rafael shrugged. "Not sure yet." He bowed his head. "I need some hot water, so I'll catch you in a bit in the dining room."

"Sounds like a plan." Leone nodded and walked out with him.

I turned and looked to Sith. "You can go if you like. I'm back in one piece."

He shook his head. "Orders are I'm with you, unless one of the royals are."

I motioned to Daxx. "She's royal, is she not?"

Daxx looked at him and raised an eyebrow.

He frowned. "Yes."

Waving her hand, Daxx sighed. "All three of you go grab a shower or whatever… we'll meet you in the dining room when the boys are back."

"Works for me." Tim turned and left.

Bronx looked at Crissy.

"I'll watch her." Daxx told him quietly.

He nodded. "Wonder what she's working out now." He mused quietly.

Turning, I watched her bouncing the ball and realized it must be how she coped with the visions.

"If it leads us to team bad, I look forward to finding out."
Daxx told him. "Go." She waved to the door.

I glanced back to Sith, who sighed and then nodded and
followed Bronx out.

After he left, Daxx looked at me. "He talks."

I smiled. "Yes. Scared me half to death the first time he
did."

"No doubt." With her eyes wide, she pointed a finger at
me. "Find out what the green eyes mean. I know red, yellow,
purple and even white... but green? No clue."

I frowned. "White?"

She nodded and crossed her arms over her chest, leaning
back against the wall. "They can get at your emotions from a
distance. So if anyone's eyes go white and you're around...
get gone."

I blew out a breath. "Good to know." I frowned. "I feel
like there should be a handbook for here."

Laughing, she threw her hands up. "I know, right. The
guys are not helpful at all... telling you bits here and there or
saying *later*..."

Crissy stopped bouncing the ball and turned. "It's stuck in
my head and I don't have all the pieces..." she frowned, "or
I'm missing a piece." She sighed loudly. "Maybe after sex
with Victor I'll find it..." She smiled. "It helps to clear my
head." Nodding, she looked at me. "You should get gloves."
Tucking the ball into her pocket she looked at the gloves on
her hands. "I don't have to wear them now for *that*, but I do
because I like them." Her eyes grew wider, "and it helps with
the cable so my hands don't get burned." She nodded again
and looked around at the empty room.

My eyes darted from her to Daxx, then back to Crissy
again. If I wasn't already emotional soup, I would have asked
for more information... to understand what she just said.

Troy appeared, startling me.

Daxx went over and tipped up his jaw. His face was
bruised, and lip was bleeding. "You blocking with your
face?"

He licked over his lip. "We found a guy hiding and he got a lucky swing before I saw him."

She scowled. "He in the cells now?"

Troy nodded.

"You want me to go kick his ass for you?" She looked serious.

Troy smiled down at her and then hugged her against him.

Victor and Arius arrived next. Arius simply bowed his head and walked out without a word, although with the amount of blood on him, he probably wanted a shower more than conversation.

Victor looked as he had going over, aside from a little blood, he didn't even look tired.

Crissy pouted, "Is it bad I'm getting used to seeing you with blood on you?"

He gave her a soft look. "No, heart, it saves me changing three times a day so you don't see it."

She bounced over to him and wrapped her arms around him, blood and all.

He kissed the top of her head and then looked around. "Where are your guards? His tone was no longer gentle and caring.

"We sent them to grab a shower." Daxx informed him. "Rafael and Leone were here." She nodded.

Chase finally appeared and where the others looked worn out, he looked exhilarated. I looked at all the blood splattered on him. "Any of it yours?" I asked.

He looked down, then gave me an offended look. "No." Briefly he glanced to his siblings, coddling their mates and then sighed. "I know you want to go see if that was really your father, but I need a shower and we'll have to separate him from the others before you can."

"Her father?" Troy asked.

Daxx nodded. "She took him down when he was going to take a swing at me, and then he called her by her mother's name."

Victor glanced from Daxx to me. "We can't just let him go."

I hugged my arms around my waist. "I realize this. I'm just thankful I was there. If I hadn't been he would have gravely injured Daxx when she turned. I do understand there is a due process, but after that I would like to see him."

Victor nodded, his look softening. "We'll move him after we've sorted through the rest."

I inclined my head. "Thank you."

Chase huffed out a breath. "Kids get away safely?"

"Yes." I offered a half smile. "Liza is the only one that knows where they were going, so they're very safe... even from all of us, for the time being."

"That may be best, after finding traitors and spies among us." He said glancing to his twin.

"It was all done in a name no one can trace, so if necessary I can keep them hidden until they're adults." I shrugged.

Chase cocked his head and studied me. "I have no doubt you're very good at it." He looked me up and down. "And how are you faring?" He frowned. "I caught the move that tumbled the giant."

I smirked. "It was a bit jarring, but it worked. I'm fine, thank you."

"That move rocked!" Daxx said waving her hand around. "I would have landed on my face."

I laughed, "Oh, trust me I did for months while trying to perfect it. My sensei asked if I'd like a helmet at one point."

Chase shook his head. "I don't want to know."

"Did you find out anything useful? A map to their secret lair would be good." Daxx asked looking hopeful.

"Michael's going through it, but there was nothing obvious." Troy nuzzled his face into her hair.

"I'm off for a shower." Chase announced. He gave me a look of inquiry.

I blew out a breath. "I believe I'm going to see if Mitz has any more of that wine."

"Cookies." Crissy blurted out. "I need cookies."

I was on my second glass of wine by the time the brothers and guards converged in the dining room again. I briefly wondered why there wasn't a large meeting room or someplace for important gatherings, and then I watched Mitz bring out trays of food and it made sense. They certainly enjoyed their food in this realm.

Between bites there were references to moves and conquests from the battle. I was quite happy I had been busy, and unaware of most of what they spoke about.

Arius grinned and pointed to me. "I caught Crissy doing her Tarzan swing and wondered *what* she was doing… until kung fu came flying in." He shook his head. "That must have taken some force to knock him off his feet, Alona."

I twisted the stem of the glass in my hand, smiling at his description. "It's all in knowing where to land a kick like that, to knock them off balance." I shrugged. "The old saying, the bigger they are…"

"The harder they fall." He finished with a big grin.

Michael came through the doorway. "Forty-two more tonight."

Quinton snorted. "That explains why my arms are tired."

"Maybe you're just getting old, brother." Rafael gave him a toothy grin.

"I'll show you old next practice you little brat." Quinton promised with a stern look.

I couldn't help smiling along with the others.

Chase appeared from the direction of the kitchen, waving his phone. "I just spoke to Emil. His son was not one of those we rounded up tonight."

"That's good news." Troy nodded. "I'd wondered about that."

Chase leaned over and looked at what was left on the tray. "It took Emil some time to reach him and make sure." He shrugged. "He's not sure where he is, but he heard cattle in the background."

"That leaves out the city." Daxx glanced around. "There are no cattle there."

"It's a cow!" Crissy jumped to her feet.

Quinton looked around the room. "What's a cow?"

Crissy shook her head. "I saw one," she frowned, "I don't know what kind it was," she looked to Bronx. "I need a book about cows." He gave her a slight nod.

"What does that mean Crissy?" Daxx asked watching her closely.

Crissy turned to her. "The book? So I can learn about cows."

Daxx shook her head. "No. The cow that you saw."

"Oh. I don't know, but it was bad." Crissy told her with her eyes-wide.

"You saw a bad cow?" Chase asked with a smirk on his face.

Crissy looked at him. "I don't know if the cow was bad or good," she looked to her mate. "How would I know that?"

Victor gave her a gentle smile. "I believe what my brother was asking is how was the beast you saw, signifying something bad?"

"Oh." Crissy frowned at Chase. "Why didn't you just ask that?"

Chase laughed, "I thought I did."

"I don't know how I know, I just do." She told him while nodding.

"If you tell us we have to rescue cattle next, little sister, I'm going to expect a steak or two out of it." Rafael told her as he leaned back in his chair.

"Maybe a few burgers too." Quinton added and then ate a quarter of a sandwich in one bite.

"Just let us know if you figure it out, Crissy." Troy suggested.

She nodded. "It's still very confusing right now."

I glanced at Leone to see that he had a scowl on his face, as he stared at the glass in front of him. I may not have followed everything that went on with these brothers, but I recognized someone distracted by their own head. I looked to Chase until our eyes connected and then slowly to his brother before meeting his hazel eyes again.

Chase turned to study his young sibling for a moment. "Maybe we could have farm talk later." He said quietly as he crossed his arms and turned to his twin. "Think you could take a look in Leone's thick head and figure out why he thinks he's hearing things lately?"

Troy sat forward in the chair and looked at Leone. "Is that why you're staring off into space all the time?"

Leone sighed and looked around at the others. "I don't know what it is, but if you can tell me how to fix it, I'll take that."

Troy nodded abruptly and got up. Going around the table, he pulled out the chair beside Leone and sat down.

Leone blew out a breath and turned in his chair, so he was facing the king.

Troy leaned closer.

I looked around and all movement in the room had ceased. Turning back, I watched Troy place a hand on Leone's shoulder, his red eyes giving him an intense look.

Troy made a noise of annoyance and leaned back. "I can't get in."

"What?" Chase shook his head. "Since when?"

Lifting his hands, Troy shrugged, "Since now I suppose."

Arius got up. "Leone's mind is one of the easiest to penetrate," he offered him a sympathetic look, "sorry, brother, but it's true."

"I know." Leone's tone was quiet. "What does it mean?"

Troy stood up. "Arius, you try."

Arius gave him a determined look and came around to sit in the chair he had been in.

"Don't embarrass me." Leone said glaring at Arius.

"I'm just seeing if I can, relax." Arius touched his shoulder and sat that way for a moment before placing his other hand on Leone's shoulder, he leaned closer.

Huffing out a breath, he dropped both hands and sat back. "I can't either."

Leone's worry was plain to see now. "What..." He shook his head. "What does that mean?"

"Have you pissed off a witch recently?" Rafael asked him. "They can..." He cleared his throat. "They don't handle some things well."

Chase gave Rafael a blank look. "I'm sure Leone wasn't sleeping with half the witches in the temple." He waved his hand and turned his eyes back to Leone. "Go see Romulus and Clairee, see if they have any insight." He turned to Troy. "And I don't want you crossing to the other side until we know what's going on... just to be on the safe side."

Victor nodded. "I agree. We know they are looking for leverage. You, distracted, hands them a perfect opportunity."

Leone rubbed both hands over his face and then dropped them onto the table. "Yeah, okay." He stood up.

Rafael did as well. "I'll go with you, just so you don't snap Romulus' neck or anything."

Leone snorted. "If he can help, I'll have to like him. And I will not be thrilled by that."

The room was quiet as they left.

"I'm off to see if the new inmates have been sorted." Arius said as he got up and walked in my direction. He paused and looked down at me. "I'll let you know when we've found the man you think is your father."

I hadn't realized they all knew, but shouldn't have been surprised. Part of their dynamic was in their all communicating everything. "Thank you." I finally said back, unsure if that was the correct thing to say.

Chapter Seventeen

I was standing in the control room to the cells, starring at the screen to my father's cell. There was no mistaking who he was, I had his eyes. Although, I think I knew that when he called me Eva.

I had expected a prison with cells and bars, but instead found clear walls, rows of them. Arius explained how all of it worked, but I only heard about half of what he said. My heart had been racing since Daxx brought me here. I was going to meet a man I thought had abandoned my mother. A man that didn't know I existed.

I heard the door open but couldn't take my eyes off the screen.

"Duchess," Chase spoke softly from behind me, "you need to be aware…"

I turned to look at him.

"Your father's mental state is not good." He said carefully.

Hugging my waist, I exhaled slowly trying to process what that meant. "My own isn't faring well at the moment either." I told him in a shaky voice.

He gave me a gentle look. "I know." He moved closer but seemed to understand I was too close to crumbling to be touched. "You can't go into the same cell." Chase told me, hunching his shoulders, so he could look in my eyes. "His emotions…" he shook his head, "Troy says that you would be debilitated by them."

I squinted, trying to focus on his words.

"You can stand in another room, you'll be able to see him and speak to each other."

I nodded.

"Whenever you're ready."

I looked back at the monitor to see my father standing in the middle of his cell. Just standing there. I turned back to Chase. "I think it's now or never."

As we walked there he explained, my father wouldn't be able to see or hear me until I was ready.

I stepped into the room Chase pointed to, and turned to see he hadn't gone past the door.

He shook his head, a weak smile on his face. "Seeing me will not do his state of mind any favors, he's *very much* against the royal family."

I took a deep breath and stepped over in front of the clear wall. I just stood there looking in at him for a moment, he was completely unaware I was there. He was a very handsome man, I couldn't fault my mother for falling for him. I clearly got the color of my hair and eyes from him.

Blowing out a breath I nodded. "I'm ready." I didn't turn to look at Chase, but knew he'd done something because Levi was now very focused on me.

The look on his face was confusion and joy almost at the same time. He moved over toward me slowly, as if he were afraid I would disappear. "You're not Eva." He said in a rough voice. "I-I had thought you dyed your hair, to hide." He stopped in front of the clear wall and looked at me. "Who are you?" His brows were furrowed. "You have her face, so beautiful…" With a finger, he traced the glass as if he was touching the outline of my face.

"I'm her daughter." I finally found the voice to say.

His green eyes searched mine and then understanding registered as he stared into mirror images of his own eyes. "We had a child?" His hand was shaking where he still held it against the glass. "She lived and… and had a child. My child." A tear rolled down his cheek.

"Yes, she did."

Covering his mouth for a moment he continued to look at me. "I went back for her, she was gone." He shook his head. "No one that knew us was still there." He paced away then came right back. "I was delayed, things to prepare before going for her… issues to resolve, but I got back… I searched the entire city… the camps…" He shook his head, looking ever more frantic.

Swallowing the lump in my throat, I felt I should explain. "She had to leave the city so she didn't get sick… and so I wasn't exposed."

He leaned close to the glass, his eyes looking hopeful. "Yes, yes good." He nodded. "Is she…" He started shaking his head, grief filling his eyes. "No, no we didn't complete the bond…" Clasping both hands to his forehead he looked at the floor. "If we had she…"

"She passed away over eighty years ago." I offered.

Levi's head snapped up. "That's too young…" He shook his head. "I couldn't find her… you… I didn't know." He turned and paced away. "I never would have stopped looking if I'd known."

A tear rolled down my cheek, knowing that he wanted me. A terribly heartbreaking feeling, after all this time. I couldn't find anything to say.

He turned and came back to the glass and just looked at me, as if he were seeing me for the first time. "What did she… what's your name?" His voice was shaking.

"Alona." I told him in a voice barely more than a whisper.

He smiled. "Alona." He nodded briefly. "That's beautiful." He touched the glass again. "As you are." His hand moved over the glass, if it hadn't been there he would have touched my hair.

I wanted so desperately to feel that touch, to feel the love of a parent I had never known.

"You're so young…" His eyes jerked back to mine. "You have my blood, are like me?"

I nodded, unable to speak a word.

He smiled. "My parents… your grandparents, will love you so much."

The lump in my throat almost choked me. I had grandparents…

All of a sudden, his eyes changed to red. "Show me your arm. Now!" He growled.

Shocked, I took a step back.

He smacked a large hand against the glass. "You wear the day king's amulet. Tell me you haven't mated with him!"

I touched the pendant on my chest, having forgotten that I had it on. Shaking my head, I backed up another step.

"Their kingdom will burn! There will be no more servitude and transporting, all will be free to leave!" Smashing the glass again, he snarled at me. "It's not too late Alona. Go to the other side and never return…"

I stumbled back further until my back hit the wall.

"Let me see her!" He screamed and hit the wall again. "Let me see my daughter!"

He could no longer see me. I slid down to the floor and stared at the man on the other side of the glass. He paced around and yelled, hitting everything in his reach. I couldn't hear him now, but could see the rage on his face. I was breathing so fast, I wasn't sure if I could catch my breath again.

"Alona," Chase was kneeling beside me.

I turned and looked at him, my hand against the pendant still shaking. "What is this that you gave me?"

He searched my face, and shook his head, I could see the regret in his eyes. "I…"

Scrambling to my feet, I reached with shaking hands to unclasp it. Holding it by the pendant I held it out to him. "Take it." I hissed.

Slowly, Chase stood up and took the chain hanging from my hand. "Alona, I should have explained before…"

Shaking my head, I backed away from him. "No. I don't want to hear it." I glanced to see Daxx and Arius standing in the door. "I'd like to go home now."

Chase sighed, his shoulders slumping as he did. "I'll have Sith…"

"No." I held up my hand. "I have no need, or *want*, of your guards."

"Alona." Daxx said quietly.

I turned to look and see she had tears in her eyes, clearly she'd heard the exchange with my father.

"I can have Arius take you back." She nodded slowly. "I'd like to come back with you for a while."

I swallowed, trying not to cry. Nodding I looked at her. "Yes." I whispered.

"Ok." She held out her hand. "We can't transport in the cells, so we'll get out of here now."

I nodded and paused to look at my father once more, he was still raging inside the cage. I turned to Arius. "Can… can the doctors help him? Please."

Arius nodded quickly. "We'll move him somewhere quieter, and get the doctor to look after him."

I nodded, placing both hands on my chest as I fought to slow my breathing. "Thank you." I went over to Daxx and took her hand and looked again to Chase. I could see pain on his face, but he didn't try to stop us from leaving.

"Come on." Daxx said softly.

Chapter Eighteen

Daxx came back out after walking through my entire apartment.

She smirked and leaned against the back of the sofa. "So, living here is a real hardship, huh?"

I shrugged. "Oh, I've had my share of dives."

She snorted. "I guess I didn't live long enough to get past the dive part of my life."

I turned to look back out the window. "I think you've moved a few steps up, living in royal chambers now."

She came over and stood beside me and looked out at the lights in the city. "It has its perks. I still miss having my own place to hide when I need quiet." Shrugging to my curious glance. "Team bad found it, and Crissy and I haven't been allowed back over here unescorted to find a new place."

"You're both welcome to hide here if you need peace." I hugged myself and watched a car go down the street.

"Cool. Criss has her tower in the realm, but she does need the internet over here to search..."

"About that," I turned and walked toward the kitchen, "I'd like to help in that search." I went to the fridge to see if I had any wine chilling. Grabbing the first bottle I came to, I pulled it out and waved it around. "Much like with those children tonight, I'd like to set up a safe haven, for others, like myself." I got one wine glass and then held one up toward her, she nodded. "I have the financial means and knowhow with the markets to fund a place like that," I poured the wine, "for many years to come."

She took the glass I held out. "That's awesome." She took a sip, and it was clear from her expression wine wasn't her favorite spirit. "We'd have to work out the security and all that, but having somewhere safe over here, that also helps those like, and to learn what they are... that's..." She blew out a breath, "an amazing thing to do."

I leaned against the counter and took a sip, thinking that through for a moment. Before I could reply, Sith appeared by the entrance. I scowled at him. "I told Chase I don't want his guards."

He shook his head. "I'm not here because I was ordered to be here, I'm here because I want to be." He shrugged. "I don't trust that Lou guy and..." he smirked. "I have a puzzle to finish."

I studied him for a moment and then smiled. "I do need help with that puzzle." His expression was sincere. "Does Chase know you're here?"

Shaking his head, Sith kicked off his boots and came over. "No, it's my downtime and the king..." he glanced to Daxx, "is too busy yelling at your king." Daxx straightened. "Don't worry Night King is yelling back just as loudly, and few of the other brothers have joined in too."

Daxx sighed. "Just as long as they're not beating the hell out of each other again."

I gave her a startled look.

She grabbed the bottle of wine and motioned to the sofa. "Come, sit, let me tell you a story that will make Chase giving you a pendant seem trivial."

Sith chuckled. "I'm going to do the puzzle while you do *that*."

Daxx looked over her shoulder at him. "Coward."

He paused and shook his head. "No. Just a man that knows when to be elsewhere."

Laughing, she set the bottle on the table and sat down.

The bottle sat empty on the table by the time Daxx was finished telling me about her introduction to the world of Alterealm. I sat there speechless. "I don't know what to say to that."

She snorted. "Exactly."

Looking at what was left in my glass I shook my head. "I'm a bit stunned." I smiled at her.

Waving her hand around, she huffed out a breath. "I was pissed, not stunned." She laughed. "I think…" She pointed to the bottle, "where I was going with this, until that hit me, *was* Chase is being…" She frowned, "very, noble? I think is the best way to explain it to you. The way he went about it may not have been clear to you…"

I sat back. "I see what you mean though. Chase was able to stop from marking you… where as your mate couldn't." I shook my head. "Which *is* surprising, he seems so unmoveable."

"Not that time he wasn't." She laughed. "I can still see the look on Quinton's face when I stomped by him in the hall carrying my raptor and wearing a sheet."

I laughed, picturing that. "But is it because Chase wasn't your true mate?"

She sobered. "No. I think he was as intended as much as Troy…" She frowned. "I don't remember what that damn book said."

"The book of prophecy?"

She nodded. "Yeah." Her eyes widened. "But I know who can probably rhyme it off for us." Pulling her phone out of her pocket she typed on it. "Crissy read it and has been studying it, comparing it to things she saw in the past to see if there are clues to lead to the other mates." She pointed to her back as she stared at her phone. "She saw my tattoo and the rune that's on her back now to stop the magic…"

I wasn't sure if it was the wine, or she just wasn't making any sense now. Something told me it wasn't the alcohol and there was still plenty I didn't understand.

"Oh good." She tapped the screen on her phone and then set it on the table. "It's on speaker."

"Hello?"

"Crissy, it's Daxx and Alona. Where are you?"

"In my tower." Crissy mumbled, "sorting, processing… I can't get this cow out of my head."

Daxx shook her head and then waved a hand. "We need to know what the prophecy said."

"Oh." There was a pause. "Which one?"

Frowning, Daxx leaned closer to the table. "You've read more than the nine sons one?"

"Yes. There are so many…" There was another long pause. "Do you want me to tell you the whole thing?"

With eyes wide, Daxx shook her head. "No. I just can't remember what it said about me."

"Oh, that's easy." She said.

Daxx rolled her eyes. "For you."

"Yes." She sighed. "So, which part about you?"

"Just start and I'll tell you to fast forward if it's not the part I want." Daxx leaned back and nodded while looking at me.

"Okay." Crissy cleared her throat. "When the marking unveils between her shoulders the sundial will validate she is the true and waiting to be found…"

"To the next part, about the king's mate or whatever it is."

"Um, okay… True mate to either twin King if the bond be made, she must select one or the other that can hold her heart right. The Huntress's reign alongside her King will change the realms forever controlling the evil of both sides and bring peace to the sun and moon."

She pointed at me. "There see, it could have been *either* of them." She snorted. "I mean *seriously* is that a bitch or what, choosing between twins?"

I opened my mouth to answer and then decided a comment wasn't needed.

"It could have only been Troy though." Crissy said sounded distracted, which I'd come to know as her main state.

"How do you mean?" I asked her.

She chuckled. "Because of Chase. If he'd been chosen by Daxx then the part about the other king makes no sense when it comes to Troy." Her tone more or less said 'duh'.

"I don't remember that part." Daxx said frowning.

"For our King not chosen, a mate lies in wait, born of human blood. She will rule over his compulsion as no other could, and bring him lifetimes of eternal peace." Crissy rhymed off without pausing to recall it.

"Oh." Daxx sat forward again and stared at the phone. "You're right. That wouldn't have worked with Troy." She made a sound of annoyance. "Too bad you weren't around to point all this out when I was losing my mind." She turned to me, an odd look on her face. "So, what part are they talking about with Chase, Crissy?"

"His compulsion?" Crissy asked.

Daxx nodded. "Yeah."

There was long silence. "I don't see much to know Chase and all the bits that are him." She finally said.

Daxx blew out a breath and looked at me. "You know he gave Alona his royal pendant, right?"

"Yes. I asked Victor and he explained what it meant." She sounded very excited.

"So, if Chase knows Alona is his mate, what is the prophecy referring to?"

I wasn't sure I wanted to know any of this, but part of me was seriously curious.

"He's got a thing with short skirts and tall boots." Daxx said with a smirk while looking at what I wore.

Crissy giggled. "I don't think that would be enough to prophesize."

Daxx frowned. "He is an emotion feeder and Alona is an emotional sponge." She snorted and looked at me. "Sorry that came out *all* wrong."

I smiled. "And yet it is true."

"That could be it... oh my gosh, that fits!" She blurted out.

"What does?" Daxx was on the edge of the cushion now.

"Victor said it was disturbing that Chase was feeding from prisoners now..."

"What?" Daxx's eyes went wide. "Seriously? Since when?"

"I don't know."

Daxx shook her head. "That's so not his M.O."

"How do you mean?" I asked, curiosity winning."

She opened her mouth and then closed it, looking at me for a moment. "The reason Chase and I didn't work out..." She waved a hand around, "later we realized it was the excessive blood he'd given me to save my life that made us think we were..." She closed her eyes, like she'd lost her train of thought briefly. "The reason we didn't work out was because of his feeding preferences. I couldn't live with it... but now he's feeding from prisoners..."

I leaned forward and gave her a hard look. "I'm not following."

"Me either." Crissy said, startling me, I'd forgotten she was on the phone.

Daxx sighed loud. "He prefers to feed off females and his emotion of choice is..."

"Oh." I sat back.

"Is what?" Crissy asked, then she chuckled. "Never mind I know."

Daxx moved over so our faces were close. "Has he fed off of you?"

I shook my head. "No. He said he couldn't or he would lose complete control. I had no idea what he meant, I thought he was talking about sex."

"Dammit, why couldn't Troy be like that?" Daxx scowled. "Even Victor was strong with Crissy, although everyone was afraid to go near him until…" she waved her hand in the air again and looked back to me. "You've broken our Chase."

"Or fixed him." Crissy added.

Daxx glared at the phone. "That's what I meant Criss."

"Oh, but you said…"

"Never mind what I said." She still looked at me. "So is there… sparks between you two."

I snorted, which I normally didn't do. Looking at the glass in my hand I set it on the table. "It is quite heated…"

"I felt like I was on fire when Victor was near, but he wouldn't have sex with me… *then* I explained why I wore the gloves and he was…"

Daxx cleared her throat. "We get it Criss." She looked at my hand and shrugged. "I didn't know enough to keep the palm of my left hand covered, so Troy couldn't mark me."

I looked at my hand. "Is that how?"

"Well, there's more that goes with it… I'm sure you can figure out *that* part, but yeah, if the flesh can't connect then he can't mark you." She pointed to the phone. "Trust me Crissy tested it out often and it works."

"It does, but when Victor took me to the field of butterflies, I knew…"

I looked down at Daxx's phone then to her. "Is that a metaphor?"

Dax shook her head. "Nope. He found a field where the monarchs migrate and took her there."

"That's romantic." I frowned, the Victor I'd seen didn't strike me as even knowing what romance was.

"I know, right," Daxx grinned at me. "I know what you're thinking."

"A flower. Oh. I have to go there's more pieces." Crissy hung up before Daxx could respond.

She looked at the phone. "Cows and flowers. This should be interesting."

I shook my head. "I don't understand most of what she says."

"It takes time to translate Crissy-speak. I've known her for five years though, so I'm the expert." She laughed and then sobered quickly and looked at me. "So, you are Chase's mate. He'd know."

I looked at my hand and turned it over a few times. "I can't do it." I said quietly and then motioned to her marked arm. "It worked out for you and Crissy. Victor better not hurt her, or I'll stab him, but..." I shook my head. "You've seen how my father is, and I watched my mother go insane and then wither and die..." I inhaled slowly. "There's an attraction with Chase, I can't deny that, but I will never agree to be his, or any man's mate, in that sense."

Daxx glanced over my shoulder and then her face blanched.

I turned to see Chase standing by my door.

He cleared his throat. "I came to apologize... in person." His voice was very rough. "I would have called first, but thought you'd say no."

"I'm going to go see how Sith is doing with that puzzle." Daxx said and got up quickly and went down the hall.

Chase watched her leave and then took a cautious step toward me. "I spoke to Arius a few minutes ago. Levi has been moved to the medical area and the doctor has sedated him for the time being."

I stood up.

"Once he's settled some, the doctor feels he'll be able to help him..."

Daxx came back out and ran over and picked up Sith's boots. "We're just going to pop out and grab a burger or... munchies. Sith says Alona only keeps girly nibbles in her cupboards." She shrugged and ran back down the hall.

Chase gave her an odd look and then turned back to me.

"Will the doctor be able to help him for the long term or... I don't know enough about this..."

Tucking his hands in his pockets, he made no move to come closer. "He'll always remember, but medication can help make him more... functional, is the term I was told."

I clasped my hands together and nodded. "Good."

"You understand he's always going to be in custody…" He titled his head and watched me. "He did intend to cut off Daxx's head when you stopped him…"

I exhaled a short breath. "Yes, I understand that."

"Once he's more stable, you will be able to visit him, if you wish."

I hugged my arms around my waist, trying to stop the shaky feeling that filled me. "I would like that."

He nodded abruptly. "Michael is looking for his parents, your grandparents. We hadn't realized they were still alive…" His eyes held mine, as if he were assessing what I was feeling. "At the time, we had only focused on finding him for you…"

"I think…" I blew out a nervous breath, "I think, eventually I'd like to meet them." I shook my head. "The very idea that I have relatives is somewhat overwhelming right now."

He took a few steps toward me and then stopped again. "I imagine it would be."

"Thank you for telling me in a more personal way." I sighed. "I'm afraid the whole texting thing still fails to enthuse me."

He nodded. "I don't think they have emoticons for what I had to say."

I smiled briefly. "I'm sorry for being rude, earlier." I waved a hand toward him. "It was all very…"

"Heartbreaking." He said softly and moved closer. "I should have told you." He shook his head. "Finding out that way was not the right way."

I cleared my throat and studied him. "I suppose it seemed right to you at the time, considering the false hope of before." I motioned to where Daxx and I had been sitting. "Daxx explained her becoming acquainted with all of this."

Chase looked surprised. "I'm sure that was colorful."

I shrugged. "It was interesting, to say the least."

We both stood there looking at each other neither moving nor speaking for several minutes.

"If you need it, I can have Arius come help you go out and feed…" His brows were furrowed as he spoke. "Until we've dealt with that Lou person, your safety is still at risk."

He was being careful with each word he spoke. I tried to feel, but it was like a wall surrounded him.

"I'm fine tonight. I'll be going to sleep shortly." I glanced toward the window to see it was still night.

He nodded, but didn't move. "Your father, he loved your mother, it wasn't just *mating*… he looked at you with adoration on his face." Chase's chest rose and fell in a silent breath. "A child born that was made without love, after these many years…" He motioned to me. "He wouldn't have looked at you that way."

I felt a tear roll down my cheek. "I have no doubt my mother loved him as well. She remembered every detail in the way he spoke, moved…" Another tear followed the path down my face. I wiped it away with an unsteady hand.

Making a soft noise in his throat, he moved over quickly and stood in front of me. With a shaking hand, he wiped the dampness off my cheek. "I'm sorry, duchess, I should have told you sooner…" He held my chin lightly so I would continue to look at him. "I wanted to be sure."

I could finally feel emotions from him, and it wasn't what I expected to feel. It was pain and sorrow. I stepped back, even though I knew I couldn't distance myself from them. How could I when they mirrored my own? "I'm sorry I can't be what you'd hoped."

Dropping his arm, he put his hand back in his pocket. "I will make sure you are kept up-to-date with regards to your father."

I nodded. "Thank you."

He studied me for a moment, his hazel eyes moving over me softly. "If you need anything, please call."

I nodded, not knowing what else to say at this point.

Chase stood there a few seconds more just looking at me and then he was gone.

I went over and picked up my phone and the device from the counter and went down the hall to my room. Setting the device on the table by my bed I messaged Daxx.

It has been a horrendous day. Thank you for the company. I am going to bed now.

I sat on the bed and stared at the phone.

Okay. Try to get some sleep. Sith says he'll work on the damn puzzle tomorrow. Yellow smiley face.

I set my phone's ringer to silence and put the phone on the table.

Chapter Nineteen

I woke up the next morning completely energized and motivated. It had been years, a decade or more since I'd felt the drive and purpose I did today. As the sun rose, I sent Daxx a message before she went to sleep.

Be sure to show Crissy how to get here, or whatever it is you do. The office will be set up by the end of this day.

A response came back quickly, reminding me that I was slow in typing my own.

Just having family meeting before bed. Are you joining us to explain to the men?

I grimaced at the thought of transporting right now. *I trust you to do that.* I sent back to her.

Okay. Will see if Victor will get Crissy a two-way device.

I made a note to inquire about one of those for myself, once I was on friendlier terms. *That would be perfect. I've ordered two more laptops and I already have a reputable VPN for us to use.* Going out to the kitchen I opened the fridge to see if there was anything for breakfast.

VPN? Came back.

I smiled, feeling somewhat better I knew something. *Hides our IP so it can't be traced.* I replied and got out the ingredients to make an omelette.

Sounds good 007 LOL

I sighed and scowled at the phone. *LOL?* I sent back. So much for feeling better.

Laugh out loud—and I did!

So did I, when I read that. *Oh!* I returned and got a bowl to crack the eggs into.

What about Michael and Quint? They help look too.

Pausing what I was doing I looked at the phone. Then typed back, *If you give all the men the keys to the castle it won't be a peaceful place for girls to hide.*

Good point! Guards and us girls…oh and Arius already knows.

I noticed she didn't mention Chase already knew. Which was fine, he could remain the elephant in the room for now. *Sounds perfect.* I replied. I had just set the phone down again when a message came in.

Warning! Incoming!

Holding the phone, I turned to look at the door expecting someone to appear. The phone rang startling me, I almost tossed it on the floor.

"Hello?"

"Good morning, duchess." Chase said quietly. "How are you doing?"

I turned back to the counter and looked at the bowl. "I'm well today, thank you."

"Okay… we'll come back to that in a moment. I am hiding in the kitchen so I can hear you. Daxx and Crissy are attempting to explain what the three of you are up to and it's getting quite loud in there."

I could hear the muffled voices from the next room. "It's nothing bad, I assure you."

He chuckled. "Oh, I trust that, and you. There are, however, a few concerns… I will go out in a moment and put you on speaker."

So much for avoiding the family meeting, I thought. "That's fine."

"First, are you doing okay, seriously?"

His concern was touching. "I am. I can't change the past I was given, Chase, but I can prevent others from the same fate. I will do all in my power to do so."

He sighed loud. "I have no doubt you will. I had hoped you'd be here this morning..."

Inhaling deeply, I stared across the room at the painting I adored. "I can't, not yet, not today at least."

There was a pause. "Just so you understand... I'm not going anywhere."

I smirked. "Is that a warning, your majesty?"

He chuckled. "Take it as you like, duchess." He cleared his throat. "I'm being glared at by a pair of eyes that look remarkably like my own. He's quite handsome too..."

I smiled. "Go put me on speaker so I can calm the natives and then make my breakfast."

"As you wish."

I could hear as soon as he stepped back into the room, there were several voices.

"Alona?" It was Daxx. "I am *so* sorry about this."

"It's fine. I don't mind putting worried minds at ease. Now, what is it I need to explain?"

"Daxx says you're going to set up an office to find others?"

I recognized Michael's voice, he was in full op mode presently. "Yes. If anyone is qualified to search for those like myself, that don't wish to be found, I think I am."

"She has a point."

That was Arius. "I'd like to set up a safe haven for them, much like I did for the children. I feel it would be needed to keep those that have gone through the change, and those that haven't, separate as well."

"That's a good point, Alona."

I knew that voice too. "Thank you, Quinton. I've ordered two new laptops and already have a good VPN." I paused. "Will I need another printer? Maybe I'll get one of those sent here as well." I mused out loud.

"I think it's amazing that you're doing this."

I smiled. "Thank you, Leone. How are you feeling today?"

Someone sighed loudly. "The same. Magic users can't figure it out."

"That's disheartening. Perhaps you can help go through records over there that we can pick up leads on this side. When others transported over regularly, and such. Until you're feeling one hundred percent again."

"Yeah. Yeah, I can do that."

"Alona, while I agree with this noble quest, wholeheartedly, my concern would be Cristy... and Daxx over there too often, at the same location..."

I nodded, even knowing no one could see me. "I understand that, Victor. Hiding any tracks from the internet is not the only measure I've taken. I can assure you, they are safer here than fortunes in a bank vault. I had an elite security system installed when I moved in." I glanced to the console on my wall. "If anyone tries to access this floor on the elevator, or via the emergency stairwell, I'll know. I even had sensors installed on the roof at my skylight and balcony."

"Damn, sister, you are safer than a bank vault."

I smiled. "I like to sleep at night, Rafael."

"Okay, before my mate stabs me, I'll agree... but Daxx still brings her guard."

"Lovely Troy, he can help Sith with the puzzle." I heard Daxx laugh.

"Puzzle?" Troy asked.

"Is Sith there now?" Chase interrupted.

I looked at the door just to be sure. "No, he's not."

"He's probably in a food coma, from the number of burgers he ate last night." Daxx chuckled.

"I'll make sure he's there shortly." Chase said and then added. "If that's all right?"

"Yes. Sith and I have reached an understanding." I could hear Crissy in the background.

"I will arrange for a two-way device for Cristy as well." Victor said, not sounding altogether pleased.

197

I smiled feeling like I'd just won some small battle. "Is there anything else?"

"No, I guess we'll figure out the rest as we go." Troy said quietly.

"Alona?"

"Yes, Chase?"

"You don't have to fund this on your own…"

I laughed. "It's perfectly fine for now, Chase, I have too much money as it is. I can afford the first few… decades, without stress."

"Damn." It was Rafael again. "You can be my sugah sistah… Ow!"

I smiled knowing, without seeing, that someone had just smacked him. "I will let all of you go, I know most of you are heading to bed shortly."

"Talk soon, Alona." It was Daxx.

I heard several byes. "Good bye, everyone." I hung up, not willing to go through another, more personal conversation with Chase right now. I still hadn't decided what I was doing with that situation. I was attracted to Chase, I wasn't going to lie, but I wasn't sure if I wanted to push my luck and pursue that attraction or not. I also didn't want to mislead him into thinking that I was agreeing to be his mate.

By early evening when Crissy and Daxx appeared, with guards, I had an entire work area set up. Sith had done most of the heavy lifting. We were sitting in the dining area, working on the puzzle when they appeared.

"We just push this other button, Tim?" Daxx asked her guard.

He nodded and leaned over her shoulder to watch them set Crissy's device.

When they were finished, Crissy grinned at me. "I can go back and forth by myself."

Bronx cleared his throat as he closed the device on his wrist.

She shrugged. "Okay, I can go back and forth with Bronx, by myself."

Daxx came over and looked at the table, smirking at Sith. "How goes the puzzle?"

He grunted. "Not as well as I hoped."

Standing up, I motioned down the hall. "Let me show you what we set up." I turned to see them follow. "I hadn't expected you this early.

Daxx snorted. "To finally get out of the realm... with permission, we got up early for *that*."

Once we reached the office area, Crissy pulled off her backpack. "I brought lists. Leone added a whole stack to what Michael and I had."

I glanced to Daxx. "How's he doing?"

She shook her head. "Not good. There is something going on, but no one can figure out what it is."

I grimaced. "I know that feeling all too well. I hope someone comes up with something for him."

"Wow, you have a serious command center set up here." Daxx went over and looked at the laptops and glanced at the whiteboard on the wall.

I nodded. "I am quite serious about finding and helping others."

"So I see." She nodded. "Okay, we have a few hours before breakfast, so show me where to start." Smirking, she sat at one of the laptops. "I usually do the legwork, but if I get to be out of the house, I'll learn how to help."

"What do we do?" Tim asked from the doorway.

I turned and looked at him and Bronx, standing behind him. "We may need research done at some point..." I glanced to the laptops then back, "how are you with puzzles?" Bronx shrugged, and Tim looked disappointed. I motioned them back down the hall.

When the girls went back for breakfast, I sent Sith back for a break. The break was more for me than him. I wasn't used to having people around me this much. The plus side was their emotions weren't overwhelming... Crissy's got chaotic from time to time, but as long as she focused and stayed on task, it wasn't too much to cope with.

I had just sat down with a glass of wine to stare out the window when my phone rang. Picking it up I looked, at it and then decided to answer. It was Lou.

"Isabell. Sorry I haven't called before now. Something came up that I had to deal with."

I smirked. I knew what had come up, I'd been there. "That's not a problem, Lou, I have been quite busy with a new project."

"Oh. That's good then." He cleared his throat. "How is your schedule for the next day or so?"

I glanced around the room. "My associates and I have just taken a break for..." I almost said breakfast and realized that gave too much away, "dinner, but I have some free time tomorrow." I bit my lip, not sure who to call the moment he hung up.

"Tomorrow would be great. I'd really like to introduce you to some of the others..."

"Is it going to involve going underground? I'm afraid the very idea of it gives me palpitations." I didn't want him to take me to another tunnel where I had no escape.

He chuckled. "No. I think we'll stay above ground this time."

"Lovely."

"What time works for you?"

I stared out the window as the sun prepared to set. "Noon would be fine. I'm not meeting my associates until later in the day."

"Good, good." There was a pause. "Do you have a fear of traveling by boat?"

My eyebrows went up. "No, I'm quite fine on the water."

"Excellent. We can meet by the harbor, on the east side, there's a small diner there where the ferry docks."

I was trying to figure out how bad an idea this was. "I believe I know the place. Are we taking the ferry?"

He laughed. "No. It's not going where we need to be."

A very bad idea. "Very well then." I frowned. "Lou, we're not going under the water, are we?"

His deep laugh sent chills down my spine. "No, Isabell, we're going to a small island."

"Oh. Sorry, I suppose I'm a little paranoid after our last outing." I bit my lip, hoping I sounded as nervous as I was trying to.

"Not a problem. Last time was a bit of a fail. After tomorrow, you'll understand so much more, Isabell."

"I look forward to it." With panic filling me, I jumped up and turned in a complete circle, needing to tell someone, but as I'd sent them all away, there was no one.

"Call if anything comes up."

"I don't foresee anything, but will if it happens. Thank you for calling, Lou." I held my breath.

"My pleasure."

He hung up and I squealed and opened the contacts in my phone. This was not going to go over well at all. I pushed Daxx's number.

"Alona?"

"Daxx." I sat down and then stood up again. "Are you in the dining room now?"

"Yeah, should I be somewhere else?" She said slowly.

I sat once more. "I'm not certain. Lou just called me."

"Interesting, and…"

I closed my eyes and spoke softly. "And we're going on a boat tomorrow at noon to an island." I held my breath.

"That's not what I expected." She was talking just as quietly.

"Nor I." I opened my eyes and stared across the room. "I have to tell them, don't I?"

"Uh, yeah. That you do."

"Drat, I was afraid you were going to say that." I sat back. "There's going to be testosterone pouring onto the floor."

She laughed. "You want to pop here, or do it by speakerphone?"

I sighed. "Let's try the phone first, then I don't have to glare at anyone."

"Okay. Guys, Alona got a call from Lou…"

Then it got loud and I knew I was on speaker.

"Where are you?" Chase asked loudly.

"I'm still at my place. I won't be seeing him until tomorrow at noon."

"Seeing him where?" Victor asked.

This was the part I knew wouldn't go well. "We're meeting at the harbor… and taking a boat to an island."

"What? An island?" That was Troy.

"That's what he said."

"You can't go on a boat with him." Chase blurted out, all pretense of option gone from his tone.

I stood up and paced to the window. "I don't want to go on a boat ride *with* him, but I don't see I have much choice if it will let me find a new location." I bit my lip wondering if they had children there as well.

"Shit. Michael, go get the maps and see if we can figure out where this island is." That was Troy again.

"There are lots of islands around the city." Crissy informed them.

"Which harbor are you leaving from?" Daxx asked.

"East side, where the ferry docks."

There was a lot of talking, none I could follow.

"There are no islands to the south of the city and the ones on the West side would be silly to take a boat from the east harbor…" Crissy said over top of the others.

"So, there's just islands to the North to worry about?" Rafael asked her.

"The East harbor goes out to the Northern edge of the lake." Crissy answered.

She was a treasure trove of information, I realized. "Does that narrow down the islands?" I turned and started to the office, to look it up for myself.

"You could come over here for this discussion, duchess." Chase suggested.

I flipped the light on in the room and went to the closest laptop. "I'm sure there will be a big meeting in the morning, I'll be at that one."

"As you wish." He said in an impersonal tone.

I opened the screen and searched for a map of the city. Expanding it, I looked to see there were four possible islands. I leaned closer. "I'm looking at a map right now. There's four islands... I think there's one that is little more than a few trees sticking out of the water, so there's three possibilities."

"That's still a boat and three islands we're not on." Arius said in a quiet way. "How are we going to cover all of that?"

"I can get some teams working on getting there tonight, to show us in the morning." Troy suggested.

"That doesn't help us know which one Alona is going to." Leone added.

"You're sitting this one out, brother." Rafael reminded him.

"I know." Leone didn't sound pleased. "Doesn't mean I won't be as worried as the rest of you."

I sat back in the chair, studying the map. "You people have figured out how to transport between realms, for god's sake, don't tell me you don't have some sort of tracking technology."

I heard a deep laugh and thought it was Quinton. "We have something like that, but we don't know if they'll be looking for something, or have magic to block it." It was Quinton.

"Of course, I hadn't thought of that." I had never had to worry about *magic* before in my entire existence, so not realizing some things wasn't surprising. "What if I have something I can turn on when I'm closer? Can they use magic to block a moving boat?" I didn't even know what kind of a boat.

"There's something that might work." Arius said in a thoughtful way. "She could turn it on before reaching the island, so we'd at least know which direction hey headed."

"A blood bond would help in this case, to know her state of being." Victor said in a matter of fact tone.

I got up from the desk. I needed to distract them from that talk. "Lou says he wants me to meet some of the others, and that after tomorrow I'll understand so much more."

"So, basically this is our way to find the key players... aside from those locked in the cells." Michael said. I hadn't realized he'd returned.

"I wouldn't mind finding out why I'm so important to them." I said, hoping the blood bond talk was done with.

"I don't fucking like any of it." Chase growled.

"None of us do, brother." Troy said sounding much calmer. "But, if what Alona's father said is true, we *need* to know."

I closed my eyes trying to grab a memory. Something about all being free to cross over or... I couldn't be certain, I'd been an emotional wreck by that point.

"We need to know, but not by putting Alona at risk!" Chase yelled.

"I don't think we have a choice, I'm the only..."

"Shit. Incoming!" Daxx shouted.

I looked all around the office and then quickly walked down the hallway to see Chase standing by my door looking larger than I'd remembered, and quite angry. "I'll talk to you shortly." I said into the phone and hung up. I walked by him and set the phone on the counter.

"You can *not* do this." He growled.

I was happy he wasn't going to yell in my face. I waved my hands around. "They chose me, I didn't sign up for this."

"You can't get on a boat with that man and go to some unknown island." He glared at me.

Huffing out a breath, I glowered right back at him. "Then what do you suggest?" I leaned against the counter hoping to appear unmoved by his anger, but I wasn't, at all. "What did my father say? Something about the kingdom burning and all being free?" He didn't so much as blink as he looked at me, I wasn't even sure if he was breathing. "What if there are more children on this island? It's the perfect place to hold them or others, with no way to get anywhere."

"So, you're going to go to this place with no way out?" He lifted a hand, finally moving. "What if your transporter doesn't work there? If it's been blocked?"

I shook my head. "If their objective is to stop the control of transporting, I somehow don't think they'll do that..." I moved into the kitchen, just to put more space between us. "Surely they have people transporting in? Taking a boat would be a little too easy to track, would it not?"

"There has to be another way than to put you at risk..."

"Then find a way." I barked back. I walked into the sitting room, feeling like I was running from him. Was I? I'd sort that out later. "Instead of standing here yelling at me, go figure out how we can do this." I turned to see he stood only a few feet away. How did such a large man move without a sound? I looked up at him, wishing I had my boots on so he didn't seem so tall.

His hazel eyes were swirling to yellow as he looked down at me. "You do not get on a damn boat with him unless and until we have figured something out." His jaw clenched.

Waves of emotions hit me and I blew out a breath, trying not to take them in. "Fine."

Someone cleared their throat. Turning, I saw Arius standing by the door. He held up a phone. "Taking your phone with you brother, makes it easier to reach you."

Chase stood there looking at him, making no sign of moving in his direction.

"We have something we think will work." Arius said calmly.

With a low growl, Chase stomped toward him. Now he was making plenty of noise as he moved. He grabbed his phone and then spun to face me. "You don't go anywhere until we have a plan."

I lifted my arms up and nodded. "Very well." I conceded, regardless of what I felt.

He looked at me for a moment more and then was gone.

I glanced at Arius, he inclined his head in a regal manner and then was gone also. "That went as well as I'd hoped." I murmured. Turning, I spotted my glass of wine sitting on the table. "Perhaps I'll just go sit down and pretend none of *that* just happened." I nodded and went to sit down.

Chapter Twenty

Despite much grumbling from the men, Daxx and Crissy came back after their breakfast. Our guards, more guards, and the brothers, were all scrambling to get to the island locations so they could transport there in a hurry if needed. I didn't understand it entirely, but knew they had to have *been* to a location previously to pop back there again. I personally wouldn't have been able to keep them all straight in my mind and get to the right spot every time.

Daxx wasn't happy she was removed from the playing field, but they still didn't know who team bad planned to kidnap to hold against them, so she begrudgingly worked at hunting down names on the internet.

"So, what's the game plan once we *find* people we think are part..." Daxx turned and looked at me, "whatever it's called, Alterealmy?" She rolled her eyes at her own words.

I looked at the screen and frowned. "I'm not entirely certain. Children will be the easiest I'd imagine, those that have been left without parents, but I don't know about just walking up to an adult and saying, 'hey I know what you are'..." I glanced to Crissy, "except with Crissy, I don't see it working."

Crissy laughed. "It doesn't really work like you think it would." She looked at me. "You didn't listen."

Nodding, I gave her a soft look. "I did, by running when you told me to."

She frowned and then nodded. "Yeah you did, too." She sighed. "Then I lost you again for weeks."

I checked at the time and realized it was way past my bedtime, but I would be too anxious to sleep until I knew there was something in place for my boat trip. I stood up and stretched stiff muscles. "I'm going to put on the kettle, would anyone like some tea?"

Crissy shook her head.

Daxx held up her hand. "I'll take one. I think I might be onto something here."

Crissy got up and went over to her screen. "Oh. You found one... I think." She scrolled the screen. "Just let me see if..."

"I'll be right back." I turned to quickly go out and put the kettle on. If we'd found one in a day, imagine what a few weeks would yield. Just as I reached the kitchen everything went blurry and started spinning, I grabbed for the counter to steady myself and missed. My head connected with the hard surface and I landed on the floor. Putting my hand to my head and then looking I saw blood. "Wonderful."

"Alona, we think— Alona?" Daxx was suddenly in my face. "What happened?" She pressed her hand to my head. "Crissy, grab a towel or something."

I heard the tap turn on and then a towel was in front of my face. Daxx took it and pressed it to my head.

"How bad have I damaged myself?" I asked feeling completely ridiculous.

Daxx was on her knees, she moved the towel then pressed it back in place. "It's not pretty."

"Perfect." I murmured.

"What happened?" Crissy asked sitting behind Daxx.

"I got dizzy." I held my hand over the towel, so Daxx would remove hers.

She leaned back and looked at me. "Is this a normal thing?"

I huffed out a breath.

"Did you eat today?" She tilted her head. "I mean like feeding, kind of eating."

I glanced at her briefly. "Not since before we went to the tunnels."

She looked at Crissy then back to me. "Isn't that kind of something you need to do at least once a day?"

I sighed. "Generally. I've skipped days before."

Leaning closer again she nudged my hand and looked under the towel. "It's not slowing. I guess you don't heal fast like the guys do."

Holding the towel again and shook my head carefully. "No, it seems my human blood prevents that."

"Oh. Uh… neither of us have magic blood and… going to get stiches would be…"

"I don't go to hospitals, they tend to disapprove when the name you give them doesn't really exist."

She nodded. "Yeah, I figured. So…" She pulled out her phone and then frowned. "I don't know where the guys are, and don't want to call in case it's a bad time to receive a phone call…"

"What about Leone?" Crissy offered and then she shook her head. "Oh, no that would be bad with her having part human essence…"

Daxx sighed, "He hasn't been here before either." She bit her lip and gave me a hesitant look. "Only one reachable is Chase, I know he's not out with the guys because he was busy getting some kind of tracking device for you…"

"Can't we just put a bandage on it?" I looked to Crissy who shook her head and then to Daxx.

"Uh, no this is more than a bandage can handle, and you need to feed." She gave me a look of apology.

"He's going to rant. There will be I told you so's…"

She grinned. "Tell him your head hurts too much for yelling."

I snorted, "pray it works."

"Okay, here goes." She tapped the screen of her phone. "Hey brother-in-law…" Her blue eyes were looking at the towel I held. "Slight problem…" She winced. "No, we're at Alona's and haven't gone anywhere." She cleared her throat. "She sort of fell and bumped her head…" She frowned. "Hello?"

Before I could turn to look, Chase was beside me, picking me up off the floor in one move. "Were you ladies drinking without me?" He asked, carrying me to the sofa.

"Uh, no." Daxx said following along behind. "She hasn't fed and got dizzy."

Making sure to hold the towel in place, I glanced over his shoulder and gave her a wide-eyed look. She mouthed 'sorry'.

Chase didn't say a word. He sat down, with me in his lap and then moved my hand so he could see what the towel was covering. "Unless you can lick your own head, duchess, you're going to have to take my blood." His eyes locked to mine. "I don't have healing saliva."

"We can't just tape it up?" I winced. The shock of it had worn off, and my skull was now throbbing.

He shook his head. "Not unless you want a bald spot on the side of your head where we'd have to shave your hair."

I jolted and then looked to Daxx. She nodded, still giving me an apologetic look.

"We'll go," she pointed to the hall, "back and double check that name." She spun and grabbed Crissy's arm, practically running out of the room.

"I thought," he reached and grabbed the hem of his t-shirt and pulled it over his head, "that you had some sort of arrangement with Arius for feeding assistance."

As hard as I tried, I couldn't keep my traitorous eyes from roaming all over his now naked, muscled chest. "I hadn't thought of it." I finally said when I realized an answer was required.

"How can you not remember to feed?" He asked, titling my chin up so I was looking at his eyes instead. He shook his head before I could open my mouth. "Never mind. I know."

He gave me a soft look. "I forget what it's been like for you." Leaning down, he pulled a knife from under his pant leg. "Let's get the bleeding stopped before you pass out."

I made a face at the mere thought of drinking his blood.

He actually smirked at me. "Three choices. Go back with me and get stiches in your beautiful head, we shave it and patch it up here... or a little blood to heal it."

I glowered at him, knowing I didn't have a choice.

"Thought you'd see it my way." He said softly.

I inhaled slowly and gave him a slight nod. He didn't make a sound as he cut into his chest, I flinched for him. Dropping the knife to the floor, he put his hand over the towel I held and with his other, pulled me closer.

"Before it heals and closes or I'll have to cut myself again." He reminded me in a hushed voice.

I looked at the blood running down his chest and leaned closer, licking it up, before closing my mouth around the mark in his flesh. He hissed out a breath as I sucked. I could feel him taking deep breaths and picked up enough of what he was feeling to know it wasn't causing him any sort of pain. This time I wasn't sexually excited, and yet the taste of his blood didn't repulse me. I wouldn't admit it aloud, but assumed it must have something to do with being mates. Yes, I acknowledged it was a fact, but that didn't mean I would tell anyone else. When it healed, I still licked over it to make certain and then lifted my head.

He looked at me for a moment, before lifting the towel to look at my head. "It's closed up."

"Don't suppose you have that bottled, and I could put in my medicine chest?"

Glancing back to me, his hazel eyes looked amused. "Afraid not, duchess, you get personalized delivery only."

"Mmm, I figured as much." I took the blood covered towel from his hand and tossed it onto the coffee table. I intended to get up as well, but he wrapped his arm around my waist and prevented me from doing so.

"Not just yet."

I turned to see he was giving me a look that said he hadn't forgotten how I'd landed in this situation to begin with.

"I know you…" he shook his head, "learned everything the hard way, but you have to know you can't go without feeding."

I leaned back as much as I could manage being draped across his legs. "I do."

"You're too young to skip feedings, Alona. Hell, I was almost two hundred before I could go past twenty-four hours."

"Well, there's good news," I drawled, "another century of infancy."

He grinned, his eyes moving over me. "Oh, I think your well into adulthood, and it's never looked so damn good."

I couldn't help smiling to that. "Feeding is just…" I sighed.

"I know." With a gentle touch, he grasped my chin. "But you *have* to, it's not optional." His hazel eyes searched mine. "Even if you want to gouge my eyes out with a spoon, I will still be available to help you…"

"What is your fascination with eyeball violence?"

He grinned. "Don't distract me. I'm being serious."

I inhaled deeply and looked everywhere but at him. "Are you saying even if I'm mad at you, I'm supposed to just grab you and bite you when I need it?" I gave him a startled look.

He chuckled. "My every fantasy lately has to do with those fangs of yours." He gave me a heated look for a moment then closed his eyes. When he opened them, they were turning yellow. "Hormones aside, yes that's what I'm saying. You need to feed, *daily*, and you won't get emotional backlash from me— okay, negative emotions, I can't promise to remain completely emotionless." He glanced at my mouth. "*Now* quit stalling. I have to get back and make sure the science geeks get this device right, because you insist on putting yourself in danger tomorrow." He pulled me closer again, tilting his head, his eyes locked with mine.

Dragging my eyes from his, I looked at his neck. It wasn't a hardship, to feed from him at all. My only concern were the strings that were twisting and knotting to tie us together, strings that I couldn't see. I leaned closer and licked over where I intended to bite.

Chase hissed out a breath. "Dammit, woman, don't make me beg like a horny teenager."

I smiled and then bit him. He cradled me with one arm, pulling our bodies closer while his other held my head in place. When I could feel his desire, I remembered we'd have a blood bond now as well. Where he may have been trying to shield me through that, he wasn't succeeding entirely. Licking over my mark, I rested my head on his shoulder for a moment. "I'm beginning to understand the appeal of feeding in ways I never had before."

He grunted. "You can feed several times a day if you'd like to explore that more."

I lifted my head and looked into his yellow eyes, he had a smirk on his face as well. "How generous of you."

"I'm a generous man." He grinned. He leaned closer and kissed my mouth softly. "I do have to get back. I'm the guinea pig so they can test it thoroughly before tomorrow."

"How so?" I moved to get off of him.

"I port all over the place and they make sure it works, mostly, but we're also checking to see if a spell can detect it." Picking up his knife, he put it back in the harness around his ankle and grabbed his shirt. Getting up, he put it on. "Will you be at breakfast in the morning to go over the plans?" He shrugged. "we're hoping we'll have some by then."

I got up and nodded. "Yes." I touched my head, feeling no pain where there had been.

Kissing my forehead, he gave me a stern look. "Try not to break anything."

I rolled my eyes. "I'll do my best."

With a grin, he motioned to the dining room table. "It's actually a puzzle."

I nodded. "Yes."

He stepped back and after a quick once over look, he was gone.

Turning to the hall, I called out. "You can come out now."

Daxx peaked around the corner. "All good now?"

I touched my head again. "Other than blood in my hair, I'm perfectly fine now."

She grinned. "Good. We found one."

I had completely forgotten. "Show me." Later, we'd have to figure out what the next steps were, but it was a good start to finding others so they wouldn't have to live through what I had.

Chapter Twenty-One

After a brief restless sleep, I transported to the landing room. Once I was certain I wasn't going to throw up, I opened my eyes to see Sith grinning at me.

"I wasn't sure if you remembered how to get to the dining room."

I returned his smile. "I had wondered what would happen if I took a wrong turn." I motioned to the door. "Lead the way." He started walking. "Are the others there?"

He shook his head. "Not yet. Most went to have a nap."

I watched, hoping to remember the way there for the next time. "I guess I've scrambled their sleeping habits."

He shrugged his large shoulders. "It's been like this since the illegal devices were discovered." He stopped so suddenly, I almost walked into him. He looked down at me with concerned eyes. "I wished I could go with you today."

"I as well. I am not relishing this in the slightest."

"The royals have a plan, and a few back up options, so you'll have assistance if you need it." He started walking again.

"That's comforting." I had a few ideas of my own, of course I needed Daxx, or someone more tech savvy before I knew if it was going to work. We walked into the room, the only one at the table was Chase.

"Good morning, duchess." He glanced at my head.

I touched where I'd hurt it. "It's fine." I went down to the other end of the table and picked up a cup filing it with coffee.

Rafael came in looking like he was half asleep. He paused and gave me a sleepy smile, then looked at my feet. "No heels today, sister?"

I looked down at my boots. "No, I'm going for functional today."

Chase chuckled. "You wear functional very well."

Setting the cup down, I place a foot on the edge of a chair and unzipped my boot. Pulling it open I revealed the handle of a dagger, tucked into a sheath made into the boot. I glanced to each male and smiled. "Functional." I zipped the boot back up and picked up my cup.

"It's amazing the human race has any males left to reproduce." Chase mused with a smirk.

"I was thinking the same, brother." Rafael nodded.

"That never ends well." Quinton said coming in the door. "You thinking, Raf." He winked at me. "Alona."

"Hello, Quinton." I sat down.

Mitz came out of the kitchen, smiling, as I'd come to know was her way. Even she looked tired. "I'm running a few minutes behind, but food is on the way."

Chase sat down across from me. "Everything okay, Mitz?"

She nodded. "Just fine, love, it's taking forever to find a plan we all agree with."

"Plans?" Daxx came in and yawned as she dropped into the first chair.

Mitz smiled at her. "For the ball, dear, to celebrate our kings' reign… it's the one hundred and sixtieth anniversary in a month."

"Wait." Daxx held up her hand. "Ball? Like gowns and all *that*?"

Chase had a huge grin on his face. Quinton coughed.

"Yes, love. It's still in the planning stage, of course, but with gowns." She smiled. "I'll be back in a moment." She walked into the kitchen.

Daxx glared at Chase. "I am *not* doing it again."

Troy and Michael walked in. "Doing what?" He asked his mate.

Rafael grinned. "Mitz just told Daxx about the anniversary ball."

"Oh." Troy looked at her, gauging her mood.

She shook her head. "I am not having a *fitting* and being squished into one of those contraptions again."

Troy poured his coffee, while nodding at her.

Michael smiled and sat down. "I'm sure if you explain it to Mitz, she'll understand."

"What?" Daxx frowned. "That's so not fair you guys." She looked down the table and pointed at me. "If I have to wear one of those bustier things again, you're coming too."

I looked around at the men and nodded slowly. "I have no problems with formal wear."

"Uh! Figures you're a girly girl." She sat back and crossed her arms.

"I'm sorry?" I offered her.

Leone came in looking like he hadn't slept at all. He glanced around. "What's wrong?"

Troy shook his head. "Just discussing the anniversary ball."

"Ugh. Is that close again? I hate those things."

"Yes!" Daxx patted the chair beside her. "*You* sit beside me."

Mitz came back in with a platter in each hand. "We were thinking crimson for the women this year, as we have women to put it on... and black for the men." She said not looking at anyone in particular.

"I'm sure whatever you decide is fine, Mitz."

She paused and gave Troy a loving, motherly look. "You know I enjoy these immensely."

He nodded.

She grinned excitedly than turned to walk out again.

"Crap." Daxx dropped her head on the table then raised her head, glaring at me. "What is crimson?"

I smirked. "It's a deep red hue."

"Guess that's better than peach. I'm not wearing peach." She mumbled and sat back again.

Crissy came in with Victor. "No, you're not. Your shirt is blue." She rolled her eyes and sat down.

"We were…" Troy began until Daxx reached over and covered his mouth.

"Not another word about it. Plans for today, that's all I want to hear." She glared at the men around the table. "As *Queen*, I demand this."

Victor actually looked at her with his mouth open. Snapping it closed, he gave a cautious look at his brothers. All of them were working hard not to smile.

Arius came in looking fresh and rested. "I just talked to Mitz, did you…"

"Sit." Daxx pointed to a chair. "Now."

Arius paused in mid-step and looked at Chase, without turning his head.

Chase gave his head a quick shake.

"Can I have coffee?" Arius asked pleadingly.

Daxx huffed out a breath. "Yes. You all suck!"

Chase lifted a finger, "I actually do *not*. But the rest of these fangers, are guilty."

Even I had to smile to that.

"Sleep deprivation is a bitch, huh?" Chase said glancing around at his siblings. "Welcome to my hell, boys and girls." He picked up his cup, raised it to me, and then took a sip.

"Let's just not discuss anything we'll need to remember for a few moments." Rafael around a yawn. "Let my brain and body synch up a bit."

Arius looked to me. "If we can come away today knowing what they're up to, it will be a successful mission."

"As long as not one hair on Alona's head is touched, it will be a success." Chase told him with a warning look.

Crissy leaned forward and looked around. "They must really want Alona, to have followed her this long."

"As far as recruiting goes, this Lou guy is an idiot." Leone said, rubbing a hand over his face in a distracted way. "Were you approached by anyone before him?"

I sipped my coffee and thought for a moment. "I was thinking about that when I couldn't sleep. I may have been but didn't realize it at the time."

"How so?" Chase

I waved a hand around. "It was creepy and random, but in hindsight it makes too much sense." Everyone turned to look at me, so I continued. "A sleaze propositioned me a few weeks ago. He said I was *just* what he was looking for, I thought he was talking about filming porn." I chuckled.

Every male in the room turned to look at me instantly. Except Crissy's uptight man. Which was good, or I'd have to stab him in the eye.

I rolled my eyes. "Down boys, I'm not a porn star, or anything close to that."

"Oh well, there goes my dream." Chase said quietly.

Daxx glared at Troy.

He lifted his hands. "You know once a male is mated he only wants his mate. I was more concerned about what they're really recruiting her for."

Daxx sighed and mumbled something that sounded like sorry.

"Wait... mated males *can't* cheat? If you could bottle that ladies, you would take the top slots on the list of the wealthiest women." I laughed.

"It's true." Leone nodded. "Except Dad, he could."

"Emil cleared that mystery up." Arius said glancing around.

Mitz came in with more platters and all the talk ceased while they heaped food on their plates. I sat there examining the two couples. Being mated meant they would never have to worry about fidelity. That was something I hadn't known.

It also explained why my mother and father hadn't moved forward well without each other.

I found Chase glancing in my direction every few seconds. It was unsettling, it made me constantly aware of his presence, a feeling I was sure was impossible for me to overlook, even if I wanted to.

"Okay, did we get people to all the islands last night?" Chase asked finally.

"Most." Arius answered. "Only one didn't allow us to get too far on, but we managed to land in several spots around it."

"Let's hope it's not that island then." Troy shrugged, "although, it most likely will be, now I said that."

"I may have another idea that I'm not certain will work, but we have time to test it." I said glancing to Daxx. "I did some *app* research last night and downloaded this," I took out my phone and opened it to the application I was still figuring it out. Sliding it toward her, I shrugged. "I'll find a way to use it."

The men near her, stood and looked over her shoulder as she checked it out. "I'll get it on my phone." She nodded and then smiled at me. "If it there's signal we can hear what's happening in real time."

I wasn't sure what in real time meant, but nodded. "It would make me feel more at ease, and then I wouldn't have to remember everything." I blew out a breath. "I would just like this to end. Soon."

"Amen to that, sister." Rafael nodded at me. "We'll run around the halls after we eat to check out the settings on that app."

"I had thought of another possibility." Victor paused and glanced around the table. "If Alona were somehow able to introduce Lou to another prospect, we may be able to get someone on the inside."

"Who do you have in mind?" Troy asked.

"Michael and I have been contemplating this for a few weeks now. We've gone through all the new guard applicants.

There is one that is relatively unknown around these chambers, she is from the other side of the wasteland…"

"A woman?" Leone frowned. "Is that…"

Victor held up his hand. "She has been screened thoroughly and passed each test through the process." He shrugged. "She is quite ruthless and doesn't appear… guard like."

"So, she's not the size of a mountain?" Daxx asked.

"Precisely. She is very *just* in her beliefs as well." He sat back and waited for comment.

I gave him a curious look. "I'm to what, just suggest this other woman?"

He shook his head. "Nothing as blatant as that. Perhaps mention you've seen another woman with red eyes at the club." He nodded to Michael. "My brother has been discussing with her a possible situation arising, and she is anxious to work for the cause of the realm. I have no trust issues, her male relatives have served the guard for many generations now."

I sat back. "I suppose that could work. I'll need her description, of course, to drop enough hints for Lou to be interested."

Victor gave an abrupt nod. "I'll arrange a brief meeting with her after we go over the rest of the plans."

"If we can get someone inside, it would stop us from chasing our tails." Quinton mused. "I'm tired of porting to discover we just missed them."

"As we all are, brother." Michael agreed.

"Has anyone heard from Emil?" Arius glanced around. "See if he found out where his son is?"

Chase sighed. "He still isn't sure. I talked to him last night, briefly." He motioned around the room. "He's still digesting all of this I believe."

I gave him a wide-eyed look. "Considering his age, I can vouch for the enormity of that task."

Chase nodded. "Three hundred years of not knowing adds weight to a man's soul."

"It must have been scary," Crissy said, "not understanding that long." She nodded. "I thought I was crazy not knowing what was wrong with me, and I'm not three hundred."

"Nothing was, or is, wrong with you, heart." Victor said softly.

She smiled at him. "We know that *now*."

"You wouldn't be you any other way, cutie." Chase winked at her.

"Thanks." She smiled and went back to eating.

After discussions of plans, backup plans, and plans within plans, and testing the application I'd downloaded, everyone finally went their separate ways.

Chase was the last one in the room with me, no coincidence there. He walked toward me slowly. "Sith will be back at your place before you leave." He stopped a few feet away and stood there with his hands in the back pocket of his jeans. "I spoke to the elders, and with more blood, they say I could trace to your location, if done right."

"You've never done it before?"

He shook his head. "Seems to be the year of firsts for me."

I thought about what he was suggesting. "While there's comfort in knowing you could do that if needed… I think the question is, should you? Just appearing in the middle of an unknown number of beings that aren't fond of you and your family …"

Chase gave me a blank look. "Oh sure, use logic against me."

I tried not to smile. "I think you're biased in this situation, so I have to be the voice of reason."

He gave me a wide grin. "I agree, doesn't mean I have to like it." Glancing around, he shrugged. "So, are you feeding here or at your place?"

"But I just…"

He held up hand. "You need to be at the top of your game in a few hours," he waved his hand to the table, "and we both know food isn't going to accomplish that."

I raised an eyebrow at him. "Now who is being logical?"

He smirked. "What goes round…"

"Fine." I almost laughed at the stunned look on his face that I'd agreed so quickly. Moving over, I touched his shoulder. "My place."

With a grin, he wrapped his arm around me and as fast as that we were standing by my door.

My stomach lurched and I regretted it. Keeping my eyes closed I stood there and breathed out a few careful breaths.

"Your body is getting used to it."

I opened my eyes and looked at him. "I won't miss this feeling if it never returns." When his arms loosened, I stepped away and went into the sitting room. "My nerves are on edge today." I stopped and looked down at the street.

"It's not too late to change your mind."

I didn't turn to look at him, but knew he was right behind me. "I need to do this. You need answers, and I do as well. I'd like to know why they want me, and I can't get rid of them if I know nothing."

"I'm surprised you didn't pack up and vanish when all this started."

Glancing at him, I shrugged. "I am as well. It's so unlike me to stick around when people are looking at me," I smiled, "or even if I'm paranoid they might be."

"Mmm, sounds like fate has its hold on you as well."

I looked to see his hazel eyes assessing me. "Does it have you?"

He sighed. "Fate has been grabbing at me since the day Daxx got her tattoo, only I didn't know it until recently."

"You don't sound happy about it." For whatever reason, I needed to know if he felt as trapped by this as I did. Some unknown force, we were labeling fate, had decided we were to be together. Period.

Slowly he looked me over, from my boots to the top of my head. "All I've wanted for close to two centuries, give or take a decade, was someone in *my* life that felt like… home. That feeling you have where it just feels right." He tilted his head and watched me. "While I have brothers to spare, I've never had that connection and I've always felt… lacking."

His answer surprised me. I couldn't think of a thing to say. I hadn't lived even half as long as he had, but had realized several decades ago, that emptiness was the worst feeling to have. It never went away, just lurked in the background all the time. The few times I thought it was gone, there it popped up again. I studied the man less than a pace from me. My assessment of him had been so far from the truth, I was speechless. *Just once*, I thought and stepped closer before I could change my mind.

Grasping his hair, I tilted his head and bit into his neck without warning.

Chase groaned and clutched the back of my head while wrapping his other arm tight around my waist.

Desire swamped me and I knew he did it on purpose, so I could feel how I affected him. Licking over the mark quickly, I pulled his head down to mine. As soon as our lips touched, he took over and kissed me with such passion, it robbed me of my breath.

He walked me backward, without breaking the kiss. As soon as the back of my legs touched the sofa, he lifted his head and turned, pulling me down to straddle his lap.

With his hands running up and down my legs, his yellow eyes held mine. I remembered what the girls had said. "Don't touch my hands." I held my breath waiting for his response.

He stared at my mouth for a moment. "I'll resist this never-ending urge to mark you."

That was close enough to a yes for me. Grasping his head with both hands, I leaned down and kissed him again. He ran his tongue over my still present fangs and groaned low in his throat. Squeezing my thighs, he pulled me tight into his body. I gasped and lifted my mouth from his.

Shoving my jacket down my shoulders, he pushed it down my arms as I shrugged out of it. He pushed my shirt up, then growled when the straps I wore to hold my dagger prevented him from moving it further. He fumbled with the straps, and I heard my dagger hit the floor with a clunk.

Grabbing my hips, he raised up and turned me so I was laying on the couch with my legs wrapped around him. Feeling his weight on me only heightened my desire to the point I thought I may catch fire.

He licked my mouth and stared into my eyes. "You are so beautiful—"

Someone coughed from across the room. Chase stiffened and blew out a quick breath.

I glanced around his shoulder to see Sith standing with his back to us, looking at my door.

"Leave." Chase growled.

"Stay." I said with a breathless voice. "I have to go soon," I whispered to the man with the yellow eyes looking down at me.

"Sith, go to another room for a moment." Chase said firmly without breaking eye contact with me.

"Yep." Sith answered.

Chase grasped my chin lightly. "I'm a patient man," he said with a rough voice. "Despite wanting you endlessly each day." He exhaled. "I won't mark you, *but* we are finishing this later." He kissed me roughly and released the emotions he'd been holding back.

My body went from a simmering that had started to cool upon Sith's arrival to such intense desire I thought there may actually be flames.

When he lifted his head, he gave me a serious look. "Nothing had better happen to you or no one will survive." Getting up, he pulled me to my feet and then straightened his clothes.

I rearranged my shirt and bent down to get my dagger and jacket.

"Sith." Chase said loudly.

As I put the straps back on for my dagger, Sith appeared at the end of the hallway.

"Sorry." He looked from me to Chase. "I came here when I had been told to."

Chase ran his hands through his hair and then looked back to me. "Transporter in your pocket, phone battery charged and tracker to turn on when you reach the island."

I nodded, all traces of desire being erased with nervous energy.

"This is your *last* outing with Lou, duchess, so make it count." He turned back to Sith. "Go do your puzzle or something." He said with an annoyed tone and then vanished.

Chapter Twenty-Two

I sat in the front of the little skiff as we traveled across the water. Lou and the man driving it were behind me. Moving just my eyes, I glanced down to the small tracker I'd hidden in my hand when we got on the boat. The tiny light was on. I planned to drop it on the shore when we reached the island.

I looked in the direction we were going, at this point it could be one of two of the islands, so that was not helpful. Turning, to look back at Lou, I smiled and then held my face up to the sun.

Suddenly, the boat tipped to the left and I had to reach out and grab the side to steady myself. A split second later, I realized I'd just dropped the tracker into the water. I couldn't very well say 'stop and go back I dropped my tracking device'. Chase was going to be a very unhappy man.

Snapping out of my internal dialogue, I looked around to see we were not going to either of the islands I had anticipated. With that turn, we could only be heading to the third and furthest away. Meaning, even if the tracker was working, where I'd dropped it wasn't going to help them figure out which island. If I wasn't mistaken, it was also the island they hadn't gotten a good location to transport to.

Taking Lou's hand, I stepped out onto the dock and then looked around the island. It was much taller than it had appeared on the map, then again, I didn't read topographical keys on a map well. Smiling at Lou, I walked off the dock to stand on the shore.

Hopefully my back up plan was more successful than the sunken tracker. "Uh." I pulled my phone out of my pocket as if it had rung. "Sorry, I thought I had it on mute." I checked and had a full signal. "Do you mind if I answer this? It's my associate and we're at a delicate phase in our project."

"Not at all." He smiled.

I tapped the screen for the app quickly as if I'd answered a call. Daxx answered. I didn't wait for her to speak. "I hadn't expected to hear from you so soon. Is it good news?"

"Tracker is a bust." She said quickly.

"Oh right." I sighed. "I figured we were sunk there." I smiled at Lou again. "So, what options do we have now?"

"The guys are freaking out. Tell me where you are."

I sighed again. "No. I don't think plan A is feasible at this time."

"Got it. Not island A."

I nodded. "Oh, that sounds much better, let's go with the last one."

"Island C it is and are you okay so far?"

I smiled. "Just lovely. I'll talk to you as soon as I get back, and you can update me with everything you hear in the meantime."

"Reception is good. Turn off your speaker and Chase says don't dawdle."

"Perfect. Talk soon." I tapped the speaker button on the app and then locked the screen on my phone. Tucking it back into my pocket, I looked to Lou. "Sorry about that."

He shrugged. "No problem. Is this a lucrative project?" He motioned to the stairs a short way down the beach.

"It's early to get too excited by it, but I have a feeling if it plays out as I hope it does, many people are going to be quite happy." I gave him a beaming grin. "Of course, the other side, our competition, won't be pleased when we beat them at their own game." I paused as we reached the stairs. "My goodness, are we walking up *all* these stairs? If I'd known, I would have worn jogging shoes." I was trying the best I could to explain the lay of the land to the brothers I knew were listening in.

Lou laughed. "No. About a quarter of the way up there's a small house. Used to be the caretaker's home. We'll meet the others there today."

I looked up to the top again. "Ah, so the top is members only?" I smiled at him.

"Exactly." He started going up the steps and looked back as I followed. "Not to worry though, there's a trail, and we use golf carts when you are allowed at the top."

"My legs will thank you for that I'm sure." With his robust figure, he was taking the stairs slowly. "I'm positively buzzing here, Lou, to finally know why I've be so vigorously pursued to be included in this, and to meet others like I am."

He stopped and turned. "I've only just recently found out why Marcus wanted you, but I'm pleased it is you, Isabell."

"Oh? That's intriguing. This Marcus is he still…"

Lou nodded. "Yes, but not for much longer now."

We started climbing the steps again. "Oh, I thought he'd been detained or something?"

He moved slowly enough that I had no problems keeping up with him allowing the others to hear what he said.

"He is. He'll be released soon, a few weeks tops."

I kept my eyes on my feet. "I look forward to meeting the man that is responsible for me discovering I'm not alone."

Lou huffed out a breath, obviously not happy to be climbing the stairs. "Shortly, you'll understand so much more."

I smiled. "I can't wait." I paused. "Are we almost there? In a hundred or less steps?" I laughed. "I'm in worse shape than I thought."

"A minute more." He said, breathless.

I paused and turned. "Oh, I can't even see the beach from here." Turning back, I caught up to him. "I hope your members-only clubhouse is well guarded." I laughed, "Or any one with nefarious intentions... and in good shape could sneak right up here."

"We have an invisible security fence, so to speak, but yes, they'd need to get up the stairs first."

"It's a brilliant plan, exhaust them with these stairs before they reach you."

Lou laughed, but made no comment. A few steps later he turned. "Here we go." He motioned to the path beside the stairs.

I smiled and stepped off the wooden step. "I wouldn't want to find this in the dark. I didn't even see it until you stopped."

He grinned. "You get used to knowing where to look."

"It's so quiet here, I may have to buy an island. This is much better than those musty tunnels, Lou."

"I agree with that. I hate those tunnels, but they're necessary for the lower ranks."

"Well then, if this is something that's for me, I plan to advance in the ranks *very* fast to avoid any more tunnel time." I joked.

"Isabell, we would never put you in the tunnels. None of the women need go down there unless it's for a meeting or some other task."

"That's a relief." I smiled at him again, all while wondering where the women were, if not in the tunnels with the rest of their army.

We reached an opening in the trees and a small little house was there. "Oh, it's like a cute little cottage." I walked beside him.

"We don't use it much, except for meetings like today."

I nodded, too busy looking around so I could remember the layout. I spotted the trail and a few golf carts. There were no guards here, so I had to wonder about the invisible security.

When we stepped inside, my heart was in my throat. A thought that I should have considered before ever speaking to Lou that first time popped up. What if someone here was an empath like I was, and they could sense what I felt? Nerves would be normal in situations like this... I hoped.

"I must confess, I'm both nervous and excited all at once." I said as I followed him into a sitting room.

A sitting room with six other people filling the small space.

"Nervous energy is perfectly normal in a situation like this. In fact, if you weren't, I'd be a bit cautious about speaking to you." A woman with long red hair said, from where she leaned against the wall. She motioned to the only empty chair. "Please have a seat."

I sat down.

She smiled, "I'm Eunice. Very pleased to finally meet you, Isabell."

"Hello, Eunice. Thank you." I tried to sound happy to be here, even though I was anything but.

I watched Lou go stand to the side, and knew I had been correct, and he was very low on the totem pole in this group.

A tall man with curly brown hair bowed his head in a polite manner. "Miss..."

"Oh, Isabell is fine."

"Isabell, I'm Lonnie. I'll make the introductions." He motioned to a dark-haired man that could rival Victor's cold, icy stares. "This is Nelson and his mate Leila."

The woman with the short, brush cut, blue hair gave me a warm smile.

I returned it.

"I believe you've met Davis before."

I turned to the man from the tunnels. "Hello again."

Lonnie waited until I looked back to him before he made a grand gesture with his hand to an older looking man, siting in the centre of all of them. He came off as very grandiose and rigid, with the posture he held. "This is Mister Hubert. Willis Hubert, for all intents and purposes, is the *true* king."

"A king, oh my." I smiled politely and made a small scene of bowing my head lower in a respectful manner. I looked around to all of them and decided other than the 'true king' and the blue haired one, they all looked like businesspeople, not warriors. "I don't want to come off as rude, but if Mister Hubert is the true king, I need to ask... king of what?"

Chase wasn't the only one that wanted this to be my last outing with Lou, so I needed as much information as possible, even as it meant acting like a completely clueless woman to get them to tell me more.

Mister Hubert waved his hand at Nelson when he made a sound of annoyance. "It's fine, Nelson, she doesn't know any better. You need to remember she was born to this side with no knowledge or guidance, just as Lonnie and Leila were."

"This side of the river?" I asked. "No, I wasn't born in the city I was..."

Leila held up her hand, a patient look on her face. "We'll get to that, dear."

"Your eyes seem so familiar." Nelson said giving me a critical stare. He glanced to Davis. "Where is Levi?"

I held my breath at the mention of my father.

Davis gave him a scowl and shook his head quickly.

"We'll come back to that." Mister Hubert motioned to me. "Have you met others like yourself, before today?"

I leaned forward. "How would I know?" I didn't want to flat out lie in case one of them could sense it, so I decided avoiding the answer would be best. "I mean, is there a way to tell without eyes changing color? Which reminds me, I've seen a few different colors since Lou has shown me around. Does the color denote different things?"

Mister Hubert nodded slowly. "Yes. You're an essence feeder, but there are emotion feeders and a few others."

"Emotions? That's..." I waved my hand around. "I don't know what to say to that." I shook my head. "It's all very hard to grasp when you find out you're suddenly not the oldest and most unusual being in a room."

A few of them chuckled.

"Yes, I suppose it is." Mister Hubert said quietly.

"I have about a hundred questions, if I'm being honest. I don't even know where to start." I gave them all a wide-eyed look.

"We have no problem answering questions." Eunice told me.

"You may regret saying that." I told her with a huge smile on my face.

Davis was studying me with a peculiar look on his face. "Before we get too far into this, I must ask if you were given something extra."

I looked from his to the others and back to him again. "Something extra?"

He nodded. "Some are given additional abilities."

I opened my mouth and then paused for a moment, trying to appear confused. "Like x-ray vision and leaping buildings in a single bound? I don't think I have anything like that." I smirked.

They continued to look at me for a few long, tense moments, at least it was tense on my end.

"I'm going to give you a bit of history which perhaps will clear up some questions." Mister Hubert said.

"Yes, that would be lovely."

He spoke so softly, I had to really listen to hear him. I wondered if the phone would pick up what he said.

"Since the beginning of existence there has always been a realm, parallel to this world we're in…"

I sat there wide-eyed, trying to look both shocked in and interested. Neither were hard, as there was still so much I didn't understand. "That's…" I shook my head, "please continue."

"We'll get into family trees and thousands of years of detail at another time."

I nodded.

"Those from our realm cross over to here when allowed. The royal family, who are imposters, like to dictate who can do what, *but,* sometimes the results of the travel are relationships being formed."

I held up my hand. "Am I a child from one of those relationships?"

"Yes, dear, you are." Eunice answered. "For millennia, our kind have left behind children, mostly because they didn't know they existed."

"So… all those from this other side are like me?"

"Most are, we do have humans over there as well. Those that didn't fit into society's norms dictated for them."

"Oh." I blew out a breath. "In all the years, I tried to imagine why I was as I am, I can honestly say this was not one of the possibilities. That being said, it feels… right." I glanced around. "Is there a gate or portal or something? I mean wouldn't that be hard to hide from discovery?"

"There's no gate, not that the eye can see." Davis answered. "But we have discovered a way to open it so anyone can come and go."

I gave him a shocked look. "That would be quite the vacation destination. I'm going to another realm for two weeks." I nodded, a smirk on my face.

"As here would be as well." Nelson stated.

I sat back. "None of this is close, at all, to why I thought I was the way I am."

Lonnie chuckled. "It does take some digesting."

"Yes. So," I motioned to Lou, "he said there were many for *the cause,* would that be working to free others or open this for all, yes?"

"That's exactly it." Eunice nodded. "There are… complications, but you have the gist of it."

"Complications?"

"Mmm, yes, the royal family isn't very receptive to losing their realm of servants." Mister Hubert said looking very angry.

"Servants?" I looked to the others. "Like housekeepers or are we talking slaves?"

"We're talking servitude." Mister Hubert said with a sneer.

I put my hand over my mouth for a moment. "That's not right." My mind was going a hundred miles a second. I hadn't seen much of the Alterealm, but I knew enough that those I'd met or seen were not being held in slavery. If that were the case, the brothers wouldn't be going into battle personally, they'd be sending others. Even their guards, like Sith, had no problem with their life. I'd think a royal guard would know if things were bad.

I realized they were all watching me. I turned to Lou. "It makes sense now, why you travel in tunnels to stay out of sight."

He nodded, looking pleased I'd included him in the discussion.

I turned back to Mister Hubert. "I think it's noble, trying to free the people." I nodded. "I still don't understand how I can possibly be important enough to warrant the special attention."

"At first, we weren't sure why Marcus thought you important to chase after as we have been," Lonnie said glancing to their leader and waiting until he nodded before continuing, "aside from being a female born to a human mother, that is."

My eyes went wide, with real shock. "That's—that's important?"

Leila gave me a soft smile. "Those like you and I can have children without being mated."

"Excuse me?" My heart was now in my throat.

"We don't force women to have children, Isabell, just encourage it." Eunice stated like it was something not serious.

"I don't understand."

Eunice glanced to the others for a moment. "Those of us born to two parents from the realm cannot have children unless we find our true mate. As you can imagine, it is a very long and lonely existence."

I gave a half nod, so many other pieces in my head clicking into place, like why eight brothers, as old as they were, had no families.

"We encourage the half-bloods to meet as many of our warriors as possible, just in case a match is made." Lonnie said matter of factly.

"Oh. I see." I answered quietly. "But that isn't the only reason I'm here?" I shrugged. "I've never even considered children, the fact that I could outlive them was heartbreaking."

Leila nodded. "I felt the same way." She smiled at Nelson, "but that's not a problem now."

Something felt so off, there was a few spikes of emotion to what had otherwise been an emotional void to this point. The women weren't kept in the tunnels, but children had been. Where were the women? My guts were tied in knots, and intuition told me if a female without having abilities they needed for their cause wouldn't be given a choice in parenthood. I didn't know if I was right, but my instincts had kept me safe for decades, so I trusted them.

"Perhaps telling Isabell she is here for more than being a broodmare will help put her more at ease." Davis suggested.

I gave him a thankful look.

Mister Hubert nodded to Davis who then started to talk. "For now, we're only in this area, to go further and expand our quest on a larger scale, which will take complex technology we haven't perfected yet."

"This opening of the gate?" I clarified.

He nodded. "Yes. We have research labs set up and trials being run, but all of that is time consuming and costly." Davis glanced to Mister Hubert briefly. "Marcus, said you were the one we needed, to help in that area."

"I hope you mean raising money, because a science professor I am not." I said with a smirk.

He smiled. "Yes. It seems your knowledge in that area is far superior then ours."

An uneasiness filled me. How did they know I was good at investments? That wasn't something anyone should be able to find out.

"She's just started a new project recently." Lou added.

I turned and smiled at his attempt to be in the conversation. "That one is too soon to know, and unfortunately wouldn't be a sound investment for your *cause* at all." In fact, it will be the end of your insanity, I thought. I turned to see the others were all looking at me. "I could take a look as what you're doing now and see... I-I suppose." I frowned. "I'm also going to be going on a short trip to look into some other possible investment opportunities, I have no problem suggesting you as key investors if they're sound." It was the only thing I could think of to drop the hint I was not going to be visiting the island every day. Today would be my only visit here, and the last time I would see any of these people, if I had my way.

Everyone watched Mister Hubert for a moment as he considered what I'd said. "Can you work with my people over the phone? The risk of someone discovering our location is too great if we're escorting you to and fro."

I nodded. "Or by email is fine too, if I'm out of reception." Which I planned on being forever, as far as they were concerned.

He nodded slowly. "I need to think about this. I trust Marcus in his assessment, but as he's not here to clarify his judgement, I do not want to take further risk." He gave me a brief smile. "No offence to you."

I nodded. "None taken. A wise business decision. Lou said Marcus would be back soon."

Davis nodded. "Yes, he will be."

"Lou knows how to reach me." I offered.

"I hope you'll consider meeting with us and the others again, Isabell." Lonnie gave me a very appraising look, leaning closer to a leer.

I smiled. "I think I would like that." I waved my hand around, going for overwhelmed in my actions. "I just need to *absorb* the fact I'm not alone, I think. It's very... overwhelming." I nodded. "Perhaps when I return from my trip."

"You're leaving soon?" Eunice inquired.

I nodded again. "Yes. I will know more about that when I get back today. I'm not fond of traveling, it always makes my stomach very upset, but I am anxious to get there and speak to my associates." That was more for the purpose of those listening in. If that didn't tell them I needed to get out of here soon, I didn't know what else I could say. "Maybe when I get back we can arrange a meet and greet or something. I'm just... wow, I'm not alone." I laughed giddily.

Leila laughed with me. "I was where you are now six months ago. You're going to be so happy when you do absorb it all."

I sighed. "I can't wait."

"Please let us know if you see any others like us." Lonnie nodding.

"Oh. Oh, that reminds me." I turned to Lou. "I meant to tell you, then got distracted with a boat ride. That club, where we met. There was a woman there, she was alone and I swear her eyes turned red." I shook my head. "I know sometimes it's hard not to, but she may be someone that is as unaware as I am."

Lou nodded. "Most that go to places like that are alone." He smirked. "As you know. Give me a description and we'll watch for her."

I smiled. "Maybe not chase after her, so she runs the other way." I laughed. "As I did the first time."

He chuckled. "Yes, that could have been handled better."

I nodded.

"Well, my dear, we have to get going, but we will be in touch with you in the next day or so to discuss those investments." Eunice glanced to Mister Hubert who nodded.

I stood up. "Yes. Absolutely." I put a hand on my chest and huffed out a breath. "I can't even tell you how I feel meeting all of you." It was the complete truth. If I told them it wouldn't go over well.

"I'll show you back down to the beach." Lou motioned to the door.

"Yes." I looked to the others. "I will see you all soon." I smiled.

Chapter Twenty-Three

The second the boat docked back in the harbor I jumped out and headed as quickly as possible to the nearest location I could disappear.   As I reached the corner of the small diner, someone grabbed me and pulled me around the corner. It was Rafael. I almost jumped into his arms. "Get me out of here." I hissed.

He grabbed me and hugged me against him. My stomach lurched and I knew we weren't on the docks now. I opened my eyes to see we were in the huge dining room. I looked at Rafael, as I blew out a breath to wait out the nausea. "I need wine. Now."

He nodded and went into the kitchen.

I had just sat when the others came through the opposite door. I stood up again. "Tell me you heard all of that."

Daxx nodded, not looking pleased at all.

I closed my eyes and sighed loud. "Good, because I am not going back to meet with those people." I opened my eyes and Chase was in front of me. It was so completely not me to encourage close contact, but I stepped in and hugged him. I just needed a moment of warmth and safety. And now, he represented safe—I'd think about the many other ways he was a danger to me, making me crave things I shouldn't give into, later.

He wrapped his arms around me. "Are you all right?" He ran his hand down my back. "I couldn't get a good sense of how you were through the bond from that distance."

I nodded. "There were barely any emotions at all."

"Not surprising." Troy said from behind me. "We know a few of those you met and they'd be emotionless through and through."

Releasing Chase, I turned but remained close to him. "There was one spike I picked up and then I just wanted to get the hell out of there."

Arius gave me a curious glance.

"The women," I glanced up at Chase, "those with lesser value, I don't think they're being given options on mating or reproducing." His brows furrowed. "None of the women are in the tunnels, but they had children down there..." I glanced around quickly, "so where are the women?"

"Holy shit." Daxx said and glanced to the others. "Other than the first few battles, we haven't seen a female since—only that witch with the light up stick."

Troy hugged her into his side and gave his twin a serious look. "She's right."

I turned back to Chase. "Who is that Willis Hubert person?"

Chase sighed and rubbed the back of his neck. "A delusional moron who swears our ancestors cheated in securing the throne." He gave his head a quick shake. "I honestly thought he'd died and would never bother us again."

Rafael came back with the glass of wine. I reached out and took it when he was close enough and took a gulp of it. Looking around, I focused on Victor. "Tell me what they're attempting to do is impossible, regardless of the money they have." I shook my head. "They're talking about combining this realm and the other into one, no boundaries, no controlling who should and should not be free, roaming among the human populous."

"I don't think it is possible." Victor said then looked to Michael. "But we need to find out."

"We need to do something else too." Troy said quietly.

"What?" Daxx looked up at him.

"We have to call an elders' council meeting." He said looking at Chase.

"Fuck. Can I bow out of that now?" Chase asked.

Troy snorted. "No. You are the only one that can shut up elder Roan, or we'll spend hours listening to how that was *then* and how poorly society has become."

"There's a council of elders?" Daxx looked from Chase to her mate. "When you guys say, 'I spoke to the elders' I thought it meant you called a mentor or something."

Troy shrugged. "We do speak to one or two from time to time, but yes there is a council of them."

"How many?"

"Twelve." Chase sighed and slumped his shoulders. "And they'll sit there the entire time and look at you like you're a bug or close to it, studying you as if they can see into your very soul."

Troy nodded. "They need to know what Willis is up to."

"How old is he?" I asked, not understanding the rest. "He's the first I've seen that actually *looks* old."

Victor frowned. "He's much older than I am. He could probably *be* an elder by now if he wasn't a lunatic."

"How old are the elders?" Crissy asked.

"You aren't even considered eligible for the council until you've reached ten centuries." Victor told her.

"A thousand years old?" Daxx gave him a surprised look. "And there's twelve of them?"

Victor nodded slowly. "Many have been on the council as long as I've been around as well."

Daxx blew out a breath. "So, I guess that's why they know so much?"

Crissy smiled. "And then they go on to watch over the library with the man that's not a man but many." She nodded.

I looked at her for a moment and decided I didn't need to know what she was talking about right now. Raising my glass to them I took a sip and then moved to sit down.

"We all need to go." Chase said looking from Victor to Troy. "All the royals. This is beyond a few illegal transporters and rogue mages."

"All of us?" Quinton frowned. "Like *all*, all of us?"

Troy nodded. "He's right *all* of us." He looked around at the others. "You'll need to wear your amulets."

I turned back to my wine.

"That includes you too, duchess."

I gave Chase a startled look.

He shrugged. "We need you in on this, and the only way through those doors is wearing a royal amulet."

"I'm not a royal." I reminded him.

He grinned. "You are, you just don't know it yet." With a wink, he turned back to Troy. "Call the meeting. I'm going to go have a stiff drink before we do this." He leaned down, his hazel eyes locked on mine. "Later we're going to discuss you putting yourself in the middle of a room of lunatics."

I raised an eyebrow, "and I'm not in a similar situation this very moment?"

"Sassy." He tucked his hands into his pockets and walked into the kitchen.

"Wait for me, brother." Arius practically ran after him.

I glanced to Daxx. "So, this sounds like a really *fun thing* that we're about to do."

She grimaced. "Yeah, like the dentist, from the sound of it."

"I don't like the dentist." Crissy said looking unhappy.

"None of us do, Criss, it's just one of those things you have to do."

"I would like to see them before they're part of the guardian of the prophecies though." She nodded looking excited.

"Can't wait." I mumbled and took another drink.

An hour later, the eleven of us were going down an endless hallway to the council chamber. I put Chase's

243

pendant back on, as all the others wore one, and I was curious to see beings as old as these council members.

Crissy was pleased she had a pendant, which was a smaller version of Victor's and not surprisingly had a sun, moon, and small scales of justice. Each man seemed to have their own symbol with the sun and moon, but unless I walked among them and stared at their chests, I hadn't seen more than a few of them before.

I leaned down to whisper to Daxx. "Maybe I missed the part where they explained why we are going to this council?"

She shook her head. "No. It wasn't explained."

"They're like the collective brain pan of literally thousands of years' worth of knowledge." Quinton said from behind us, "we need to know if what Willis is trying to do can be done, and they're going to want to know he's back."

"Because he was thought to be dead?" I slowed to walk beside him.

"That and every uprising, or war, we've had in the last thousand years there was a member of his family in the forefront."

"Ah, so this Marcus isn't the leader."

Quinton shook his head. "No. He's the main cause of many of the problems we've had tracking them. Somehow Willis hooked up with him, and got to him to believe his crap. I'm guessing together their broken minds came up with this new *take over the world* scheme."

"It's usually just trying to take over this realm." Michael said over his shoulder.

"If it was just here, it would be a hell of a lot easier to catch him." Daxx said with a thoughtful tone.

I glanced to the front of the group to see the twin kings walking together, speaking quietly. "So, is there a protocol to be followed with this council?"

Quinton shrugged. "Technically we're higher on the food chain then they are…"

"But they do warrant a certain degree of respect, considering their ages and status." Michael finished.

"Someone sit near me that knows their names." Rafael said looking around. "If I have to address one of them, I never know the name."

"They all start with elder, if that helps." Leone patted him on the shoulder. "I'll sit next to you, just nudge me if I do that blank out thing. Sitting with them staring at me is worse than fifth grade when the teacher asked a question and you were too busy zoning out to pay attention."

"Then don't sit near Chase or Troy, and they won't even notice you're there." Arius said in passing as he went to speak to the kings.

"I hope they don't ask me anything." Crissy said, a worried look on her face. "I have too many answers."

"That's still better than having none, because you have a voices in your head distracting you." Leone complained.

She grinned. "No voices, just pictures."

Everyone stopped walking and stood there. I looked to see the kings waiting by a large door. Troy held out his hand to Daxx, she went to him and took it. Chase turned to me and did the same. Hesitantly, I took it.

"The four of us sit first." Troy said turning back to the door.

I expected more instruction, but instead Chase opened the door and we walked into a large chamber. It consisted of two long tables. One with twelve undecorated wooden chairs and the second had at least twenty chairs, adorned with suns and moons.

Chase led me to one of the center chairs and motioned for me to sit down. After sitting, I glanced to see Troy and Daxx sit beside us. The kings next to one another. The others stood in front of their chairs.

The fact that Chase continued to hold my hand under the table lead me to believe he didn't want to be here at all, or he was holding onto me so I couldn't run, I wasn't sure which.

A door on the opposite side opened and the elders filed through it. They all looked older, but I wouldn't have said any looked near to a thousand, although I had no reference to be certain. Most had white hair and wore unadorned black robes.

"I feel like I'm in a sci-fi movie." Daxx whispered.

I bit my lip so I wouldn't grin.

"Should have worn long sleeves, brother." Troy said turning to look at him.

Chase gave him a curious look, but didn't say anything.

Once the twelve were in front of their chairs, they bowed in a slow, formal manner. As they were raising their heads to sit, the rest of the brothers sat down.

A woman with a long white braid seated at the center of the elders smiled. "Your majesties." She bowed her head again. "It is an honor to be here." Her blue eyes moved over the eleven of us. "It has been over one hundred years since a formal council was called." I noted she looked at Quinton when she said that. She nodded her head abruptly to him, and then looked back to the kings.

"Thank you for assembling so quickly, Elder Varus." Troy said in a regal tone.

She smiled. "We were very pleased to do so."

"Tell us, Night King, what is so dire that we had to assemble without notice?" A man with squinty brown eyes and very thin grey hair said loudly. "As you can see, we stopped to attire ourselves according to tradition, I see you did not."

Troy glanced to Chase, who sat forward.

"We didn't waste time getting our formal wear out, Elder Roan, the things we have just discovered were too important to wait." Chase told him, looking bored.

"I see." Elder Roan appraising him and then glanced to me, squinting further. "Perhaps my eyes are failing me, which can happen at my age, Day King, but I don't see your mate's mark and yet you have a woman at your side wearing the Queen of Light's pendant."

I turned to look at Chase, not so much waiting for an answer, but the *Queen* part was something I hadn't been informed of in all of this mate talk.

"Told you to wear long sleeves." Troy whispered.

Chase looked to him. "Would have been nice if you'd said *why*." He said in a hushed tone. Clearing his throat, he looked back to Elder Roan. "I realize it is breaking tradition to give the pendant before the mark," He looked down the table at the other elders, "it couldn't be helped, as my mate had been approached by Marcus's followers and has been getting information for us." He waved his hand in a carefree way. "Had she born my mark, this would not have been possible."

Elder Roan sat back and glanced to those sitting near him. "Are you certain that she is your only true mate?"

Chase sneered at him. "As certain as I am that I hope to *die* in battle at the age of nine hundred and ninety-nine, so I'm never called to sit where you are."

Troy smirked and then gave his brother a wide-eyed look.

I just looked at the table, not sure what the reaction was going to be with Chase, more or less, telling him to get stuffed.

A man with white streaks through his dark hair frowned. "Is it wise to put your mate into such a dangerous position?"

Chase took a deep breath and exhaled slowly.

Before he could reply, the woman at the end with white hair spiked in a brush cut, spoke. "Elder Moire, do you really believe the prophecy would have spoken of meek women that needed coddling as the mates to the royal brothers?" She snorted. "Perhaps your old memory is failing you, but the female warriors in our history have always been, and will always be, the true strength of Alterealm."

Chase and Troy put their heads down, probably to hide the grins on their faces.

"I wasn't suggesting the queen was meek, Elder Drusla. I was just taken back that such chances would be taken." He sat back looking much like a chastised child.

Chase cleared his throat. "I can assure you every precaution possible was taken to ensure her safety."

Elder Drusla gave an abrupt nod and sat back. There was no doubt in my mind, with the way she held herself, she was a woman that had seen many battles in her time.

The man with long wavy grey hair and pale green eyes held up his hand and leaned forward. "I really *must* ask," he looked to me with an anxious expression, "we have spent hundreds, too many hundreds, of years trying to solve the mystery of the second twin king's prophecy." He smiled at me. "You have an ability. What is it my queen, if I may be so bold to ask?"

I glanced to Chase, he gave me a nod and whispered. "Elder Nodin."

I looked back to the man and offered an awkward smile. "I am an empath, Elder Nodin."

"Ah." He threw up his hands and glanced down the table to the woman with the spiked hair. "Of course, it all makes sense now."

"Perhaps we could get to the point of the meeting. I'm sure the royal family did not call it to settle bets and clear up queries." The man seated next to the woman with the long braid said. His white hair was pulled back tightly, his face appeared to be etched and emotionless, his dark eyes cold. Turning, he glanced to Victor and it became clear that the two were connected.

"Elder Segos," Victor said loudly, "there are many reasons this meeting was called today. To start, we have discovered who is truly behind the illegal devices and the challenges we have been facing."

"Please continue, Justice." He said inclining his head.

Victor glanced to his king brothers, both gave him a slight nod.

"Alona," he looked to me, "our Queen of Light, was able to obtain a meeting with the key members of this mad scheme."

"Marcus was not the perpetrator?" Elder Segos asked.

"While he was involved at the highest level, he was not at the head of it." Victor said in a low tone.

"Are these members known to us?" Elder Varus asked, her blue eyes wide.

"I'm afraid most of them are." Arius said quietly. "We knew there had to be more, when they continued to elude us after we took Marcus and the witch into custody."

"You were able to get information from Marcus?" A man that seemed to be the youngest at the table asked. His hair was still brown and eyes gentle.

"I was not, Elder Landry." Arius told him.

"Who are the others?" Elder Nodin asked, leaning forward on the table in front of him.

Troy cleared his throat. "Willis Hubert seems to be at the head of it all."

The shock on their faces was clear, all twelve of them.

"As well as the mage Davis, Nelson and his sister Eunice." Troy finished.

"Him... again." A woman with fading red hair said. "We had hoped in all these years he had crawled under a rock somewhere and expired." She said venomously. "Nelson and Eunice have always been right on his heels." She looked down the table at another woman who hadn't spoken yet. Her eyes were a washed out grey, almost appearing white. "You couldn't see this coming, Elder Faran?"

The woman turned and looked at her slowly. "No, Elder Udela, I'm afraid it doesn't come with a channel guide that I can just tune into." She turned and looked to Crissy. "As I'm sure our Seer of Truth can attest to, visions come when they're ready, not when you want them to."

Crissy nodded. "I wished they came with a guide." She sighed, "Or at least instructions."

Elder Faran gave her a soft look. "Your burden is much greater than mine, as I only see select events to come, but I have no doubt you can bear the weight of it."

Crissy glanced to Victor and then back to her and nodded. I was shocked that was all she was going to say.

"Do we know what Willis is trying to accomplish? I'm presuming the illegal devices was not the overall objective."

A man with black and white hair and eyes almost blacks asked.

"We do, Elder Marinus." Michael answered. "They are planning to bring down the barrier between our realms. What we need to know is, if that is possible."

All of the elders turned and talked to one another, no longer sitting motionless. I glanced to Chase and then Troy, both looked concerned, and weren't taking their eyes off the elders as they waited for the answer. My heart was beating faster in my chest, I may not understand the complexities of this barrier, but knew enough to understand it was the worst possible scenario.

Chase took a hold of my hand under the table again, and brushed his thumb back and forth in a soothing manner. Even while focused on all that was happening, he still noticed when I was stressed. Of course, we were going to be discussing this Queen of Light nonsense, just as soon as we found out if the world needed to be saved from maniacal lunatics.

He leaned closer to me. "You can stab me later for being a bad boy, again."

I turned to see him smirking at me. "You can count on it, your majesty." I whispered back.

The elders quieted again as the woman seated near the end held up her hand. She had white, curly hair and just looking at her, I knew she was a science person. All she lacked was a pair of glasses and a pocket protector to fit the stereotype of geek.

"While I'm not one hundred percent certain the entire barrier could be taken down, even if they managed a portion of it, the result would be chaos... for both realms."

"Do you know what they would need to do this, Elder Arian?" Quinton asked.

She shook her head, "No, Captain, I don't know the precise list of items needed to do it, but I can find out." Looking down the table of royals, she cocked her head to the side. "What was said to lead you to believe this is what they are intending to do?" She shrugged. "It may assist me in my conclusions."

Chase sat forward again. "When my *Queen* was speaking with them, they said they'd discovered a way to open the barrier so anyone can come and go." He looked to me briefly, "that it would take complex technology, and they have research labs set up and are doing trial runs."

Elder Arian nodded her head slowly. "So, they have started trials already." She shook her head. "That's not a good sign, they may have found a method to make it possible."

"Elder Arian, my expertise isn't science, but even I understand that this method would, more than likely, be quite violent and intrusive." The only elder that hadn't spoken said. His pale brown eyes were showing concern.

"You are correct, Elder John, there would be casualties on both sides," she held up her hand as if she were pausing to think, "I'm not certain on the radius, but it would take a great force and any in that area would be gravely injured, or killed."

"Do we know where this place is? Where they'd have to blow a hole?" Rafael asked to no particular elder.

Elder Arian shook her head. "Any number of areas could be plausible." She paused for a moment. "The barrier isn't a physical *barrier*, so to speak. It's a presence of sorts, and the exact workings of it are too complex to explain in a brief meeting."

"Not to mention, we'd all fall asleep while she explained it." Elder Drusla said with a smirk.

Ignoring her comment, Elder Arian continued. "I will speak to the scholars once this council has ended, and find out if I can bring back any useful information."

"Thank you, Elder Arian." Elder Varus said then looked to Troy and Chase. "There's more?" Her brows were furrowed together.

Troy inclined his head. "There is." He glanced to Chase, like he wasn't sure what to tell them next.

"With some other facts my mate found, we've come to a realization." Chase said, giving my hand a squeeze under the table. "There was talk of those women born to the other side, with one parent from our realm..." He turned and looked at me, uncertainty on his face.

I realized he wasn't sure how to explain it. I turned and looked at the elder I believed was in charge. "Elder Varus, it was plainly suggested that once I joined their ranks in this ludicrous quest, that I meet as many males as possible from Alterealm, with the end goal of procreation, as they've realized those with one human parent can breed with someone other than their true mate." I cleared my throat, feeling a bit nervy speaking to them. "I caught a spike in emotions during this conversation that leads me to believe the women, not as useful as myself would not be given as much leniency or freedom of choice in *mating* with someone."

"We haven't seen any women during any of the skirmishes since the first one, either." Daxx added, backing me up.

"I seen a baby... in my head, before Alona was found." Crissy said suddenly. "I thought it might have been her, because her father didn't know she existed... but the aura around it... I know now, was all wrong for that." She nodded.

I looked back to see most of the elders seemed to understand what she said. I clearly had some Crissy speak to learn.

Elder Varus glanced to Chase. "When we spoke last, you said their numbers were three hundred or more?"

Chase nodded.

"Do we know how many of these are woman, such as your mate?" She asked him.

He shook his head. "We do not."

I sat forward. "Regardless of being born to one human parent... I believe even just human women will be at risk in this faction of... lunatics."

"I tend to agree with the Queen of Light." Elder Udela said quietly. "The very suggestion of this transpiring is barbaric, and must be dealt with."

"Yes, Elder Udela, we can all agree on that, but the question remains… how?" Elder Faran inquired.

"Alona…" Michael glanced to me, "has set up a project to find more lost to the other side, like herself." He paused. "So, we can find them before Willis does."

"Do you see this working?" Elder Roan asked, the scepticism clear in his tone.

"We already found one." Crissy said quickly. "I'm just working on finding out who they are now." She nodded. "Like I did with Emil, who went through many names in three hundred years."

"I was a little disappointed your lost brother wasn't with you today." The soft-spoken Elder Landry said.

Troy cleared his throat. "He is still adjusting to the fact that nothing he knew was all of the truth."

"He's had children?" Elder Faran asked.

Troy nodded slowly. "Yes, three of the five have lived beyond a human lifespan, Elder Faran."

"They will need to be found." She stated with no further explanation.

"Are you planning to just bring all you find to Alterealm? Without knowing them?" Elder Segos queried in a cold tone.

"Not at all, Elder Segos," Victor replied in a tone much the same. "Our Day King's mate has set up a safe house for them, and we will monitor each recovered."

Elder Segos gave an abrupt nod. "Very wise."

Elder Faran turned quickly and looked at Leone. "Enforcer, you are well?"

Leone straightened and inclined his head in neither a nod nor denial of the question. "I have been having a few issues, that can't be explained." He finally said.

"Perhaps some time in solitude would help to clear the matter up." The elder suggested with a smile.

"I will consider it, Elder Faran." He slumped back in his chair again.

"Warden of Justice, when we spoke a few days past, you were concerned with this plot to barter the release of Marcus the mage and his human witch, have you found out more pertaining to this?" The warrior, Elder Drusla asked.

I leaned forward wondering who she was talking to.

Arius shook his head. "We have not learned more."

"I was told they expect Marcus to be free in no more than a week or two." I informed them.

Elder Drusla studied me for a moment. "They did not hint at how they're going to do this, aside from trading someone?"

I shook my head. "I fear they weren't chatty enough with those details."

"The outcome of that plot is in the hands of fate." Elder Faran said thoughtfully.

Several of the elders turned to look at her, a look of contemplation on their faces.

"Indeed." Elder Varus said quietly.

"Night King, we have been studying the prophecies to ascertain which Marcus the mage believes is his. We have not been able to unravel why he believes he is important enough to think he has one." Elder Nodin said looking to Troy.

"Criss... the Seer of Truth hasn't had any luck there either." Troy told them.

"I'm beginning to think he misinterpreted a prophecy, and thought it was meant for him. Now that we know Willis Hubert is in the picture, can assume Marcus was nudged in his misguided t conclusion in service of Hubert's cause." The elder said, glancing to the others for their thoughts.

"It would fit his past transgressions." Elder John agreed.

"I also see that as a probable outcome." The squinting Elder Roan added.

Crissy shook her head. "None of them fit for Marcus, I have read them all..." she tapped the side of her head, "they're in here now and nothing comes to me."

"You remember all that you read?" Elder Udela asked her.

Nodding, Crissy sighed, "read and see... it's all up here." She tapped her had again.

"How exhausting." Elder Faran said, giving her a sympathetic look.

Crissy shrugged. "It's just me."

"Indeed." Elder Segos said glancing to Victor and then to his tattooed arm, an emotion crossing his face that made it appear to soften for a brief moment.

Elder Varus looked down the table of brothers, a contemplative expression on her face, she stopped at Daxx. "Your arrival has been much celebrated, Huntress Queen, I pray I am still of this plane when the next chapter unfolds."

Daxx glanced to Troy with one eyebrow cocked and then offered the elder a polite smile.

"If that is all, we have much to research to help with your fight." Elder Arian said looking all too excited, considering the details we'd just shared.

"We will find out if there is anything to assist you." Elder Moire inclined his head to us and then stood.

"If I may be so bold," Elder Nodin said softly, "perhaps not mixing with those working with Willis Hubert may be advisable, my Queen of Light."

Despite his calling me that title, I nodded. "I have no intentions to see them again, Elder Nodin, but thank you for your concern."

Elder Roan stood up and smiled at me. "I am delighted you are so properly spoken, my queen," he gave Chase a hard glance, "I believe you will have a hard task before you to instill some of that in your... king." He stood up and bowed. "Your majesties." Then turned and walked to the door, and stood waiting for the others.

Elder Segos stood up and looked at Victor, "I do miss our sparring, Justice." He smirked. "Although I fear you would surpass the teacher by now."

Victor stood as well and bowed slightly. "I highly doubt that, Elder Segos."

With a nod the elder went to the door.

As we stood up, Elder Faran paused and turned, she looked to Leone.

"Enforcer." She waited until Leone looked to her. "Your questions will have answers soon." She smiled. "I feel it."

Leone took a deep breath, like he was going to speak, but then inclined his head and said nothing at all.

When the last Elder went out and the door was closed, Chase looked around. "Well, that was as fun as ever." He smiled. "Anyone care for a drink before you all run off to nap?"

There were several positive responses.

He glanced to me. "I may need two by the time our Queen of Light is done with me."

"You could have warned me." I said and then glanced to the others. "Any of you."

"In our defense," Quinton said carefully, "we don't get hung up on all the titles." He shrugged. "I forgot that pendant on your neck came with such a large one." He smirked.

I lifted the pendant in my hand. "The weight of it increases each time I wear it." I reached to undo it and Chase stopped me with a shake of his head.

"Best leave it for now. Their digging is going to light a fire under a lot of asses, and people will be racing around the halls all over the place." He gave me a serious look. "I'd rather you hate me for not telling you it's meaning, than have you detained as a trespasser."

Troy nodded. "He's right. Everyone keep theirs on for the time being."

"Uh." Leone groaned. "People will be bowing their heads every time we walk by them."

"Really?" Daxx asked, her hand on her pendant. "Like, *everyone* everyone?"

"Afraid so, kitten… you have to play the queen sometimes, it can't always be stabbing and kicking." Chase said with a smirk.

"Awesome." Daxx mumbled and motioned to the door. "About those drinks."

Chapter Twenty-Four

I sat and watched the various conversations taking place, everyone had their own idea on how to proceed. Chase stood there, arms crossed, watching me. I didn't know what he was thinking, but if body language was any indication, we were going to have words later, most likely hostile ones, while he tried to control me and I refused to allow it. Then there was this whole Queen of the Light thing… With a scowl, he pulled out his phone and then walked to the other side of the room.

Daxx came over and sat beside me. "What are you thinking?"

I looked at her for a moment, tiredness was showing in her posture as she slumped in the chair. "A few things. First, I think I need a nap." I tapped the empty wine glass. "I may have had one too many… it's been quite the drama filled day."

"I agree with a nap." She grinned.

"I was also wondering if there was a way to delay Mister Hubert from gathering the capital needed to continue, am I being naïve? I imagine he'll just take it from someone, or somewhere, if desperate enough."

She nodded. "There is that chance, but if they are trying to stay off the radar…"

"I'll think on it some more and see what I can come up with, if they do contact me about investments. I may not understand everything… well, very little with this and that realm, but I understood what the elder meant by there being casualties on both sides."

She sat straighter. "You're not planning to see Mister Hubert again, are you?"

"Oh no. Not a chance." I glanced at the empty glass again. "Which puts me in an unfamiliar situation."

"How?" She frowned.

"I can't very well leave my apartment if I've told them I'm on a trip."

"Oh yeah…"

"Normally I'd just move on in a situation like this. I don't like being confined."

She nodded. "I hear that."

"So, what am I to do with my time? I can't sit in front of the screen and look for others all day long, and if we can't go out, how do we find the others before they do?"

Daxx blew out a breath, exhaustion clear on her face. "Is it safe for you to go out here?"

I hadn't considered that, so far, *here* was an elaborate maze of halls and grand rooms. "I don't know. With several of them being from here… How do we know if they don't have people over here right now? Being seen on this side is a neon sign that says *liar* and it's pointed at me…"

Leone came over and sat down, laying his head on the table.

I looked to Daxx, who didn't seem to be concerned. "Voices louder?" I asked him.

He raised his head and looked at me. "No more than the last few days. Actually, I had a few hours today—which was nice, I'm just not sure what Elder Faran meant."

"What do you mean?" I hadn't retained a great deal of what was said. Probably because I'd been in a room, in another realm, with twelve individuals that were older than ten centuries. It was a lot to process, to say the least.

"She said solitude... is that, hang out in my room, the witches' temple or go to the mountains?" He shrugged. "Did she see it or was she just trying to be helpful? She said my questions would have answers. *All* questions have answers." He waved his hand in the air. "And what's in fate's hands now? That we're just to let one of us be taken, or was she talking about something else?" He scowled. "Why does she talk in riddles? Crissy doesn't."

I glanced to Daxx for input, but she had a blank look on her face, much like Leone did now. I was just about to try to offer some comforting words when Michael sat down looking much like Leone did. I was no expert, but it seemed the elder's council meeting stirred up confusion more than anything else.

"I just want to sleep." Michael said. He held his phone up. "Every time I think I'll go lay down, it rings."

"What's going on?" Daxx asked, leaning her elbow on the table and resting her cheek on her hand.

"We're searching for any that were associated with Willis or Nelson and his sister in the past, to see if that are more here helping them." He shook his head. "We may have half of Alterealm in the cells at this rate."

Arius came over and leaned on the back of a chair. "We have lots of room, still." He winked at Daxx and I. "Even if we run out, I'll make room for more." He nodded to me. "Which reminds me. Your father is doing much better now. The doctor feels in a week's time you may be able to visit him again."

"Oh. Thank you, Arius." I wasn't sure how I felt about that. I'd gone my entire life without my father and now he was here. Another thing that was going to take some adjustments.

"I completely forgot." Michael moaned. "We found your grandparents, but we haven't contacted them yet because..." He looked to Arius briefly, "we don't know if they agreed with what Levi was doing." He shrugged. "They could be completely unaware, but until we know for sure…"

I nodded. "That's quite all right. I've gone this long with no family. I'm sure I can wait a while longer."

He nodded abruptly. "Good enough. Well, I'm going to go nap and turn my phone off." He grinned at Arius and got up.

I watched Michael leave then turned to Arius. "Daxx and I were discussing what I'm to do now. I can't go out at home if I've told them I'm on trip." I motioned to the door, "Michael is concerned there more here working with Mister Hubert… so what am I to do?"

Arius opened his mouth and then closed it again and stood there with a thoughtful look on his face. "I'd suggest cloaking, but we don't know who is on the other side, and if they can see through it.

I gave him a blank look, having no idea what that was about. "Perhaps something I understand?"

He sighed. "I don't know. Going out on either side, for all of us, is risky right now."

"I'm so sick of being under house arrest." Daxx moaned. "Even if the house is this large, not that I know my way around yet like Criss." She glanced around. "Where is Crissy?"

"She said something about pieces and her tower." Arius informed her.

"Oh."

I looked from him to her. "Pieces of?"

"Whatever she's seeing. Keep your fingers crossed it's something that will put an end to this." She said sounding drowsy.

Arius straightened, a serious look on his face.

I turned to see he was watching Chase talk on the phone, in a corner away from the others. Chase's expression was one of the utmost focus. I didn't know who he was talking to, but it was quite serious.

"I hope this isn't a let's go phone call. I need a nap before I can kick any ass." Daxx said in a hushed tone.

I looked around to see Troy, Victor and a few of the other men also watching him. "It's something. That silent brother connection has them all paying attention."

She looked at the men. "I'm supposed to be part of that silent connection thing, but I can't figure out how to listen in yet."

"I'm sure it's just that they've had many decades to hone it."

"I suppose." She motioned to Troy. "I'll go ask."

Chase hung up the phone and came back over to the table. "That was brother Emil." He waved a hand. "Who doesn't understand any of this…"

I rolled my eyes. "Welcome to our club, it's small but contains plenty of confusion."

Chase smirked. "Sassy *Queen*," he winked and was serious a second later. "His son, Ellis," he nodded, "has been on *this* side working with a purpled eyed freak, his son's words," he shrugged, "setting up boundaries, for what, he doesn't know, but he told his father he thinks they're up to more than he's been told."

"Does he know where these boundaries have been set up?" Troy asked.

"In the middle of nowhere, which doesn't help, we have large areas of nothingness here.

"Think he could show us on a map?" Rafael stood up.

"I don't know. Our brother wants us to detain him so he's out of this. I briefly explained what they're really trying to do, and he just wants his son safe." Chase crossed his arms and looked to his siblings.

Quinton leaned back in the chair. "Detain him how?"

Chase shrugged. "That's why I'm saying all this, so we can figure it out."

Arius nodded slowly. "I'd be happier knowing I wasn't going to cut my nephew in half if we find another location."

"There's that too." Chase agreed.

"I wouldn't feel right putting him in the cells, not when he knows something is wrong and he wants out." Arius leaned back down on the chair.

"I agree, but that still leaves the question of how?" Chase glanced to Victor.

"It has to be on this side, we have control over here." Victor said in a thoughtful way.

Chase raised one eyebrow at him. "Apparently our control over here is lacking, or none of this would be happening."

"There's the guard training grounds. It's very secure, limiting who enters and leaves." Rafael suggested.

"That would work." Chase looked around. "Where is Michael?"

Daxx yawned. "He went to bed."

Chase chuckled. "Sleep deprivation. None of you can handle it as well as I do." Nodding to Quinton. "You go talk to Ira about this."

Quinton got up. "Will do." He went out through the kitchen.

"We can't just transport him to the landing room." Victor crossed his arms over his chest and looked quite stern.

"I'm aware. Emil was going to kidnap him the way duchess did him, but with everything going on, I'd prefer a different landing location, not one in the royal chambers." Chase looked at Troy, who nodded.

"Which means, we somehow have to meet him on the other side." Daxx mused. "I'd say my place, but I don't have a place anymore." She gave Troy a hard look.

"You're certain this isn't some sort of set up? To get closer to one of the royals?" I turned in the chair so I was looking at Chase.

His jaw clenched for a moment, then he shook his head. "No. On Emil's part, I am. He understands the danger this presents to everyone, but I can't be sure about Ellis."

I thought for a moment. "It would be hard to control the situation in a public place." I was more or less thinking out loud. "How would you know if he was being tracked or traced?" I lifted my hand, looking for a way to explain. "Magically, I mean. Electronically can be dealt with…"

"Good point." He glanced to Rafael. "We can get Clairee to check."

"Which still leaves the where." Troy pointed out.

"Can this Clairee put some kind of protection on my place?" I looked from Rafael to Chase.

"You want to use your place?" Chase's brow furrowed.

I shrugged. "It's private, high security. If you and a few others are there, and Emil gets rid of his son's phone or a transporter device…" I looked around at the others.

Troy nodded. "It's a solution, a good one."

The two kings exchanged a look.

Chase nodded. "As it's technically my watch, I'll call it." He turned to Rafael, "you get Clairee over to the duchess' penthouse, send her with Tim. I don't care if she has to block magic from the whole building, make sure anything magical can't enter."

Rafael got up. "I'll go get her over there now."

Chase turned to Arius. "You, Bronx and Sith are going to be there with me." He glanced to me next.

I smiled. "I have to be present. The security is biometric, so unless you have my *red* eye signature and thumb, you can't even open the door."

He glared at me for a moment. "You do love complicating things while pushing boundaries, don't you?" He stood there for a second more. "You do what you need, then stay clear of him. We don't know…"

I held up my hand and pointed to myself. "Big girl, but your concern is noted."

Growling, he turned and slowly looked at Victor, then Troy. "You two will be on this end at the training office, where I'll be bringing him. Having our little Seer of Truth there to check out his aura or whatever she does, would be helpful."

Victor nodded, turned, and walked out.

Chase motioned to Daxx. "I guess you, Leone and Michael will be on duty for the first part of the night shift, so you may want to grab a nap now."

She sighed and then nodded.

Troy smirked. "You love bossing us around."

Chase gave him a smug look. "Last I looked it is still daylight out, so *my* watch."

Mitz came out of the kitchen. "Oh good, Alona, you're here." She smiled and came toward me carrying a small package. "Crissy asked me to get these for you."

I stood up. "Oh?" I hadn't asked for anything.

Mitz handed it to me and patted my arm. Waves of love were coming off her. "I suggest you open it later, love, she didn't feel her style was your style." With another sweet smile, she walked back into the kitchen.

I looked down at the package. It wasn't much larger than an envelope. I looked to see that Daxx was grinning and decided if they were both in on it, perhaps I'd open it later when the men weren't standing there staring at me.

"Oh, you'll need to send Emil my address." I turned to Chase and smiled.

He glanced to the package and then held up his phone. "We'll do that now, so we can meet my nephew."

Chapter Twenty-Five

I sat in my favorite chair by the window and looked at the five large men standing near my door, I couldn't even *see* the door at this point. They weren't dressed for battle, but they still had some weapons, and their stance said they were prepared for anything. Glancing to Clairee, I gave her a blank look and then back to the men. "You could sit, or at least clear a path to the door, so I can find it when they get here."

Sith was the only one that looked amused.

I turned back to Clairee, I liked her. She seemed quiet, but there was something about her that led me to believe she wasn't a woman to be messed with. I picked up a trace of emotions, but nothing I couldn't handle. "So, you've done something to prevent magic here?"

She shrugged. "Not prevent mine, but anyone else's, yes."

"On the building or just my place?" I knew nothing of magic.

"I placed a few short-term enchantments in the area first," she smiled, "if they are using something, we can't have it suddenly cut off at your door step—it defeats the purpose of having them not know the location."

"Very smart."

She grinned. "Thank you."

"So, you've done all this and you're still planning to check Ellis?"

"Mmm, yes, after what the mages did to Crissy, I'm not taking any chances."

"Crissy attempted to explain that, but I didn't quite grasp what she meant."

Clairee smirked, "That's not surprising, keeping up with her on a slow day is hard enough. I don't know how, or even what they did, but even after I thought we'd cleansed her, they managed to track her." I picked up anger. "The pain they caused her…" She shook her head. "We had to tattoo over it to block it for good."

"And how does one avoid such things? In case I'm ever allowed to go out again." I glanced over to where Chase stood.

She looked at the men for a moment, then turned back to me. "Best advice I have for you is, if you encounter anyone with purple eyes, go the other way as quickly as possible."

"So, your eyes?"

"Go purple." Clairee grinned.

"Ah, well then, so pleased you're on our side." I looked back to the men once more for a second, they all stood by the door, still. Sighing, I gave her a wide-eyed look. "Would you like coffee, tea?"

"Tea would be great."

Chase cut me off when I reached the kitchen.

I waved him aside.

"This isn't a time for tea." He said looking annoyed.

When I went to go around him, he stepped in front of me again, his eyes now bordering on yellow. "Get your emotion suckers out of my face." I gently pushed his face away with my hand.

He gave me a startled look. "This is serious…"

"You need to stop preparing for a fight."

"We don't know anything about him." He crossed his arms over his chest.

"As he knows nothing about you." I put the kettle on and got the tea pot out. I'd always kept a tea pot, and never once had the chance to use it until now. That was something I needed to think about, I have people around me more now than ever. I turned back to see Chase standing there with his arms crossed, looking large and on edge.

I sighed. "Have you never done something and realized it wasn't right before?" I heard a chuckle and turned to see Arius leaning against the wall. Chase didn't look impressed. "He's your nephew, one that you've never met, give me the benefit of a doubt?"

I watched him take a deep breath and turned to the guards. "Spread out around the room."

I smiled when he looked back at me. "Tea?"

"No. I could handle a coffee though."

"I'll put some on."

Chase moved over to stand in the sitting area. I gave Arius an inquiring look. "I suppose it's a normal thing to have a nephew the same age as you."

He smiled. "It happens. The average age of most adults is around eight hundred, that's a lot of time to have children."

I laughed. "When I met all of you, I thought your mother must have been both brave and insane to have eight male children."

"She may have been a little of both." He shrugged.

"I always wanted children, then that hope died when I realized I wasn't normal."

"I guess normal depends on which realm you're in." The kettle whistled, so I turned back to deal with it and give myself a moment to think. Setting the teapot and cups on a tray, I carried it out. Chase stood watching Sith as he stood over the puzzle with a focused expression on his face.

"What have you done to my guard?"

I set the tray down and motioned to it for Clairee to help herself. "I haven't done anything to your guard, it happens to be a very complicated and challenging puzzle."

Chase shook his head and went back to the kitchen.

I had just sat down when he came out and waved his phone. "They'll be here in a minute.

When Emil and a tall blond man walked in, I felt like I should apologize for the hovering giants standing there staring at them.

Ellis, despite being Emil's child, was not a child. He was most definitely a man. His hair was the same pale blonde as Chase's and there was no questioning the family genes when I looked into grey eyes like his father and Uncle Arius.

I stood back and watched Clairee wave a stone around in her hand, as she walked around him slowly.

His emotions weren't hard to pick up even without my ability, the uncertainty in his eyes said it all. "She's checking to see if they're tracking you." I offered when no one seemed to be saying anything to him.

His eyebrows went up. "They'd do that?"

"And more." Chase said in a low tone.

Ellis lifted both his arms and watched Clairee with a look of concern on his face. "I left that watch thing and my phone at Dad's." He glanced to Chase and then back to me. "I didn't stop to think they could do more than that."

Clairee lowered her hand and looked to Chase. "I sense nothing." She looked up at Ellis. "Have you had any burns or burning sensations?"

He shook his head no.

Chase went toward him, but stopped a few feet from him. Ellis wasn't as large as the brothers, but he wasn't a small man either. "We'll be taking you somewhere they can't find you until this is over."

Ellis rubbed a hand over the back of his neck and nodded. "That would be good. I don't know what they're planning, but I'm pretty sure it's not what they told me."

I motioned to the sitting area. "Come and sit down." I sent Chase a quick look, everyone standing around him a foot inside the door was ridiculous. "I'm sure you can answer questions there just as easily as here surrounded by guards."

Ellis gave Sith and Bronx a hesitant look, then noticed Arius leaning against the wall by the hallway. "I always wondered what you'd look like with long hair, dad."

Emil shrugged. "It wouldn't help me go unnoticed, would it?"

"Guess not." Ellis moved cautiously toward the sitting area and sat in the chair where his back wasn't turned on anyone else present. "So, who are the uncles and who are the guards?" He motioned to Arius, "except Dad's look alike, of course."

"I'm going back now." Clairee said.

Chase nodded. "Tim will go back with you. Thank you."

She smiled. "It's not a problem. I love getting out of the temple, and your family keeps it interesting."

He snorted. "I could do with a little bit of dull from time to time."

Tim stepped to the door and Clairee touched him. He pushed the button on his transporter and they were gone.

"Damn. Seeing that never gets old." Ellis said quietly. "Although I can do without almost tossing my cookies on the landing part." He looked at me and then to Arius. "What is that about anyway?"

Arius smirked.

"I agree with that completely." I told him, then I motioned to Chase. "This is your uncle Chase, who also happens to be one of Alterealm's kings." I waited for a reaction, he wasn't surprised.

"Yeah, I didn't get much of the history from those guys I was with, other than you're supposed to be some overbearing, slave master. The whole royal family is…"

Chase snorted. "That would be *your* family."

Ellis's mouth opened, then he closed it and frowned. "I guess it is." He turned to his father. "Rena's going to love that, being part of a royal family."

Emil sighed. "I haven't contacted her yet to explain any of this."

"Yeah, just leave her on that mountain for now. Have you talked to Abe?"

"Abraham and I spoke last week, he's away right now on business, so I'll call him when he's back." Emil rubbed a hand over his jaw, a contemplative look on his face.

Chase heaved out a breath and sat on the arm of the chair I'd sat in. I noted he placed himself between Ellis and I. "We need to know everything you know about any locations they might be in, what they're trying to do has to be stopped or many—on both sides of the realms will die when they try to breach the barrier."

Ellis' eyebrows shot up. "*That* part I know nothing about. I was just a grunt, because I'm a *half blood.*" He rolled his eyes.

"You were on our side doing what?" Chase asked, not commenting on what he'd said.

"The purple eyed freak... and I don't call him that because of his eyes, it's more his personality..."

"What's his name?" Chase looked to Arius briefly.

"Herman—I know he's a mage or whatever, but there's something wrong with him, like serious brain flaw, kind of wrong with him."

Chase sighed and looked to his brother. "I think we need to talk to Romulus and find out how many of his are missing."

Arius nodded. "One we can deal with, more than that and," he huffed out a breath, "unless we can cripple them so they can't move their hands, we're in trouble."

Chase rubbed the bridge of his nose and then nodded. "Yeah, we need to get the magic community working on that." He turned back to Ellis. "What were you helping this mage do?"

"He was making some kind of barrier, or perimeter, around a house."

"For what?" Chase leaned forward.

Ellis shrugged. "I don't know, he just said it had to be secure for a V.I.P."

The brothers exchanged a look. "Maybe a meeting?" Arius came over and stood behind the sofa.

Chase gave Ellis a curious look. "A perimeter to keep someone in or out? Or an alarm?"

Ellis shook his head. "I have no idea. The vague answers I got is one of the reasons why I called Dad, there's a lot they're not saying." He shrugged. "I don't share either, but I'm not some organization recruiting people for a *cause*."

"Do they know about your father or siblings?" I asked, not caring if it was my place or not.

"No. I didn't tell them anything about my personal life." He smirked. "You get used to keeping certain facts to yourself, if you know what I mean."

I smiled. "I understand completely."

Chase gave him a hard look and leaned closer to me.

"So, you are like us?" He looked from one uncle to the other. "I was beginning to think my sister was a rare female or something." He shrugged, "a few of the others said there were lots of women, half-blood and true-blood, but I was never anywhere they were."

I sat straighter. "Do you know where the women are?"

He frowned. "None of the places I was, but the guys talked about some island."

I looked at Chase, judging by the way his jaw was clenched, I knew they were going to figure out a way to get on that island.

"If we showed you a map can you show us where you were on our side?" Arius asked him.

Ellis made an odd face. "I can try."

"Do you know locations on this side? Arius crossed his arms over his chest and stood there.

"I've been to a few, and I know some others where they go to recruit."

Chase and Arius's expression both hardened. Ellis had given them new targets.

"So," he looked between his uncles, "they know where I live, I can't go back there."

"No, you can't." Emil said. "Your uncles will keep you safe on their side until this is resolved."

Ellis nodded. "I still can't believe I have uncles... a whole royal family." He looked at me and then to Chase. "Do I have Aunts?"

Chase smirked. "A few, but I'm pretty sure if you call any of them *aunt* you may get stabbed, well, by one of them at least."

Ellis sat back and blew out a breath before turning to his father. "It's just so weird. We're not some genetic fluke at all."

Emil nodded slowly. "I'm still coming to terms with all of it myself. The fact that I have eight brothers is just... shocking."

Arius made a sound of annoyance and turned to glare at Chase. "Will you *please* call Troy." He rubbed his forehead. "When did he get strong enough to invade my head this way?"

Chase pulled out his phone and started typing on it. "Is that what that noise is?" He smirked and glanced at his younger sibling. "I thought I was just getting a headache."

Emil and Ellis both look confused. "The brothers are able to communicate with each other by silent means..." I stopped, not knowing more to explain it.

Arius chortled. "It's not very silent when it's like he's standing inside your head, screaming."

"That..." Emil lifted a hand and then dropped it, "is beyond my comprehension."

I nodded. "I don't understand it either, well, much of it. I've known of this for a few days more than you have."

Chase stood up. "Okay. They're waiting for you at the guard training facility." He gave Ellis a brief nod, "no one will get near you there." Looking at Emil, he tilted his head in question, "are you going back with him?"

Emil stood up. "If that's all right, I wouldn't mind." He looked to Arius. "Small doses, and eventually it might all sink in."

Arius grinned at him. "Some days it's better to be clueless."

Chase chuckled. "We're not discussing your dating choices, brother."

Rolling his eyes, Arius gave me a polite nod. "Are you coming back with us, sister?"

"We'll be along shortly." Chase told him, not giving me a chance to speak.

Chapter Twenty-Six

Two minutes later, we were alone. I looked at him. "*We'll* be along shortly? I didn't realize I was needed over there."

He stood there for a moment. "I don't think staying here is a good idea right now."

"I don't plan on going anywhere…"

"In light of everything we've learned today, there's no way you're staying here until we know they think you're away."

I looked at the window. "You think they know where I live?"

He shrugged. "We have no idea who is working with them."

"Are you still worried about them tracking Ellis?"

"No," he paused, "yes, but this isn't about him." He ran a hand through his hair. "I *know* some of those people you met with today—I've seen the carnage they're capable of. They may seem reasonable when they spoke to you, but they're not. Willis and his two sidekicks are responsible for more deaths…" In two strides, he was right in front of me. "The very idea that they're here on this side," he huffed out a loud breath, "let's just say it's a worst case scenario."

I could feel fear from him and that shook me more than his words. "What if I called…"

He grasped my chin before I could finish. "You are *not* seeing them again. If they didn't need you to help them make money, you wouldn't have gotten off that island." He took a deep breath and I felt him rein in his emotions as he gentled his hold. "I was fit to be tied, by the way, when I had to listen to that conversation. My brothers had to stop me from doing something stupid. Knowing I had no way of getting to you if you needed me..." He released my face and dropped his hand to rest on my shoulder. "I know you don't understand mating and all that goes with it, but you *are* mine and it's the single hardest thing I've ever had to do, to not mark you as mine." Chase's expression softened, as his hazel eyes searched mine. "I'm aware after what happened to your parents it's everything wrong in your eyes, but it's not like that." He offered an understanding smile. "I don't even know how to explain it so you'll understand, but you need to know that I am struggling non-stop to not toss you over my shoulder and carry you away."

I smiled at that. "That sounds like a caveman tactic."

He smirked. "My twin would laugh if he knew that's how I feel, it wasn't long ago he went caveman on Daxx."

"Yes, I've heard that story, or parts of it."

Chase smiled. "I'm trying hard to not carry you around the royal chambers over my shoulder like he did to his mate."

My mouth dropped open. "He didn't."

"Oh, he did. It was very amusing. However, I now understand what he was going through at that time."

"He marked her but they didn't do the blood bond?" I frowned. "Did I get that right?"

With a look on contemplation, he nodded. "Yes. I don't know how your parents bared the mark, but didn't complete it, Troy was a madman." He shook his head. "How your father left your mother to return to our side without marking her... I can't even..." He shrugged. "All of it would have ended differently if he had..."

"Are you saying my mother would have lived?" I hugged my arms around my waist. "I doubt she would still be..."

"That's just it, if your father had of marked her, he would have been able to find her. Tying each together through the blood bond, with the mating mark, would have extended her existence…"

There was still so much about this I didn't know. "Why… why would he have left her that way?"

His expression hardened. "I don't know. Arius thinks he'll be easier to talk to now that the doctor has him under control. The madness he was suffering was because his mate was gone, he'd have sensed it."

"There's so much I don't know." I said quietly.

"I'd like to help you find answers but, I'm not as impartial to mating issues as I once was…" He shrugged.

"Daxx just gets frustrated because her mate was a Neanderthal and Crissy isn't much help either." I remember the package from Mitz. She wouldn't have? I looked around his large body to the island counter where the package sat.

Chase turned and followed where I was looking. "Ah, yes, the mysterious packet. What is it?"

"I'm not sure, and I must admit I'm a little hesitant to find out." I looked back to him. "I still need to take you to task over this *queen* thing."

He smirked, "I had hoped you'd forgotten."

I shook my head. "As if I could." I touched the pendant I still wore and paced away from him, having trouble finding clear thoughts when he was near. "I've spent my entire life living in the shadows, so to speak," I glanced over my shoulder to see him watching me carefully. "Suddenly becoming a queen is the exact opposite of that. I'd be known." I turned to look at him.

He titled his head and gave me an amused look. "Well, yes, being queen is hard to keep a secret."

"What if I don't want to be one?" It wasn't lost on me how strange this conversation was.

"You already are, duchess," he waved his hand toward me, "we just haven't gone through the formalities. You are my mate, so as long as I'm king, you are a queen."

I frowned. "You do know, in all of the history of monarchies, the spouse is chosen?"

"Fate made the choices for my brothers and I... I will only have one mate and that is you." He crossed his arms and studied me. "The only way out of being a queen is if I step down..."

"You can do that?"

He glanced at the floor for a second then back to me. "I have no idea. I suppose one of my brothers would get the title... since Troy and I were crowned, it was decided there would always be two rulers for Alterealm."

"You would do that? Step down?" I found that had to believe.

"I don't know, honestly. Troy and I have always known who we were and what our place was, but as I'll never have another chance to not spend eternity alone, I think one of the others could help rule the realm if it was what I decided."

"See, I don't even know how big Alterealm is? Are we talking a small country size, or bigger?"

Grinning, he shook his head. "Does size matter? Would you agree to be queen to a small population?"

I scowled at him. "It doesn't matter, I'm just saying there is so much I don't know."

He sighed. "I know and I wished I could fill in all the blanks for you, but its taking all the focus I have to stay this far away from you, so I may not be the best option for twenty questions."

I studied his face for a moment, he didn't look like he was struggling. "It's really that difficult?"

"You don't feel inclined at all to be near me? I don't enter your thoughts?" His hazel eyes locked on mine while he waited to answer.

"Mainly when I'm thinking things such as 'he's not going to be happy with this'," I paused when he gave me a hard look, "I'm drawn to you, I just—my past relationships haven't been..."

"This isn't a relationship that may last a few months. Simply put this is *the* relationship, the only one for us." He moved closer, but stopped when he was a few feet from me.

"That didn't exactly work out for my parents." I reminded him.

He exhaled slowly. "I know. There's something there that we're unaware of, your father leaving your mother without completing the bond, there's got to be a reason, Alona."

I hugged my arms around my waist. "I need to know it. I've spent my life thinking one thing and now, to find out there is a chance it's wrong," I took a ragged breath and let it out quickly, "it would mean a lot to me to know."

"And we will find out the answers, as soon as your father is well enough for you to visit." His eyes searched my face. "We can go see your grandparents as well, that may shed some light."

"I thought it was too risky…"

He stepped over, so he was right in front of me, a serious look on his face. "If it helps you, then we will." He smirked, "you'll be surrounded by guards, but we…"

"We?" Each time he said it I felt a part of me inside wanting that, but not at the same time.

"Yes." He gave me a soft look. "There is no more you or I, only *we*. I told you I'm not going away."

"I've never had that before."

With a gentle touch, he pulled my arms apart, so I wasn't hugging myself. "I know. In this sense of the word, neither have I." His voice was soft, barely more than a whisper. "I'm so completely distracted by you," he cupped my cheek with his hand, his touch warm against my skin, "so completely lost in you." Hazel eyes watched mine. "I should be with my brothers finding out what Ellis knows, but I can't drag myself away from you…" His thumb brushed over my lip, "you should really put me out of my misery." He stared at my mouth.

I licked my suddenly dry lips. "How so?" Whenever he touched me, my heart sped up.

"Kiss me, bite me, agree to be mine…" his eyes moved back to mine, "I have a list if you'd like to hear it."

What was it about this man that prevented me from logical thought when he was this close. "I don't think I need the list." I answered in a whisper.

"Is that a yes?" The color of his eyes were closer to yellow now.

I felt my mouth fill with fangs. "No. I just don't need your list."

He growled soft in the back of his throat. "Before you lie to yourself, remember I can feel what you do. Your desire, your needs…"

I found myself watching his mouth as he spoke. "Something else I'm not used to. Usually I am the one that feels everything."

"We're wired differently, most of us can control our emotions. I struggle near you though, so we're both in a new territory." His eyes moved all over my face, but kept going back to my mouth. "I think I need you to bite me more than you need to feed." He smiled. "Can one become addicted to that I wonder?"

"I don't think so, most wouldn't enjoy fangs in their throat." I found myself wanting to lean into him.

"Mmm, must be a mating perk." He mused quietly.

"You shared what you felt, I don't think it's the biting, but more the possibilities."

He leaned closer, his breath on my face. "*So* many possibilities, all of them X-rated."

I bit my lip for a moment. "How do you know this isn't just a draw because of being mates?"

His eyes were on my mouth again. "Oh, a large part of it is. Imagine being mated to someone you weren't attracted to. Rest assured, my sexy duchess, I wanted you before I realized we were mates, more than I'd ever wanted another."

"Really?"

"Mmm, then you threw me to the mat and stepped on my chest. I fell in love at that moment."

I smiled, something I'd never remembered doing while my fangs were present.

With a growl, he grasped the back of my head and kissed me, his mouth anything but gentle. Flames traveled through my body and a moment later feelings of desire and lust swamped me, I didn't know where his ended and my own started. I wanted to give in, just let this go where it may, but I was afraid of the repercussions.

Despite clinging to his neck and drowning in him, when he lifted his mouth to take a breath, I leaned my head back. "I need to know more."

He gave me a heated look, "I'd be happy to show you as much as you want, duchess."

"I said know, not do."

Exhaling slowly, he frowned and looked down at me. "I believe you are trying to drive me mad. Know more *what*, exactly?"

"Everything. Feeding, mating, expectations I suppose. I don't understand all the details."

His hands continued to knead my hips, but he didn't pull me close again. "Don't suppose I could fill in all the details after, while recovering in bed?" His mouth twitched.

I smiled and shook my head. "After may be too late. I'm not sure how this works…"

He hunched down and looked into my eyes. "I can assure you *that* works just the same as with a normal human."

"I didn't mean sex."

Sighing, he dropped his hands and stepped back. Tucking his hands in his pockets, he studied me for a moment. "I'm trying—clear thought is a struggle right now."

"I'm sorry, I don't mean to keep leading you on." I motioned up and down his tall body. "I just can't seem to help myself."

Nodding, Chase smiled. "Then we're on the same page there." Closing his eyes for a few seconds, hazel ones looked at me when he opened them. "What is it you need to know?"

I sat on the arm of the chair. "Feeding to start. What are the ramifications if I've already fed from you and you feed off my emotions, and then we have sex?"

He crossed his arms over his large chest. "We're both satisfied in more than one way?" He smirked.

"That's it? There's nothing more binding?"

He shook his head. "Nothing. I'm sure we'll feel a further connection, but it's not a bond."

I sighed. "There needs to be an instruction manual for all this." I looked down at my left palm and studied it. "A blood bond is just temporary unless marking is involved?"

Chase moved over and knelt in front of me. "Yes. We can have a blood bond, it will wear off if I haven't marked you." He gave me a tender look. "I won't do what your father did to your mother, Alona. I will not, unless you consent." He shrugged. "I may follow you around like a mopey puppy, but I would rather die than do what your father did to your mother."

I could feel the emotions attached to his words, and he meant every word he said. That was another check for him on the plus side. I was too used to others saying one thing while their emotions told me differently.

Chase gently grasped my chin, so I would look at him. "What else do you need to know, Alona?"

"There's so much," I sighed, "feeding. You said you couldn't feed from me or you'd lose control. I don't understand. Daxx told me you prefer women, but Crissy said you've been feeding from prisoners."

He frowned. "Seems people have been saying plenty where I'm concerned."

"They were only trying to..."

"Help you understand." Standing, he grasped my hand and pulled me to my feet. "I'm beginning to regret being part of a large family." He pulled his phone out of his pocket. "If I don't call Troy my brain may very likely burst." With jerky movements he tapped the screen. "This better be something important that will allow me to hurt someone, brother."

I watched his eyes move over my face as he listened.

"Can we confirm this before we go charging in?" With a gentle touch, he brushed the hair back from my face, the hardness in his eyes fading briefly as he did it. "There's still a few hours of light left today, I suggest you all go get some rest and I'll send someone to scout the possible locations." He nodded, a bored expression on his face. "We'll meet at next dawn and make some decisions then." With a quick grin he rolled his eyes at me. "They're not going to take over the world in the next twelve hours. and you are too tired to be of use. I know this because you haven't called me that since we were kids. Go rest brother king and send our siblings to bed as well." He sighed, giving me a brief appraisal. "I will be back shortly." Chase gave an abrupt bob of his head and ended the call.

"Ellis knows where he was?" I wrapped my arms around my waist.

"A few potentials." He rubbed the back of his neck, a look of indecision on his face. "I really want to stay and talk, answer some of your questions…"

I shook my head. "I will survive a day without having them. You may possibly have the location of a meeting, Ellis said VIP, it could be who is working for their cause on this side… you need to focus on that."

He gave me an exasperated look. "You always toss logic at me when I'd prefer you didn't." Grasping my hips, he pulled me against his body. "Feed. Then go soak and take the evening to rest and relax… at least then I'll have an image of you naked in the tub to entertain me."

I smiled. "Your entertainment at a moment of such dire consequences is first and foremost on my mind."

"As it should be, you sassy woman." He kissed my mouth lightly. "Now feed, before I'm otherwise distracted, or worse my brothers show up here looking for me."

"What about you? Did you want to feed—from me?" Butterflies filled my stomach when I thought of it.

"Mmm, I do, but I won't, yet." He gave me a heated look. "I'm sure mutual feedings between us will not end at life sustaining sustenance, and I've promised you I'd behave."

I felt slight disappointment, yet excited at the same moment by his words. "I feel you could be very bad for me."

Chase chuckled, "Oh, I plan on it, in many, very good, addictive ways." He grasped the back of my neck lightly. "Now put those fangs in me, so I can go focus on being a king in charge again."

My fangs filled my mouth, I smiled. "Yes, your majesty." I bit into his neck.

Chapter Twenty-Seven

Daxx dropped to the sofa with a dramatic flair. "I've been benched. I can't believe it."

Crissy perched on the arm beside her. "I don't mind the bench, there's no blood."

They both looked at me. I shrugged. "Don't look at me, I've never had a team before." I motioned to our office. "We could go see if we can find an address for the women we've located."

"Oh," Crissy jumped up. "I think I found a third one."

"I got up after too little sleep to go kick some ass." Daxx sighed and stood up. "I guess finding people is better than sitting here planning how I'm going to punish my mate for leaving me behind."

I gave her a sympathetic smile. "You can't be too upset they're trying to keep you safe."

She snorted. "In case you didn't notice, you're here with us and under guard as well."

I looked over to where Sith stood with the other two guards. "Might as well get comfortable." I told him.

He gave me an abrupt nod and went toward the table with the puzzle.

"I may have to get a new puzzle soon." I said to no one in particular.

An hour later, we stood there looking at the computer screen.

"All three live at the same location? Daxx repeated.

"Safety in numbers?" I offered.

"I guess." She leaned against the table. "I wasn't expecting it to be that easy."

I wrote down the address and went over to my laptop. "I doubt it will be this easy every time."

"I'm worried." Crissy glanced from Daxx to me. "If we found them this fast..."

"Team bad can too." Daxx finished.

Crissy nodded, an apprehensive expression on her face.

I entered the address into the map screen and waited to see where it was. "It's an apartment complex about fifteen minutes from here, a decent neighborhood."

"We're going there?" Crissy's eyes were wide.

Daxx's face lit up. "The guys won't like it."

I glanced at the door. "I could request a van, and we could take our shadows with us."

Daxx chewed on her bottom lip for a moment. "It's within our orders of confinement. We were told no *wandering* around." She shrugged, "we'll be in a van and then at an apartment building. That's not wandering."

"What do we do when we get there?" Crissy fidgeted with a small red rubber ball. "I don't know what we do." She frowned. "We never talked about what comes after."

Both looked at me. "I suppose we'll have to figure that out according to what we discover, after speaking to them.

"How old are they again?" Daxx looked down at the print outs.

"One is fifty and the other two a little younger." Crissy nodded.

"So they already know they're not normal humans, or should right? They won't be aging and should already be displaying," she shrugged, "feeding preference?" Daxx said with a look of contemplation on her face.

I nodded. "I guess that's where my expertise comes in." I said as I motioned to the door. "You can explain to our guards we're going on an outing."

"Are we telling the kings?" Daxx asked, pausing in the door.

"Won't they almost be to the location they were checking?" Crissy asked with a concerned tone.

"She has a point." I agreed. "Pausing mid-battle to answer their phone may not be advisable."

Daxx nodded. "We'll tell them after then." She smirked, "they'll yell less that way."

"Better to ask forgiveness." I said with a grin.

"Exactly." She laughed and walked out.

The driver kept checking in the mirror ever few seconds, probably the first time his van taxi had men this large crammed into it. I focused hard so I didn't pick up his feelings. I glanced to Sith again, if his expression was any indication he wasn't happy we were doing this. I leaned in and offered him a smile. "We'll go right back to my place when we're finished."

He made a non-committal grunt.

"Once we are certain they are safe, we'll call the others and see how to proceed. Does that work for you?"

He nodded, but I could tell he really wasn't placated.

"What could go wrong? We have you guys with us." Daxx offered.

"Famous last words, huntress." Tim said quietly.

"Oh, we're here." Crissy almost didn't wait for the van to stop before she had the door open.

Handing the driver a large tip, I got out and closed the door.

"Looks like a nice place." Daxx mused and she wasted no time walking to the door.

I was just about to inquire what we were going to say to gain entry into the building when a couple came out, and Daxx hurried the last few feet to grab the door.

"We're taking the stairs." Bronx said in a tone that left no room for argument. Whether for a tactical reason or from fear of elevators, I wasn't sure, but they allowed us this adventure, so I wasn't going to complain.

By the time we reached the door to the apartment, the guards were standing so close I felt crowded. I looked at the men. "Perhaps you should stand to the side, so you won't frighten them?" They moved to stand off to the side.

My stomach was knotted with anticipation, but there was something else. As I was trying to sort through the emotions, a feeling flooded me. I held up my hand so Daxx wouldn't knock while I examined the sensations closer. It was fear. Stark terror, and something darker. "Something isn't right in there." I whispered, "They're terrified."

Our guards moved closer to the door while still remaining out of sight.

Daxx checked everyone's position and then knocked on the door. There were muffled voices on the other side.

It opened a few inches. A small woman of Asian descent looked out.

I offered my most polite smile. "Hello. We're looking for Alyssa, Brittany and Kristin, we're from the neighborhood welcoming committee." It was the first reason I could come up with. More than once in my life I'd had such committees on my doorstep.

"I-I'm Brittany."

I didn't need to rely on my empathic abilities to know this woman was afraid. She barely looked at me, and kept glancing to what or whomever was beside her. "Wonderful. We have the right address." I patted Crissy's backpack. "We have so many wonderful offers and welcome gifts for you."

"I-I..."

"Are the others home as well?" I interrupted.

Daxx silently motioned for the woman to step out of the way, her other hand was behind her back gripping the blade she always wore.

"Yes." The woman said hesitantly.

Crissy moved back out of her guard's way. I stepped over to give Sith access to the door while trying to decide if I needed my dagger or not.

As soon as the woman moved, Bronx kicked the door open and rushed in. Sith and Tim were right behind him, followed by Daxx. Crissy and I hurried through at the same moment, she shut the door and leaned on it.

Two large men came rushing into the room. Bronx was wrestling with one. Huddled in the corner was the woman who had answered the door, and two others beside her.

Crissy yelped, I turned to see her ducking out of the way as Tim tossed one of the men against the wall. "Go watch the women." I told her but didn't stand there to watch if she listened.

Bronx and Sith were struggling to get one very large male to the floor while Daxx was dancing around trying to avoid a blade the other man had. She stepped on the sofa and jumped at him. He caught her mid-air and flung her. I cringed as her head hit the wall. Deciding she needed my assistance more than the men, I skirted around the others and went to help her. Sliding down, I swung my leg out and tried to knock his footing out from under him. He stumbled, but didn't go down. If I'd known I would encounter giants, I may have trained differently.

He turned and jabbed at me with the blade. I felt a burn on across my arm and kicked out to knock him out of reach.

"Where's my damn zapper when I need it." Daxx grunted as she tried again to knock him down.

Glancing at my arm, I saw the blood. That was enough motivation to try harder. Stepping back, to give me the distance I needed, I crouched slightly and then sprung up. Landing a two-footed kick against his chest, he hit the floor, flat on his back a moment later.

Daxx knelt on his chest, her curved blade at his throat. "Don't even breathe heavily." She huffed out a breath. "Crissy find me something to tie him up with."

I glanced over my shoulder to see the guards had the other two pinned to the floor as well. I could feel the blood running down my arm, and held it out to see a gash down the side of my arm.

Crissy came rushing over with what looked like scarves to tie up the men. She stopped and looked at my arm and handed me one of them. Taking it, I awkwardly wrapped it around my arm to slow the bleeding as I went over to the women huddled in the corner.

"That wasn't quite the introduction we wanted." I glanced at the one with curly black hair to see oven mitts taped to her hands. "Are you all right?"

She nodded and turned as the petite blonde woman started taking the tape off.

Their fear was almost smothering me. "You're safe now." I allowed my eyes to turn red and looked at them until I was certain all three had noted their color. "You're among friends now."

The fear was immediately replaced with relief. "How did you find us?" The one that had opened the door asked.

"It wasn't easy, but once we did we knew we had to come," I motioned to the man Sith was all but sitting on, "Just in case they found you before we did."

"We need to get them to the cells." Daxx came over rubbing her hand over the side of her head.

"Are you all right?" I turned to check on Crissy.

"I'll have a headache later, but as fights go, that's nothing." She chuckled. "Troy is going to be pissed though."

"Huntress the devices aren't working." Tim pulled the man he'd tied to his feet.

Daxx frowned and looked to Bronx who was shaking his head. She looked to the women. "Are any of you mages?" They shook their head.

"They had someone here that did some kind of block or spell or something to the apartment." The short blonde said quietly.

"That's annoying." Daxx mumbled. She pointed to the hall. "Tim take him and see if you can transport in the hall."

He shook his head. "I'm not leaving without you."

She rolled her eyes. "I'm fine… now. These guys need to get back to the cells. Get a hold of Arius so he can find out what they were doing here."

Pressing my hand on my arm, I turned to look at Sith. "Go and get them where they can't hurt anyone."

"My king…"

"Will be quite upset if he finds out you're dallying with them here where we are." I told him.

"She has a point." Bronx said as he dragged the man to the door. "You come right behind me Crissy."

She nodded. "Okay. I will. With Daxx and Alona."

Bronx dragged the man out the door. He looked down the hall and then opened the device on his arm. Both he and the man vanished.

"Oh my god." One of the women gasped.

I turned back to them. "It is something to see, the first dozen or so times."

"Watch him." Sith growled and shoved the man against the wall beside Tim. He stomped over to me and gingerly held up my arm. "My king is going to have my heart for this."

"It's fine. Go. Get him back and I will be along in a moment."

He frowned, the indecision clear on his face.

"Go. I-I order you." I said, even though the hesitation in my tone told him I was only going through the motions, and not ordering him at all.

"Be right behind me, please." He said with worry and then went and grabbed the man whose hands were tied with a neon pink scarf out the door.

After the guards and men were gone, I went over and slid down the wall to sit.

The women with curly black hair came over. "I'm Alyssa." She knelt and pulled the scarf off my arm.

"Alona." I glanced to see Daxx sitting on the floor on the other side of the room wincing as she touched her head. "You ladies need to pack anything you want to take with you. I have a safe place you can go."

"I'll help you pack if you like." Crissy offered.

"I'm dizzy." Daxx said. "Do you have your transporter on, Alona?"

I shook my head. "No. I didn't think to put it on, we were with the guards who all wear them and you..."

"I don't think I can focus enough to take us back." Crissy came rushing back into the room with the woman that had opened the door. "Criss, do you have your transporter on?"

She bit her lip. "No. Victor didn't want me disappearing on my own, so I took it off."

"Lovely." I mumbled knowing what that meant. "Can the guys come to us?"

"Not if some kind of blocking spell has been put on here, and we can't exactly go wandering without the guards." She slid further down the wall and gave me a look I understood well enough. She didn't want to call the men either.

I motioned to the hallway, so Alyssa would go. "Go pack." She got up and rushed down the hall.

Crissy came over and looked at my arm. "Chase isn't going to be happy."

Daxx snorted and then winced. "That's putting it mildly, he's going to freak right out. After this Troy is going to lock me in our room."

Getting up, Crissy went over and examined Daxx's scalp. "It's not bleeding, but it's not good either." She sat down. "I don't want to call Victor for help—again. He'll get that look."

"I'll make the call." I didn't want to, but the amount of blood coming from my arm wasn't going to get better if we sat here debating. "How mad can they be? We rescued three women and found three more team bad members."

Crissy and Daxx both gave me a blank look.

"Okay, wishful thinking. I'm going to message first and make certain they're not mid-battle." Getting my phone out of my purse, I quickly sent. *Is this a bad time to call?*

The phone rang before I could exit the screen. I answered it.

"Duchess anytime is a good time for you to call me."

"I wasn't sure if you would be beating on people. I wouldn't want to interrupt that."

He chuckled. "I would beat them one handed if you felt inclined to talk. We just found another deserted location, so I have time to spare." I could hear several voices in the background. "Alona, why is Victor ranting about killing the three guards that are supposed to be with you and my brothers' mates?" Gone was his playful tone.

"I was just going to get to that."

"In the future, perhaps you should lead with that and save the trivial banter for later."

"Noted." Both Crissy and Daxx watched me intently.

"Before Victor snaps my neck, maybe you could shed some light on the situation."

I could hear the voices behind him go silent. "Short version?"

He cleared his throat in the way he did when he was annoyed. "Fastest version."

"We found three women." I offered, while trying to explain the end result of such.

"Excellent... and?"

"They were being held by three men, from Alterealm, I am guessing by their sheer size," Daxx wasn't looking well at all. "Our guards have taken them to the cells, but we've hit a slight snag in transporting back."

I could hear someone speaking, they must have been standing right beside him. "What sort of snag, and I'm warning you now, my patience are almost gone."

"We are still at the apartment, but neither Crissy nor I have out devices on and we sent..."

"Your guards back with prisoners."

I nodded. "Yes, but Daxx hurt her head and can't seem to focus and devices don't work here regardless, so we're not even sure she could transport us, there is some sort of block placed on this apartment…"

"Stop. Hurt her head?" There were muffled voices. "Troy can't trace her, where are you? Are you all right?"

I looked down at my arm and then over to Daxx and Crissy. "I have a small cut on my arm. Criss is fine." Crissy nodded at me.

I could hear him blowing out a loud breath, probably trying not to say what he wanted to. "We are going to meet the guards so they can bring us to you." He said it in a quiet precise way. I knew he was trying to stay calm, but I could hear the rage beneath the surface.

"I have the women packing. Could you have Michael get in touch with Anthony so he can come and pick them up and take them somewhere safe? I haven't had time to set up another safe house…"

"Alona?"

"Yes?"

"I'm going to hang up now. I will call you back once we are on that side."

"Okay, Chase."

The line went dead. Hanging up, I looked at the screen of the phone and then to the girls.

"We're in deep shit, aren't we?" Daxx asked.

I nodded. "I believe we may be."

"Awesome." She said and then closed her eyes. "This is *so* going to suck."

Crissy got up. "I'm going to help them, so they're ready when the guys get here, because I don't think we'll be staying longer than that."

My arm was starting to throb more. "I believe you're correct in that assessment."

Chapter Twenty-Eight

Chase didn't call back, I had to wonder if that was a good or bad thing. Most likely the later. I hadn't watched the time but knew it couldn't have been ten minutes when someone knocked loudly on the door. Alyssa came out holding a broom. She stood beside her friend, Kristin, and raised it in the air. Kristin looked out the spy hole.

She turned to look at Daxx and I. "It's one of the big guys that was here with you."

"Crap." Daxx mumbled.

Alyssa sent me a hesitant look. "Is that a crap, don't let him in?"

"I doubt that door will stop them, you had better let them in."

"There's more of them and they look very angry'." Kristin said quietly.

"I'll see you in twenty years when I'm allowed out again." Daxx said and then sighed.

Lowering the broom, Alyssa stepped back from the door as Kristin opened it. I watched as they came through the door, and I had to admit if you didn't know them, you would give them a very wide berth. Chase and Troy were clone visions of anger and concern. Victor came through last, and was the scariest male I've ever seen in my life. I was almost relieved to see Michael come in, really knowing we were in trouble when he looked the least threatening. Our guards came in last and closed the door, standing in front of it like silent statues.

Troy scooped up Daxx without a word and went back over to the door as Crissy was jumping up to hug Victor.

Chase dropped down beside me and moved the cloth covering my arm.

"Is it bad?" Michael asked while towering over us.

Chase made a sound of annoyance. "Blood should heal it."

The fact he hadn't looked me in the eyes was unnerving. I sensed no emotion, either from him or his brothers. Just the cold void of no emotion. Similar to when they fought.

"I'll wait here with the guards until Anthony arrives." Michael looked at the women standing as far as possible from them all. "I sent a message for Leone to track down Romulus, to check the apartment." He waved a hand around. "We'll make sure all of their belongings are moved."

Chase picked me up into his arms. I looked at Sith. "Stay here with them until Anthony arrives." I held my hand up, so Chase would stop. "Tell Anthony to have Liza use the account to find a house and email me the details. Until then Alyssa, Kirstin and Brittany can stay at a rental unit."

Sith nodded.

Michael opened the door. "I'll find a guard to stay with them." He glanced at them. "A female one."

"Thank you." Chase started for the door.

I looked around him to Alyssa. "Get my number from Sith and I'll talk to you later."

She nodded. "Thank you." She looked at the guards. "All of you."

Chase barely stepped through the door before I found myself being carried to the counter in my kitchen.

His silence was worse than any verbal reprimand could ever be. Despite my stomach rebelling against the transport, I was hoping for some vocal confirmation that he wasn't as angry as I suspected.

He carefully took the scarf off my arm, his face showing his displeasure clearly. Reaching around me, he grabbed the cloth off the counter and wet it in the sink.

I tried not to wince as he dabbed at the blood on my arm. "Are you planning on being silent for much longer?"

Glancing at my face, he tossed the cloth into the sink and leaned a hand on either side of me. His pale eyes holding mine. "I didn't ask one of my red-eyed brothers to heal your cut," his tone was lower than a whisper, "with their saliva, because we are going to do a full blood bond, you and I."

I opened my mouth to object, he interrupted before I could utter a syllable.

"If Michael hadn't known the area I would have had to ride in a taxi reach you. A *taxi*, through traffic, for who knows how long." He searched my eyes briefly. "I'm a patient man, Alona, but that is wearing on me in ways I can't even describe." Straightening up, he crossed his arms over his chest and towered over me. "You don't want to wear my mark—fine, but you *will* at least have a connection that allows me to know when you're getting yourself into trouble the next time." His handsome face turned into a scowl. "I have no doubt there will be a next time." Inhaling deeply, he let it out slowly. "Do not fight me on this, please." He whispered with such angst in his tone that my heart skipped a beat.

That small tell revealed more of his internal struggle then sensing emotions ever would. I'd never had a connection to anyone in my long life. My mother, perhaps, from time to time, but she was so fragmented it was never what a mother and child should have. Would such a connection fill the void that always seemed to haunt me? There was still that part of me that needed to know the details. "Is that permanent or something…"

"It's not unless you're marked, so if you're worried I'm trying to irrevocably tie you to me, don't be." He sighed loudly. "Every cell in my body tells me to mark you, and I'll continue to fight that, but you have to give me something to calm the beast inside, Alona."

I studied his face. His eyes were still mostly hazel, with that slight blurred coloration that happened before they turned to yellow. He was genuinely struggling to stay calm. "All right."

Surprise flashed in his eyes. Recovering quickly, he shrugged out of his jacket, the straps holding hidden blades were undone and the blades hitting the floor echoed in the silent room. Taking his shirt off, he dropped it on the floor as well.

I couldn't help looking at his bared chest, as I finally sensed the first emotion from him since he arrived at the apartment, desire. My mouth filled with my fangs. Later, much later, I needed to seriously ponder why this kept happening where he was concerned.

Coming back to the present, I watched him score his chest with a sharp blade.

"Take it before it heals." He reminded me softly.

Sliding to the edge of the counter, I leaned forward and ran my tongue over the blood trickling down his toned chest. The taste didn't bother me, another thing to ponder. Why? As I gently sucked his life blood into my mouth I felt his tongue licking the cut on my arm. I hadn't even noticed he'd lifted my arm. All it took was a touch and I was consumed with this man.

When the cut healed closed, he grasped the back of my head and guided my face to his throat. I needed no further encouragement as I sank my fangs into his flesh. He made a guttural noise in the back of his throat and suddenly his emotions were merged with mine. Desire ignited in a way I'd never felt in my life. Licking across the bite, I lifted my head and looked at his yellow eyes. I needed to know. "Feed from me, let me feel what you do."

His hand still rested against the side of my face, his thumb stroking along my jaw. "That will be dangerous, my lovely duchess." His voice rasped. Holding my look, he lowered his head and brushed light kisses along my jaw and down my throat. My whole body responded to his touch.

Running my hands up the warm flesh of his chest, I reached around his neck and released the tie holding his long hair. Feeding my fingers into it, I closed my fist and pulled his head down so I could reach his mouth. He required no further persuasion and kissed me with more passion then I knew a person could have. His desire and my need mixed inside me, and I thought we may burst into real flames.

Lifting his head suddenly, he looked into my eyes, his yellow ones holding mine captive. I could feel him absorbing our longing, combined. With the blood bond and combined with my empathic ability, I was taking it right back from him, an endless cascade of erotic heat. I heard a moan, and realized it was my own.

"Fuck," Chase hissed out and closed his eyes and rested his forehead against my own. "We are truly in danger of killing each other with passion."

Trying to steady my own breathing, I didn't reply. There was nothing more I could say to what I knew was true.

"I am *very* sorry to interrupt." Arius' voice said quietly from the doorway.

Chase lifted his head up and looked down at me. "You may have just saved me from getting stabbed, brother. What is it?"

I watched his eyes swirling back to normal as he held my own in his stare. I could feel what he did, and I could only describe it as adoration. Something I'd felt before, but never had it directed at me.

Arius cleared his throat. "Is Alona's arm healed?"

The mention of my injury brought both Chase and I back to reality. I lifted my arm, and he looked at it. There was a slight red mark, but there was no pain.

"It's well enough, now." Chase answered him finally. Taking a deep breath, he stepped back and finally turned to look at his sibling. "How are the others?"

"Daxx will have the headache from hell for a few hours, but nothing permanent. And Crissy, well is Crissy."

Chase nodded and then picked up his shirt and pulled it over his head. "And the women they rescued?"

"Anthony and Michael are taking them to a hotel until a house is found. They're going to lay low for now."

I got off the counter and went around the island to the sink. "I didn't get a chance to speak to them."

"No, you were too busy bleeding out on their floor." Chase said with a snap to his voice.

Dabbing my arm with a damp towel to wash off the blood, I looked at him and rolled my eyes. "I was hardly bleeding out."

He leaned on the counter so I would have to look at him. "One drop of blood is too much where you're concerned."

I was going to snipe back when a warm feeling washed over me. Stopping, I made eye contact with him and saw the soft look. This blood bond thing was really quite fascinating.

Arius came further into the room and leaned against the doorframe. "I just spent some time with the three men the guards brought back, I can't be certain until Troy takes a look, but I don't think those three women were the only ones being paired with Alterealm men."

Chase and I both stopped and stared at him. I tossed the cloth back into the sink. "What do you mean paired up?" I looked from him to Chase for a second. "Are we talking what I suspected from the meeting with Mister Hubert?"

Arius sighed deeply and nodded. "I believe so."

Chase went and picked up his blades. "Because feeding off innocent humans, or fucking up the world by dropping the barrier isn't bad enough, let's take it one step further and force women to have sex with our kind."

A wave of anger rushed through me. I inhaled sharply and Chase swore again. Before I could build a barrier against it, the emotion was gone, as if it had been blocked.

"Sorry." He looked at me. "It got away from me before I could shield you from it."

I shrugged. "It's nothing. My own emotions weren't far from yours." I glanced to Arius. "So, what do we do?"

Chase swore again and pulled his phone from his pocket. He glanced at the screen and answered it. "Michael." Setting his blades on the counter, he gave Arius a stern look. "A what?" Rubbing a hand across his forehead he blew out a breath. "Is there a way to follow it back to the source?"

I looked at Arius to see if he had a sense of what they were saying. He was scowling at his brother, which told me nothing, other than he understood his brother's stance and expression, or this internal family link was involved.

"Let us know. I'm heading back in a few minutes." He turned and looked at me. "She's fine now." He nodded. "Call Anthony and fill him in. Make sure he checks all their electronics." Hanging up he leaned on the counter and looked at the floor for a moment.

I could feel faint emotions from him, none of them were positive.

"What is it? Arius finally asked.

Chase blew out a breath again and then turned to look at him. "Michael went back to the apartment to meet Romulus to see if he can trace the magic used," he glanced to me, a look of concern on his face. "They found hidden cameras."

Inhaling sharply, I put my hand over my mouth. Whoever was on the other end of those cameras would now know I was involved with the royal family.

"Shit." Arius lifted both hands and held them to the side of his head for a moment and then looked at me. "You're burned." He held out his hand. "Give me your cell phone. I'll get you a new one with a new number."

Nodding, I pulled it out of my pocket and handed it to him. "Is there a way to find out who was watching?"

Taking my phone, he opened it and pulled out the little card in it. "I think we all know who was watching." He shrugged, "even if we find and follow where it leads to, they'll clear out before we get there."

Wrapping my arms around my waist I looked from him to Chase. He stood there watching me. "So, what now?" I suddenly didn't feel safe in my own high-tech security home.

Chase came over and wrapped his arms around me. "Grab anything you need for now, you're staying in the royal chambers until we figure out the next step."

Normally I would have argued, but every instinct I had told me it was better if I wasn't here. Nodding, I leaned back. "Is this ever going to end?"

A hard look appeared on his face. "It will." He said quietly, and then kissed my forehead softly. Releasing me, he turned to Arius. "Stay here until she's ready to come over. I need to talk to Troy and Victor."

Arius nodded. "We'll be there shortly."

Chase picked up his blades and coat. Turning back, he kissed my mouth softly. "I'll see you shortly." He grasped my chin lightly. "Stop."

I didn't have to clarify what he was referring to, I knew he could feel the panic building inside me.

"I would bleed to protect you, as would any brother of mine." He said softly. Kissing me once more, he stepped back and vanished.

"Do you need a hand packing?" Arius stepped out of the doorway.

Inhaling deeply, I counted to three to feel this long-lost feeling. "I have bags ready for emergency relocation." I walked past him. "If you could grab the red case and laptop from the office, I'll get the rest." I didn't pause to see if he followed, just walked with sure strides to my room. Opening the closet, I pulled out my run case, as I referred to it. Inside was everything I'd need to move on with short notice. I stood there and looked around the room out of habit. Usually when I needed this case, I would never see the room I stood in again.

"Check your security is set before we go." Arius said from the doorway. "You'll be back enjoying your wine soon."

I smirked at him. "Will I though?" I went to the dresser and picked up the box on top of it. Favorite items, with the recent addition of elbow length satin gloves. I'd barely had time to consider the meaning behind that gift from Crissy.

"Things are different now, Arius." I stopped and looked at him. "Question remains, is if I wish them to be that way."

He smiled. "Seems to me when I arrived, you weren't objecting loudly to how different things are."

I felt my cheeks flush and paused in the door. "I've been discovering many flaws in my usual immoveable resolve as of late." I gave him a bold grin.

"Mmm, I'm sure you have." He glanced around. "Got everything you can't live without?"

I nodded. "As long as I have my boots, I can replace anything else."

Arius laughed. "Tell me that case isn't filled with boots."

I walked to the closet by the front door and opened it. "Don't be silly." Setting my bag down, I pulled another, larger case from the closet and started putting my boot collection in it. "That one isn't big enough."

Looking over my shoulder, Arius hissed out a breath. "You're coming back, Alona, you can pop here if the six pairs you've put in there aren't adequate enough."

I paused and then straightened up. "Old habits I suppose." Grabbing my absolute favorite pair, I sighed. "Okay the boots stay. Let's go before I change my mind."

Chapter Twenty-Nine

"I have to be honest, I'm a bit disappointed you picked the room on this side."

I jolted and turned to see Chase leaning against the doorjamb grinning at me. I glanced around the room I'd been brought too when I'd been so ill. "This one has the closet mall."

"I'll have them begin building a mall on my side immediately to entice you to come over." Straightening away from the door, he walked slowly toward me.

I could sense him trying to figure out my emotional state. "If you're anticipating dramatics, you'll be happy to know there won't be any." I shrugged. "Sudden life changes are something I'm *very* used to." I motioned around the room. "Although I must confess, I've never had somewhere so vast to hide in on short notice."

He walked slowly by the dresser and noted my belongings on it. "I pictured you having backup locations and safe houses scattered all over the world."

I turned back to the case open on the bed. "Oh, I do, but most are just small places of no significance, easy to get to when the situation seems irrevocably dire."

Chase stopped and stood beside me. Tucking his hands into his pockets he watched me take things out and fold them. "I don't suppose I can have a list of those places."

"For what purpose?" I set the shirt on the bed and looked at him. He had an odd expression on his face. Not a strange odd, but one of hesitation. "You think I'm going to disappear and move on?"

"The thought has crossed my mind, more than once since meeting you." With a gentle touch he held my chin and searched my face. "Am I wrong?"

I couldn't lie to him. "I have considered it a few times, but it's different now. I know I'm not alone—in how I am. I've never had that before."

"You'll never be alone again, in any sense."

Taking a deep breath, I held it momentarily then released it. "I don't think that's sunk in completely yet. It's…" I gave him a wide-eyed look. "I suddenly have a father and people I care about."

"And that I'm sure is something you had given up wishing for."

"More like yearned for." I grimaced. "I had my woe-is-me period during my sixties."

He smirked. "Have I mentioned you are the sexiest young woman I've ever seen?"

I laughed. "I will never get used to knowing there are others so much older than I am."

"We are children compared to some." He dropped his hand away and put it back in his pocket. "We have some time until the others are back or awake," he frowned, "I don't even know who should or shouldn't be sleeping at the moment." Shaking his head, he gave me a tender look. "I thought we could go see your father, if you like."

"Oh, he's doing well enough?" My heart beats increased.

He nodded slowly, "I just spoke to the doctor and he believes his condition is under control now, so a short visit would be allowed."

"I-I…" I held my hand over my heart beating faster. "Yes, I'd like to see him."

He held out his hand, paused and reached to tuck his pendant I still wore into my top. "The doctor says not to ask too many questions at this point, just let him choose what he wishes to talk about."

I took his hand and nodded. "All right. Honestly, I have so many questions, I wouldn't know where to begin." I looked up at him. "Speaking with my father was something I never thought I would be doing."

"I know. I'm going to be there. The doctor may feel he's under control, but I'm not taking any chances."

I remembered Levi's reaction the last time. "I am a quite nervous."

Lifting my hand, he kissed it then winked at me. "I know. I can feel what you feel."

I stopped abruptly. "That is odd, usually I'm the one doing that."

Chase chuckled. "Emotion feeder, remember?"

We started walking again. "You could feel them before the blood bond?"

He smirked. "More like taste them, but now I feel them as well."

I glanced at him for a second, before turning my attention to where we were going. "More for me to think about."

"If I could get you thinking less and feeling more, I'd be a happy man."

"Can't always have it your way, your majesty." I inclined my head in a mock bow.

"As you say, my Queen of Light." he murmured teasingly.

Glaring at him, I offered no reply. I did, however, note that despite all that was happening he always made me feel better.

We stood outside my father's room for several minutes. He was reading on a screen built into his wall. Chase explained he was now in what was considered the medical wing of the vast cells, and was allowed some privileges. I had to wonder if he'd been given special attention because he was my father. After all, he had intended to decapitate Daxx, something I'm sure her mate wouldn't forget. He seemed more at ease than the last time I'd see him.

"Whenever you're ready."

I glanced to the man patiently standing beside me. "A moment more." I whispered, still feeling far too much uncertainty to go in and speak to a man I'd never thought existed.

Chase did something on a panel beside the door and stepped into the hall. "I'll be right back."

I watched him go into the cubicle-sized room with my father.

"Mister Berg. Do you know who I am?"

My father stood slowly. "I do."

Chase continued to stand just inside the door, looking very much a ruler at that moment. "Do you remember meeting your daughter when you were brought to the cells?"

A pained look appeared on my father's face. "I-I do, vaguely. I thought I'd imagined her until I spoke to the Warden of Justice. Did I…" He frowned, "Did I frighten her?"

"She was upset."

"I didn't mean to, I was consumed with grief all over again."

"We understand that, Mister Bergs, I may not know what you've been through, but I do sympathize with it, what you've been through."

"Thank you, my king."

"Am I?" Chase studied him for a moment. "Your king? Last time you mentioned my family, I do believe you said our kingdom would burn."

My father bowed his head. "I don't recall exactly what I said or thought then. I'm sorry, my king, I still have moments of little clarity."

Chase stood there watching him for a minute. "How are you feeling right now, in terms of your clarity?"

"I am doing well today." His voice was barely a whisper.

"Well enough to have a short visit from your daughter?"

My father's head snapped up. "Yes. Yes I am. Please."

Chase closed the distance between them. My father was only a few inches shorter than Chase, but lacked the confidence the blond king had, seeming more drawn into himself and much smaller. "There are a few things you need to understand before she comes in." He paused and watched him. "Your daughter is an empath, so if you have another episode similar to the last time, you will cause her distress, and I will *not* allow that."

Levi's eyes widened. "She has an ability? That's…"

"Do you understand Mister Berg?" Chase's tone wasn't allowing any doubt of who was superior in their relationship.

"Yes. Yes, I will control myself."

"I will be staying in the room the whole time to ensure that you do. Your daughter is *very* important to me, and is under my protection."

The expression on my father's face changed to concern. "Is she in some sort of danger?"

"The faction you were working with is after her…"

"What? No." Levi paced to the other side of the room. "No, you can't let them near her." He spun around. "You must keep her safe."

Chase watched him carefully as he moved around the cell, returning to stand in front of him. "I intend to." He waited for my father's stance to relax. "At a later date, when you're feeling better, anything you can recall to assist us in stopping them from taking other father's daughters—it would work in your favor."

I realized what he was doing. Knowing my father's awareness of having a daughter brought new light to the situation. Having heard and felt what I had in the last few weeks, I couldn't find fault in a king using any tactic available to him to protect innocent people.

"I will try to fit the fragments together, my king. Just please keep her safe from them."

Chase nodded abruptly. "I'll go get her." He spun on his heel and left the cell. I watched the door close behind him. He came in and stood in front of me. "Ready?"

I glanced back at Levi. "He's so much more lucid than before."

"He'll always require the medication. Losing your mate is a grief that never subsides." He offered his hand.

I nodded and took it. "I know." I whispered. The years with my mother would never fade from my memory. The desolate months with her barely existing—consumed with a grief that I had mistaken for mental infirmities.

He paused before opening the door. Lifting my chin, he kissed me softly. "If it becomes too much, let me know."

I nodded, too anxious to speak.

When we stepped in, my father straightened and smiled. He motioned to the chair and little table in the corner. "Please sit."

I went over and sat on the edge of the chair.

He quickly sat on his bed.

Chase remained in front of the door, his arms crossed over his chest, his expression a rigid warning.

"I don't..." Levi shrugged, "I don't know what to say. Where to begin."

I offered a small smile. "Neither do I."

His eyes were so much like mine, it felt like I was looking in a mirror.

"You have your mothers' features, it's haunting."

"If it's too much, I can go and come back another time."

"No." He shook his head. "It's not unbearable." He looked at Chase. "I suspect I'm being given a large dose of drugs to keep it manageable."

"Is it helping then?" I asked him.

He was quiet for a moment. "As well as it can, I imagine." Placing his hands on the mattress, he leaned against the edge of the bed, looking at the floor and then back to me. "I have many regrets in my long life. The latest, of course, you're well aware of." He shook his head, his expression lightening briefly, "I didn't feel it at the time, but now after much thought, I feel pride—the way you took me down in that underground cavern." He sat there looking at me, the pride shining in his eyes.

A lump formed in my throat. I'd never had someone look at me that way.

The smile faded, "I will never forgive myself for leaving your mother behind." The words came out fast, as if he had to say it quickly or not at all.

I felt tears fill my eyes at the emotion in his voice. A feeling of warmth filled me, and I knew Chase was helping me keep my own feelings under control.

"I'd like..." Levi blew out a shaky breath. "I would like to explain, if I may?"

I nodded, unable to find my voice.

"I loved your mother, with all of my heart." He looked back to the floor. "Even before I realized we were mates. I courted her for months before we even held hands—" He closed his eyes, a small smile on his face. "Which is quite the struggle when fate brings you a mate." He glanced to Chase then back to me. "Resisting instinct." Exhaling slowly, his eyes searched my face. "We had been discussing her coming over with me, it was both elating and exciting—then things," he looked uncomfortable, almost embarrassed, "took their natural course and I unintentionally marked her. We spent a few weeks after that planning. We didn't do the blood bond because I knew it would cause too much discomfort to be separated so early in our mating."

Levi stared at the floor for several minutes, many expressions appearing on his face during that time.

I could find no words to speak, so I waited in the heavy silence.

"When I came back here, I applied to bring my mate over, then quickly set about finding us a home..." He shook his head. "Many fell ill, in a matter of days—then it stretched into months." He blew out a ragged breath. "My sister," his eyes returned to mine, "your aunt, became sick." His face filled with grief. "We lost her."

A tear rolled down my cheek.

"My—your grandparents were devastated." He sighed softly. "I think because of her vulnerable state; my mother became ill. She lived through it, but there were months for her to recover her full strength again." His eyes connected with mine. "I didn't want to risk bringing Eva over during the epidemic—I didn't want to lose her." He stopped and squeezed his eyes shut.

I could feel his pain as tears began to roll down my cheeks.

"Alona?" Chase inquired quietly.

"I'm all right, Chase."

My father looked from Chase to me slowly. "I'm sorry. It still hurts me. I had no idea how bad it was where you and your mother were—I never would have left her there that long if I'd known." He stood up and went to the small sink. Filling a cup of water, he sipped it for a moment. "Everyone we'd known in that neighborhood was gone when I went back. I don't know if they moved or died…" He set the cup down and went back to the bed. "I had no way of finding her. I knew she was alive, I could feel it through our mark, but I couldn't find her…you." His voice cracked with emotion. "I traveled from city to city. I searched camps—records of the dead. I just—she—I-I couldn't find you." He kept waving his hand around, his voice getting louder with each word.

I could feel his emotions becoming more chaotic. These emotions resonated inside me, the same I'd felt from my mother for months on end. She'd go from melancholy to frantic, to barely moving for hours. My heart sped up. I looked to Chase, he was watching me, a serious expression in his eyes. He moved away from the door.

"Mister Berg, Levi, you need to settle down or Alona will have to leave." Chase said it quietly, but there was no mistaking his authority.

"I know," Levi looked at me. "I'm trying—I don't think—" He took deep breaths. "You should go for now, my lovely daughter."

I could feel him trying not to come apart in my presence. I got up. I wanted so much to comfort him, but I couldn't when he was so upset, I would absorb it all. "I'll come back in a few days...father."

He looked at me, his face filled with pain. "Yes." He said hoarsely.

Chase put his hand on my back and guided me out of the room. When the door closed, and my father could no longer see, he spun me and pulled me into his arms.

"It wasn't his fault." I whispered more to myself then him.

"No, it wasn't." Chase ran his hands up and down my back in a soothing motion.

I could feel waves of warmth filling me from him through the bond. "It changes everything I believed." I said against his chest.

"I know. It's going to take time to digest." He kissed the top of my head. "How does a glass of wine and a hot bath sound?"

"What about meeting the others?'

He wiped the dampness from under my eye. "I'll stall them while you have some quiet time."

"How will you do that?" I was in no hurry to move further from his warm body, it was comforting.

He winked. "I can be very distracting and entertaining when need be."

I smiled and looked up at him. "I have no doubt you can be." I gently tugged his goatee. "It must be this flirty beard."

His eyes went wide. "Behave, or I'll move the meeting to outside your bathroom door while you're relaxing."

"You wouldn't."

He smirked. "Oh yes, duchess, I would."

Chapter Thirty

I'm not sure how long I lay back in the large tub. I didn't even drink the wine, just started at the wall, letting the water relax me. I tried not to, but couldn't help thinking, just how different my life would have been if my father had found us. If I'd lived my entire life with loving parents... it was overwhelming, the difference I would have experienced. It had almost got to me when I snapped out of it, refusing to dwell on it a moment more. It was not my parents' fault. It was no one's fault that the epidemic happened.

After soaking in deep contemplation of the things I'd learned, I got dressed and decided I'd kept the others waiting long enough. I hadn't even realized it was well into the night realm's shift. I wasn't tired at all; my mind wouldn't allow for sleep anytime soon. The entire day had been a complete haze of events.

Opening the door, I stopped abruptly and looked at Sith standing across the hall. "You are a welcome sight. I have no idea how to get to the dining room."

He smirked. "I figured as much, but after the events of earlier, I'm not to be more than ten feet from your presence for the rest of my life."

Closing the door, I sighed. "He took it out on our guards?"

"I think we're the least frightening ones to deal with." He motioned down the hall.

I laughed. "Are you saying the giant, alpha men are afraid of us women?"

Sith bobbed his head. "Yes."

"Well, I don't know about that, but I will try not to put you in a bad situation again."

Pointing which way to turn, he shrugged. "I know you will, just please try not to get injured next time."

"I will do my best." When we turned the next corner, I recognized the hall and realized we were there. "I'm going to need a map of these halls." I said as we walked in.

"A map shouldn't be required if your guard is with you, as he should be." Chase said from the far end of the room.

A warmth spread through me, and I wasn't sure if it was from seeing him, or sent by him through the bond. "Am I not secure inside the royal chambers' halls?" I glanced to the others around the table, "I thought any allied to Mister Hubert had been found."

Daxx rolled her head to glare at her mate. Troy scowled.

"To our knowledge they have been, sister." Rafael shrugged, "being cautious isn't a bad thing."

I sat down beside Daxx. "So, you gentlemen have guards following you around the halls?" I made an exaggerated move to look around at each corner of the room, as if the guards were hidden well.

"We don't..." Raf started until Quinton nudged him with his elbow.

Michael leaned forward and looked down the table at me. "We're less likely to," he sent Arius a look, "require..."

"You guys should stop while you're ahead." Daxx said softly, leaning back in the chair and crossing her arms. "Dig, dig, dig."

I smirked at her reference and sent Chase an inquiring look. "I am certain you're not about to tell us you can take care of yourselves but we are weak, feeble women that need watching over."

Chase tilted his head, giving me a contemplative glare. "I—we," he motioned to his siblings, "would never be stupid enough to utter those words." He said slowly.

"As none of us brothers are rarely without the company of another brother, we don't require guards." Victor said as he poured more coffee into his cup. "Is this settled for the moment?" He took his time making eye contact with those seated closest to him. "As I have information to share, and Michael and I have raid parties to organize to check other locations."

"What information?" Troy sat back, casually holding Daxx's hand in her lap.

Such a small gesture, but it made me realize that was something I'd never had. I unintentionally looked down the table at Chase. His eyes met mine, a soft look in them. A look meant just for me.

Accepting the other matter was put to rest, Victor gave an abrupt nod and set his cup down. "The female guard from the Hinton family has been successfully recruited to their *cause*."

"I'm still not sure we should have gone with that plan." Quinton set his fork down and pushed his plate back. "Not after what we've found out about how they treat women."

I felt a brief flare of anger from him.

"She's a very well-trained, quite skilled in combat." Victor assured him.

Michael nodded, "and she has a very useful ability, so I'm confident she will be able to hold her own if needed."

"Oh?" Arius looked from Victor to Michael. "What sort of skill?"

Michael shrugged. "We didn't get into specifics, but she tossed a dozen objects at Victor in a matter of a few seconds—without touching any of them."

Chase grinned. "Really? That would have been amusing to see."

Victor gave him a blank look. "At the very least, she will be able to deter anyone if she chooses."

Michael paused before taking a drink. "We have a few plans set up as well, so she can communicate with us when she's able."

"What is fire without flames?" Crissy said quietly.

Everyone stopped and looked at her, I'm sure it was to see if she was asking or just blurting things out as she seemed to do that a lot.

"I don't understand the question, heart." Victor gave her his undivided attention.

Crissy blew out a breath. "I keep seeing fire, but it's not fire—," she waved a hand around, "there's no flames." Nodding, she looked at Chase. "How can it be fire without flames?" Turning in the chair, she picked up her backpack and started to dig in it. "And the daisy, I don't know what the connection between flameless fire and daisies are." Pulling out her notebook, she set it on the table and the continued to dig in the bag.

Victor, without looking away from her, reached into his jacket pocket and pulled out a pencil and held it out to her.

"Oh." Smiling, she stood on her chair to kiss him. "You always know what I need." Nodding she squatted on her chair and opened the notebook.

"Can you describe this flameless fire?" Chase leaned on the table, watching her. "Is it sparks?"

I frowned, wishing I could understand better how her mind worked. "Could it be a flash of sorts? Bright enough to look like fire, without flames."

Crissy stopped and looked at me. I could feel the swirling emotions pouring off her. "That might be it." She stood on the chair, picking up her bag and clutching her notebook. "I need to go to my tower."

Victor stood and held out his hand to help her step down off the chair. "I'll call you before I head out."

She nodded, obviously distracted.

Everyone watched her walk out, Bronx right behind her.

Victor sat down. "She's exhausted." He picked up his cup. "She only sleeps for a few moments at a time, the visions won't pause long enough for her to rest." He rubbed his hand over his forehead.

"She's been worse, Victor." Daxx offered. "At least now with the bond between you, she's not completely absorbed in it." She snorted. "There were times she'd babble so much, not one word was coherent."

Rafael nodded. "That's a fact."

Crissy's mind and feelings were chaotic, in my opinion, if this wasn't bad, I don't think I'd survive it worse.

"I do all I can to help her, when she allows it." Victor said with a note of displeasure in his voice.

"She'll figure it out, brother." Chase nodded. "She always does."

"I don't know how she does it." Leone said sounding exhausted. "I have *a* voice in my head, no pictures, just a voice, and I can't focus on a damn thing."

"It's no better?" I asked.

He shook his head, "The mages and witches have tried several things." He shrugged. "No luck yet." Rubbing his hand over his short-spiky hair. "I'm about done with people messing in my head though. I've been thinking about what elder Faran said though, maybe a few days of fresh air and quiet might help."

"You're going away?" Rafael looked from one king brother to another. "Alone?"

Leone shook his head. "No, I don't think that's a good idea right now." He glanced at Chase and then Troy. "I was just going to go for a ride tomorrow—during daylight and see if it helps." He motioned around the room. "I've been stuck inside for days now and the walls are starting to close in on me."

I noticed the brief look between the twin kings. Chase nodded slowly. "As long as you're not going outside the kingdom border boundaries, I don't see a problem." He turned to Michael. "Those are still patrolled regularly?"

Michael nodded. "We've increased frequency until this maniacal uprising is resolved."

Chase shrugged and gave Leone a look. I could feel the concern through our connection and wished I knew how to send the warm encouragement to him that he sent to me often. He glanced to me for a second and I had to wonder if I'd managed it without more than thinking. "Just take your phone and a device, in case something comes up."

"I agree." Troy said in that tone of authority.

"Yeah. Okay." Leone blew out a long breath. "Figure it can't hurt, right?"

"I'm sure it will help." I offered him a small smile.

"Could be worse," Daxx said under her breath, "you could be under house arrest and not allowed to go *anywhere*." She glared at Troy.

Troy sighed. "No one said you weren't allowed to go anywhere, just nowhere without first letting us *know*."

She sat forward. "So we can go to Alona's and research?"

Troy looked to Chase, who turned to give me a thoughtful glance.

"I want to send Clairee and Romulus over to check her apartment before anyone goes back." Chase held my look for a moment. "Do you agree, brother king?"

Troy took a moment, indecision on his face. "If they can clear it and find no evidence that someone is watching, I'd agree to that." He gave Daxx a hard look. "*Research* only, not going to *rescue* anyone."

"I'll take Romulus and Clairee over." Arius offered as he stood up. "If that's all, I'd like to get back to the cells and see if our new *guests* are ready to share yet."

I couldn't believe I'd forgotten about the men that had been holding those women. "Have you found out anything? Perhaps whether there are more in that situation?"

Arius shook his head, Daxx answered before he could speak. "They've given us diddly so far."

I took that to mean nothing helpful. "Has anyone checked on the women?"

Quinton stood up. "I met Anthony with a personal guard a few hours ago. She's going to send us regular reports." He walked to the end of the table. "Your friend Liza told Anthony she had a house in mind, and once she got the go ahead from you she'd begin the process."

"I'll have to check my email." I looked to Michael. "Is the I.P. secure here?"

He nodded. "Yes, no one can trace it."

"Good. I'll make sure those women and any others found have a safe place." I looked to Victor. "Aside from guards, I'd like a security system installed."

Victor's eyebrows went up. "We are more prone to use magic barriers."

I nodded. "That's fine too, but an honest to goodness alarms-sounding-lights-flashing system will be installed."

"As you wish." He gave Chase a brief look and then stood up. "Keep me informed. I'm going to vet a few more of our female guards that have passed training to reside at the house."

I smiled. "I will. Thank you." I shrugged, "For using female guards. I have no idea what these women have been through, but I'm sure a male-free environment will be reassuring."

Daxx snorted but said nothing.

Victor gave me an abrupt nod and then turned on his heel and left through the kitchen.

I went back to my large temporary room. Everyone had other places to be, I had nothing to do. My mind was restless, processing so many things I knew sleep was going to elude me through what remained of the night. To pass the time, I browsed through the endless closet. Daxx had explained why there were so many clothes of every size, but I was still amazed by the variety. Having been told to help myself, I tried on anything that caught my eye. At the rate I was going, I would need another closet to put it all in.

I looked in the mirror and turned. With my hair up, this top would look soft and feminine. After the years of fashion trends I had lived through, I liked this era the most, almost anything was acceptable. Except bell bottoms, thankfully. There had been a few tense years when flare bottoms were in style, that I feared those floppy-out-of-control bells would make a comeback.

My mind was bouncing around like one of Crissy's little rubber balls. Levi—my father, what he'd said and just the mere fact that he was alive, and I'd met him kept me spinning. Chase was also on my mind more than I was comfortable with.

I paused on a simple short black skirt and stared at it. Was that him pushing somehow through the bond, making me think of him so much? Holding the skirt to my waist I decided I'd try it with this top. Of course, I was only half trying to put the blame on Chase. I knew it had nothing to do with the bond, and was my own weakness causing him to be at the forefront of my thoughts.

Securing the zipper, I smoothed it over my thighs. It was quite short, but not obscenely so. Turning, I looked in the mirror trying to decide what type of boot would go with it. A knock on the door had me looking out of the closet. I knew who was on the other side without opening it. I couldn't feign I wasn't here either with all the lights on. "Come in." I called out, deciding I was going to stay right here in the closet doorway.

Chase walked in and closed the door behind him. He paused and looked around for a moment.

I had clothes strewn all over the room. "It may look out of sorts, but it's a system."

Smirking, he walked over. "A system to what, is the question?"

I pointed to the bed. "Those I'm keeping. The sofa is undecided, and the two chairs are down further on the list unless I find something that goes with them."

Tucking his hands in his pockets, he nodded slowly. "And here I thought you'd be asleep, but instead you've gone on a shopping spree."

I had to smile to that. "A *free* shopping spree."

"Ah, yes that would do it."

As he spoke his eyes were appraising every inch of my body. "I think you should keep that skirt."

"You're just saying that because it shows a great deal of leg."

"Indeed it does." He motioned for me to turn around.

I did until I was facing him again. I could feel his desire even though it wasn't showing on his face.

"It's missing something," he mused quietly.

"I was thinking boots." I looked into the mirror again.

"Boots." He came up behind me to study my reflection over my shoulder. "Heeled?"

I stared at my legs in the mirror. "Low heel I think."

"Mmm, what style of boot?"

"I suppose that would depend on if I was going for flirty with an ankle boot or something higher and more daring." This was one conversation I would never have anticipated having with the large, very masculine king standing behind me.

He moved close enough I could feel the heat from his body. "You could definitely get away with more daring...in a tasteful way."

I glanced to his eyes in the mirror, his met mine immediately. "You don't think a tall boot would be too fetishist?"

Crossing his arms, he looked as if he was seriously contemplating it. "I'd have to see it to decide."

"I didn't bring anything like that. They're at the apartment."

He stepped back. "Apartment...your sexy legs distracted me from the reason I'm here. Your apartment has been cleared. No trace of anything that shouldn't be there."

I took a moment to consider how I felt about that. It was good, yet I didn't feel comfortable being there just yet. Turning, I looked up at him. "Is it all right if I stay here longer? Just—" I glanced down at my hands clasped in front of me. "Knowing they had a camera and were watching—it's unnerving." I returned my eyes to his.

Chase gave me a soft look. "You can stay as long as you want." He motioned in the closet, "after all you still have half the closet to try on."

I laughed.

"Not to mention a rather large mess to tidy up."

I grimaced as I took stock of the clothes scattered about. "Yes, I do."

Clearing his throat, his expression went serious again. "I stopped to tell you about your apartment—and you should feed again. I feel like reminding you that you can feed whenever you want is necessary, after past *incidents.*" He reached out and ran his fingertips lightly over my arm where the cut had been. "Feeding a few times after an injury will help it heal, on the inside too."

I glanced at the red mark on my arm. "I don't have the fast healing you men do."

"It's reasonable to assume a properly fed body functions better…"

Turning my head, I gave him a disbelieving look. "You just want me to bite you."

He grinned. "I won't deny that, ever, but I am concerned for you as well."

My mind, without permission, immediately went back to the earlier *feeding*—the intimacy of it, the heat… Did I want to chance that again? I wanted to continue to think I was resisting the pull between us. That I was resisting him, but I knew inside I was only lying to myself. Each time we had been close, there had been some sort of dire situation pending, or an interruption.

"I think you're running more from yourself than from me." He said softly, standing close enough I could feel his breath against my hair.

"I can feel them you know." I said out loud and then realized I had. Turning on the spot, I faced him.

"Them?" He tilted his head in that patient way he had, not pushing for immediate response.

I felt what I could only describe as butterflies in my stomach, knowing I was about to admit things I had been trying to hide. "The invisible threads, weaving us together."

"Yes."

That was all he said, no denial, no arrogant satisfaction. "I'm not..." I stopped, trying to decide what I wanted to convey. "I'm not sure I'm willing..."

He smirked to that. "I know you're not a liar, Alona, don't tell me what I've felt isn't there."

Clasping my hands, I glanced down to them while I gathered my thoughts. "I won't deny there is chemistry between us."

He raised one eyebrow. "You're going to make this scientific?"

Frowning, I shook my head. "That is not what I meant at all, I don't know the first thing about science." I shrugged. "What I was trying to say was I don't want to give you the wrong idea. I wasn't trying to deny there is an attraction between us."

He nodded slowly, considering what I'd said. "Attraction might be a slight understatement." Stepping closer, so there was barely an inch between us, he tucked his hands in his pockets and looked down at me. "And *what* wrong idea are you afraid to give me?"

My heart was skipping inside me. I picked up no emotion, just that carefully guarded void of nothingness he seemed all too capable of achieving. "If we," I paused to choose the right word, "sleep together, I don't want you to misconstrue that to mean I'd agreed to..."

"Be marked as mine for whole realms to see?" He finished quietly, with no infliction of emotion at all.

Nodding, I took a quick breath. I hadn't thought about this conversation prior to now, or if I had, I was in denial. Now that I'd just laid it out on the table, there was no going back and every nerve in my body tensed waiting for the conclusion.

"I know you feel what I do, the only difference is I am not denying it is there." His eyes searched mine. "We have been the embodiment of taking it slow, despite what our bodies, instincts are saying." Pausing once more, he just watched me. "Why would you think I would take one thing to mean the other?"

His breath on my face was very distracting and I was having trouble focusing on his words.

The expression in his eyes become softer. "I know your fears. I may not be able to read minds as my twin can, but I have felt the gauntlet of emotion you have felt in a multitude of situations, or felt the spike of them during conversations. I would never take advantage of you, beloved Alona."

As he spoke my whole being was filled with—I wasn't exactly sure, love, adoration? I felt like I'd been wrapped in a cocoon of emotions I'd never personally felt in my long life. My heart began to change rhythm again when he touched the side of my face with a feathery touch.

"I will *not* mark you until you ask me to, of that you have my word." With a gentle pressure, he tilted my face up to his. "If you never feel assured enough for that step, I will learn to accept that." Kissing my mouth briefly, he looked back to my eyes. "I know you've been feeling different sensations since the bond, as well as sending out your own—*that* is only the start of what we could have, there's so much more."

Focusing on what I wanted to say was becoming more difficult. "I don't want to hand over my entire life to someone, to allow them to decide what I can and cannot do…"

"If you're referring to my brothers ruling over their mates, I can assure you what we see is a fraction of what the situation actually is." He smirked. "I have a connection with them, and feel what they do if I focus. They are not getting off scot-free in the telling their mates what they cannot do." His face became serious again. "There is much bending and giving on both sides there, duchess. We are not rulers to our mates," he grimaced, "Mitz alone would stab each of us if we tried that, never mind what our mates, or intended mates, would do."

His thumb's steady caress of my jaw was mesmerizing, ensuring I was solely fixated on him.

"I've taken a lot of missteps in my life, rushed in without thought of consequence," his eyes were swirling between one color and the other, "but in this, with you, I am—have been taking it one step at a time, and will continue to do so until told otherwise."

The fact that he was taking the time to reassure me and put my doubts to rest, all while keeping the emotions that went with his words at bay, meant a lot to me. I could *see* his emotional state as he was fighting his eyes from changing color. Taking a deep breath, I exhaled slowly. "What," I licked dry lips, "what are the steps?" I was having my own struggle, trying to keep my fangs from protruding while this close to him.

He stepped closer, so our bodies were barely touching. "Right now, I'm just talking about you feeding—what comes after that is entirely up to you."

My fangs filled my mouth. "Is it?" I bit my bottom lip between my teeth. "I don't feel like anything is up to me anymore."

His hand moved gently up to cup the back of my head. "It's all up to you." Tipping his head to the side, he offered his neck to me.

I knew he stood there waiting, wanting my mouth on him as much as I did at this moment, but he was showing restraint as well as showing me that the next move was mine. His fingers moved in my hair, but he made no move to push my face closer to his bared flesh. His eyes were almost yellow now as they held mine. The tension of the moment was almost as stimulating as our earlier moments in my kitchen. I didn't know why I was hesitating as long as I was, I wanted nothing more at this very moment than to sink my fangs into him. Chase's nostrils flared as he looked down at me, his jaw was clenched now as he waited out our silent battle of wills. I leaned closer and inhaled the scent of his essence into my body and a buzz went through me. Reaching up slowly, I buried my hand in his hair and then closed my fist around it as I bit into him.

He gasped out a breath and then growled and pulled our bodies tight together.

The slight rush I'd feel from feeding was amplified when it was from Chase. He added to it through the bond, taking advantage of my empathic ability. Releasing his neck, I licked across my marks and pulled his head down to mine.

Our mouths clashed with the same need. I wasn't sure if either of us were controlling the direction of the kiss. When the intensity of the combined sensations hit me, I pulled my head back. "Do you need to feed?" I was quite breathless.

His lips traveled along my throat. "Feeding is *not* what I need right now." He grasped my hips, grinding his into me so I couldn't help but feel his arousal.

My knees were already shaking from the desire, I was afraid they'd give out completely as his mouth trailed along my skin causing me to quiver with need.

Lifting his head, he crushed my mouth with his. I found myself being lifted, then my back was against the wall. He lifted me further, bracing me with his leg. Wrapping my legs around him, I was rewarded with a deep groan. His tongue invaded my mouth, brushing against my fangs—that I hadn't realized were still out.

Chase's hand found their way to my bare skin under the hem of my top. Just his skin touching mine increased the heat inside me. I needed to feel more of our bodies touching. Reaching between us, I pulled his shirt open. The sound of the buttons popping off added fuel to the fire inside both of us.

Shoving the shirt over his shoulders, I ran my hands along the toned muscle of his chest and shoulders. A feeling of reckless abandonment came over me, for the first time in my life I wanted to bite someone, not for feeding. I pulled my mouth from his and leaned down. Without warning, I sunk my fangs into the flesh of his shoulder.

"Fuck," he hissed, grasping my hair, he pulled my head back up.

Our breathing was ragged.

"Stop now or not at all," he whispered, his yellow, lust-filled eyes locked on my own.

I knew he was keeping his word and letting me choose how far this went. Inside me was a blazing fire—just for him. I'd never felt close to this powerful desire before, and I feared if we stopped I may never again. "Don't stop." I said against his lips.

His eyes grew heavier, then the full force of his lust swamped me. Leaning closer, almost in slow motion, he kissed me in a very passionate, yet controlled way. I felt consumed by the depth of it.

Grasping my hands, he pinned them against the wall above my head. My whole body quivered. *My hands...* I pulled them out of his and leaned my head back against the wall to break the kiss. "I need my gloves."

He closed his eyes for a second, I could feel him reining in his desire, before he lowered me to the floor.

I walked as quickly as I could on unsteady legs, to the dresser and opened the box on top of it. Pulling out the long black satin gloves. I fumbled to get them on.

As I pulled the second one up my arm, I turned to see Chase stood just where I'd left him. He looked at the gloves and then his eyes moved down my body.

In a few long strides, he was in front of me, grasping my waist. "Hang on. We're going to get those boots." His mouth covered mine, flooding passion into me at the same moment.

When he lifted his head a few moments later, I panted to catch my breath. We were in my apartment. Chase pulled his shirt off and dropped it to the floor.

My stomach felt giddy, but there was no nausea. I'd been so distracted when he transported us, my body didn't rebel.

He continued to look at me. "Boots."

Blinking, I tried to get my brain to function again. Turning, I went to the closet and pulled the long boots out of the case Arius had persuaded me to leave behind.

Chase came up and pulled them from my hand. When I turned to ask why, he dropped to his knees in front of me and held one of them out so I could put my foot in.

It took a moment to coordinate my shaking leg so he could pull it up past my knee. Either he was moving in slow motion or I was in a daze.

When the other boot was on, he stood slowly, his eyes devouring each inch of my body. Grasping my hips, he boosted me up so I could wrap my legs around his waist again. "The gloves and boots stay on." He growled and started walking down the hall.

As he crossed the threshold to my room, I couldn't stand not having his mouth on me a moment more. I pulled his head down, tugged the tie binding his hair, and with a handful of his silky mane guided his mouth to mine. The kiss reeked of desperation, but I didn't care. I needed the man, like I'd never needed any other.

Chase turned and pushed me against the wall again, our bodies so close, there was no air between. He rocked his hips into me and I broke the kiss, gasping. Reaching, I pulled my top over my head and tossed it aside. He made quick work of ridding me of my bra. I was struggling to get the strap off my arm when his mouth closed over my nipple.

Shaking the bra off, I clutched his head and held him there. "Chase," I gasped, "it's too much—the bond—the intensity…"

Lifting his head, he turned and carried me toward the bed. "I want you to burn for me, beloved." He nipped at the side of my breast with his teeth.

I gripped his hair. "I am."

Grinning, he turned and sat on the bed, holding my legs so I was straddling him. Cupping both breasts, he licked over one nipple, then the other.

I was done waiting. Shoving his shoulder, he lay back. I got up, undoing his pants quickly. He lifted his hips so I could pull them off. When I got stuck at his boots, he sat up and helped to remove them, and the blades strapped to each ankle.

He lay back again, I could only look at him. My eyes took their time moving over him. I'd never seen a man that looked as good as he did before. His body was toned and in perfect balance, from the top to the bottom.

He sat up and grasped my hips, pulled me to the edge of the bed. Without a word, his hand moved under my skirt until he felt the scant material of my underwear. With a quick jerk he tore the fabric and pulled it from my body.

Pure unadulterated lust filled me, burning from the inside out. I didn't know where his ended and mine began, but if he didn't touch me soon, I was going to scream out my frustration.

"You're in control for as long as I can stand it." He whispered roughly.

Laying back, he pulled my hand so I'd follow. Straddling him, I leaned down and kissed his chest, pausing to lick across his nipple.

"Now, woman." He growled.

Looking up into his heavy eyes, they blazed with a warning, I realized my time in control was going to run out soon. I lowered my hips slowly until he was inside me. Both of us moaned.

"We'll just grab the lists and get back before anyone notices we're gone."

Both of us froze as Daxx's voice traveled down the hall.

"Okay. Victor won't be happy if he finds out. He took my device, so I couldn't go anywhere."

Crissy was here too.

Daxx's laugh echoed through the silence. "Good thing I don't need a device."

Chase swore softly, then pulled me down to him. "Hang on." His mouth crushed mine.

I knew he'd transported us somewhere else, I didn't care where. I was flipped onto my back with him still inside me and then my whole existence began to blaze and swirl out of control.

There were no words between us, no awkward moves, the two of us were in complete unison, our minds, emotions and bodies joined as one.

When I thought I might go crazy from the need, I heard myself cry out, followed by a deep animalistic moan from Chase.

I had no idea how much time had passed. It didn't matter. We gasped, trying to catch our breath. Sweat dripped from his body onto my own damp one. Even my feet were soaked.

"Boots," I panted, "too hot."

He turned his head, his hot breath brushing against my shoulder. "Give me a minute, I'll take them off." He kissed me softly. "You were so fucking sexy in those. I thought I might explode just looking at you."

Opening my eyes, I looked at him in the dim light. "I don't think I was in a much better state."

Lifting up on his elbows, he looked down at me. "Later— when I can feel all my extremities again… we're going to look at your boot collection."

I laughed. "There are a lot."

"I will buy you more. Every color, style and fabric you want."

I looked around. "Where are we?"

"My room." He smirked. "Was the only thing I could focus on in that moment."

"It's very dark in here."

"I'll turn on a light when I can move." He kissed my mouth, lingering for a moment. "That was…"

"Yeah, it was. Is that from the bond or because we both absorb emotion?"

He squinted for a moment. "I don't know, but I don't want it to change."

I tried to sort through how intense it had been and gave up. "I can't think right now. I need a nap."

He lowered his mouth to my throat.

"After the boots are off," I reminded him.

"Right." He kissed me again.

Chapter Thirty-One

When I woke up, I didn't remember where I was until a large arm wrapped around me and pulled me against a warm chest.

"It's too early to be awake." Chase mumbled against my ear.

I felt a warmth move through me. "How would you know? It's so dark in here. Why aren't there any windows?"

"Underground chambers."

"It's so dark." I hadn't realized until this moment the entire royal chambers were underground. I needed windows and light.

Chase sighed and rolled away. Low lights lit up all around the large room.

It was a tastefully decorated room, clearly masculine and all in dark tones.

He picked up a small clock from the table and held it above his face. "Did we sleep at all? It's after dawn."

I felt my cheeks heat. "I think we must have. We did just wake up."

He set the clock back down with a clunk. "I'm going to need more coffee than usual." He rolled back over and wrapped his arm around me again.

"I'm going to need clothes." I said with a smirk.

Kissing me mouth softly, he sighed. "You have clothes."

"Boots, gloves and a skirt aren't going to be sufficient."

He lifted the cover and looked down it with a grin. "I'll loan you a shirt."

I pulled the cover out of his hand. "Oh yes, no one will notice if I'm wearing one of your large white shirts and black boots *at all.*"

He held his hand up and closed his eyes. "Wait. Let me savor that image for a moment." Dropping his hand, he looked at me again. "I will take you to your room for clothes—after." He pulled me tight against his body.

"After? Really, again?"

Chuckling, he nuzzled into my neck. "You need to feed."

I playfully shoved against him. "I did, twice already, as well as renewed the blood bond." Amused hazel eyes met mine. "We'll kill each other inside of a week, you know."

"I can't think of a better way to die." He was quiet for a moment. "I'm out of reasons to stall getting out of bed." He frowned. "Perhaps I can declare today a national holiday…"

"Coffee." I stated, trying not to laugh.

Leaning up on his elbow, he smiled. "You make a very compelling case…"

A loud knock on the door startled both of us. Chase turned and stared at it.

"My king?" Sith's deep baritone voice came through the door.

"Yes, Sith?"

The door opened and inch, so he wouldn't have to yell.

I slid down further in the bed and pulled the covers up, almost covering my entire head.

"I can't find, Alona." Sith said barely loud enough to hear. "I went to her room, she's not there and it's… very disordered."

I grimaced and remembered the clothes all over the room. Chase grinned.

"I went to her apartment, she's not there."

"She's not?" Chase said, his smiled widening. He intended to play it out.

"No, she's not." Sith answered. "I tried to call you, sire."

Chase frowned. "My phone," he looked at the table, "I don't have it…"

"I found your phone, my king."

Chase glanced at me and then got out of the bed. He didn't pause to get robe or clothes. I wasn't about to object as I watched him walk to the door. He looked just as nice naked from behind as the front half did.

Just before he reached the door Sith stuck his arm in, he was holding Chase's pants and shirt we'd left at my apartment. "I believe it's in the pocket of these, my king." I could hear the amusement in Sith's voice.

Chase took them out of his hand. Sith's arm appeared again. "I also have the Queen of Light's new phone."

Chase took that also and sent me a quick look. "We'll be to breakfast shortly, Sith."

"Yes, my king." Sith's voice was no longer serious.

The door closed and Chase turned and smiled at me. "Busted." He laughed.

We were quite late getting to breakfast, Chase assured me no one would notice or care. He was wrong. As we stepped in, Troy raised his cup to his twin.

"Sleeping late today, brother?" He grinned.

Daxx also grinned.

Chase brushed by me, with a soft touch to my back and went down the table to the coffee urn. "So it would seem, *brother*." Pouring a cup, he glanced to me as I took my usual chair beside Daxx. He tilted his head slightly, the only sign he'd hoped I sat elsewhere. Taking a sip, he looked at Daxx. "How's the search with the *lists* going?" He made a point of looking at Crissy then back to his twin's mate.

Daxx frowned and looked at me, then back to Chase. "Fine." She said carefully.

Giving her an abrupt nod, he turned to sit down. When he did, he winked at Crissy, who quickly put her head down and looked at her plate. "Brothers, what is the play of the day?"

Michael pushed his plate aside and leaned his forearms on the table. "We have three sites to check out. Ellis was able to remember enough details about camps here."

"And what of the house he was at?" Chase looked around the table. "Where's Leone?"

"Left at first light to go for a ride." Rafael mumbled around a mouthful of food.

"I hope it does him some good." Chase said then looked back to Michael.

He shook his head at Chase. "We couldn't find anything about the location of the house." He motioned his head to Victor. "We're hoping if we find members still at these camp locations Troy or Arius can find out the location from them."

Mitz came out and set a plate in front of Chase with a smile. She glanced to me. "The usual, my dear?"

I nodded, not wanting to voice I was starving and to pile it up the same as Chase's. "Thank you."

"My pleasure, love." Mitz hustled back into the kitchen.

"What time do we leave?" Chase asked, waving a piece of toast around.

"Why are you so cheery today?" Quinton asked. "Not one sarcastic word has come out of your mouth."

Chase's eyes briefly connected with mine and then he smirked at his older brother. "I'm sorry, how lax of me. Must be from lack of sleep."

Quinton gave him an odd look and then shook his head. "We have to wait for the last guard change and then we'll head out." He motioned to Rafael, "we want to make sure the guards are fresh and alert anytime we're not here." He shrugged. "Which allows us a brief time to sleep."

Rafael nodded. "Until we know more about their abduction plans, all of the local villages are being regularly patrolled."

"Anything useful from our new inmates?" Chase took a bite and looked down the table at Arius.

Sighing, Arius leaned back and crossed his arms over his chest. "Unfortunately not. They only knew about their part. They know of others in the same situation, but no details."

My heart ached knowing there were other women out there being held as Alyssa and her friends were. How would we find them all? I felt the warmth of reassurance fill me and looked to Chase. He was watching me with a pained expression. Sighing, he stood up, and picking up his plate and cup to walk around the table and sit down beside me.

I glanced to see the expressions around the table, everything from surprise to smirks.

Picking up my hand in my lap, he squeezed it. "We will find them. All of the women being held against their will." He said softly.

"Count on it." Daxx nodded.

"Cristy and Daxx have been working on it through most of the night." Victor assured me. "We decided focusing on the easiest to locate would be the best course of action. The faster we can find them, they can as well."

Crissy nodded. "I've been going through my notebook too, with Daxx, checking for anything that could be related." She sighed loud. "Or not, there's too many to know for sure." Shaking her head, she glanced to Victor, "I hate the not knowing part."

He clasped her small hand in his large one on top of the table. "I know, heart, but you will prevail, you always do."

I felt hope as I looked around at the determined faces. I may not know all there was to about this family, but I did know if they said something would come to be… it was going to happen. "Okay. How do we narrow down the search?" I glanced to Chase. "There are so many possibilities."

"I feel that way about these halls."

Everyone turned to see Emil standing in the door.

"I took three wrong turns trying to find my way here." He said, exasperated.

Chase turned in his chair. "Brother. Is there a problem?"

Emil shook his head and quickly sat at the empty chair at the end of the table. "No. Aside from this maze of damn hallways."

Mitz came out of the kitchen and set a plate in front of me. She paused and smiled at Emil. "Can I get you anything, dear? Some green tea perhaps?"

A surprised expression appeared on Emil's face. "Yes. Thank you."

She bobbed her head and went back into the kitchen.

Emil gave chase a curious glance, Chase shrugged. "It's Mitz."

Someday when there weren't women to find and evil men to stop, I needed to find out more about the woman that oozed nothing but pure love while seeming to know everything.

"I spoke to Ellis last night." Emil glanced down the table at Victor. "He's taking in some training while he's here."

Victor nodded. "As he's part of the royal family, combat skills are never moot."

Emil frowned. "That's not reassuring, but I agree, learning to handle himself won't be a waste."

"Aside from your awesome switchblade skills, do you train?" Rafael asked, standing to reach a plate of biscuits across the table.

Emil shrugged. "I've had training. None that I was required to use in the last few hundred years though."

Chase chuckled. "Better hone them, lost brother, more hands on our side will help ensure this ends quickly."

Quinton snorted. "Have to find them to end anything."

Michael leaned back in his chair. "We know more of what we're up against, and their plan at least." He sent Quinton a look. "That's more than we had a few weeks ago."

"We've stopped many." Crissy said rubbing her forehead, "I just wished I could see more."

Daxx turned to look at her. "You *see* any more than you already do and your head is going to pop off your neck."

Crissy smirked. "It can't do that." She shook her head and then picked up her notebook in her lap. "I'm going to my tower until it's time to sleep."

Victor leaned over and kissed her before she could get up. "I'll be along to collect you shortly."

"Okay." Grabbing her pack, she almost skipped out of the room.

Mitz came out and set a cup in front of Emil. She stood there with her hands clasped. "I'm so happy to see you." With a gentle smile, she turned and walked back to the kitchen.

Arius pushed his chair back and looked to Emil. "Grab your cup, brother, I'll show you the cells and fill in the latest before you go see Ellis."

Emil stood and picked up his cup. "Filling in any blanks is always welcome." He glanced around at the others and gave an abrupt nod. "I will no doubt come across you later," he turned to follow Arius, "somewhere in these halls."

Daxx tapped a hand on the table and then looked at me. "After you eat, get Chase to bring you to Troy's office, that's where we're set up for now." She glanced to her mate, an unenthusiastic expression on her face. "Until we're *allowed* a weekend pass again."

Troy sighed loudly and stood up. "I have some things to look into." He bowed his head to Chase. "Until later."

Everyone filed out with one reason or another, until Rafael was the only left sitting at the table with Chase and I.

"So," Rafael smiled across the table at us, "how's things?" He glanced to Chase's arm and then my own, looking for a tattoo to be evident.

I paused in taking a bite and looked to Chase, who had a hard look on his face.

"Things are fine, Raf, don't you have somewhere to be?" Chase asked him in a bored tone.

Rafael shook his head. "Nope. Well, just have to check in at the temple with Clairee about keeping a mystical eye out on Leone, but other than that my shift is over."

Chase picked up his cup. "I hope he gets through whatever is going on."

He leaned closer to me and I had to wonder if the seasoned king needed his own reassurance. I reached under the table and rested my hand on his knee. Warmth filled me as I met his soft understanding look.

Placing his hand over mine he looked back at his brother. "I keep hoping it's only a relapse—he had some pretty wacked out illusions when he was kicking his addiction."

Rafael rubbed a hand over his face. "I've thought the same, but I don't think he's fallen back into it, Chase, I really don't."

"I agree, despite hoping for the easiest answers." Chase released my hand and stood up with his cup. Going back down to the coffee urn, he topped off his cup.

I could feel the worry from him. "Could it be—" I waved my hand around, "I don't know about such details of magic and other abilities your people..."

"Our people." Chase added walking back to sit down.

I blushed slightly. "Our people have, but could it be some woman is trying to get his attention?" I shrugged and held it. "Leone is very—he has tunnel vision, and is quite focused from what I've seen, perhaps he's just missed some interested counterpart trying to get his attention." I sat back and clasped both hands in my lap.

"Huh." Chase's brow furrowed. "I hadn't even thought of that." He looked at Rafael. "Has he been dating at all since..." he huffed out a breath, "I can't even remember when Leone last kept female company."

Rafael leaned on the table, his head resting in his hand. "I don't know either. He's all about work, work, work." He rolled his eyes.

Chase leaned over and kissed my cheek. "I pray you're right, my beloved." Straightening, he motioned to Rafael. "Stop by the library on your way to the temple and see what his prophecy says—maybe we've all just missed something that's been staring at us for millennia."

Rafael smiled and stood up. "I hope you're right, sister." He winked at me. "Better be keeping her brother, or someone else might have to."

Chase growled, "Over their dead, quartered body."

Rafael laughed. "I thought so."

We could hear his laughter as he went down the hall.

Chase motioned to the plate in front of me. "Eat. Then I'll take you to Troy's office." He gave me a heated look. "You could work out of mine today."

I felt my cheeks heat. "Then neither of us would get any work done."

He raised an eyebrow. "And that's a problem?" Leaning closer, he brushed a kiss on my lips.

"My king."

Chase jolted at Sith's voice coming from the door.

"What?" he asked, not hiding the annoyance in his tone.

"You're needed on our side, there's a group with *complaints* about the frequency of guards riding through."

Chase huffed out a breath and turned to look at him. "If they're complaining, then it means they have something to hide the patrols are disrupting."

Sith bowed his head slightly. "That was my thought as well."

Standing, Chase leaned down and kissed me quickly again. Picking up his plate, he took a step and then grabbed his cup. "Stay here with Alona, take her to Troy's office after she eats."

"Yes my king."

When Chase stood beside him near the door, he paused and looked at him. "This morning was not funny."

Sith smirked. "My king." He bowed his head in a more exaggerated manner.

"Hate being out pranked by a guard." Chase murmured as he left the room.

I motioned to the table with much food still on it. "Sit. Eat."

"We have a guard's kitchen…"

I pointed at the chair with my fork. "I don't care. Sit, eat, keep me company while I eat." I looked around at the empty chairs. "This room is haunting when it's empty."

"As you wish, my..."

I glared at him. "Do *not*."

He grinned and sat down.

Chapter Thirty-Two

Exhausted and frustrated from fruitless searching I retreated to the large workout space. I had bypassed lunch and the big send-off as the men left to search for those camps. I was still processing everything that had altered my life so drastically in such a short time. How did one begin to process all this? There were moments when I felt like I'd stepped into the pages of some fantasy novel. How was all this possible and no one knew? Exhaling slowly, I internally rolled my eyes at my own thought. Wasn't that the very meaning of the kettle calling the pot black? I was one of those things no one would ever imagine.

"I don't know much about tai chi, but aren't you holding the poses just a little longer than you should?"

I dropped my arms and turned to see Daxx, Crissy and their guards in the door. "I was lost in thought."

Crissy smiled. "You looked like a statue." She nodded and went over to the wall of weapons and set her pack down. "We needed to do something."

Daxx followed her path and studied the wall. "Sitting still wasn't going well for either of us." She picked up a long bo and glanced at Tim over her shoulder. "Might as well be useful and not just a shadow."

I looked to where Sith stood. "I offered to teach him the poses, but he wasn't keen on it."

"I don't need that kind of discipline and focus." Sith said with a hard look, "I bash, that is my style of combat."

"You just didn't want to look like a big awkward ox." Bronx stated and went to the wall and pulled down two small batons, he held them toward Crissy. She grimaced. "Our Justice wants you to learn some offensive moves."

Crissy sighed and took them. "I don't need offensive, I just climb out of reach."

Daxx walked by and patted her on the back. "What if there is nowhere to climb."

A panicked look cross Crissy's face. "That would be scary." She tapped the two batons against each other. "Okay, I'll try."

"I'm not sure why our guards aren't helping the guys." Daxx lifted both arms. "We agree to be good little women and stay in the royal chambers."

I tried to relax and start the cycle from position one again. "I believe it has something to do with never being farther than twenty…"

"Ten." Sith corrected.

I gave him a blank look. "Ten feet away from us, for the rest of their lives."

Daxx snorted. "Good luck with that."

"Just as long as you don't get us sent to the far side of the wasteland for disobeying the kings' wishes, I'll be happy." Tim said and motioned for Daxx to come at him with the bo.

Accepting I was not going to succeed in this today, I went over to where I had set my bottle of water. I was just going to take a sip when a burning pain went through my side. I dropped the water, splashing it on the mat. Gripping my side, I breathed through it.

"Alona?" Daxx came rushing over.

I shook my head. "It's just a stich or something." I could still feel it, but not in my side. I pressed into my side where it had been. Then sent Daxx a look of concern. "I don't think it was my pain." I looked to Crissy as she walked over, then back to Daxx. "Is-is that possible? To feel Chase's pain?"

Daxx's brow furrowed. "With a strong blood bond, if he let it through…" Her eyes widened, and she looked to Crissy. "Can you sense Victor?" She closed her eyes and exhaled, probably trying to focus.

"I can. Which is wrong." Crissy said anxiously. "Victor doesn't allow for that ever—unless it's…" she shook her head. "Never mind."

"Troy is mad. Like livid-I'm-going-to-eat-your-soul kind of mad. I've never felt him feel that." Daxx said opening her eyes.

I turned to look at the guards. "Something is wrong."

"Shit. I hate the wastelands." Tim cussed.

"What do we do?" I asked, trying not to let the feeling of distress overwhelm me. If Chase was in trouble, I didn't want to add to it by sending my panic to him.

Daxx looked to Tim. "Do you know the locations?"

Tim shook his head. "We were to stay with you, so they didn't bring us in the loop."

"Men." She huffed out a breath and then nodded. "Okay. We need weapons."

I looked at the wall.

"No, real weapons." She motioned to my boots and Crissy's pack. "Get your stuff." She started for the door. "Tim, go get my zapper box. Sith, get Ira to the armory. Bronx, find me a few more guards, meet us at the armory." She pushed open the door. "Five minutes, people, let's move!"

I grabbed my boots and dagger and jogged with Crissy after her. As we ran down the hall, Crissy was securing a belt to her waist. On it were two boxes, I recognized the one as the pulley she used in the cavern when we saved the men.

"I need a bo." Crissy said excitedly beside me. "I can't do the two sticks, but a bo I can use to get higher."

I had no idea what she meant, just nodded and ran after Daxx.

When we reached the armory, she grabbed a vest and put it on quickly. Turning she tossed one at me. "Get this on and pick something larger than your dagger."

I pulled it over my head and did up the strap and quickly put on the strap for my dagger. Bending down, I pulled on my boots and zipped them up. "I'm not good with large weapons." I didn't bother to mention the emotional backlash of using one almost debilitated me.

"Pick something." She said as she strapped thin katanas to her back.

Tim and Bronx came running in with two other large men. Daxx nodded. "That will work.

Mitz came running in, a large older looking man right behind her. Sith was through the door last, sliding his sword into his belt as he went.

I turned and looked at the vast amount of weapons. Holding my breath, I hovered over a few and then shaking my head at the lethal blades, I grabbed a polished pair of nunchakus, or nun-chucks I suppose they were referred to more frequently.

It had been years, I backed up and looked at them, hoping the endless hours of practice with them allowed for muscle memory. Holding a breath I went through a few moves and was pleasantly surprised that it was as if I'd done it the day before. Nodding I stopped and looked back to Daxx.

She raised her eyebrows. "I approve." Then she turned to Mitz. "How do I find them?"

Mitz came over and gave her a quick hug. "You ladies focus on your men and then you will get there, love. I have faith." She turned to the large man. "Go with them, Ira, bring the boys back."

He leaned down and kissed her cheek. "I will, my love."

I realized this one was Mitz's husband. The pain hit me again. "We need to hurry." I said and went over and grabbed Daxx's hand.

Crissy took her other hand and the various guards simply touched one of our shoulders.

Daxx nodded and took a few deep breaths. "I got this." She whispered. "Focus on them."

I closed my eyes, drawing on the feelings Chase always managed to draw from me. The pain was there, something else, it was faint. I'd never felt him so distant since the first blood bond. He had to be all right. I felt something whisper over my skin but didn't open my eyes until my stomach felt like it dropped. Opening them, I let go of Daxx's hand and looked at the scene before us. The brothers were outnumbered. It was a commotion of madness.

Victor was scrambling trying to zap, or whatever as many as he could.

"Jerks." Daxx muttered. She pulled her one blade free. "Let's help." She charged into it without hesitation.

"Bronx." Crissy said and ran after her.

The other guards went without comment, taking on the first body they encountered.

"Sith, where is he?" I tried to see through the rush of bodies.

Sith touched my shoulder. "I can't see him, but head for Troy, he won't be far if Chase is injured."

Nodding, I pulled out my dagger and started moving toward the only blond I could see. The clash of Sith's blade was right by head and I knew there was no way I was getting through this without getting close to all the wrong emotions. Taking a deep breath, I erected a wall in my mind and came to an abrupt halt when a large, dirty man swung a hand with large knife at me. Dropping low, I flicked the chucks at his arm and then jerked so the blade fell to the ground. Executing a very improvised spin kick, I knocked him to the ground and then stepped on his chest, my dagger pointed at his face.

"Got him." I heard Daxx coming from beside me and got up. "Go help Troy." She said as the man vanished.

I didn't stop to chat, jumping up, I headed toward Troy again. As bodies moved I could see him momentarily. His stance could only be described as rage, as he swung his blade and knocked one body after the other back. I dodged a man flying past and then slid to a stop when another blocked my path, he had a blood-soaked blade in each hand and I was meant to be his next target. I only paused to wonder if any Alterealm males were normal size. Widening my stance, I braced for his move. He wasn't graceful as he gave a rebel scream and lunged at me. Dodging his blade, I jumped up and using Sith's large body as leverage, I launched myself at this large man and kicked him in the head, he stumbled back out of my way.

"I got him. Go." Sith growled.

I moved through the next bodies and ducked under Quinton's' wide swing. Out of nowhere Crissy appeared, flying through the air and landed beside me. "He's behind Troy." She said hurriedly and was gone, sliding under Quinton's' legs.

I ran past him only to be stopped again by another large man. He had a loathsome snarl on his face. His vile feelings tried to invade my mind, but I wasn't in the mood for that right now. Swinging the chucks, I aimed for the closest body part, and winced when they connected and reflected back against my hand. He dropped like a doll to the ground, clutching his own parts between his legs. Not taking the time to observe his discomfort any longer, I turned to see Troy beating back two men. The wrath of his expression was frightening. Beside him was Chase, using only one of his swords while he clutched his side. I could see blood pouring over his hand.

Chase stumbled when his sword connected with his opponent's. Having seen enough, I rushed forward. Squatting as I reached him, I swept my foot out and knocked the footing of his assailant out from under him. Jumping up, I tucked the chucks under one arm and separated my dagger to twin blades in one smooth motion. Dropping to my knee, I stabbed the one into the man's chest, using the momentum from dropping to drive it in deep. He howled and grabbed for it.

"Got him." Daxx appeared again and the man disappeared while I was still holding the blade that had been in him.

The clang of metal rang over my head had me jolting only to see Sith blocking the blade that was intended for Chase as he rushed to get to me.

Getting up, I went to him, he was barely able to stay upright.

"Miss me, duchess?" He asked sounding out of breath.

"Why didn't you transport back?" I leaned down and tried to assess the damage he was trying to hide under his hand.

"Can't leave them a man down." He gritted his teeth against the pain.

I honestly debated hitting him and then decided the backlash wouldn't do me any good, glaring at him instead. I turned back to assess the commotion around us.

Troy's battle cry had me spin around. A man was trying to take on Daxx and Troy wasn't having any of that.

Rafael appeared beside me. "Get him home." He said hurriedly.

I felt panic. "How? I don't have a device."

Chase lunged past us as a man aimed for Rafael. Sith was right there protecting his king and my mate.

Swearing, Rafael stabbed one of his blades into the ground and held out his wrist. I quickly took the device off his arm.

"Go." Victor yelled as he rushed over, he grabbed Chase under the arm and more or less dragged the stubborn fool over to me. "We cannot lose a king to their cause." He ordered, not even sounding winded.

Chase was panting.

Troy moved past him, blocking anyone from reaching him. "Alona cannot be here in all this, Chase."

Chase's head snapped to me, a dawning realization on his face. He conceded with a slight nod.

I hurriedly put the device on my wrist and went over to him.

"Fight well, brothers. Come home." Chase said.

Rafael patted his shoulder and then winked at me. "Sister."

Leaning into him, I wasted no time pushing the button. As we settled in the landing room, Chase dropped to one knee and hunched over. Dropping my weapons, I knelt and tried again to see the damage.

"They ruined my favorite vest." He made a sound of annoyance.

Mitz came running in. "How bad is it?"

"I don't know." I turned as she came over and pulled on his arm to help him stand.

"Let's get him somewhere where I can clean him up and look."

I got up and helped him to his feet. Mitz took off her apron, moved his hand to push the apron against the bloodied area. Nodding to me, I put his arm around my shoulder and started walking. I didn't know where we were going, so I glanced to Mitz's silent directions.

"They weren't expecting us," Chase huffed out a breath, "they had a full unit there still."

"Is everyone else alright?" Mitz looked to me.

I gave her a wide-eyed look. "I think the extra men we took evened the odds."

She nodded. "Good." She tsked and looked at Chase. "You should have come back immediately instead of bleeding out on the ground."

He grimaced and paused in walking for a second. "I couldn't leave my brothers…"

"Nonsense." She said with an exasperated tone. "You are lucky the girls sensed what was happening and went to lend you aid."

Chase hissed out a breath. "They were like avenging angels."

I shook my head. "That's questionable."

Turning his head, he looked at me for a moment. "Later when I'm done ruining the carpet, we're going to have words…"

"Ha, the only words we'll be having is about you trying to get yourself killed." I took a deep breath and swallowed the fear that went with those words.

We reached the dining room and went through to the kitchen. "Try to hold him up on a stool, while I wash off some of this mess." She went over to the sink. "One of the boys will be back shortly and give him some blood to help this along." She glanced over her shoulder, "unless your blood has healing properties?"

I shook my head and held Chase with a hand on his shoulder as I tried to look under the blood soaked cloth. "Not that I'm aware of."

She came over with a bowl of water and cloths. "Let's get his vest off." I held him while she undid straps and belts to get to his vest. "What about your saliva, love? Does it heal?"

I paused to answer.

"Yes or she couldn't heal her bite so thoroughly." Chase said with distaste in his tone.

I looked at him. "Are you sure?"

He nodded slowly. "Have you ever left a mark behind when you feed... before me?"

I opened my mouth and then closed it. Aside from a few failed flounderings when I first craved biting people, I couldn't recall leaving bite marks behind. "I guess I do have healing saliva."

He gave an abrupt nod. "Help me to a bed. I'm not going to have you licking at me in the kitchen when my brothers come back with their bragging to harass me.

"Just let me wash some of this off." Mitz said putting her hand on his shoulder. "Make sure it's only one."

Chase snorted. "You think I'm dumb enough to let them slice me twice?"

"You were dumb enough to stay while injured."

Frowning, he looked at me. "No sass right now, I'm not up to it, duchess."

Mitz straightened and dropped the bloodied cloth into the bowl. "We need to get that sealed up, now." She gave Chase a hard look. "Any higher and it would have been fatal."

I swallowed the lump in my throat and moved quickly to get him to his feet.

As we reached the hall Crissy came running up. She was covered in dirt and blood.

"Can you run ahead and clear my bed?" At least I hoped it was the closest room.

She nodded and jogged down the hall.

"Where are the others?" Chase called out in a weak voice.

She didn't stop. "Cleaning up the mess." Taking a turn, she disappeared from our sight.

Once Chase was on the bed, Mitz straightened. "I'm going to see if the others need help."

Crissy nodded and went out the door without a word.

I looked down at the man with blood running down his side onto the bed. "I don't know how to do this."

He held out his hand. "I'm assuming there's no trick to it." Taking his hand, I sat on the edge of the bed, he reached and pulled my head down to kiss me quickly. "Let your fangs out, beloved."

I nodded and slid off the side of the bed. His eyes held mine as I did. Though I could feel his pain, I felt him pushing to fill me with his warmth. His eyes turned yellow and my fangs were immediately present.

"There." He smirked, "sexy red eyes." His voice was so weak, which brought me back to the severity of the situation.

Leaning over him, without looking away from his face, I ran my tongue over the torn edge of his flesh. If someone had of told me I'd be doing this, digesting this much blood on purpose I would have laughed, before today. He winced several times as I moved over his injury, but never broke eye contact with me. It was the most intimate feeling I'd ever had.

It dawned on me that somewhere between kicking that man in the face and this moment I had come to terms with the fact that Chase was my one and only, and that I would do whatever it took to always have him. A tear rolled down my cheek, causing him to lift his head.

"I know you loathe the taste of blood…"

Pausing I shook my head, "that's not it." I inhaled a shaky breath. "Just shut up and lay there and heal." I told him.

An amused look appeared on his face through his pain. "Yes, beloved, shutting up."

With a soft smile, I leaned down and with tender affection used my own saliva to heal this man that was mine.

Studying the wound, until I was assured it was sealed enough that no more blood would fall, I got up to sit on the bed beside him. With a soft sound, he pulled me down to lay beside him. His mouth crushed mine in a soul-wrenching, passionate kiss.

"The last few minutes were pure hell, I think you dallied on purpose." He smirked at me.

I smiled back at him. "I can't have a damaged mate, it's unacceptable."

He leaned back, an unsure look on his face. "I only have to get sliced open to hear you say that?"

"I've done some deep soul-searching in the past twenty-four hours." I confessed.

"Do tell." He hugged me tighter against him.

"Seriously, are you healed?" I leaned up and looked at his side.

He was quiet for a moment. "It's more or less healed. I'm just a little drained at the moment." His eyes caressed over my face. "I can't believe you came rushing in to save me." He frowned, "exposing yourself to all those vile emotions when I'm too distracted to protect you."

I tugged gently on his goatee. "It has to go both ways. That's rule number one."

"Rules?" His brows drew together.

I nodded. "If I'm to be tied to you for an eternity, then there will be rules established prior to said binding."

Chase was quiet for a moment, several emotions crossing his face. "Let the negotiations begin." He touched my lip in a light caress, his eyes swirling to yellow. "Rule one, it goes both ways. Agreed." Leaning, he licked over my bottom lip. "What is number two?"

"You're distracting me."

He smirked, "Yes, trying to hurry it along before you change your mind."

I laughed. "I'm not going to change my mind. The very thought of almost losing you shattered me in ways I didn't think possible." I gave him a wide-eyed look. "I kicked a man in the face and stabbed another. Not to mention where I hit that third one."

"Yes you did, you vicious, beautiful woman." A gave me a daring smile. "I was so distracted watching you wield your vengeance I was almost hit again." Kissing me quick, he looked at me. "Get on with it, next rule…"

"Brother." Troy came rushing into the room, Daxx right behind him.

Chase sighed. "I'm fine."

Ignoring his twin completely, Troy was on the bed on one knee so he could look at Chase's side. "You need to feed." He said with concern.

Making a noise of annoyance, Chase released me and turned to face him. "I was working on it, brother before you charged in."

Daxx looked over Troy's shoulder and then sent me a look. "You have healing saliva."

"Apparently." I slid up on the bed, so I was sitting, and not in such a compromising position.

"Chase." Rafael came through the door next.

"Should have gone to your apartment." Chase said glancing at me.

Rafael came over blood, grime, and weapons included and dropped onto the bed by Chase's feet. "You crazy beast." He said to his brother, "I hope you finally realize you're not indestructible."

Chase shrugged. "There were three of them…"

"Still." Rafael gave him an unhappy look before turning to me. He bowed his head to me as a subject would to royalty. "Thank you, sister, only you could have saved him from himself."

Quinton came into the room before I could reply. "I hope you're healed enough before I beat some sense into your head."

Chase chuckled. "I may need a few more minutes, brother."

Stopping at the end of the bed, Quinton pointed a finger at Chase. "Don't *ever* do that to me again."

"Oh, well, I'll try not to get sliced up on you again." Chase muttered without inflection.

"King or not, I will ground you to your quarters if you're going to be so callous with your life." Victor came striding in with Crissy tucked under his arm.

Chase sat up further and glared at him. "It wasn't like I ran among them all willy-nilly saying catch me if you can."

"I'd pay to see that." Michael said walking in carrying a tray. "From Mitz." He walked around and set it on the side of the bed where I sat. Turning, he bowed formally to me. "Thank you, my queen." Straightening, he nodded to Daxx then Crissy. "If you ladies hadn't showed up when you did we would have had our asses handed to us."

"As if."

"Whatever."

The men objected.

Chase held up his hand to silence them. "Michael is right. We've never found a full cell, and have grossly underestimated their strength."

"Did he hit his head?" Arius said quietly coming into the room.

Chase rolled his eyes at him. "You know it's true."

Arius stopped at the end of the bed, his eyes moving over his brother, assessing his state. "What I know is true is that our women are totally kickass, and we owe them." He smiled at me. "Caught the chuck action, you've been holding out on me."

I laughed softly. "Daxx said grab something, so I chose the least lethal," I motioned to my head, "for the least backlash."

"And that guy you dropped with a shot between the legs—how was the backlash to that?" Daxx asked.

I shrugged. "Gratifying."

"I missed that." Chase murmured.

It seemed everyone started talking at once, Chase included. I listened to the ribbing, the threats that were given with the deepest love, and felt my heart jerk in my chest. When a tear rolled down my cheek, Chase immediately looked at me with a questioning look on his face. With a soft smile I shook my head letting him know it wasn't anything bad. He picked up my hand and lifted it to his mouth and kissed it softly.

Glancing over I saw the three guards standing, hovering by the door. I gave Sith a slight nod to let him know I and my mate were well. He smiled and backed out of the room again.

Chapter Thirty-Three

Watching the brothers and the two women, I came to realize they were meant to be my brothers and sisters—maybe not of blood, but of the heart. Overwhelming emotion came close to smothering me. Chase looked at me. I leaned closed and kissed his lips softly. "It has to be now, Chase."

It was a delayed moment before he realized what I was saying and then he turned to his family. "Everybody out. Now." He moved to the edge of the bed and motioned to the door. "Thanks for coming, go bathe, all of you stink." He was pushing Troy along with a hand on his shoulder.

Mitz appeared in the door with a bottle of wine and two glasses. She paused, her full hands resting on her hips. "All of you out. Chase needs time to recuperate."

Quinton stopped and looked at the bottle. "Since when does that require wine? I only got juice when I was recuperating."

I felt my cheeks heat.

"Out." She moved into the room as everyone walked past her until she was in front of Chase. Handing him the bottle and glasses, she smiled up at him. "Lock the door after I leave."

He nodded. "I intend to."

She gave me one of her loving looks and a motherly smile, then left.

Nerves took over when he turned and gave me a heated look. His eyes were yellow again. "So," I licked dry lips, "how does this work."

He smirked, "one step at a time, remember?" He walked to the bed and set the bottle and glasses on the table. "First, we both need to feed or this isn't going to happen." He touched his side gingerly.

I couldn't believe I'd forgotten he wasn't completely healed. I scrambled off the bed and was next to him before the next breath. He gave me a serious look. "Is it terribly painful?"

He shook his head, "no, I'm just tired." His eyes moved over my face, "someone kept me up all of last night."

My cheeks grew hot again. "I'm fairly certain I didn't force you."

Pulling me closer, he kissed my forehead. "No I was quite willing—am quite willing." He looked to the bed, "I think the coverlet is ruined."

Turning I looked to see dirt and his blood on it. "A shower room is needed by the landing room." I leaned down and pulled the cover off into a heap by our feet.

He chuckled. "That might end up being complicated." He sat on the end of the bed and looked up at me, "mates ramped on adrenaline taking showers in a public room…"

"Oh." I frowned. "Right." I dropped to my knees and looked at his side. "It's still so red looking, maybe my salvia is diluted."

Grasping my chin, he lifted my face so I'd look at him. "It's not you, I need to feed to replenish and it will heal further." He leaned down and kissed me. "Now, not to sound like I'm rushing you—but I am really, we need to feed and then…" he gave me a suggestive look. "Kiss me." He whispered.

Stretching up those few inches, I brushed my lips over his. When I would have pulled back, his hand was behind my head holding it, deepening the kiss. Fangs filled my mouth, his tongue brushed along them.

Leaning back, he broke the kiss. "Last chance, beloved." His yellow eyes searched my red ones, "before I bind us together in all ways."

"I have no doubts." I answered out of breath from the anticipation.

"I'd like to tell you I will make this as romantic and gentle as possible, but it's not going to be." He blew out a breath. "I want you too much—been waiting a few hundred years to find you."

I smiled. "That's a very substantial reason."

Chase smiled. "I thought so." He nodded and then motioned to the bathroom. "Step one, we shower off some of this..." he looked at the vest I still wore, "everything." Getting up, he took my hand and walked to the bathroom.

"Do you suppose Mitz went back and got my dagger from the landing room?"

Dropping my hand, he smirked as he undid my vest. "That's not instilling confidence, I'm taking you to the shower and you're wanting your dagger."

I pulled the vest off. "Mindless things to keep me from being nervous."

He assisted pulling my shirt over my head. "I'm nervous." He confessed.

"You?" Bending down, I undid my boots and slipped them off.

He went over to the corner and opened the shower door. "Yes. Once this is done I have to forever try to keep you happy, without getting stabbed when I screw up."

I realized he was teasing me. Pulling the yoga tights off, I tossed them into the corner with my shirt. Momentarily I realized I went rushing into a battle in my workout clothes, a leather vest and slouchy boots. My good fashion sense was failing.

Chase tilted his head and looked at me. "Your emotions are all over the place." Reaching in, he flipped the water on.

Snapping out of it, I rolled my shoulders. "It's been a day." I nodded.

"It has." He held out his hand. "Let me distract you from it."

Pulling my arms out of my bra and slipping out of my underwear quickly, I walked over to him.

Taking my hand he held it in the air and leaned back to look at me. "You are so beautiful."

"You are still dressed." Was the response I gave him.

He looked down. "So I am."

I suspected he wasn't feeling as well as he was letting on. I watched him slip out of the dirty leather pants and kick out of his boots. His hands were shaking ever so slightly. "Chase," he looked up at me, "can you feed in the shower?"

He raised an eyebrow. "With you I can feed anywhere, everywhere."

I held out my hand and he stood up. Stepping into the shower, I moved back into the spray of warm water tugging on him to follow. He stood just out of the water and smiled at me.

"You're so many dreams come true."

I tugged his hand again. "Show me."

I watched as he let the water cascade down over him for a few moments, the tension visibly draining from him as he did. Seeing the water trail over his form wasn't exactly a hardship on my end either. My body stirred, needs rose. My fangs filled my mouth just looking at the man. With a smug smile, I stepped over so our bodies were touching. Reaching up, I grasped his hair and gently tugged so his neck was exposed to me. Stretching up on my toes, I sank my teeth into the corded muscle of his neck.

He pulled me tight into him and cradled my head in his large hand. "Only the fates could give me everything I've ever desired in one woman." He whispered near my ear.

Lifting my teeth, I didn't lick over his neck. I didn't need to pull his mouth to mine either, he covered mine before I could take the next breath. His lips were demanding, his tongue lashing my own.

When he pulled his mouth from mine, his yellow eyes blazed with lust. He turned and pressed my back against the cool tile, pining me there with his hips. Holding my head against the wall, his thumb under my jaw to keep it there, his eyes held my own. With his other hand, he reached down between my legs and stroked over me.

I sucked in a breath from the intimate contact. The feelings began to consume me, our combined desires. This time I wasn't startled by it, I let it take me and release all inhibitions. Chase groaned and reached to pull me tight to his body, he rocked his into mine, causing the passion to blaze through us both and then back again.

With a loud gasp, he closed his eyes for a moment, his breathing so erratic that it e excited me to know that I'd done that to him.

Opening his eyes, he gave me a heavy-lidded look. "Aroused beyond all limits without touching each other." He grinned, "We are so fucking perfect for each other."

I nodded. "Less talk."

The smile he gave me was almost evil, in a good, stirring way. Grasping my waist, he lifted me, I wrapped my legs around his waist. Turning he stood us under the fall of the water, my shoulders resting against the wall.

Clutching his shoulders, I tried to lift my body so I could have him inside me. The need filling me from him, from my own wanton body was almost unbearable."

Biting his lip in concentration, he shook his head. "Your hand." He said in a rasping voice.

Letting go of his shoulder, I held out my left hand. Our eyes were locked as much as our bodies soon would be. He grasped my hand in his left and slowly raised it above my head. I held my breath, my heart may have even paused.

Leaning in he took my mouth with his and shifted his hips so he slipped inside me. The onslaught of too much pleasure crushed me and I moaned into his mouth. He tore his mouth from mine as he thrust inside me.

"Bite me, my beloved, now." He panted, a beautiful expression of passion on his face.

I leaned forward and bit into his shoulder, his hips surged harder. When I thought I'd become boneless from the pure pleasure, my hand and arm started to burn. The mix of so many sensations had me release his shoulder and cry out. I felt like I shattered so completely moments later. The water hitting my skin no longer registered as I became weightless.

Letting go of my hand, Chase held me tight to him as he continued to move with hard, intense motions. He growled against my throat as his whole body became rigid.

Gasping, I tried to breath without inhaling water. Dropping my head onto his shoulder, I clung to him. "Well," I panted and then could find no other words.

"Mmm." Was his reply.

"Maybe in shower was…" I blew the water out of my mouth, "not the best idea."

"Yeah." He shook his head. "We're going to drown."

I started laughing. "Quite likely."

"Can you stand?" His chest heaved against mine.

"I don't know." I was trying not to laugh more.

Slowly, I was able to unwrap my legs as he lowered me to stand. I leaned back against the wall and used it to hold me upright. Chase smiled down at me with that adoring look in his eyes.

"You're supposed to stop me from doing things that endanger me." He grinned.

I brushed the wet hair back from his face. "How was I to know it would be debilitating and potentially deadly?"

He shook the water from his face. "Solid point." Straightening, he tested his balance and then put a bit of distance between us. He held up his arm and looked at it. From shoulder to hand was covered in an intricate design. "I never thought I'd see this on my skin." He said with emotion in his voice.

I looked at my own, turning it to see the same pattern as his. "I never thought I'd ever understand why my mother had one." I looked up to see his hazel eyes considering me carefully. "I'm not regretting it, Chase."

He huffed out a breath. "Good, because even a magic eraser can't erase these." He grinned.

I blinked the water out of my eyes. "I don't know what that is, but I'm glad it can't." Stretching up I kissed him. "I'm never hiding it like my mother did." I told him with much conviction.

Grasping me by the waist, he hugged me tightly against his body. "Alona?"

"Mmm?"

"When did the water get cold?"

I pulled away and laughed. "I have no idea."

Reaching around me, he flipped it off. "I need food."

"Of course you do. All of you always need food." I stepped out behind him and took the towel he offered. Drying off I paused and looked at my arm again. "At least it's black."

Wrapping the towel around his waist, he gave me curious look. "And that's good?"

I nodded. "Yes. It means it will go with my boots."

"Ah, of course." He chuckled and pulled me into his arms. "I need to pop to my room for clothes or I'm going to have to walk these halls wearing nothing but a towel." He grimaced.

Pulling out of his arms I looked at his side.

He shook his head. "It's fine, completely healed. I just realized we're going to need a truck to get all of those clothes out there to my room—our room."

Moving away, I wrapped a towel around my hair. Standing up again I looked at him. "I'm keeping my apartment."

He raised an eyebrow. "That's fine. Gives us somewhere to hide." He grinned.

I shrugged, "because that worked out so well for us last time."

Leaning down he kissed me. "I'll be right back." He winked at me and then vanished.

As we walked toward the dining room, Chase would pause often and kiss me.

He paused again and looked down at me. "You are glowing."

I felt my cheeks darken. "This is the most complete I've ever felt in my life."

Smiling, he pulled me against his side and started walking. "If I wasn't half starved, we'd be discussing that over a bottle of wine."

"Discussing?" I gave him a disbelieving look.

"Mostly." He grinned again.

When we reached the door, he paused and looked at me. I nodded and we went into the room filled with many voices. The room went silent.

Crissy squealed and was out of her chair, practically launching herself into my arms. "I'm so happy for you."

I hugged her, then blew out a breath as her emotions came close to flooring me. "Thank you."

Victor got up and came over to peel his excited mate off me. "You're going to kill her with your excitement, heart." He tapped Chase on the shoulder and then ushered Crissy to the other end of the table again.

Before anyone else could obstruct Chase's path to the food, he took my hand and walked to his chair. Michael stood up and grabbed his plate and went the other way, sitting down beside Daxx where I'd normally sat. Chase pulled out the chair he'd vacated for me to sit in. I sat down, hoping if I did the awkward silence would cease.

Sitting beside me, Chase reached over and grabbed the nearest platter. As he heaped food onto his plate, he looked Troy. "How many did we get?"

As if none of it had happened, his injury, our marks, Troy swallowed what he'd been chewing and shrugged, looking to Arius. "Thirty-five?"

Arius nodded. "Yeah. Four didn't make it."

Chase put some food on my plate and nodded. "Thirty-nine against the seven of us." He shrugged.

I glared at him.

Rafael chuckled. "Only you could piss off your mate in the first hour of your union."

Waving his fork around, Chase grinned, "she forgives me, mostly."

Mitz came out of the kitchen. In her hand was a glass of wine. She smiled at me, her eye moving over my arm. Setting the wine glass beside me, she leaned down and gave me a quick hug. "Welcome to the family, love." Without another word, she turned and went into the kitchen.

Picking up the glass I took a sip and glanced to the empty chair beside me. "Leone not back yet?"

Quinton shook his head. "I messaged him, but no answer." He stabbed the food on his plate. "Might be in a dead zone, or could be passed out in his room again."

Michael set his glass down. "I stopped there, he's not back."

"Should we be concerned?" I asked no one in particular.

Daxx pointed to Rafael. "Clairee is keeping track of him?"

Rafael nodded. "Yeah, she said she'd check up on him every hour or so."

I took a small bite and chewed it slowly. Washing it down with another sip of the wine. It wasn't my favorite, but it was good. "This is quite lovely." I said before looking around. "How does she track him?"

Michael looked up from his plate. "The temple has a store of our blood." He motioned around the table. "Just in case."

"Oh." I sighed. "I have so much to learn about different things."

Crissy bounced in her chair. "I have books, books on every ability that's common here." She nodded.

"Well, I may have to peruse some of those." I told her.

"Please take some of them." Victor said in a teasing tone, one I hadn't heard from him before. "They're taking over our room. I may have to knock out a wall and build her a library of her own."

"Oh." Crissy looked at him, her mouth open, as she was bouncing excitedly.

"I think your building her a library now, brother." Chase said chuckling.

Victor looked at his mate, his expression softening. "Well, I did give her a tower, so I suppose a library is next."

Crissy squealed and scrambled over the corner of the table to climb into his lap.

"I'm building a shopping mall closet." Chase said with a smirk.

I leaned and rested my head on his shoulder. "You were serious?"

He shrugged. "It will have a whole boot section."

My cheeks went red.

"What have you given me?" Daxx demanded of Troy.

He looked shocked. "You have every weapon known to man at your disposal, do I need to give you more?"

Daxx grinned. "This is true, you rock." She leaned over and kissed him.

Clairee ran into the room. "Leone has vanished." She said breathlessly.

Troy and Chase stood up in unison.

"What do you mean vanished?" Quinton demanded. "People can't vanish and be untraceable when blood is used."

Clairee waved a piece a paper that looked like a map around. "I had two others try, very strong magic... he was there an hour ago and now nothing. We even tried a seeking spell."

"Fuck." Chase put his head down and blew out a breath. "That's why we found so many of them." He looked over to his twin. "They wanted to keep us busy."

"Shit." Troy looked to Victor as he stood, setting Crissy to her feet on the floor.

Victor motioned to Clairee. "Go get Romulus, we'll meet you at the temple." He looked at Michael. "Wake up the guards off duty and get everyone out there. Find out where he was and start from there."

Michael nodded and jumped up, pulling his phone from his pocket as he went out the door.

Chase paced away and then turned to look at his twin again. "You and Arius get to the cells, I don't care if you have pry apart every mind there, find out something to lead us to our brother."

Troy nodded. "Was just thinking that." He leaned down and dropped a kiss on Daxx's head and strode from the room.

Arius took a deep breath and stood up. He glanced to me. "Sorry if you pick up any hostile emotions, sister, this is hard to contain."

I held up my hand. "I'll be fine. Go find your brother."

He nodded and left without another word.

"I almost pity the fool that tries to resist him." Daxx said quietly then looked to Chase. "What can I do?"

He closed his eyes and breathed deeply for a moment. I could feel the shakiness of his hold on his emotions. Opening them he looked at her. "Go keep my twin from exploding someone's head."

With her eyes wide, she jumped up. "Good idea." She jogged from the room.

Crissy picked up her backpack. "I'm going to my tower." She patted Victor on the chest and looked up at him. "The flameless fire, cows and daisies must mean something."

He gave her a nod. "Try, my heart."

"I will." She ran out of the room.

I got up and went to Chase. "Can I do anything?"

He hugged me against him tightly. "I don't know. I just know we have to find my brother."

KEEP READING FOR AN EXCERPT OF

The Witch

The Alterealm Series

Book 3

By J. Risk

COMING SOON

Prologue

"Why are you just sitting here?"

I looked at the food on the plate in front of me, figuring it was self-explanatory, then back to Davis. "I need to eat and rest occasionally or I won't be able to do *crap.*" I told him wishing he would just go away. He was a magic user himself, or I'd try to make that a reality. I didn't know enough about this mage stuff to be sure it would work, and worry that he would do something worse in retaliation. Then again, if he kept getting in my face I may have to find out what I could do to him.

If it hadn't been for him talking my best friend Erin, into meeting all these power hungry, demented morons, she would be here still—then I could drag her, kicking and screaming if need be, far, far away. So yeah, Davis was at the top of my wish list to have something bad happen to him.

He gave me an unamused look.

Like I cared what he thought of me.

"It *is* working though, isn't it? You assured me you could work it from this distance."

It had been working for over a week, and he just thought to ask me that now? Sighing, I set down the sandwich I *really* wanted to eat, deciding if I answered him, he'd go away. "Yes. It took a few days to find one that I was *able* to get into." I'd never encountered so many closed minds as I had in that search. I was almost afraid to see the bodies that went with them. Good thing for me I didn't have to. Other than the one I was mesmerizing, I'd never have to see these royals Davis and his crew had so many issues with.

"Are you certain it's one of the royals? If you're tapped into some servant, it's completely useless."

My first thought was to pour my juice over his head and walk away—but then I'd be thirsty, and he'd probably just follow me. "You make it sound like it's as easy as scrolling through a list and picking one." I cocked my head to the side and gave him a blank stare. "People don't walk around thinking my name is Bethany. My name is Bethany. All day long." Great, now *my* appetite was gone. "Yes. It took me an entire day to find his name and reversing it. Just to do that, and *be* sure, cost me another day to recharge." I scowled at him. "Magic—*my* kind of magic comes with a price, using my magic too much, knocks me out." He continued to stand there and look at me like I wasn't even speaking. I sighed again. "His name is *Leone*." I waved my hand at the door. "What's his face said that was one of the royal brothers." I pointed a finger at him. "Are *you* sure they'll trade Erin for *him*?" A look of what may be described in a comic book as 'pure evil' appeared on his face. It was creepy, to say the least.

"Oh, they'll trade one of their brothers for anyone we say." He grinned. "Tomorrow we'll move you to the other side so you can draw him in."

I shrugged. "Sure. Just as long as I get Erin back, I'll," I made quotes marks in the air, "draw him in." Dropping my hands to the table, I gave him my best 'go away' look and held it, hoping he'd go be creepy in someone else's face.

He nodded and then turned to walk out of the room.

I exhaled, letting my shoulders sag. The sooner I was rid of that guy, the better it would be. Looking back at the plate, I picked up the sandwich again. I wasn't hungry now, but I knew if I didn't keep up my strength, I'd never get Erin back.

Taking a bite, I chewed it slowly. It was like chewing cardboard, no flavor at all. I looked at the drab colored walls of the wrecked building they had some of us in. Talk about no flavor, this crumbling place had seen better days.

Pausing with the juice bottle raised to my mouth, I checked to see if Leone was still sleeping. He was and I was happy about that. I took a few sips and picked up the bread again. A mesmerizing spell could almost be left on autopilot when the person was sleeping, taking very little effort. But when he was awake, it took every ounce of my energy to stay in his head. If he hadn't had a weak moment, I never would have gotten in to begin with, so there was no way I was losing it and starting all over again. Usually when doing this spell, the person was within sight—I still didn't know how I'd managed to without even having a visual target, but somehow, I had.

I didn't know where we were going. The *other side* didn't tell me much. Other side of the city, other side of the lake? Who knew? If it was closer to him, it would take no time at all to draw this Leone into the trap creepo and his friends had been working on. I frowned at my juice bottle, I didn't have any more details than that. I should be asking more questions. Just like I should have dragged Erin out of here when she'd brought me to some of them. Any and every sixth sense alarm had been going off when she did. The warning bells in my head, a feeling of dread in my stomach, my skin crawling, and just about every other descriptive phrase that meant 'run the other way'.

These people were lunatics and should all be locked up. And *what* was with the weird colored contacts these people used? Sure, getting a bit freaky for a rave or party was doable, but they did it for no reason at all. To add to their complete weirdness, half of them were deep into medieval roleplay and dressed like they should be running a dungeon.

This crap about bringing down the gate, or wall, or whatever they called it, to allow people to cross over... I snorted out loud. Pretty insane. Dropping what was left of the sandwich, I rubbed my temples. My head had a dull ache that wasn't going to go away until this was over. Grabbing the juice, I got up and walked to the corner where my cot was. Laying down was the only way I could maintain contact when he woke up. If I tried standing, my legs would just give out and I'd do a face plant on the floor.

I thought of Erin for a moment. She was going to owe me for a long, *long* time after this. Setting the juice on the crate, I sat down and rolled my shoulders. "Okay, Leone, lets pick up the intensity a bit." I lay on my back and looked at the cracked ceiling, that I knew every mark on now. "What am I saying to you today?" I closed my eyes, "not that it matters, all you want is me out of your head." I felt bad, but there were no other options.

Chapter One

I stood there staring at Davis, some creeper named Herman, and some big sweaty, bald guy whose name I couldn't remember. The bald one stood there watching the other two walk around the room waving their hands in the air. Usually, I was the strangest person in the room. I mean I could do magic, and that just wasn't something you ran around telling people. These guys here were mages and aside from waving their arms around like they were guiding planes to land…I really didn't know what it was they could do.

I glanced out the window and left them to do their thing in the bedroom. They'd already done their little dance in the hall and bathroom. I decided I was wasting my time watching and hoping they'd do something to jazz me. We'd *crossed over* last night and after I threw up, I realized we'd actually teleported. To where? No idea. A tiny little house in the middle of nowhere, was all I knew.

When my brain wasn't throbbing from staying connected to Leone, I'd have to find out a lot more about that. Imagine being able to get from one end of the city to the other without riding buses or subways full of people crammed together. Wouldn't that be something?

Lifting my arm, I looked at the strange watch thing they'd told me to keep on. When I asked what would happen if I didn't, they told me 'bad things', so I was wearing it.

"Are you sure he's coming out this morning?"

Davis practically yelled in my ear. Scared the crap out of me. I turned and stepped back, putting some space between us. "Yes. He'll be up shortly."

He nodded like a bobble-head. "Good. Draw him to you, then we'll sedate him to get him inside."

"And then what?" I watched the other two go out to the kitchen.

"Don't worry about that. All you have to do is stay here with him until we call you with the time for the trade."

I crossed my arms over my chest. "How am I supposed to make him stay here?"

He waved me off like I was an idiot. "He won't be able to leave the house."

My brain was prodding me to ask more, but right now I just wanted to get away from these guys. "I'm going outside to find somewhere to get comfortable before he wakes up."

"Fine, fine. Just let us know when he's close."

I watched him go to the kitchen. Shaking my head, I went out the door and then stopped and looked around. Endless fields, no matter what direction I looked. Turning I started walking to the one and only tree beside the house. Whoever lived here, they clearly didn't like people—or anything.

Sitting down, I leaned back against the rough bark and tried to relax. Staying tethered to Leone since we'd teleported had been a lot easier. I don't know where he lived, but he was much closer than before.

"Okay, Leone, time to wake up. Let's get this done so we can both get back to our regularly scheduled lives."

Not that I had a phenomenal life to return to. After bailing on my job when Erin was taken, I was definitely unemployed—which was no big deal. Being a cashier at the supermarket wasn't exactly my dream job. I had two weeks to come up with rent or Erin and I were homeless. Our one-

and-a-half-bedroom apartment wasn't the Ritz, but it was a roof over our heads. The creativity of calling a one bedroom with a room the size of a closet a one and half bedroom still got me.

I blew out a breath to focus. Maybe Leone's life was a little more interesting than mine. Closing my eyes, I reached for him. Suggesting he should wake up now. It was a beautiful day today. Perfect weather. Great time to get out for some fresh air…

I stood in the door listening to the commotion. Something crashed and hit the floor. I cringed at another sound that sounded like a yelp of pain.

"Did you give him the proper dose?" The bald one asked, sounding like he was doing some serious straining.

To me, it sounded like they were wrestling. Then again Leone turned out to be some kind of giant. I hadn't expected that at all. His thoughts and persona, internally, didn't come off as some sort of he-man body-builder.

"I gave him a full dose." That was Davis.

"Give him…." Creeper dude grunted, "*more.*"

Hurried footsteps echoed the hall. Davis came running into the room and opened his bag. He glanced at me, a panicked look on his face. "Come and help us."

I jolted like he'd slapped me. "Do what? Get trampled by a giant when I get in the way?" I'd always felt like my body had forgotten to grow. At five feet tall, there was no way I was going to try to help them 'tame the beast'.

He filled a syringe from the little bottle. "No. I'm going to give him more sedative. We need a sample of his blood."

"For?" Warning bells were chiming in my head again.

"Proof it's him we have."

As far as proof went, that was solid. I guess the one thing you can't fake would be someone's blood.

He held out a small vial and another needle. "Take these, stay out of the way until he's more compliant."

I snorted as I took them. "Good luck with that." I was really feeling like this was a bad plan, but still followed him to the bedroom.

The room was wrecked from the four of them wrestling. Leone had been groggy when they carried him in, but he was wide awake now.

I stood in the door as the three of them tried to hold him still so Davis could drug him again.

Baldy went flying into a wall as Leone snarled and shoved him with one arm. The Herman guy was trying to hold his other arm, unsuccessfully. Leone raised it up and Herman's feet left the floor, as he dangled from it.

If this was the drugged version of this man, how many did it take when he was alert? My mouth was probably hanging open—but seriously this guy was a brute.

Using his shoulder, Leone knocked Davis back again. Swinging he caught Baldy in the jaw. I stood there, eyes wide, waiting to see if he hit the floor from the force of that blow.

"Bastard, Davis," Leone growled.

Davis had gotten close enough to stab him and empty the contents of the syringe into him.

A few seconds later, Leone shook his head like he was trying to clear it. The three men dove on him and down he went. The cracking of the little table by the bed filled the silence in the room.

"Now." Davis looked over his shoulder at me.

I rushed in and held out the needle to him. There was no way I was sticking that in anyone.

Leone moaned and tied to swing his arm, but it ended up giving Davis the access he needed when Herman grabbed on and held it.

Leone kicked out when Davis started to draw his blood, I stepped back further.

Getting up, Davis came over. "Here." He nodded to the vial I held.

I pulled the stopper and held it out for him. He started emptying the blood into it. Leone kicked out again and bumped Davis, who squirted blood on my hand.

"Uh, watch it with the bodily fluids." I handed him the vial and wiped my hand on my jeans. Looking around him, the other two were lifting the rest of Leone's body onto the small bed. He didn't exactly fit. "Now what?" I looked back to Davis who stood looking at the vial of blood.

"He can't leave the area from the bathroom to the bedroom, so all you have to do is watch and feed him."

I nodded. "I can do that." I looked at Leone and again and the feelings of guilt started to hit me. "How-how long do you think?"

Davis glanced to Baldy and then looked back to me. "We're supposed to give them two days to panic and try to find him, then deliver the message and blood."

"Try to find him? What if they do?" My heart was beating so hard inside my chest I felt like a cartoon character-where you could *see* it beating.

"Don't worry," Herman said pushing past us, "this house is so well cloaked even people that know it's here can't find it."

I followed him. "Does that wear off?" This would teach me for not asking questions *before* I agreed to do things. If the people looking for Leone were even half the size he was... I would not stand a chance.

He shook his head, then stopped and shrugged. "In about fifty years."

I smirked, feeling relieved. "Okay. So-so, two days, no biggie."

Baldy came in wiping the sweat off his face. "Kitchen is fully stocked for you. We'll call you as soon as we have a time."

They headed to the door.

"Okay. See you in a few days."

They left without another word.

I closed the door and locked it. "Jerks." Turning, I leaned back against the door. The silence was a bit eerie after the last few weeks of being surrounded by the contact-wearing-role-playing crew. "So, Bethany, what would you say is the weirdest moment in your life?"

Pushing away from the door I went to check the kitchen. "Well, there was that time I was in an invisible house with an unconscious giant…" I nodded and opened the fridge. It was full. At least in all this bizarre crap, I'd fallen in with people that liked to eat. After too many times of living on gross handouts from soup kitchens and food banks—I wasn't going to complain.

Closing it, I looked toward the bedroom wondering how long he'd be out. The next few days were going to be awkward. I should check on him, right? They didn't exactly measure the dose they pumped into him. Wouldn't that be the worst move ever if they killed the hostage needed to get my friend back?

I looked around for a weapon and then stopped and shook my head. "Stupid, you *are* the weapon." With my hands raised in front of me, I walked cautiously to the bedroom. I stopped in the door. He was still out. His large chest was rising and falling. So, still alive. I glanced down at my own petite one and felt a bit inadequate. So what if his pecs were bigger than my breasts, he was a giant right? His everything was bigger than me. I stepped closer and looked down at him. His hand could probably wrap around my whole head.

With my hands on my hips I checked over the rest of him. He had red hair, not the bright orange-red, but a deep rust color. My own was a brighter, deep red, more like dark fire. His was cut into spikes of red all over his head. I wondered if it was meant to be that way, or if it was a brush cut left too long. Whatever, the style suited his jaw of steel. I wondered what color his eyes were. It had been a little hard to see them while he was wrestling three guys—and winning, for the most part.

He made sound and I almost tripped, stumbling backward. "Great, now you're turning into a creeper." Spinning on my heel, I went back out to the kitchen. For the first time in two weeks my head wasn't pulsing in time with my heartbeat. I could eat and rest without having to hurry back into his head.

They'd stocked the fridge well at least, so that was a bonus. One thing I appreciated was food. I'd gone too often without it, or very little of it. Most would binge after living the way I had, but I savoured the abundance and would make it last. Life could talk odd turns without warning, and it was better to always be prepared.

I found a pan and figured out what to make. Scrambled eggs, couldn't go wrong there. As I waited for them to cook, I stared off into space.

That nagging feeling was back, the one that kept trying to tell me there was something wrong in all of this. Sighing, I stirred the eggs around. If I were being honest, I'd known from the moment I agreed, that it was all wrong. I didn't have a choice. If not for Erin getting me off the streets eleven years ago when I was fifteen, I'd probably be dead by now. I still remember when she offered to let me stay in that crumbling building she'd been squatting in. It was condemned and falling down, but it was dry and out of the weather. Not to mention, it kept me away from all the weirdos on the streets. We'd sealed it up, so no rodents could get in and that had been out home for a year. When they'd torn it down, we worked odd jobs, saved money, then lied about our age and found the one and a half bedroom apartment. I couldn't abandon her when she needed me.

Scraping the eggs onto the plate, I set the pan in the sink and sat down. Davis and his crew weren't telling me the truth, I knew that, but no one was getting hurt. Leone would be home again in a few days and Erin would be free. Then I was done with all of this, and if Erin thought for even a millisecond I was letting her see any of these douchebags again, she was in for a really big surprise.

About the Author

J. Risk is a pseudonym used by Jacqueline Paige

I wanted to write a story that would fit into new adult levels as well as adult. Something that was serious with fun elements-- paranormal / fantasy that everyone could read and enjoy.

I've decided to use J. Risk as the pen name for this to separate this series from my other writing which is definitely adult reading material.

Jacqueline Paige lives in Ontario in a small town that's part of the popular Georgian Triangle area.

She began her writing career in 2006 and since her first published works in 2009 she hasn't stopped. Jacqueline describes her writing as *all things paranormal*, which she has proven is her niche with stories of witches, ghosts, psychics and shifters now on the shelves.

When Jacqueline isn't lost in her writing, she spends time with her five children, most of whom are finally able to look after her instead of the other way around. Together they do random road trips, that usually end up with them lost, shopping trips where they push every button in the toy aisle, hiking when there's enough time to escape and bizarre things like creating new daring recipes in the kitchen. She's a grandmother to eight (so far) and looks forward to corrupting many more in the years to come.

Jacqueline loves to hear from her readers, you can find her at

http://jacquelinepaige.com

Printed in the USA
CPSIA information can be obtained
at www.ICGtesting.com
LVHW041252151023
761121LV00001BB/84